Postcards From a Stranger

Postcards From a Stranger

IMOGEN
CLARK

LAKE UNION
PUBLISHING

Text copyright © 2017, 2018 by Imogen Clark
All rights reserved.

Published by Lake Union Publishing, Seattle

Previously self-published in Great Britain in 2017. This edition contains editorial revisions.

www.apub.com

Amazon, the Amazon logo, and Lake Union Publishing are trademarks of Amazon.com, Inc., or its affiliates.

ISBN-13: 9781503902497
ISBN-10: 1503902498

Cover design by Emma Rogers

Printed in the United States of America

Postcards From a Stranger

PROLOGUE

1987

The post hits the doormat with a thud.

He hears it, his ears tuned by months of careful listening. He should go and retrieve what has been delivered, sort through it, check. But the egg that he's been frying is almost perfect. If he takes it from the heat now, the white will stay slightly viscous. If he leaves it, the yolk will go hard and spoil that pleasing moment when he pierces its surface with his fork.

He listens but he can't hear the children. They must be upstairs. The post can wait for a moment or two. Who's to say that there'll be a postcard today anyway? It's not like they arrive every morning.

He returns his attention to the egg, watching as the edges begin to crisp, holding the fish slice poised. At precisely the right moment, he flips it out on to the waiting plate. Then he goes to get the post.

His daughter stands in the hallway, her nappy hanging heavy from her tiny three-year-old hips. In her hand is a postcard.

'Daddy,' she says when she sees him, her pretty face lighting up. 'Look what the postman bringed.' She shows him the postcard. It is a picture of a chimpanzee cradling its baby safely in its arms. 'What do the words read?' she asks, passing the card up to his waiting hand.

He turns it over but he knows what the single line of script will say. It is always the same. He doesn't let his eyes settle on it.

'I've told you before,' he says firmly, her question ignored. 'You must not touch the post, Cara. It's for Daddy.'

He picks up the rest of the letters and buries the postcard among the manila.

'Now, go and tell your brother that breakfast is ready.'

He watches as she trails off up the hall and makes a mental note never to let that happen again.

CHAPTER ONE

Cara, 2017

'I can't do this on my own anymore!'

I shout it down the phone. I don't mean to shout. It's just how my voice comes out. 'I need some help,' I say more quietly.

I put my hand over the mouthpiece to muffle my voice. 'Dad!' I plead. 'Stop making that racket.'

Dad looks at me, his eyes mildly curious, but he does not stop. The crack of metal spoon on wooden table continues to pummel my delicate nerve endings. I remember the advice that I got from the specialist-care team and take another deep breath. 'Please!' I add with the best smile I can muster.

I remove my hand and continue the conversation with my brother.

'Can you hear that?' I ask, even though most of the country must be able to hear it. 'That sound is our father banging a spoon on the table. He's been doing it for the last hour and a half. He won't stop and he won't give me the spoon. Honestly, Michael. I'm not sure I can cope for much longer.'

I can feel the tears pooling behind my eyelids but I don't want Dad to see that I am upset so I press my lips together tightly and take a deep breath through my nose.

'Just stay there, Dad,' I say as calmly as I can. 'I'm talking to Michael. I'll be back in a minute.'

I scan the room for stray knives or anything else that Dad might be able to harm himself with then I gently tap the top of his greasy head and go out into the hall, leaving the door slightly ajar. The banging continues.

'I can see it's difficult for you, Cara,' Michael says from the safety of his office hundreds of miles away. 'I would help more if I could but you know how it is . . .'

His voice trails off but I can't detect anything in his tone that's even close to guilt.

'I know,' I snap back. 'And I'm not asking you to help with the day-to-day stuff. But I can't carry on by myself. I'm out of my depth here, Michael. He keeps getting worse and worse. Sometimes, I get so angry with him that I'm worried I might . . .'

I stop before voicing what I might do and let it hang menacingly in the air between us. Michael doesn't reply.

'We need a nurse,' I continue. 'Someone who's trained to look after people like Dad. They don't need to live in – well, not yet – but I need someone here during the day so that I can work and do the shopping and, well, go to the loo without worrying what he'll get up to when I'm away. Dad can afford to pay. There's no point him just sitting on our inheritance. I'd rather we find some care for him. Some proper care.'

There is no sound on the other end and I wonder if the line's been cut.

'Michael? Michael? Are you still there?'

'Yes.'

His voice sounds distant.

'Okay,' he says eventually. 'You know best. If you really can't cope and a nurse is the only solution then go ahead. How will you go about finding one?' he asks.

'There's an agency in town,' I say. 'It comes highly recommended.'

I don't add that the recommendations were on Twitter and made by someone I don't know from Adam. I can do the research now that I have Michael's say-so.

'I'll give them a ring and set up a meeting,' I say.

I can hear muffled talking at Michael's end. He isn't on his own anymore and I know that I've had the best of his attention.

'I have to go,' he says in his unfamiliar telephone voice. 'You go ahead and fix that up and let me know how you get on.'

He might have been talking to some stuffed-shirt client about a takeover rather than his sister about his seriously ill father. I am about to put the phone down on him when I hear him whisper: 'Keep going, Ca. You're doing a great job.'

The line goes dead.

I stand in the hall and breathe deeply, trying to get my thoughts to line up neatly despite the noise coming from the kitchen. Dad has stopped banging now. He is singing something. I listen harder and it is the first line of a hymn that I learned at school.

'Oh, when the saints . . . go marching in . . .'

His voice is clear, as if the tangles in his brain have smoothed themselves out for long enough to let him remember how to carry a tune. The words, however, are beyond him.

'Cara!' he shouts. 'Cara!'

I try singing the hymn from the beginning myself to see if I can help but I can only get as far as Dad got before my mind goes blank. It can be hereditary, you know, Alzheimer's. God knows who will be there to look after me.

Dad starts on the hymn again from the beginning. 'Oh, when the saints . . . go marching in . . .'

Then the spoon starts up its relentless beat on the tabletop, not in time with the words but raggle-taggle, like new recruits out of step with their platoon. I look at my watch. It won't be long before Social Services arrive to take Dad away to the day centre. I just have to stay calm and in control until then. I can't blame Michael, not really. He escaped. His life is in London now and he can't come running back up here at the first sign of trouble. It might be nice if he came back occasionally but Michael's solution to the problem of what to do with Dad is to leave it to me. It's not unreasonable, I suppose. I am the one left here trying to hold it all together. But, like a little girl, I still feel like I need my big brother's blessing. I'm scared to forge ahead on my own, make the difficult decisions, but that is exactly what I'm going to have to do. I know that Michael gave up worrying about what happened to Dad a long time ago.

There is a knock at the door, the confident rap of a frequent visitor.

'Dad, Brian is here to take you to The Limes,' I shout, hoping that Brian can't hear the relief in my voice. 'Maybe he knows the next line of "When the Saints"?' I add. The tune is still chasing its tail in my head.

I open the door and there stands Brian, short and stocky with hands like shovels and a voice you could grate cheese on.

'Come in,' I say. 'We're nearly ready. Right, Dad . . .'

I push open the kitchen door and Dad is standing by the sink pouring a full pint of milk on to the floor. Teabags are scattered around him like fallen leaves. He smiles at me, a toddler with a new painting.

'Tea,' he says.

'Oh, Dad!' I say as I take in the devastation.

I'm trying to see where the outlying milk has trickled so I can make sure it is not going to seep into anywhere that I can't clean up. Last time he did this it took weeks to get rid of the stench.

'Brian will get you a cup of tea when you get to The Limes,' I say, smiling through gritted teeth. 'Come on now. Let's not keep him waiting.'

I take Dad's hand and give it a squeeze. There is no response. He follows behind me, splashing straight through the milk and to the door, where Brian takes control.

'Come on now, Joe,' Brian rasps. 'Let's get gone. Patricia's in the minibus already. She's a bit frisky this morning. I think you might be in there.'

I pull a face at Brian. I can't quite believe that he said that but he just winks at me. Whatever it takes to get you through the day is okay, I suppose.

As the minibus pulls away, I set to with the mop to clear up the milk lake.

◆ ◆ ◆

Outside, a stranger approaches the house. The street looks nice, the stranger thinks: affluent but not too pleased with itself. She has checked and double-checked the address and memorised the route from the bus stop so that she won't have to ask directions. It wouldn't do to draw attention to herself. This is a small town and she can't be sure who might know who.

She edges up the pavement, squinting at the houses. Three, five, seven . . . Her heart pumps hard in her chest and she sucks in deep lungfuls of air just to keep upright.

When she reaches the house next door but one she stops, opening her bag and pretending to search for something. She peers out from under the brim of her hat. She can see the house clearly from here: a three-storey Victorian townhouse with a handkerchief-sized front garden and a picket fence. How does this tally with her mind's-eye version of where they've been living all these years? The windows are dirty, she notices, and there are dead leaves clogging up the foot of the downpipes, but the curtains look nicely made. A stone urn by the front door had been filled with summer bedding but now the plants are straggly and brown, savaged by the early frosts. Still, someone cared enough to plant them in the first place, she thinks.

She feels a little braver now that she's here. What would she do if someone were to look out from an upstairs window? Would she smile at them, chance a wave?

A minibus turns into the street, slowing down as it approaches. She drops her head and walks on. It pulls up just behind her and she hears the door open and the driver get out. He says something to his passengers and then strides up the path to the house, knocking confidently on the front door.

She crosses the street and heads back the way she came.

CHAPTER TWO

The nurse from the agency is due to arrive at 2 p.m. and I am as ready for her as I will ever be. The house where Dad and I have lived for the last thirty years or so is big and tricky to keep clean by myself, particularly when I'm just not interested in the task. It has high ceilings, draughty window casements and far too many nooks and crannies for dust and spiders to settle in. Frankly, the place feels unkempt and unloved. Even though we barely use half the rooms now, the ones we do inhabit seem to have slithered out of my control. I am not naturally tidy but I have tried because that was how Dad liked things. When Michael and I were children, Dad ran a pretty tight ship. Partly, I suppose, this was because Mum wasn't around and he didn't want to be accused of not looking after us properly, but mainly I think tidiness was just embedded in his DNA. Since Dad has been drifting further and further from me, my handle on the house has done the same. He no longer notices the dust and disorder and it doesn't bother me either so that works just fine.

I do want to make a good impression on this nurse, though, so I put a few things away and surge around with the vacuum cleaner and a duster. I even have a go at the inside of the windows, but now that it is light outside I see the half-moon smears on the panes. Waves of soured milk keep wafting over from the kitchen but I am hoping that nurses are used to that sort of thing. As I straighten a pile of bridal magazines on the coffee table, I tell myself again that the woman is not coming to judge me on my housekeeping skills – and yet, out of a sense of loyalty to Dad, I want the old place to look its best.

The hands on the mantelpiece clock move closer to two and a scene from *Mary Poppins* plays in my imagination. I adored that film when I was small. I longed for a magical nanny to love me. And now here we are again, with me searching for someone to swoop in and make everything better with a spoonful of sugar.

I have decided to get the ball rolling with the nurse when Dad is at the day centre. That way, if she turns out to be a disaster then he need never know that I tried to fob him off on a stranger. I know that's not what I am doing but it's how it feels to me. I retrieve the agency's letter from its hiding place between the pages of one of my magazines. On paper, Mrs A. Partington looks just the ticket, with plenty of experience and excellent, recent references. I wonder what the 'A' stands for? Alison maybe? Or Abigail? I'm glad she is married. Somehow it makes her sound more experienced, which I know is ridiculous. I catch myself hoping that she's older than me too but I cannot really put my finger on why.

At bang on two o'clock the doorbell rings. Through the opaque glass of the front door, I can see the outline of a woman in dark clothing. She's not wearing a hat or carrying a brolly so it is unlikely to be Mary P. Yet again the thought that I am failing Dad punches me so hard in the stomach that it takes my breath away and I have to gather myself before I lift the latch. I screw my guilt deep down inside me where I can't feel it. Dad is very vulnerable and this woman is a total stranger but no one is saying that I have to give her the job. This is just a chat. I open the door.

She must be in her fifties, so she passes my first test. She is wearing a tidy gabardine mac in a smart navy blue and is carrying a matching leather handbag under her arm. Her hair, gunmetal grey and slightly wiry, is short and neatly cut. She's not wearing any make-up. I don't look down at her feet but I just know that she's wearing sensible shoes.

'Hi,' I say and smile broadly with my best welcoming smile. 'I'm Cara. Please come in.'

'Angela Partington. How do you do?' she says.

Her voice doesn't have the harsh consonants of a Yorkshire accent but I can't identify where she's from. Somewhere south is the best I can do. She holds out her hand and her handshake is firm, her skin cool and dry. I'm aware that my own palm feels slightly clammy but I resist the urge to snatch it back. I feel her fingertips linger over the rough ridges and crevices of my damaged skin and her eyes widen slightly but thankfully she doesn't pass comment.

'Dad's not here just now,' I add as I see her scanning the parts of the house that are visible from the hallway. 'He goes to the day centre most days. He's got a few friends there and the staff keep him busy. It's good for him to get out and it gives me chance to get things done.' I pull a face to show how tricky my life is and immediately worry that I will come across as unsympathetic, uncaring, but she doesn't seem to notice. 'I thought it might be best if we met when he's not here. He can be a bit . . .' I search for a word that will describe his behaviour without sounding too disloyal. 'Disruptive. Well, you know what I mean, don't you?' I add.

'I do indeed,' she says, her head nodding to show that she's with me. 'That's only to be expected, given his condition. He can't help it, of course, but it does make it a bit difficult to get on with everything else.'

I am immediately less nervous. She understands what it has been like for me all this time and I feel the pressure lift just a little.

'We all have our moments,' she continues. 'I know I certainly do. It's just a matter of knowing how to deal with them. Through here, are we?'

As she smiles widely at me, I see that her front teeth have a gap between them that modern dentistry wouldn't have left alone. She pushes open the sitting-room door before I have chance to show her. In any other part of my life, I would find this directness uncomfortable, but as I watch her make herself comfortable on my sofa I realise that this is exactly what I am looking for. Someone to play the grown-up so I don't have to.

'Can I get you a cup of tea?'

'No thank you,' she says, dismissing my question with a flick of her hand. 'I'm awash with the stuff. Now, why don't you tell me something about your father and how things work around here?'

And so, before I know it, I am telling her everything: my frustration with Dad's unpredictability, my inability to cope with his constant questions, the guilt. As I speak she nods like she's heard it all before, which she probably has. From time to time, she interrupts with phrases like, 'He does that, does he?' or, 'Oh, he's one of those,' which gives me confidence. And the more she seems to understand, the more details I share with her until my feelings of disloyalty have completely left me and I have laid bare our life together, such as it is.

'I work from home, too,' I add, 'which makes things a bit tricky.' I nod at the pile of bridal magazines on the coffee table. 'I'm not about to get married,' I say when her eyes dart to my left hand. 'I design wedding dresses for a living. I have a workroom here in the house.'

She nods but she doesn't ask any questions about me, which I find strangely disappointing even though I usually hate talking about myself.

'Anyway,' I continue quickly, 'I talked it over with my brother, Michael. He lives in London now and we don't see that much of him.' I don't tell her why. I don't want to scare her off before we've even started. 'And we agreed that the time has definitely come to call in the professionals. And so here you are.'

I sit back a little in my seat, smiling at her like a schoolgirl with a headmistress, and it crosses my mind how much I want to please her. Things would be so much less complicated if I could just offer her the job and get on with it but I remind myself that I need to be sure. This is about Dad and his needs, not me and mine.

'Well, I'm happy to go ahead if you are,' she says, as if reading my mind. 'I can work whatever hours you need,' she says. 'Evenings too, at a rate to be agreed, and I can live in to cover the nights when we reach that point. That's if you don't want him to go to a hospice, of course.'

A lump rises in my throat like a stone. Having someone talk in such matter-of-fact terms about the end of my father's life is like a stab to the heart but at the same time it's almost comforting to hear her practical honesty.

'Oh, I'm sorry,' she says when she sees me struggling to hold back the tears. 'I know this must be hard for you, but never you worry. I've seen it all before. My job is to make things as painless for you as I possibly can.'

'Thank you,' I reply, my eyes pricking. 'It's just that . . . well, you know.' Swallowing hard, I return to practicalities, pushing the pain back down. 'When he was diagnosed with early-onset Alzheimer's five years ago, he was okay really – just a bit confused sometimes. But now he seems to be declining quite quickly. He's not safe to be left on his own anymore. He gets muddled really easily and then he gets upset. He doesn't tend to be violent but he can be.'

I'm suddenly worried that my honesty will put her off, which makes me realise how much I want her to stay.

'That's not a problem, is it?' I ask quickly. 'It's not very often – the violence, I mean. It's really quite rare. Maybe once a month or something. And he's never hit me. He tends to throw stuff. I suppose it's more frustration than anything else.'

The nurse nods, like she understands exactly what I am trying to say.

'That's okay,' she says. 'It's very common. It can be a little bit frightening but it's just a matter of knowing how to handle it. You'll see from my references that I've plenty of experience of nursing people with Alzheimer's. I do understand how hard this must be for you. Entrusting the care of someone you love to a stranger is a difficult thing to do but hopefully I won't be a stranger for long.'

Even though this sounds like a well-rehearsed speech, I decide there and then that I'm going to offer her the job.

'Shall I show you around?' I ask her. 'I'm afraid it's a bit of a tip. Things have got slightly on top of me.' I smile apologetically but she dismisses my fears with a wave of her hand. I like her more every minute. 'Dad's room is still upstairs,' I continue, 'but there's a room that we can use down here when he can't make the stairs anymore. We've already had various alterations done, handrails on the stairs and in the bathroom and what have you. You can see and then, if you're happy to go ahead, we can arrange for you to meet Dad.'

She looks at me with a kind, broad smile.

'That would be just fine,' she says.

CHAPTER THREE

Annie, 1969

Annie dreams of running away to Frinton-on-Sea. She has never actually been to the smart little seaside town but her mother received a postcard from there once and Annie liked the look of the place. For a few weeks, the card was proudly displayed on the mantelpiece in the best room and Annie would stare at it for as long as she could get away with, losing herself in the row of wooden beach huts that lined the shore. Her favourite was painted a delicate shade of pistachio green. She pictured a tiny bed nestling inside, with a pink satin eiderdown, a rocking horse and stripy seaside curtains that she could draw against the world. Her perfect home.

The postcard sat propped against the carriage clock until one day her father snatched it down during some row or other and ripped it neatly into four pieces. Annie wanted to stop him, to explain about the tiny bed and the rocking horse. But in the end it was easier just to let him tear it up. She was already learning that her dreams would often end up in tiny pieces in the dustbin.

When she told her older sister, Ursula, that she was going to run away, Ursula laughed at her. How could she possibly escape? There was nowhere to go. Annie spat back, telling her about her beach hut in Frinton-on-Sea. For just a moment, Ursula looked confused. How could there be a safe place that Annie knew about and she did not? Then she just laughed at her again because she was older and knew everything and Annie cried hot, angry tears of frustration. She never mentioned Frinton again but she squirrelled it away in her memory for use in emergencies, for when things got really tough.

Of course, Annie can't run away anyway. She's only ten. It's just a stupid dream. Ursula, at thirteen, stands a better chance of escape but she never seems to crave it as deeply as Annie does. When things are bad, Ursula just takes herself off to her room and sketches until it's safe to come down again. Later, Annie comes to realise that that was Ursula's escape, into her art. Annie had to rely on her mind to get her out of there. She comes to see, though, that her mind was a false friend, sometimes on her side but more often leading her down blind alleys and into dark places where she should never have been.

Right now, Annie is in the kitchen of the family home in East London peeling the potatoes for dinner. The peeler is blunt, the string unravelling from the handle and getting in her way, and the pile of potatoes still to be peeled seems to be growing not shrinking, as if someone keeps adding one when she isn't looking. She puts her hand into the cold, muddy water and chases a potato around the sides of the washing-up bowl, finally catching it and lifting it out with a flourish. She examines it for eyes and green bits but this one is blemish-free. She is just sliding the peeler across its skin when she hears the front door bang. Her eyes flick up to the clock on the kitchen wall. It is only half past four. He's early. She lowers her head and peels more quickly. She can hear him moving about the house, dropping his keys in the bowl on the hall table, hanging up his coat, opening the door to the front room. She knows he will come into the kitchen next. She peels faster still, removing far more flesh than skin even though she knows that will land her in trouble too.

The door opens and there he is, her father: a short, compact kind of man, with thick, sandy hair that sits in tight waves under the Brylcreem that he uses to keep it under control. Everything about him is solid.

'Hello there, sweetheart,' he says. 'What's for dinner?'

She can tell as soon as he speaks that, for now, things are going to be normal. She allows herself to relax slightly but steals a glance up at him, just to check. He is standing steady in the doorway, a broad smile showing his tobacco-yellow teeth.

'It's egg and chips, Dad,' she says. 'I'm just peeling the spuds.'

'Good girl,' he says.

That pleases her. She craves his praise, despite everything.

'Where's your mother?' he asks, with no hint of irritation, and she relaxes a bit further.

'Not back from work yet,' Annie says. 'And Ursula's gone to the shop to get more eggs.'

'Good girl,' he says again. 'Be a treasure and make your old Dad a cup of tea.'

He is loosening his tie as he leaves the room, signalling the end of one part of his day. She nods and puts the peeler down smartly in order to fill the kettle straightaway. Muddy water splashes back on to her blouse, telltale brown spots staining the blue fabric. She holds her breath but he has already turned to leave and does not see the mess she's made. Her panicked mind is racing with solutions to the potential stain before the water has even fully soaked in. She'll put her cardigan back on when she takes him his tea. He'll never notice. She fills the kettle and places it on the hob, struggling a little with the weight of it. As she is lighting the flame beneath it carefully, the front door bangs again. Ursula is back.

'That miserable old sod in the corner shop tried to sell me cracked eggs again. I think he thought I wouldn't notice,' she shouts as she comes through to the kitchen. 'But I was on to him. "I might be young," I told him, "but I'm not stupid. I'll have half a dozen of your best eggs. Or at least ones that aren't cracked." He must think I was born yesterday.'

'Dad's home,' Annie says, cutting across her tirade to give her chance to be quieter, but Ursula does not miss a beat. She puts the eggs down on the table with some coppers. 'He's all right, though,' Annie adds.

Ursula shrugs as if it is no skin off her nose how their father is but, as she takes her coat off to hang on the hooks on the back door, Annie sees her wince ever so slightly.

'Does it still hurt?' she asks quietly.

Ursula scowls at her and Annie braces herself for more trouble but then Ursula's face softens a little.

'It's not too bad,' she says. 'Just a bit sore.'

'Do you think we should tell Mum? It might be broken or something.'

Ursula's scowl is back as fast as it had disappeared.

'Fat lot of good it'll do telling her,' she says, the words spitting from her mouth like hot fat from a pan. 'It'll be fine,' she continues, her voice gentler. 'It just hurts sometimes, if I catch it wrong. It'll get better. It just needs time.'

'We could tell someone at school,' Annie presses on. 'Mrs Williams says that if ever there's anything worrying us we can always talk to her.'

'That's junior school. It's different when you move up. No one cares there. They've all got problems of their own. Don't worry, Annie. It'll heal. It always does. The important thing is just to stay out of his way. Now you get on with those chips and I'll set the table.'

'He wants a cup of tea,' Annie says.

Ursula's expression blackens yet again and Annie thinks for one terrible moment that she is going to explode, but then she seems to think better of it.

'I'll do it,' she says through gritted teeth.

Annie fishes a half-peeled potato from the brown water and continues stripping away the muddy skin in steady, firm strokes, keeping her head down.

CHAPTER FOUR

Cara, 2017

'So, you think this nurse is what you need?' Beth asks me when we meet for coffee in our favourite café in Ilkley later that week. Beth, best friend and confidante, has been constantly at my side since we were at primary school. We have scrambled over each and every developmental hurdle together and she is the person with whom I share the most memories. It's hackneyed to say that she's the sister that I never had, but she is.

The café, tucked away at the bottom of town where only the locals can find it, is tastefully decorated in muted shades of grey with mismatched tables and chairs. Huge plate-glass windows are perpetually steamed up by the coffee machines and the breath of women. The aromas of roasted coffee and toasted teacakes mingle deliciously in the fuggy air.

'I think so,' I say, picturing the nurse in my mind's eye as I speak. 'She's got the right experience and she seems really down to earth. I like her. We clicked.'

I take the last mouthful of my coffee but it's gone cold in the cup. I resist the urge to spit it back.

'What's her name?' asks Beth. 'We can't keep calling her "the nurse".'

'Angela Partington,' I say. 'But I can't call her Angela. It just doesn't feel right somehow. And Partington is such a mouthful.'

'Well you have to call her something,' says Beth, wrinkling her nose in thought. 'How about Mrs P? It gives you a touch of distance but it's not quite as formal as the full thing.'

I turn the name over a couple of times, feel how it sits in my mouth. It makes me smile.

'What?' Beth asks.

'Mrs P,' I say. 'Like Mary Poppins. Right. I'll get us some more coffee and then you can tell me your news.'

I scoop up our empty cups and make my way across to the counter. When I get back, Beth has kicked off her shoes and is sitting with her legs curled beneath her. She's studying her phone, her dark hair flopping down in front of her face.

'Greg never answers my texts,' she says as I sit down. 'I sometimes wonder if he even reads them. I suppose they aren't really important. It's not life-or-death stuff. But when I message him and he doesn't bother to reply it makes me feel so needy.'

She seems to shrink a little into her seat, like someone has let a little bit of air out of her. It is my job to boost her back up.

'He's probably just busy with a patient or in surgery or something,' I say as brightly as I can.

I suspect Greg is playing games with her. He strikes me as the sort but it's not going to help matters to tell Beth that. She rolls her eyes at me, the briefest flash of irritation as she tightens her lips.

'I'm not entirely stupid. I do work in a hospital too,' she half snaps, and I can tell that I'm going to have to tread more carefully where Greg is concerned. Of course, she can't maintain her anger because she's Beth and it's vanished before I have chance to reverse out. She changes the subject and the atmosphere recovers.

'So, what does Michael think of this nurse? Mrs P?'

She emphasises the letter, making a popping sound with her lips.

'Oh, you know Michael,' I say. 'He's basically left me to get on with it. He agreed in principle but I get the impression that he thinks I've failed somehow.'

Beth bristles, the emotion of a few moments ago now turned against my brother.

'That's rubbish and you know it. If he really thinks that then he should come up here and try to deal with your dad himself. See how long he lasts. It's all very well being judgemental way down there in London. I'd like to see how he'd cope with a week at the coalface.'

I raise my coffee cup to my mouth and hold it there until the heat starts to burn my lip.

'I suppose there's always been that thing between him and your dad,' Beth says, and I feel a shiver run all the way down my spine.

That's the trouble with childhood friends. They have long memories.

We both sip our drinks, at ease with the gentle silence between us. Behind us the coffee machine hisses and the sound of chinking crockery mixes with the low murmur of conversation.

'What are you up to at the weekend?' I ask.

Her face brightens again.

'Greg's taking me away,' she says. Her dark eyes sparkle as she speaks and I fear this must be love, the real deal. 'He won't say where,' she continues. 'He just said to pack something gorgeous.'

'And your passport?' I ask.

Her shoulders drop a little. 'He didn't say anything about my passport so I took that to mean that I wouldn't be needing it. What do you think?'

I have to agree. 'There are still loads of fabulous places that he can take you,' I add.

'I know! I've been trying to think where it might be. It can't be too far because he's on call on Sunday but there's that country house place at Bolton Abbey. The one with the spa, you know? Or maybe one of those boutique hotels in Harrogate?' Beth bites her lip. 'Can you keep a secret?'

'Beth!' I say, feigning indignation. 'I am your best friend. I know all your secrets.'

She looks around her as if there might actually be someone spying on our conversation and then she lowers her voice to a whisper.

'I think he's planning to propose. I mean, he hasn't dropped any hints or anything but it just kind of feels right, you know?'

Of course I don't know. I have no idea what it feels like to be in love but I nod supportively.

'And what will you say? If he asks, I mean.'

Underneath the table and out of Beth's sight I cross my fingers firmly.

Beth just stares at me, wide-eyed.

'Well, yes! Of course!'

CHAPTER FIVE

Annie, 1976

Annie meets Joe Ferensby when she is seventeen and he is twenty-five. He lands in her life like a box of firecrackers. He makes her heart race and her palms sweat and from the very beginning she is never entirely sure what is going to happen next. In many ways, Annie thinks later, this just mirrored the way her life had always been but with Joe, instead of being frightened of the explosions, she positively relishes them. His unpredictability is exciting and snatches her breath from her lungs and, while she is never entirely sure where he is taking her, it has to be better than where she's been so she buckles up and follows him.

They meet on a bus. She's on her way to her job selling ladies' gloves in Selfridges. It's a nice little job that is never going to be a challenge but that suits her just fine. Katrina, her friend from the Men's Shirts department, is sitting next to her.

'Don't look now,' Katrina whispers to her from behind her hand. 'But that bloke down there is eyeing us up.'

Of course, Annie has to look and Katrina is quite right. She spots him at once through the sea of office girls and schoolchildren. His head and shoulders emerge like Poseidon. He has unruly dark hair, cut long to sit on his collar, and a five o'clock shadow even though it is eight thirty in the morning. There's an air of confidence about him, like he knows secrets that nobody else has worked out. Annie's eyes catch his and he winks at her – one of those cocky winks, set off by a slight turn of the head. Annie drops her eyes again, angry at the schoolgirl blush that she can feel creeping up her neck. The bus draws to a halt, he jumps down to the pavement, waving his thanks to the driver, and then he turns back to look at her as the bus pulls away.

'That's him hooked!' says Katrina with a smirk.

Annie doesn't reply, just shrugs her shoulders. Easy come easy go, she thinks, but she replays that wink in her head until the memory gets wobbly. The following week, he's there again, sitting this time and focused entirely on a copy of the *Racing Post*, a stubby pencil clamped between his teeth. He doesn't look up as Annie walks past and sits down a little further back, but when Katrina spots him she makes such a commotion of being discreet that he raises his eyes from his paper to see what all the fuss is about. He sees Annie just as she turns away to sit down and throws her such a delicious smile that, for a moment, she thinks she might keel over. This time, though, she's more prepared for his charm. She nods at him coolly, as if he were someone she once met at a party but whose name she can't now recall.

He stands and sways his way down the bus towards her, the newspaper tucked under his arm. Coming to a rolling stop next to Annie, he perches on the edge of the seat opposite, blocking the aisle for anyone else, his knees touching Katrina's thigh. Annie registers that her friend does not move her legs away and feels a stab of irritation, but he shows no interest in Katrina and focuses his gaze entirely on her. She sees, now that he is closer, that his eyes are a pale blue that sits a little unnaturally against the darkness of his hair. There is something of George Best about him.

'We meet again, ladies,' he says. 'Joseph Ferensby.'

He holds out his hand, cocksure. Annie is reticent, not sure what to make of this overt display, but at the same time she can feel herself being sucked into his orbit almost against her will. As she tries to pull back and regain control, Katrina dives straight in.

'I'm Katrina and this is Annie,' she says.

She offers her hand to the stranger. He takes it and kisses her knuckles lightly. Annie's nose wrinkles. He might be handsome and considerably older than the boys that she knows from school but even to her this seems a touch nauseating.

'Hello, Katrina and Annie. And where are you two off to?'

'Work. We work at Selfridges on Oxford Street. She's in Ladies' Gloves and I'm in Men's Shirts.'

Annie nudges Katrina. She feels uncomfortable giving a stranger so much information but Katrina ignores her, totally in her element.

'Are you indeed?' says Joseph Ferensby, his eyebrows rising until they disappear into his dark hair.

Even though Katrina is doing the talking, it's Annie he's watching. She resists the urge to look away and holds his stare, lifting her chin a little higher.

'Well, this is me,' he says without warning, and stands up. Despite her reserve, Annie feels her heart sink a little as she watches him stride back down the bus and bound off. As they pull away, he turns and salutes her.

'Well, he's a bit pleased with himself,' she says to Katrina, trying to sound unimpressed.

'Tasty though,' says Katrina. 'Did you see them eyes? Oh, I could lose myself in them eyes.'

'Give over. You sound like something out of *Jackie*,' says Annie, but she knows exactly what her friend means.

A week later he turns up at Annie's work. It is a slow day and Annie is dusting the stands, more to pass the time than because the job needs doing. She flicks the feather duster in and out between the gloves, trying not to dislodge anything apart from dust. The minutes tick by so slowly that she checks to see if the clock has actually stopped.

The first time she hears the noise she doesn't really take it in. It's only when she hears it a second time that she looks up and tries to work out what it is.

'Psssst.'

It's a sound like gas escaping from a tap.

'Psssst.'

Then she sees him. He's hiding behind a pillar, his head peeping out.

'Psssst. Annie.'

He beckons her over with urgent little gestures, as if he's in real peril. Annie looks back at her supervisor but she's busy talking to a customer so she takes a couple of steps towards him.

'What are you doing here?' she asks when she is close enough to be able to whisper and still be heard.

'I've come to see you,' he says.

'Well, I can't talk now. If my supervisor catches me I'll be for it.'

He looks crestfallen.

'But I've come all this way, traversed dangerous rivers and fought bears to . . .'

'Okay, okay,' she says.

This man is an idiot but there is something about him that makes her smile despite her determination not to.

'You'll have to pretend to be a customer,' she whispers. 'Stop skulking behind that pillar.' And then, in a slightly louder voice, 'How can I help you, sir?'

For all his usual confidence, he seems unsure of what is required of him in this new role and Annie has to prompt him.

'So, you'd like some gloves, sir? For your . . . girlfriend?'

'Er, yes,' he replies.

'And what kind of thing does she like?' Annie asks, trying not to laugh.

'Well . . .'

He pulls a face that suggests to Annie that he needs more of a steer.

'Is it leather you're wanting, sir?'

'Oh yes. Definitely,' he says, nodding and starting to warm to the game.

'And what colour, sir? We have some lovely baby pink that has just come in. Does she like pink, sir? Your girlfriend.'

'Yes!' he says, seizing on the idea. 'Pink is her absolute favourite colour.'

'And would sir be wanting a lining?'

He looks confused again. Annie is having fun, enjoying having the upper hand for once.

'In the glove, sir. A silk lining? Or cashmere?'

Joe raises his hands in a gesture of confusion and Annie smirks.

'If sir would like to step this way . . .'

She leads him across to a bank of drawers a little away from the main display area. Her supervisor doesn't even look up. She drops her voice as she bends low to open the second drawer from the bottom.

'What are you doing here?' she hisses. 'I'm working.'

Joseph makes no effort to speak more quietly.

'Like I said, I'm looking for some gloves for my girlfriend.'

He winks at her and her stomach turns over. He was such a charmer in those days. Annie never stood a chance.

'And what size would sir be needing?' she asks him.

'Size? Gloves have sizes?'

'Of course, sir. How big are your girlfriend's hands?'

Before she knows what is happening, he has taken one of her hands and is examining it, turning it in his own.

'Tiny,' he says.

Annie snatches her hand back, worried that someone will see, but no one is interested in her. Except this man.

'Will you come for a drink with me?' he asks quickly. 'Friday after work? I'll pick you up here. Six o'clock.'

'Six fifteen,' she says. 'And they're a size seven, in case you ever need to know.'

'I'm not sure you have quite what I'm looking for,' he says in a louder voice. 'Never mind. Thank you anyway.'

He grins at her, pleased with his performance, and then he walks away from the counter, turning back to mouth 'Friday. Six fifteen' at her, and then he is gone.

They went for that drink. The next week it was the pictures and after that they just fell into a sort of routine. He was fun to be with and he made her laugh. He gave her something to talk to the girls at work about but he also made her realise that there might be a life for her away from home. Slowly, she began to let herself think that this might be her escape route. She knew he was a charmer from the very first moment she saw him on the bus, but there was nothing wrong with being charming. She liked to be fussed over and he really did make a fuss, pulling her chair out for her before she sat down, always standing when she stood. It was a bit old-fashioned but what was wrong with that? She thought then that she was operating on her own terms. As she lay in bed at night, listening to Ursula snoring gently through the wall, she would make elaborate plans for her future. When the front door slammed just after eleven thirty and her father made his unsteady progress through the hall, clattering his keys not into the wooden bowl on the table but on to the tiled floor, she would lie as still as she could even though there was no way that he could tell that she was still awake, and dream of a life where she did not have to pretend anymore.

CHAPTER SIX

Cara, 2017

By the time Mrs P has been with us for a week, it is as if she has always been here and I can't remember how I coped without her. She slots neatly into our daily routines and doesn't try to change anything, which is vital for Dad's state of mind. Something as simple as a new person in the house could really upset the apple cart but she is so gentle that even he adapts.

A structure for our days soon builds itself around us like scaffolding. The cobwebs that I've grown accustomed to are gone, as are the smeary windows. I'm not quite sure when she finds the time to do the housework but I'm very grateful.

One day, in the second or third week, I am in my workroom trying to finish a wedding gown. Outside my window the day is damp and grey. At this time of year, the street is submerged in the shadow of the moor, the sun never getting high enough for its rays to hit the gardens, but I can see glimpses of brightness on the hills. The purple haze of heather, so beautiful in the early autumn, is just starting to die away and soon the moor will be cloaked in a dull brown shroud.

The wedding dress is stunning, even if I do say so myself. It's a traditional gown in ivory duchess satin that I'm making for a bride who giggles in excitement through every fitting. The boned bodice is to be covered in tiny seed pearls, which all need sewing on by hand. It's a fiddly, time-consuming job, made more difficult by the lack of flexibility that the taut skin on my right hand creates, but is the sort of detail that makes the difference between a dress bought off the peg and one of mine. I don't mind the task as long as I'm not having to rush. It's quite therapeutic and there is something about the monotony of picking up each tiny bead with the needle and letting it slide down the thread to the dress that relaxes me.

As I sit there, pricking the tiny beads on to the needle one by one, the phone starts to ring. The call turns out to be something and nothing, a young person scratching a living in a call centre like a battery hen. I'm polite but firm. When I get back, the door to my workroom is standing ajar. Panic rises in my throat as I approach. I see Dad standing in the middle of the room. He has the dress in one hand, its heavy skirt trailing all over the floor, and the box of seed pearls in the other. The box is empty. The pearls are skittering across the floorboards like so many grains of rice.

Before I can think, I shout at him. I can't help it. All the skills that I have learned about caring for a person with Alzheimer's desert me in my anger.

'Dad!' I yell. 'What the hell are you doing? Oh God! Look at the mess. Put that dress down. You'll ruin it!'

Dad looks at me, totally bewildered. He doesn't know where to put the dress or what he has done wrong. Normally I would soften at this point, his confusion blunting the edges of my anger, but I'm so incensed by what might have happened that I can't.

'Here!' I snap. 'Give it to me. Oh, for God's sake!' I try to snatch the dress out of his hands. Dad starts to shuffle forwards, kicking the scattered beads in all directions. His slippers catch on the train of the dress and I think that he's going to tear the fabric. 'Watch what you're doing!' I shout again. 'Bloody hell, Dad! You're kicking them everywhere.'

He looks so hurt but I can't feel any compassion for him. All I can see is the danger to the dress and the devastation that he's caused in a few short moments alone. Right now, I could cheerfully murder him.

I untangle him from the dress, placing it out of harm's way on the work table. Then I drop to my knees and start trying to rescue all the beads while Dad just stands there. I am still shouting at him when Mrs P bursts in.

'What on earth is going on?' she asks before she has even crossed the threshold. She casts her eyes around the room, quickly takes in what has happened and then gently slips her arm through Dad's and starts to lead him towards the door, the beads crunching under their feet as they go. He is mumbling something. I catch the odd word but 'sorry' isn't among them. I let them go and carry on picking up the beads, licking my index finger so they will stick to it and then dropping them, one by painstaking one, back into the box with shaking hands. There is no real damage done. The dress is bit crumpled but it's still clean and in one piece.

I am under the table finding yet more pearls when Mrs P comes back. I don't hear her but when I look up there is a pair of sensible shoes attached to legs just next to the table.

'Is he okay?' I ask, without emerging.

'He's fine,' she says. 'He's just taking a nap. Do you want some help with that?'

Without waiting for a reply, she drops to her hands and knees and starts picking up the beads and dropping them one by one into the scoop of her hand.

'I dealt with that really badly, didn't I?' I say to her broad back.

'It was a tricky situation,' she replies quietly. 'Perhaps you should keep the door locked when you're not in here?'

I feel chastened.

'I do normally,' I say, sounding like a child who is making some feeble excuse for an avoidable misdemeanour. 'I only popped out for a second. I should have known.'

Mrs P stands up, pushing her arms into the small of her back and stretching.

'I'm too old for grovelling around on the floor,' she says.

'I think we've nearly got them all,' I reply. 'They're so tiny. They get everywhere.'

Mrs P moves over to the dress, reaches out and tentatively strokes the creamy satin.

'It's so beautiful,' she says so quietly that I barely hear her. 'I had no idea.'

'Thanks,' I say and a little electric current of pride sparks around my veins.

'And this one?' she asks, pointing to a calico mock-up on the tailor's dummy.

'That's for next summer. It's going to be in shell pink. Hang on,' I say, getting to my feet. 'I've a fabric sample somewhere.'

I open a drawer and pull out a square of raw silk, the pink so pale that it almost looks like a trick of the light. I hold it out to Mrs P and she takes it from me like it is a butterfly that she might damage. She runs her fingers over the fabric and they falter over the burrs.

'You're so talented, Cara,' she says and I swell a little more under her praise. 'Your father must be so proud of you.'

My bubble bursts.

'Well . . .' I begin.

I suddenly feel the need to be honest, to tell her something of how things have been in this house over the years. I want to share how Dad has driven away my friends with his tongue and belittled my work to the point that it took every inch of determination that I had to keep going. I want to tell her how his getting ill has made my life easier and not more difficult. Then I change my mind and revert to the safe and standard answers that I might give to anyone who shows an interest.

'Dad's always thought my work is kind of frivolous and a bit of a waste of time, to be honest,' I say with half a smile. 'He could never understand why women would pay hundreds, sometimes thousands of pounds for a dress that they only wear once when most marriages end in divorce anyway. When I went to art school, he told me I was wasting the opportunities he'd given me and that I should go and do something useful instead.'

I shrug dismissively, like this is just a fact of life – which of course it is – but I can see Mrs P shaking her head ever so slightly.

'But he could see how determined I was so in the end he gave in and let me have the workshop here. To start with, I didn't make enough money to afford the rent on a house of my own, let alone a studio, so it suited me. Then when he got ill my being here killed two birds with one stone. He's never seen it as proper work, though. According to Dad, this . . .' I sweep my arm around, taking in my workroom with its tables and bolts of fabric and pots of beads and spools of thread. 'This is just a hobby that he finances.'

'But surely you make enough to live on now?' Mrs P asks, looking at the notice board where I keep snaps of all the brides that I have dressed, the pictures all layered on top of one another so that only tiny portions of some dresses can be seen.

'Of course,' I say. 'I could keep both of us very well on what I earn, but Dad either can't or won't believe that. Well . . .' I rephrase. 'He wouldn't before. It's different now, of course.'

Mrs P nods.

'I like to think that my mum would have been proud, though,' I add. 'I told you that she died, didn't I? When I was two.'

'Yes,' she says. 'You did mention it. Such a tragedy to lose your mother so young. Do you remember her at all?'

I shake my head. 'No, nothing. I know her name was Anne but that's about it. There are hardly any pictures either. I suppose there just wasn't any spare money for film back then. There's a wedding photo and a couple of holiday snaps but that's all.'

I point to a picture of Mum and Dad together. It is a square Polaroid of the two of them sitting on a blue-checked picnic blanket, the colours overdeveloped and garish. Mum is wearing a dress with roses on it and a yellow and blue scarf ties her straw-coloured hair away from her face. She is beaming at whoever was taking the picture but her face is less than a centimetre across.

'It says on the back that it was taken in Brighton in 1980. They look happy, don't they? I wasn't born in Yorkshire,' I continue. 'We used to live in London, but after Mum died Dad moved us away. I think it was too difficult for him to stay where we were. And we had no family to speak of. I suppose there was nothing keeping us down there so Dad got a job in Leeds and we moved here. A fresh start for the three of us. Like I say, I don't remember any of it. As far as I'm concerned my life has always been here.'

Mrs P doesn't say anything. She just sits and listens, twisting the calico of the mock-up dress though her fingers.

'Anyway,' I say, suddenly feeling slightly awkward, 'I hope she would have been proud of me. Mum, I mean.'

'I'm sure she would,' says Mrs P. 'What kind of a mother wouldn't be proud of her daughter?'

Then she stands up, smoothing the skirt of her blue uniform down with her palms.

'Now,' she says, readopting her usual, efficient tone of voice, 'I must be getting on,' and she leaves my workroom with tiny, quick strides, pulling the door shut behind her.

Something glints on the floor and I see yet another pearl. I know that I will be treading on the ones I've missed for weeks. I pick it up and pop it back into the box.

CHAPTER SEVEN

Michael, 1992

It's raining. It's been raining for days, not the dank mizzle that drifts down from the moor but water in biblical quantities. It hammers on the windows, demanding to be let in. It engulfs gutters and bounces off the surfaces of the newly formed lakes on the lawn. It's what they call 'raining cats and dogs', Michael knows, except that it isn't and he is scornful of the inaccurate and frankly ridiculous expression.

He and Cara are caged indoors and their resources are running low. As with everything in the house, there are rules attached to where they can play. Michael's room sits directly over the lounge and so if they jump around in there, drop anything or even talk too loudly, threats of punishment from their father waft up the stairs. Cara's room is better positioned but too small to swing a cat in and so only any use for Top Trumps or reading. The attic, which would place an entire floor between them and their father, would seem like the ideal space. However, playing there or even on the wooden stairs leading up to the two rooms is banned. Michael once suggested that they clear a little bit of space to make a den but their father shook his head.

'I don't want you two poking around up there,' he said. He was smiling but there was just enough menace in his voice to let them know that he was serious. 'There are too many things for little fingers to get caught in.'

'What kind of things, Daddy?' Cara asked.

'Things that you shouldn't be messing with,' he said, leaving so much to their imaginations that the attic became like a siren, luring them in to crash on the rocks.

Today Cara looks at Michael, her hazel eyes wide with hope and expectation that he will make her day better.

'What shall we do?' she asks him.

'Let's play the French Resistance.' Cara looks unconvinced but is nodding loyally and waiting for more details. 'We can be Resistance workers,' he continues, warming to his theme, 'and we can try to get our soldiers over the enemy lines and back home.'

'Is it very complicated?' asks Cara, her small mouth taking its time over forming the long word. 'Will I have to be the prisoner again?' She narrows her eyes. She may be young but she's not stupid.

'No,' he says, shaking his head. 'And the attic can be the enemy territory.'

'But Daddy says we're not allowed to go in the attic,' Cara says, shaking her head earnestly.

'I bet there's nothing up there. He just doesn't want us making a mess. We won't touch anything. We'll just rescue the men and get out. Dad'll never know anyway; he's too busy watching the golf.'

Cara clearly isn't convinced and screws up her little nose. 'I don't think Daddy will like that game,' she says.

'Tough.'

They creep towards the attic steps, casting wary glances up and down the corridor for the enemy. Michael feels that he, as mission commander and the oldest, should go first. He picks his way up the forbidden wooden staircase gingerly, avoiding the third step and carefully testing the others for creaks before putting his full weight on them.

Cara takes a deep breath and then sets off, mimicking Michael's careful tread. When she reaches the second-from-top step, the heavy torch that Michael has attached to her mission belt with his school tie somehow works its way loose and drops from her waist. It lands on the wooden step with a clatter. Panicked, Cara reaches out to try and break its fall but it slips from her small fingers and thuds down the remaining steps, each bang louder than the last. There is nothing to do but stand and watch it go.

The torch has still not come to rest when they hear the lounge door open. Cara throws a horrified look at Michael, her eyes wide and the colour draining from her cheeks fast. Michael's brain freezes with panic. He is rooted to the spot. They should run. They should run as fast as they can to Michael's room or the bathroom and come up with some story as to how the torch ending up clattering so loudly. They should do something but instead they just stand there, frozen, as they hear their father's heavy footsteps approaching.

'What on earth is going on up there?' he shouts, long before he makes it up the first flight of stairs. And then, when he realises where they are, he adds, 'I do hope you're not in that attic because if you are, so help me God, I'll tan your hides.'

Michael is shaken from his terror first.

'We're not, Dad,' he says, trying to make his voice even and calm. 'We were just playing here on the stairs. We didn't go in, did we, Ca?'

'No, Daddy.' Cara backs him up, shaking her head as hard as she can. 'I dropped the torch and it fell and made all that noise but we haven't done anything wrong, Daddy. Honest.' She looks at their father, opening her eyes as wide as she possibly can to show how innocent they truly are, but this seems to make him even angrier.

'Get away from there!' he hisses, his voice sharp with an anger that Michael has never heard before. 'How many times have I told you not to go in the attic? It's dangerous and you must not . . .' Their father reaches out a huge hand and slaps Cara hard across the thighs.

The blow takes her legs out from under her and she has to grab at the banister to stop herself following the torch down the stairs. 'You . . . must . . . not . . .' he repeats, each word separated from the others, the consonants spat out, 'go . . . in . . . there. Ever. Now get down and go to your rooms. There will be no supper tonight. You can think about your disobedience when you get hungry.'

Cara makes her way down the stairs. She keeps her head down but Michael knows that she's fighting to hold back the tears. Despite the obvious danger, she rubs at her thigh as she walks, determined to show how much it hurts. With each step she takes, Michael feels anger building inside him. He follows his little sister down, his shoulders tensed and his arms ready to lift in self-defence in case he needs to shield himself against a blow.

'I'm sorry, Daddy,' Cara says again, more warily this time, as she passes their father and heads towards her bedroom.

Michael stops three steps from the bottom. He is at his father's eye level but he pulls back so that he is just out of easy reach. He takes a deep breath and stands as tall as he can. 'You shouldn't hit us,' he says. He tries to sound calm but there is a tiny catch in his voice. He hopes his father won't hear it. 'It's against the law. They told us at school. And Mummy wouldn't like it.'

His father looks as if he might explode. His eyes narrow and he thrusts his lower jaw forward at Michael. 'I will do what I flaming well like in my own house,' he shouts. 'And you know your mother is dead. She doesn't care about you. Now, get to your bedrooms and don't come out until I tell you.'

Michael has no intention of moving. He searches out his father's eyes and then holds their stare with his. He can feel the insolence radiating out of him but he doesn't care. His father reaches out, grabs his arm and yanks him down the stairs. Michael loses his footing, first his ankle and then his leg crumpling beneath him, and lands in a heap at the bottom. Cara, from her safe vantage point down the landing, gasps and Michael immediately worries that this will draw their father's attention back to her. He stands up slowly. His right ankle is screaming out at him but he ignores it. He lifts his head and looks at his father, channelling his venom straight into his soul. He thinks for a moment that he will be hit again for his cheek, his father's arm beginning to lift but then dropping back down. Michael can see the muscles working as his father flexes his fist.

'Go to your rooms,' he says, anger resonating with every word.

Then he turns and stamps back down the stairs, slamming the lounge door behind him.

As soon as he is gone, Cara runs straight to Michael and throws her arms around him but he cannot hug her back. His anger seems to have turned his body to stone. He stands bolt upright and stiff as her reedy arms wrap themselves around his waist. He can feel her heart beating hard in her chest.

'I. Hate. Him,' he mutters. 'As soon as I can, I'm leaving this house and going as far away as possible.'

The next day, their father went up to the attic with his toolkit and fitted a padlock to the door. Michael and Cara didn't go up there again.

CHAPTER EIGHT

Cara, 2017

It's not like I haven't been up to the attic since I was a girl and it was banned. The padlocks are long gone. I went up with Dad's ancient toolkit and removed them when I was pretty sure he would no longer remember why they were there in the first place. He never comes this high anymore. It is as if this part of the house and its contents have been entirely erased from his memory. I rarely make the climb either. Even though I'm an adult now and this is my house, to all intents and purposes, something about being up here makes me feel anxious. It's like Dad's warnings are still hanging in the musty air. It's silly. I know now that Dad just didn't want us messing with his stuff but I sometimes wonder if he ever realised just how much damage he did to his relationship with Michael by laying it on so thick. In any case, I have never had any desire to mess with Dad's stuff. It's just old boxes filled with old things, after all.

Anyway, something that I heard on the radio has sent me up here now. The programme said that it can be helpful for people with Alzheimer's to have familiar objects to touch. I fear that Dad might be a bit beyond this stage but there's no harm in trying and it might give me new things to talk to him about. So, I venture up for a snoop around his stuff in search of memorable treasure.

It's the heat up there that always hits me first. The air is dry and warm, claustrophobic somehow, even when it's cold in the rest of the house. The room at the front is almost completely empty but for the cobwebs and dust motes dancing in the spiked light. When I first discovered it, I was so angry with Dad. All this space! What would it have hurt to let Michael and me play here? Surely he could just have locked the room that housed the things 'that little fingers might get caught in'.

While the first room is empty, the second is filled to the rafters with the detritus of almost an entire life. It's like the forgotten storeroom of a long-defunct business. There are shelves along two walls filled with cardboard storage boxes, each with a neat, white label facing outwards and describing its contents. My eyes settle on a couple – 'Slides from Holiday in Arran Aug 1993', 'Spare Belt Buckles'. How could anyone have spare belt buckles and why did it justify a whole labelled box in a long-forgotten attic?

The answer to this is easy. Dad. There was nothing in his life that he didn't have full control of. That's why the Alzheimer's is so cruel. It's robbed him of his entire raison d'être. This space represents the last vestiges of his power. Were it not for these neatly labelled boxes, it would be easy to think that he's just an elderly man who has fallen foul of a common affliction of old age. It is only when you see this room that you get some idea of the man that he once was.

As I stare at the regimented boxes, I wonder, yet again, if there might be some of Mum's things up here too, although I know the answer to that. When I was small, I was constantly asking. I longed for photos of us as a family or an old handbag that might have further treasures inside. Each time I asked, Dad became more angry than the time before so that it got so I had to steel myself before I brought it up. Michael would shake his head in silent warning but it didn't stop me asking. Dad's answer never wavered, though. He always said there was nothing and I never found anything of Mum's anywhere in the house.

I peer at more of the labels – 'Tax Returns 1990–99', 'Instruction Manuals (Electrical)'. I cannot see how far the room goes back because of the towering stacks of boxes, which create a huge, beige wall. I move a few until there is a gap that I can hop over. Back here the boxes are less regimented, and instead of purpose-bought office storage, Dad seems to have used whatever he could get his hands on. Many of them are shoe boxes, some of them tiny. I suppose they must have held my little shoes originally. I run my fingers down them, smiling at the sketches of the shoes once contained inside. They're all so familiar even though it's more than twenty years since I wore them. Then I spot a box in the corner. It is not like the others. It is metal for a start: a dull, khaki grey, like a large cash box. There is no white label either. A battered luggage tag hangs from one of the handles. It simply says 'A'.

I feel my heart beat a little faster. 'A'. Anne? Mum.

There's barely room to turn round in this darkest corner, let alone to squat down to investigate the box properly. I have to rearrange some others to give myself space to manoeuvre. I am aware of my breath coming in quick, shallow snatches and I tell myself to calm down. This box could contain anything and might be nothing to do with Mum.

When I have made a big enough space, I kneel on the floor next to the box. Dust has settled over the lid so thickly that I could write my name in it. Clearly no one has touched it for quite a while. Then I see that it has a lock and my heart sinks. Am I going to have to search for the key in all these boxes? I am about to take it downstairs to see if I can prise it open somehow, but when I go to pick up the box by the handle the lid just opens without any resistance. I'm holding my breath and I take a couple of slow gulps of air before I allow myself to look inside.

Unlike everything else around me, there is no tidy order to the contents of the box. It is half-full but no attempt has been made to stack things neatly. Each item has been thrown in carelessly without thought as to where it might land. It looks like dozens of photographs, but when

I look more closely I realise that they are postcards and I feel deflated. This can't be a box of my mum's things after all.

I pull one of the postcards out at random. On the front is a picture of the Post Office Tower in London. I can tell from the quality of the image that it's old. I turn it over and see that it is addressed to me and Michael at this address. Again, my heart sinks a little. Mum died before we moved here so it can't be from her. My eyes flick to the short message, which is written in a stilted, jerky script.

My darling babies. I love you more than you will ever know.
Please forgive me.

That is all. The card isn't signed and the only other clue is the postmark. Thoughts race round my head so fast that I hardly have a chance to catch one before the next one has set off. I squint at the postmark. It is smudged as they usually are but I can just make out part of the date – March 1992. That would make me nearly eight when this was posted, so it can't be from Mum, but who else would write us a card like this?

I fish out another. This time it is a picture of Big Ben with black cabs passing by in the foreground and a big, red Routemaster bus. I turn it over with shaking hands. Again, the same message.

My darling babies. I love you more than you will ever know.
Please forgive me.

This one is dated September 1995. My hand dives into the box again and retrieves another. This time it's from Mombasa, an African elephant waving its trunk high in the air. It's dated 2001. The message is the same as the others.

I pull out card after card. They all say exactly the same thing. My head is spinning with questions. Who are they from? Why are they all addressed to me and Michael? Why are they hidden in this box in the depths of the forbidden attic?

There is nothing else in the box – just the postcards, hundreds of them, in no particular order, just lying where they have fallen. I scrabble about, looking for the oldest card. I cannot find a single one that was written before March 1987. Mum died in the February.

It makes no sense. I take the box and settle myself down on the dusty floor in the other room, where there's more space, all thoughts of finding what I came up here for forgotten. I begin to pull out hand-fuls of cards. I make piles – one for each year, so that I can get them into chronological order. They span from March 1987 to July 2002. The cards seem to be from England at first, mainly London. There are a few from touristy places – Paris, Amsterdam, one from Moscow with snow settled on the brightly coloured turrets of the cathedral in Red Square. There are lots from Italy – Rome, Naples, Bologna – and America too . . . But then later, after 2002, nothing. The cards just stop. I wonder whether they stopped arriving or whether Dad stopped saving them. I reason that they must have actually stopped arriving as I've been dealing with the post for years now and I would have seen a postcard like this.

I empty the box out completely but there's nothing else hidden at the bottom. There are just the postcards. I pick one up at random. It is a garish shot of a sunset. The colours look artificial. I tap it rhythmically against my lips as I try to calm my racing mind into some kind of order. But there is no order. It makes no sense. I can think of no one who would send us postcards like this for so many years. No one, of course, except the one person who couldn't possibly have sent them.

CHAPTER NINE

Annie, 1976

Joe is coming for Sunday lunch with the Kemps and Annie has worried herself into a frenzy. Her desperation for them all to like one another is almost visceral. If they could just not shout at each other long enough to eat the meal that would be a start, she thinks.

Her mother has invited Joe for pre-lunch sherry. Annie shudders at how bourgeois this sounds but decides not to say so in case her mother loses her nerve and cancels the whole thing. She spends the morning chopping veg and constructing a trifle and becomes so distracted by trying to make everything perfect that when the front doorbell rings at a minute after twelve she can't think who it could be.

'He's very punctual,' says her mother from the lounge, where she is plumping the cushions on the sofa for the third time. 'I do like that in a man.'

She supposes that her mother's tick list of qualities for an ideal mate must be pretty short, given that she settled for her father.

'Well, answer the door then!' her mother adds, standing frozen to the spot like the proverbial rabbit. She must be as nervous as me, Annie thinks.

She knows as soon as she opens the door that everything is going be all right. He stands on the front step polishing his shoe on the back of his trouser leg. He is wearing his good suit and a blue and grey tie that Annie has not seen before. His dark locks are neatly combed and he has had a shave recently. A glow of pride both for him and that he has chosen her radiates out from her somersaulting stomach.

Shyness creeps over her, as though she, not he, is the one on foreign territory. She gestures towards the lounge and he steps over the threshold, gently placing a little kiss on her cheek as he passes. She inhales the woody overtones of his aftershave.

'Something smells good,' he says, momentarily confusing her until she realises that he means the lunch.

'It's roast beef,' she says. 'Mum likes to do a full roast on a Sunday.'

Actually, what her mother cooks on a Sunday depends almost entirely on how sober her father is, but it sounds better to pretend that Joe has just stepped into a typical day at the Kemps'.

'Please. Sit down,' she says. Her voice sounds formal and strained to her but Joe does not seem to notice. He drops into the sofa, squashing one of her mother's over-plumped cushions. Annie winces involuntarily. 'Did you find us okay?' She sounds like the receptionist at a job interview. 'I'm sorry,' she adds, twisting her mouth into a grimace. 'Ignore me. I think I'm a bit nervous.'

Joe smiles his wide smile at her, no hint of apprehension in his face. 'Don't be,' he says. 'I'm great with parents. They'll love me.'

Before she has time to worry about that as well, the door opens and in strides her father. She tries to look at him through Joe's eyes. A middle-aged man with the start of a beer belly and hair slick with Brylcreem. He is wearing a sleeveless cardigan over a tired green shirt and brown slacks, clearly having made no effort for their guest.

'You must be the new squeeze,' he says and Annie winces again. 'Malcolm Kemp.' He nods, as if his identity is so obvious that he really has no need to introduce himself to anyone.

Joe, who had stood up quickly when her father came into the room, now offers him his hand to shake.

'Joseph Ferensby,' he says. 'Very pleased to meet you, Mr Kemp – and may I say how delightful your daughter is?' He oozes confidence, just like he did that first day on the bus, and she envies him his easy manner.

Her father regards Annie thoughtfully, as if it has never occurred to him that she could be considered delightful. Annie tries to second-guess his thoughts and fails as her mother bustles in. She is carrying a silver tray holding five rattling glasses of amber sherry and a bowl of salted peanuts. 'Sherry, anyone?' she asks and begins to offer the tray to Joe. Then, at the last minute, her mother changes her mind and pushes the tray towards her father, who takes a glass, sniffs its contents and knocks it back in one mouthful.

'Joe, this is my mum, Pam,' Annie says quickly. 'Mum, this is Joe.'

'Lovely to meet you, Mrs Kemp,' said Joe. 'I can see where Annie gets her good looks from.'

Annie very nearly chokes. Her mother blushes instantly and almost drops the tray, casting a nervous glance at her husband. She offers the tray of glasses to Joe and he's about to take one when her father speaks.

'You don't want to be drinking that muck, Joseph. They're open and we're wasting good drinking time. We'll just nip out for a quick pint, Pam. We'll be back in time for lunch.'

Her mother, who clearly hasn't anticipated a trip to the pub before the meal, is momentarily thrown. She rubs at the knuckles of her left hand with her right as if they are sore. 'All right,' she says quietly, 'but I need you back to carve the meat at twelve forty-five, Malcolm. Please.'

Annie can hear the pleading tone of her voice and hopes Joe can't. Her father just nods and then, snatching a handful of peanuts as he passes, ushers Joe back out of the front door. Now all they can do is wait and hope.

Annie takes a glass of the sherry and a handful of peanuts, which she tips into her mouth in one go. Her mother begins to re-plump the cushions.

It is closer to one thirty by the time the men get back, both having clearly had more than a pint but in high spirits and seemingly getting along just fine. At the sound of the door banging shut, Ursula appears from her room and comes halfway down the stairs, stopping just out of reach. Annie's father waves his arm towards her.

'And this young beauty, Joseph my boy, is my firstborn, Ursula. Now, she's a proper firecracker. You'll be wondering whether you've picked the right sister by the end of lunch. Ursula, my little chickadee, come and say hello to young Annie's new beau.'

Ursula scowls down the stairs but makes no effort to move any closer. 'Hello,' she says. Nothing about her tone is welcoming or friendly. She turns to their mother. 'Is lunch ready yet? I'm starving.'

'I think it may be slightly past its best,' says her mother under her breath, but her father is already making his way through to the dining room.

'My belly thinks my throat's been cut,' he says, pushing his way past her mother.

'Shall we sit boy, girl?' asks her mother brightly as they gather around the table awaiting instruction. 'I'll sit here by the door so I can bring things in and out. Do you want to sit next to Annie, Joseph?'

'This isn't going to work out,' says her father, shaking his head deliberately. He points a tobacco-stained finger at each chair in turn, counting them off one by one. 'It's basic maths, woman,' he says to her mother and then turning to Joe adds, 'You'd better not be looking for brains as well as beauty, Joseph. They're in pretty short supply around here.'

Annie hears Ursula clear her throat and thinks for one terrifying moment that she is going to contradict him, but instead she says, 'Oh, we're both as thick as planks. Not a brain cell to rub together between us.'

'Well, I don't think that's really true,' says her mother quietly.

'The boy knows I'm joking, Pam. Don't be so sensitive.'

Annie sees her mother shrink a little, her shoulders rounding and her head dropping so that Annie can no longer see her face. 'I'll just bring the food in,' she says in a voice barely above a whisper. 'Could you help me please, girls?'

'I don't know,' says her father, leaning back in his chair and looking over at Joe as he speaks, as if the two of them are communicating in a language that the women cannot follow. 'How can I show my daughters off to Joseph if you keep dragging them away? Can't you manage in the kitchen by yourself? Anyone would think you'd never made a Sunday roast before, the fuss you're making.' Her father is clearly enjoying himself, belittling her mother and showing off to Joe. 'And Joseph and I need a drink. There's some beer in the pantry. Bring us each a can, would you?'

Annie can see her mother starting to flap, unable to cope with so many tasks at one time.

'I'll get them, Dad,' she says and then slips out of the room before he can complain again.

Her mother follows her out, head bowed.

'I've had to carve the meat myself,' she says once they are safely in the kitchen. Nerves make her voice high and breathy. 'I couldn't wait any longer. He won't like it but what could I do?'

'It'll be fine, Mum,' Annie replies. 'I bet he doesn't even notice. I'll just take these drinks through and then I'll come back and give you a hand.'

She scoops up the cans and a couple of glasses, more for appearances' sake than anything, as she is certain they won't be used, and heads back to the dining room. Her father is holding court, Joe laughing roundly at something that he's said. Ursula is still scowling and looks as if she would rather be anywhere but there.

'That's true, isn't it, Annie?' her father is saying as she enters the room. 'Ursula could turn milk with that face of hers. It's no wonder that young Joseph here has set his cap at you. You might not have the looks of your sister, or, let's face it, the figure . . .'

Annie is mortified. She sets the cans down on the table, places a glass next to each and then backs away, her arms folded tightly across her chest. She shoots a glance at Joe, hoping to see horror or, at the very least, sympathy on his face but he is focused on her father and is laughing even louder than before. He can't be being taken in by him, surely? She risks a glance at Ursula, who shakes her head with a minute movement. Leave it, she is saying. Just leave it.

'. . . but at least our Annie knows how to smile,' her father continues.

'I'll just go and help Mum,' Annie mutters and retreats.

'Joseph seems nice,' says her mother when she gets back to the kitchen. Her voice sounds calmer now. 'And your father likes him,' she adds. 'Which is good.' Annie notices the sherry bottle, open and almost empty, on the side but doesn't mention it. 'Can you just carry the veg and I'll bring the roasties and the meat,' her mother adds, handing Annie a tea towel. 'I'll come back for the gravy.'

Annie picks up the hot tureens and follows her mother through. She sets the dishes down carefully on a mat in the centre of the table, the serving spoons placed with their handles towards her father.

'Oh, silly me,' her mother is saying. 'I've forgotten the plates. What was I thinking?'

'You weren't thinking,' her father says. 'You never do. See what I have to put up with in this family, Joseph? I'm surrounded by incompetent idiots.'

Joe laughs again but he sounds less sure this time. He looks at Annie, one eyebrow raised quizzically. She just shrugs. What could she say? Welcome to the Kemp family.

'I'll just go and get them. They're warming. I won't be a minute.'

Her mother's voice is once more shrill with the strain of trying to keep control. She disappears yet again and returns seconds later with a pile of plates and the gravy bowl balanced on top. Annie holds her breath, expecting disaster, but her mother manages to deposit them all on the table without accident. She raises her hands over the food, checking that everything is as it should be. It's almost as if she's blessing it.

'So, Joseph,' she says, finally raising her eyes to her guest. 'What can I get you?'

'Oh, a bit of everything would be lovely thank you, Mrs Kemp,' Joe says and gives her one of his trademark winks.

Her mother blushes like a debutante. Ursula rolls her eyes but Annie feels a little shiver of pride. This handsome man is hers and hers for keeps. Joe's plate, piled high with food, is passed round to him.

'Gravy?' Annie asks.

Joe nods and winks at her too, a small conspiratorial gesture that tells her that he understands and that they will get through this together.

'What the hell have you done to that meat?' Her father's anger comes suddenly and out of nowhere. The atmosphere shifts immediately to something much darker. Annie bites her lip. 'What did you carve it with, woman? A nail file? Hacked at it with a spoon, did you? You've ruined a perfectly good piece of beef, you dozy cow – and it didn't come cheap you know, Joseph. None of your skirt or brisket for us. That's proper topside, that. Might as well have been skirt, though, for the mess she's made of it.' He pushes back from the table, preparing to stand.

Her mother retreats into herself, the tiny sliver of confidence that had built back up evaporating.

'I'm sorry,' she mumbles. 'I did my best. It was just that you weren't here and it needed doing or everything else would have spoiled.'

'I see,' her father replies, nodding his head slowly. 'It's my fault. My wife is incompetent with a carving knife and somehow I end up taking the blame. Do you see what I have to put up with, Joseph?'

'You could have done it yourself if you'd been back from the pub when Mum asked you to be. As it was, we had to make do,' says Ursula calmly.

Annie stiffens and drops her gaze to her place mat, suddenly fascinated by the hunting scene depicted on it. Her mother takes a sharp breath. They all wait for what will inevitably come next but it is Joe that breaks the silence.

'Well, it all looks delicious to me, Mrs Kemp,' he says. 'My mouth is watering like you wouldn't believe.'

Annie's father falls back in his chair and grunts but he doesn't complain again. Her mother quickly piles food on to a plate and passes it to him. He accepts it without thanks. Then she serves Ursula and Annie and finally herself and soon they are all tucking in, noises of appreciation coming from Joe in lieu of conversation.

When he has finished his plateful, her father pushes his plate away and leans back in his chair.

'So, Joseph. What do you do to earn a crust?'

'I'm a bookie, Mr Kemp,' says Joe.

Annie sees her father sit up a little.

'A noble profession,' he says. 'You have to be smart to be a bookie. It's all mathematics, you know, girls. Calculating the odds, working out probability. Clever stuff. Bit beyond you, though, Annie. Not the sharpest knife in the box, our Annie,' he adds in an exaggerated stage whisper.

'Oh, I don't know,' interrupts her mother bravely. 'Annie did very well in her O Levels. She got nine you know, Joseph.'

'Fat lot of good it did her, though. Selling gloves to women with more money than sense for a living? I don't call that a career success. And Ursula's no better.'

'I'm at art college, Dad,' says Ursula.

'Against my better judgement. Where's that going to lead, I ask you? Nowhere that'll put a roof over your head and that's for sure.'

'You should be proud of your girls, Malcolm,' her mother ventures. 'They're both doing very well.'

Her father looks about to disagree but Joe jumps in.

'Well, I'm very proud of Annie,' he says. 'She'll do for me.' He smiles at Annie then, his pale eyes twinkling despite being slightly unfocussed. 'That was a delicious lunch, Mrs Kemp,' he adds.

Annie's heart does a little leap in her chest. She sees her mother glow too. Even her father looks less angry. Ursula is still scowling.

'Oh, please, call me Pam,' her mother says, sitting taller in her seat. 'Another drink, Joseph, before I serve the dessert?'

CHAPTER TEN

Cara, 2017

After I discover the postcards, things become very confused in my head as I struggle to process what I think I know. Questions chase each other around my mind like squirrels in an oak tree but there are no answers. I retreat to my workroom but I can't settle to anything. I sew and unpick a sleeve setting three times before I decide that I am on a hiding to nothing. Abandoning the dress on its mannequin, I sit and stare out over the sleeping garden, hoping that the answers will be just outside the window.

Dad and Mrs P are in the kitchen. I can hear cupboards being opened and closed and Dad is singing hymns again. He has never been a churchgoing man, or at least not as far as I know. Just where he learned all these hymns, which seem to be lodged firmly in his memory to the exclusion of almost everything else, is another mystery that may never be solved. This now troubles me in a way that it didn't before. Until this morning, I thought I knew everything there was to know about the man with whom I have shared a house for more than thirty years. Now I am not so sure.

Obviously, I've thought about talking to Dad about the postcards and the idea pushes its way to the front of my mind again. I reject it. Hymns he may remember but a lot of the time he has trouble placing me, his daughter. I can tell from the quizzical looks that he throws me when I speak to him. To start with, I thought he was just chasing my name around the dark recesses of his memory but now I realise that it's my entire identity that escapes him. So there is no point asking him about the metal box in the attic. I know that he's becoming increasingly frustrated by his own failings. Just yesterday, the last of the blue Denby china bit the dust as he hurled his dinner plate across the kitchen without warning. I can replace the plates with something cheap and anonymous but I do not want to make things any worse for him in his fragile state.

I keep turning the possibilities over and over in my head but each time I come to the same conclusion. What if Mum didn't die? What if she's been alive all this time, sending me postcards, trying to keep in touch? When I think about what this might mean, a knot grows in the core of me, hard as a nut, making it impossible to breathe. My mother is dead – this is a known fact. It has been the truth since I was two and yet what if it isn't true? Would Dad really lie about something like that? None of it makes any sense. I flounder around in the dark waters of my imagination, desperately searching for something to hold on to.

Three or four times, I find myself standing with the phone in my hand, dialling Michael's number; but each time, I cut the line before it starts to ring. What would I say to him? My parents may suddenly be a mystery to me but I do know my brother. I need to have more information at my fingertips before I talk to him or he'll just dismiss the idea out of hand.

Then it strikes me – a moment of clarity in all this confusion. If my mother is dead there will be a record of it. People don't just die. They leave a trail of bureaucracy behind them. I know my mother's name, approximately when she died and that she lived in London. There will be a death certificate. All I have to do is search online. Even as I think this, I am crossing the few short steps to the workroom door and closing it firmly behind me. My hand lingers on the brass key in the lock but I decide against. There have been enough locked doors. If they walk in, I'll just close the search down. No one need know what I am up to.

My hands are shaking so violently that I can barely open the laptop, let alone type in my password. I open Google and type 'How to find a death certificate'. The first couple of pages are adverts for family-tree hunting sites but I scroll past those and find the official government page. Without giving myself time to reconsider, I click on it and then on 'Births, Marriages and Deaths'. Almost at once, the page for ordering a death certificate is before me. My hand hovers over the mouse but I am shaking so much that I must click without realising because then a page requesting payment pops up. I am confused. This isn't right. If my mother isn't dead then there won't be a death certificate to pay for. I need to approach this in a different way. I go back to the ancestry sites. It was only thirty years ago when my mother is supposed to have died but surely that counts as ancestry? I select a site at random. It takes me straight in and there, at the top of the screen, is the offer of a free search. All I have to do is enter a name and a date, plus or minus ten years.

'Cara! Cara!'

Dad's voice cuts through my thoughts and I jump as if he's standing right behind me. Guilt washes over me like it did when I was up to no good as a child.

'Cara!'

I can hear him approaching, his tread heavy and unsteady. I mini-mise the screen.

'I'm in here, Dad. In my workroo— In your study.'

The door opens and Dad is standing there. He has his sweater around his neck like a muffler. The empty sleeves dangle uselessly at his sides.

'I can't . . .' he begins and then, defeated by both sentence and sweater, he flops into the armchair, narrowly missing a newly cut out paper pattern. I stand and manage to sweep it out from under him just in time.

'Oh, Dad. You seem to have got yourself in a bit of a pickle. Here. Let me help you.' I begin to right the sweater and he wriggles like a recalcitrant toddler. As I thrust his arm into the correct sleeve, a task I must have done for him dozens of times, I recognise that something about helping him feels different. A tiny kernel of doubt is hanging over me. Has Dad lied to me for all these years and about something so important? My sympathy for his confusion feels, for the first time, tainted by some other emotion that I can't quite place.

'Where's Mrs P?' I ask, trying to shake the feeling, which I don't recognise and don't like.

'Who?' he asks.

'You know. Mrs P. The nurse.' I help him back to his feet and pull the sweater down his back.

'No nurse,' he says shaking his head from side to side gently.

'Come on, Dad,' I say, leading him by the arm out of the room. 'Let's go and make a cup of tea.'

I close the door carefully behind me. My search will have to wait.

I catch myself being short with Dad – well, shorter than usual. Everything he does makes my nerves jangle and I mutter under my breath uncharitably at the slightest provocation. Deciding that fresh air might help, I head out to tackle the leaves. Our garden is surrounded by mature trees, which give us shade and privacy in the summer and blocked drains and leaf-rot in the autumn. Dad used to sweep away the dead leaves as soon as they fell and somehow knowing that the old Dad, my real dad, would not leave them lying there spurs me into action. I work methodically, raking them from one section of the lawn into a tall pile and then moving on to the next. Soon the grass is spotted with brown humps, like giant molehills between the green patches. I go to get a sack from the shed and when I get back, my beautiful piles are strewn all over the lawn again. It is as if I had never begun. There, in the middle of the mess and having a rip-roaring time, are Dad and Mrs P. He leans into her to stop himself from falling over and kicks at the leaves with his foot, swinging it back to get as much momentum as he can. He has the body of a geriatric man but the smile on his face as his foot flies through the pile shines with sheer delight like a child's.

I see red. There are a million better things that I could be doing this afternoon rather than wasting my time on things that are undone as quickly as I can do them.

'Oh, for God's sake!' I shout as I approach them. 'Dad. Don't do that!'

Dad turns towards the sound when I speak but shows no sign of having understood what I said. His leg keeps swinging, even though the pile he is standing over has been reduced to a few leaves. Mrs P, her hands tucked around Dad's arm to keep him upright, catches my eye and gently shakes her head. She is telling me, without any words, to let this go, that it is just harmless fun, that I should live in the moment. I look at the leaves and Dad standing in the middle with a smile on his perpetually confused face. I know I should be treasuring this moment, taking a mental snapshot because there will not be many more smiles and surely this should be more important than a few minutes of wasted effort. But all I can see standing amid the mess is the man who has lied to me for my whole life, kept things hidden in the dark when they should have been out in the light.

I drop the sack. I would hurl it at the pair of them but it's empty and doesn't have the weight behind it to do more than fall at my feet.

'You two can clear it all up,' I say, knowing how ridiculous a suggestion this is but really not caring. Then I turn and stalk back to the house. They don't call after me. I hear the rustle of leaves as they move on to another pile. I am like a petulant child. I want to join in, be part of the fun, but I am too stubborn to turn back and risk losing face and this makes me angrier still. I know that there was more to my outburst than just some spoiled leaf piles but I leave the thought where it is. I daren't examine myself too closely. I'm just not ready to go there. I need to move forward one step at a time.

Later, with dinner made, eaten and cleared up after, and with Mrs P getting Dad ready for bed, I go into my workroom. The search page is still there in the bottom of my screen. I click it back up and then, with shaking hands, type 'Anne Ferensby 1987' into the boxes.

My finger hovers over the mouse. What if there is no death certificate? That will surely mean that I still have a mother. A living mother. I click. Now I have come this far, how could I not know? I've put myself in an impossible position. I watch as the little hourglass fills and empties. Then the screen refreshes itself and a message typed in red shouts out at me.

Sorry, we could not find any results matching your search criteria.

For a moment, my heart sinks until I realise that no results means that there is no death certificate for my mother. My mother is not dead. My mother is not dead. Not dead. Alive.

I do the same search again and again. Each time the result is the same. I try moving the date five years either way, even though this makes no logical sense as I know exactly when she is supposed to have died – February 1987. Nothing. Then I try with the current year but this time my hand hesitates. What if my mother didn't die in 1987 but is dead now? What if I had lost her, to find her, to lose her all over again?

Now I have to know. I have to know everything. I click and wait but the same response fires back at me. No results.

Tears began to prick at the back of my eyes. I blink them back as I stare at the message. No results. The words blur behind my tears until the screen becomes a mass of coloured pixels. Can my mother really be alive? It makes no sense but what other explanation is there?

I must sit there for half an hour or so, just staring at the screen. At some point, the laptop goes to sleep because when I finally come round from wherever it is I have been, the screen is black. I am vaguely aware that a thought has occurred to me and that this is what has pulled me back to the here and now. I try to focus on what it might have been but I cannot seem to be able to hold it in my head. It's like trying to catch the seeds from a dandelion head. Every time my hand reaches out, the breeze that my movement makes floats the seeds a little further out of reach. I struggle to think back and recapture the idea. When I finally catch it, it is so simple that I cannot quite believe I ever lost it. If she is alive then maybe I can find something out about her, some other detail that will make all of this less confusing.

A fresh surge of adrenaline powers through to my fingers. I wake the laptop and start a new search. I type 'Anne Ferensby' into the box and wait anxiously for the response.

'Do you mean Anne Hornsby?' Google asks me, as if I don't know my own mother's name.

My eyes skim across what the search has brought up. Anne Browne, who came from a place in Yorkshire that is not even spelled the same way, and then various pages relating to the town. There is nothing that could possibly be my mother. Immediately, I am thwarted. How can there be nothing? Everyone has some kind of digital footprint. It can't be avoided in this day and age. I refresh the search. I know that it is pointless but I have to do it. Then I try searching against her name and the date of her supposed death. Then her name and the year that she was born. None of them throw up anything.

I bang on the keyboard, like that's going to do any good, and the keys rattle in protest. How can my mother be not dead and that be the end of it? There must be more out there. If she's alive then where is she? What is she doing? How is she living? There are millions of other questions that will come to me later but at the moment I'm just focusing on the basics. And then suddenly I can barely keep my eyes open. When I look at the clock it says 2.30 a.m. and everything around me is silent. I close the laptop and make my way to bed. As I clean my teeth, I look at my reflection in the mirror. Do I look like her? Would she recognise me in the street? Would I recognise her?

As I climb into the bed, the exhaustion lifts as the ideas start pulsing around my head again. I just lie there, in the dark, until the edges of the curtains turn pale with the new day.

CHAPTER ELEVEN

It turns out that Greg did propose to Beth on their romantic weekend away. I get a handful of texts from her, all hurriedly typed in the ladies' loo. They're full of abbreviations and exclamation marks and positively squeal with excitement. I'm not surprised that he asked her. Beth is a great catch. Who wouldn't want to marry her? But as I'm driving over to Greg's house for a celebratory dinner with them both the next day, I can't help but feel a bit sorry for myself. The inevitable pairing off of people seems relentless. I know it's in the natural order of things but, despite genuine best intentions, Beth will gradually slip away from me as the gravitational pull of her new life becomes too strong to ignore.

I turn into Greg's road and pull up outside. His sleek, black Porsche is standing in the drive next to Beth's bashed old Peugeot. The house, a newly built executive home, is clad in manmade concrete blocks designed to imitate the smooth, honey-coloured local stone. The house next door is almost exactly the same, and the house next door to that. The flagged drive reminds me of a child's drawing and there are no plants to soften the frontage other than two regimented box trees standing sentry over the glossy black front door. Despite its obvious high price tag, the building is bland and featureless. I much prefer Beth's little cottage with its wildflower garden and the huge wisteria creeping over the tumbledown trellis. I suppose that she will probably sell that now to move into Greg's mansion and the thought makes me feel sad all over again.

I grab the bottle of champagne that has been rolling about under the passenger seat and check my hair in the vanity mirror. There is something about the way that Greg looks people up and down that makes me feel uncomfortable even though I don't actually care what he thinks of me. I run a finger over the corners of my mouth to catch any stray lipstick, and take a deep breath.

When I knock at the big, black door, Beth opens it almost immediately.

'Who is it?' I hear Greg shout from inside.

'It's only Cara,' says Beth.

'Charming!' I say and then throw my arms around her and give her a huge squeeze. 'Come here you! Congratulations!' I plant a kiss on her shiny hair, breathing in her familiar perfume. Despite my concerns for myself, I cannot help but be pleased for her. 'Right. I want to hear all about it,' I say. 'Leave nothing out. But first, a drink. I've had a hell of a day and I need alcohol to revive me.'

She grabs my elbow and steers me towards the kitchen. It always takes my breath away, Greg's kitchen. It is a shrine of chrome and granite with every surface reflecting the next. I once commented on the cleanliness of all the appliances – Greg strikes me as the obsessive type – but Beth informed me that he doesn't actually cook there.

'It's all for show,' she once told me. 'He can't boil an egg.'

'Let me see if I can find some glasses,' she says, opening cupboards in turn.

After several attempts, she locates a cupboard filled with glasses and mugs. She is just reaching up for the champagne flutes when Greg appears at the door.

'Not those, darling,' he says. His voice makes Beth jump so that she almost drops the glass on to the tiled floor. I see her breathe out in relief that the glass is still in her hand. 'This is a special occasion,' he continues. 'I think it calls for the crystal, don't you?'

He opens another cupboard. The cut glass sparkles in the harsh light from the overhead spotlights. 'These, I think,' he says, taking a tall flute from the shelf and holding it up to examine it. 'Just give them a little polish.'

For a moment, I think that this is a direction to Beth but he opens a drawer, takes out a chequered tea towel and begins the task himself. Beth stands down and watches him patiently.

'Shall I pour.' It's more a command than a question. He takes the bottle from me, runs a critical eye over the label and then pops the cork expertly. The champagne bubbles and froths and, just too late, I remember its bumpy journey here. 'That's a bit frisky,' he says as he struggles to keep the wine in the glass.

We all hold our breath as the bubbles edge closer and closer to the lip and then begin to retreat back down again just before they escape over the edge.

'And so,' he says when all three glasses contain millimetre-perfect quantities of champagne. 'A toast. To my beautiful bride-to-be.'

I echo his words and raise my glass. Beth bounces on her toes, pointing at her chest and mouthing, 'Me! That's me!'

'Congratulations to both of you,' I say, and then to Beth, 'I'm so pleased for you.'

Beth takes my hand and squeezes hard.

'I can hardly believe it,' she says. 'It was such a surprise.' She winks at me roundly. I flick a glance over to Greg, who is totally oblivious as he basks in the moment. 'Come and sit down.' She links arms with me and virtually drags me towards the sitting room. She's like a puppy, all wide eyes and bounce. I relinquish my self-will and follow her.

The sitting room is large and brightly lit. There are three sofas, each small and neat with highly polished wooden arms and feet like little conkers. They don't look tempting. They are upholstered in a rich claret striped with gold and fringed with gold tassels. It reminds me of an old-fashioned country hotel, the sort that doesn't allow children.

Beth nudges me towards a sofa. I sit down, finding myself perching on the edge rather than sitting back. Beth immediately squeezes herself in next to me, kicking off her shoes and tucking her feet up underneath her.

'I want all the details,' I say and I mean it.

Every inch of Beth seems to be smiling. She hugs herself tightly as she speaks.

'Oh, Cara,' she begins. 'It was so romantic. The hotel was just perfect. We had a suite overlooking the golf course. The bathroom alone was almost the size of my cottage. So, when we arrived we . . . well. You can guess that bit.'

I smirk at her.

'And then . . .?'

'Then we went down for dinner. We had a drink in the bar first and I should have known that something was going on then. The waiter just served us champagne without us having to order it. Greg had already told them what was going to happen.'

I'm struggling to see the romance in something so staged but I want to be delighted for Beth and so I nod enthusiastically.

At this point Greg walks into the room. It is almost as if he has been waiting in the wings for his moment of glory and has timed his entrance for maximum impact.

'I was just telling Cara how you gave the nod to the waiters, darling,' Beth says, turning her whole body round in the sofa to face him.

Greg grins and looks at me like he is waiting for praise. I ignore him and pointedly focus all my attention on Beth.

'Anyway,' she continues. 'Then we went through for dinner but halfway through the starter . . . I had the scallops with pea foam. They were fabulous, so succulent and . . .'

Behind her, Greg makes a low tutting sound.

'Cara doesn't want to know exactly what we ate, darling,' he says.

'Actually, I do,' I reply but Beth is already apologising.

'Sorry. Anyway, halfway through, a man appeared with a violin and he came straight to our table and started to play some classical thing. What was it again, Greg?'

Greg shakes his head, smiling indulgently at her. 'It was Albinoni's Adagio,' he purrs.

'That's it,' she says. Her smile is now so wide that I'm surprised she can still talk. 'So he started playing his Adagi-wotsit and everyone was looking over at us. The dining room was full, wasn't it, Greg?'

Greg nods. His smile has shifted from indulgent to something approaching smug.

'So, then Greg leaned over and took the rose from the vase. Oh. Did I mention the rose?' I shake my head. 'Well, there was a single red rose on the table when we got there. Anyway, he took the rose from the vase. Then he got down on one knee and, in front of the whole restaurant, he asked me if I would do him the very great honour of becoming his wife.'

I think we've got to the climax and so I'm about to hug her but she's still talking.

'And then he gave me the rose.'

Greg jumps in.

'That's where the plan went somewhat awry,' he says, looking point-edly at me with eyebrows raised.

He talks like a character from a bad historical drama. A blush starts to bloom from the hollow of Beth's throat.

'I'm such an idiot, Cara. I didn't even notice the ring. It was just sitting there in the rose. I don't know what I was thinking. I mean, just look at the size of it!' She holds her left hand out for my inspection. The ring is spectacular. There is a ruby in the centre that is almost the size of a five-pence piece, set high in a rose-gold setting surrounded by brilliant cut diamonds. It would not have been my first choice. I'm not sure it would have been Beth's either.

'Wow!' I say, as both of them are clearly waiting for a reaction. 'Not sure how you missed that, Beth.'

'Absolutely, Cara,' Greg agrees.

'Maybe it was the colour of the rose that confused things,' I add. 'A white one might have been better.'

Greg sniffs.

'Well, if Beth had just opened her eyes . . .' he mutters.

'So,' I say. 'Greg proposed. Beth found the ring . . .'

'Eventually,' says Greg.

'And then . . . ?'

Beth looks at me like I've got a screw loose. 'I said yes, of course, and then the whole restaurant started clapping and the violin man played "Congratulations".'

'I'd forgotten about him,' I say under my breath.

Greg clearly hears me because his smile slips.

'And then Greg bought champagne for everyone. Well, it was waiting ready, wasn't it, Greg? So the waiters brought it out as soon as I said yes.'

'Wow,' I say again. 'It's a good job you did say yes.'

'Of course she was going to say yes,' said Greg and his eyes flick round the well-appointed room. 'Why wouldn't she?'

Why indeed, I think. 'Show me the ring again, Beth,' I say.

Beth holds out her hand and I hold it steady in mine.

'It was my mother's and my grandmother's before her. And it fits just perfectly, doesn't it, Beth?'

'Well, I still think it might be a little bit tight,' Beth says quietly.

'And have you set a date?'

'Oh, just as soon as we can get everything sorted. Greg doesn't believe in long engagements, do you, Greg? And you'll make my dress, won't you, Cara?'

Greg's smile freezes. 'Don't you want to go down to London for your dress, darling? I mean, I'm sure Cara's dresses are perfectly adequate but money really is no object here.'

'No,' says Beth with a determination that I recognise and am relieved to see. 'It's my dress and I want nothing more than to have my best friend design and make it for me. We'll pay you, of course,' she added. 'As you just heard, money's no object.'

I cannot help smiling at Greg, who has been hoist by his own petard, just so that he knows his wife-to-be is not a complete walkover. Then I turn back to Beth.

'I would be delighted and honoured to make the dress,' I say and I hug Beth tightly.

I look at Greg over the top of Beth's head. He gives me a tight little smile.

CHAPTER TWELVE

Annie, 1978

It's funny how your mind rewrites history with the benefit of hindsight. It will become obvious to Annie eventually that it was a mistake to marry Joe. She was searching for a way out, for a new life for herself, and she thought Joe was it. When she first tells Ursula that Joe has proposed, however, she isn't prepared for the response. It's not like she was expecting her sister to crack open champagne, even if they had any to crack. Ursula is the elder sibling and, in the ordinary course of things, would probably have been expecting to leave home first. When they were children they'd even talked about leaving together, speaking in whispers under the bedclothes while their father raved downstairs. Those weren't real plans, though; at least Annie had never thought so. They were childish daydreams like getting a pony for Christmas or becoming a ballerina. They would each break away on their own, chasing their chances for escape. She'd expected her sister to be delighted for her and so Ursula's reaction comes as a shock.

'You can't marry him!' Ursula screams.

'I'm an adult. I can do what I like!' Annie screams back.

They aren't actually screaming. Even though they spit their words out at each other like venom, the volume is only a little above a whisper. Their father is slumped at the table between them, his forehead resting on a wrist, the other arm hanging loosely at his side. His breathing, slow and nasal, might have suggested that he was dead to the world but they know from bitter experience that this can never be taken for granted. At any moment, he might wake and find them arguing over his head. This possibility is to be avoided at all costs.

'Why shouldn't I marry him?' Annie says, in a hoarse hiss. 'He's handsome and charming. He's got a good job and a place of his own. And he loves me.'

She finishes on her trump card, hearing and enjoying the note of triumph in her voice.

Ursula rolls her eyes.

'Loves you?' she mocks. 'Loves you! You wouldn't know what love was if it strolled in here, fell to its knees and started licking your shoes. You don't love him, Annie, and he certainly doesn't love you. Open your eyes. Can't you see what's happening here?'

Annie cannot, for the life of her, see what's happening. As far as she is concerned, she has met her soul mate and is going to gallop off into the sunset with him.

'You're just jealous,' she hisses back, jabbing a finger at her sister across their father's slouched body. 'You're jealous because I have found someone who wants to take me away from here and you're going to be left behind.'

'Oh, is that what he is? Your knight in bloody shining armour? You're as bad as Mum. Can't you see how this is going to work out?'

Annie, her arms folded tight across her chest, sees something slacken in her sister, as if she has lost the will to attack. Her face, which had been pulled taut in anger, slips into something closer to compassion.

'Look, Annie,' she says more gently. 'I know that you want your life to start. God knows, I understand that. But are you sure this is the answer? Really sure? You're so young to tie yourself down. You've got your whole life ahead of you. Go out and live a little first. If he loves you as much as you say he does then he'll wait for you.'

Annie hugs herself tighter still. She won't let Ursula talk her out of this. She's completely sure about Joe, been sure for months. She'd just been waiting for him to pop the question. She'd even practised looking surprised and delighted in the mirror so that when he picked her up from work one night with a twinkle in his eye, she was ready. He walked her past their usual tube stop and on to a side street where they picked up a cab. He handed the driver a small piece of paper, rather than announcing their destination out loud, and then took a silk handkerchief from his top pocket and bound her eyes so that she had no way of knowing which way they were heading. When the cab stopped, he helped her out on to the pavement and ignored her laughing protestations. He guided her gently to their destination. She could feel the ground switching from concrete to grass and the gradient increasing beneath her feet but still he kept her eyes behind their silken mask. Finally they stopped climbing and he instructed her to take off the blindfold. They were, as she had guessed, at the top of Primrose Hill, the lights of the city twinkling beneath them like a giant treasure trove. He was on one knee in front of her and she felt her heart flip. He took her hand in his and she realised that she was trembling just slightly.

'Annie, would you do me the honour of becoming my wife?' he asked, and before she could reply he thrust a dark-blue box towards her. The ring, a ruby cluster, was delicate and feminine. Annie pushed the tiniest sliver of disappointment out of her mind. In her imaginary version of this moment, he had not yet chosen the ring and they would go to the jeweller's and select a diamond together. It was beautiful, though, and she had to admit that there was a possibility she might have picked it out herself, if it had been pointed out to her.

She said yes – of course she did – and he picked her up and spun round with her in his arms as if she were a child. Annie wanted the whole of Primrose Hill to stop and look at them. In fact, proposals up there were two a penny. The only person to notice that her life had just changed beyond recognition was an old man with a poodle on a red lead.

She floated back down the hill, Joe holding her hand tight; she felt the new, strange ring digging into the side of her finger as he squeezed. She smiled randomly at everyone they passed, dog walkers, joggers and recalcitrant teenagers alike, until her cheeks ached. She was going to be Mrs Joe Ferensby and she wanted the world to know and share in her joy.

And now here is Ursula telling her that the whole thing is a mistake. She is nineteen years old, for goodness' sake. Totally old enough to know her own mind, make her own decisions. And this one is a good one. She knows it in her heart.

'I know you think I'm young, Ursula,' she says. 'But I'm not like you. I haven't been to college. I'm ready for the next stage.' She's expecting some sort of protest from Ursula at this statement and pauses, waiting for the interruption, but Ursula doesn't speak and Annie feels slightly wrong-footed. 'I'm ready to make a home for myself,' she continues, 'have some children of my own. And I know Joe's a charmer and he flirts like mad with everyone. He wraps Mum and Dad around his little finger. But it's all a front really. He's kind and caring and fun to be with and I know he loves me. He really does.'

Annie reaches across the table to touch her sister's arm. It's an awkward gesture and she needs to stand on her tiptoes to achieve it. She feels Ursula withdraw slightly and then accept her touch.

'Can't you just be happy for me, Urs? Please.'

Ursula takes a breath to speak but is interrupted by a deep, guttural snore. Their father shudders in his sleep and Annie pulls her hand back quickly, preparing for flight. Ursula's face hardens again, her thin lips narrowing into tight, white creases.

'You do what you like,' she says. 'As soon as I've finished my course I'm out of here too. I'm going as far away as I can get. You won't see me for dust. Marry him; don't marry him. It makes no odds to me. But don't come crying when you're tied down with children you can't look after and your life is over by the time you're twenty-five. This is your choice, Annie. Your mistake.'

Ursula storms out of the kitchen, quietly. Annie is left alone. Her father is drooling now, a thin ribbon of saliva snaking its way down his cheek and pooling on the table. He looks so vulnerable. Annie could just take a cushion and . . . But none of that matters now. Joe will protect her. Her father will never be able to hurt her again.

CHAPTER THIRTEEN

Cara, 2017

Somehow, I know that my mother is still alive. I can't explain why but I feel it deep inside me. Somewhere out there in the big, wide world, I have a mother who is not dead. I have no proof though, no reason, beyond a box of old postcards, to reach such a startling conclusion. Even as I think this, the butterflies inside me grow into dragons that flap their wings so violently that I'm having difficulty breathing and I have to suck in large gasps of air through my mouth. The best word I can think of to describe how I feel at this possibility is joy: deep, unadulterated joy.

Of course, that feeling does not last. Breakfast is the usual muddle of spillages and misinterpretation. I think Dad wants cornflakes. I discover that he does not when he upends his bowl on the table. I set to with a cloth. It doesn't take long to clear up the resulting mess. I've learned not to overfill his bowl. I start again with Weetabix. That's not right either but he seems to lose interest in his objection halfway through it and finally gets on with eating. He's at the point where he still wants to feed himself but isn't quite able to. When the Weetabix mush finally makes it on to his spoon, it at least stays put – but more of it then ends up down his chin than in his mouth. Eventually, frustrated and hungry, he allows me to help him with what is left in his bowl.

I need to talk to Michael. Even as the thought materialises in my mind, I know that I must do it now, this minute. I have to tell him what I have discovered. This woman whom I might just have resurrected from the dead with the click of a mouse is his mother too. More than that, though, it's too big to carry all by myself and my brother is the only person who can know what it feels like. Beth would be empathetic and make all the right noises to support me but her mother has not been dead for thirty years only to be rediscovered. No. The only person with whom I can possibly discuss how this feels is Michael.

But how? Michael's in London. It's not like I can pop over for coffee, and I can't do this by telephone. I need to see his face as I tell him so I can judge his reaction. I have to talk to him properly without him clamming up or, worse still, putting the phone down on me. It wouldn't be the first time that he's dealt with unpalatable information by sticking his head in the sand. All of a sudden, my need to get to London becomes all-consuming. I stand up as if I'm about to set off there and then. I do it so quickly that Mrs P turns round from the sink to see what's happened, turning back wordlessly when all seems well.

'I have to go to London,' I announce. 'Today.'

As soon as I've said this, the practicalities start to dawn on me. Trips like this require days, maybe weeks of careful planning. I can hardly leave Dad to fend for himself – and, while Mrs P and I discussed her staying over when Dad needs that level of care, it's not something that I've mentioned since.

'I need some silk,' I continue. 'And I'm running low on other things too. I usually order online but . . .'

My voice trails off. Even to me it sounds like a feeble excuse. I work on wedding dresses that have a lead time of months, almost years. I am well organised – well, in my work at any rate. I'd never get to a situation when I needed things now, at once. I should've been more honest. I should've said that I wanted to see Michael from the outset. There is no need to say why. I'm about to do a U-turn when Mrs P turns from the sink, wiping her hands on a towel.

'Would you want me to stay with your father?' she asks. 'I had nothing planned for this evening. If I nip home when he's at The Limes, then I can pick up a few bits and pieces. I'll stay the night and then you don't need to worry about racing back.'

I evaluate her offer as she speaks. It seems genuine. There's no sense of her being put-upon or pushed into something that she's reluctant to do – and anyway, it's not like I'll be asking her to do it for free. I am sure the agency's night rates more than cover the inconvenience.

I realise that I still haven't replied. She's staring at me, waiting, and the longer I delay in accepting her offer, the more it looks like I don't quite trust her somehow. I see doubt start to flicker across her face and I leap in before it has time to take hold.

'Well, if you really don't mind, then that'd be fantastic,' I say, smiling as widely as I can to show her how much confidence I have in her ability to care for Dad while I'm away. 'I don't normally need to go on such short notice. This is a bit of a one-off. But if you could step into the breach . . .'

'Don't you worry,' she says. 'We'll be just fine here without you. There'll be less mess for a start.'

This pulls me up short, but when I look at her I can see the joke playing around her hazel eyes and I know that this is going to work out just fine. Then I remember Dad, who is sitting waiting for someone to tell him what to do next. He has not been following the conversation flying in the air over his head.

'Would that be okay with you, Dad?' I ask him. 'If I go away for a night and leave you here with Mrs P?'

'We'll get along just fine, won't we, Joe?' Mrs P adds.

Dad looks from one of us to the other. I'm pretty certain that he's not grasped what we said but I am not about to look a gift horse in the mouth. If this doesn't work then I won't get a chance to speak to Michael and suddenly this is the only thing that matters.

'That's great then,' I say before he has a chance to catch on.

Dad's blank face just stares up at me.

'I'll just go and pack a few things and then check the train times,' I say. 'Thank you so much.'

I have to stop myself from bouncing up and down. Mrs P nods and I race from the room and into my workroom, where I have loaded up the train website and worked out when I need to leave before you've had time to say 'Jack Robinson'. Then, suddenly, I start to doubt myself. What will I say to Michael? It's not like I have any real proof that our mother isn't dead. A box of unsigned postcards and the lack of a death certificate is a pretty good starting point but what does it actually tell me for certain? At the moment, all I have is some circumstantial stuff and a feeling in my gut, and I'm going to need more than that to convince my brother.

CHAPTER FOURTEEN

As I leave the house, my overnight things hastily stuffed into my bag, I turn back to see Dad sitting in the front-room window, watching me. My heart lurches, seeing him there like a little boy waiting for his daddy to come home, until I realise that he sits there every morning while he waits for Brian and the minibus to take him to the day centre. Any emotional agenda placed on top of that is entirely of my own making. Dad will have forgotten that I'm going anywhere. He won't give me a second's thought until he gets back and finds I'm not there for tea – and maybe not even then.

The train pulls into Wakefield and I toy with how best to approach Michael. I sent him a hasty text message before I left, just to make sure that he was going to be there.

Hi. In town today. Any chance of a bed? Arriving around five. C x

Michael texted back, his message curt but saying I'm welcome. He'll have been slightly surprised but not thrown by my short notice. As long as they are at home, their door will always be open to me. As the train races towards Doncaster, I think through how the evening will pan out. I picture dinner with Marianne and their twin girls, my nieces. They all eat together much later than we ever did at home, testament I suspect to the new life that Michael has built for himself in the south. The children call the meal 'dinner', not 'tea', which always makes me smile. I suppose I would have been the same if Dad hadn't raced us up north, leaving our London life and all trace of my mother behind. After we've eaten I'll need to get Michael on his own for a bit. Much as I like Marianne, I can't do this in front of her. It needs to be just Michael and me. Maybe if I tell her that it is something to do with Dad she'll be happy to absent herself on the pretext of getting the children into bed.

At this point, my plan falters. When I do get Michael to myself, what will I say? How do you tell someone that you think their mother, dead for the last thirty years, is actually alive? It's hard to imagine how that can be casually dropped into the conversation. As I play this all out in my head, I can feel moist patches forming under my armpits and beginning to seep into my top. But beneath this anxiety there's a frisson of excitement. I try to imagine how Michael will react. He won't believe it, not at first, but he'll have to wonder when I show him everything I've found. The idea that I know something that he doesn't makes me feel a bit smug. Being the baby sister never really leaves you.

The train pulls into Doncaster. It is a tall, old-fashioned station. It makes me picture soldiers with sweethearts, steam and bustle. A woman gets into my carriage. She must be around sixty, although I'm not great at guessing the age of anyone more than ten years older than me. I'm going on her hair, which is shot through with steely grey, and her clothes, which are mainly various shades of beige apart from a resolutely red polyester scarf tied around her neck.

The woman is quite heavily built and has to turn herself sideways to get down the narrow aisle between the seats. I am sitting alone at a table and there are plenty of free seats so I am annoyed when she stops next to me and squeezes herself into the seat opposite. Her legs bang mine as she tries to get herself comfortable in the limited space. It's only when she has arranged herself that she looks up at me.

'No one sitting here, duck, is there?'

I am tempted to tell her that my travelling companion has just gone to the buffet car and will be back shortly but then I'll be embarrassed when she moves and my companion never reappears. I shake my head and turn to look out of the window, hoping to avoid any further conversation. The woman steadies her breathing – she must have been running late for the train – and then starts to get things out of her bag. Despite my fear of catching her eye, I can't help but watch surreptitiously. First she finds a dog-eared book of logic problems and a stubby pencil with a well-worn eraser on the end and then a rather squashed Eccles cake in a cellophane wrapper. She opens the Eccles cake and starts to eat the sugar from the top by licking her finger and pressing it down on the sparkling little clusters. I want to look away but I find my eyes drawn to her. As if sensing my gaze, she looks up at me and smiles. Then she blushes and wipes her sticky finger on the fabric of her skirt.

'Ooh, what must you think of me?' she asks, shaking her head. 'Eating my Eccles cake like that.' Her eyes twinkle as she shrugs her shoulders. 'Still,' she adds. 'It's the only way to eat 'em. Next you have to bash the top in and pick out all the currants.'

As if to prove her point, she gently taps at the pastry and the crust breaks, revealing the shining, dark fruit within.

'When me mam made 'em, she always used to stick a sprig of mint inside before she baked 'em. Tasted marvellous. You don't get that in these shop-bought ones but they're nice all the same. Want a bit?' she says, pushing the flattened cake towards me.

I shake my head.

'Don't blame you, duck. Doesn't look that tasty, does it?'

She goes back to picking at the top of the cake and putting tiny, mouse-sized portions into her mouth. I see her catch sight of my hand. I could pull it out of sight but I have learned that the best way to deal with the staring is to face it head-on. I leave it on the table in front of us. The woman doesn't snatch her gaze away, as people usually do. Instead she studies the rough contours of my skin.

'That's a terrible scar you've got there, duck,' she says. 'Does it still give you any bother?'

I am touched that she asks about the aftermath rather than how it came about. Usually those who can't resist asking are entirely focused on how I ended up with such an injury.

'It can get sore if it gets too hot, and the damp weather sometimes sets it off,' I say.

'Well you're living in the wrong part of the world if you want to avoid the damp,' she says with a wide, open smile.

Then she opens the puzzle book, pressing it down along the spine, and sets to reading the clues. She takes the pencil and bangs it gently against her forehead as she reads. Two minutes later she puts the pencil back down and sits back in her seat.

'I don't know why I'm bothering,' she says to me. 'I can't make head nor tail of it. My daughter says I need to do puzzles to keep me brain active. I think she's worried I'll go doolally and she'll need to look after me. She seems to have forgotten all those years that I spent looking after her. Still, she has a point, doesn't she? There's a lot going senile these days. They say it's getting worse and worse.'

Even though she is a stranger, there is something about this woman's straightforward, direct chatter that draws me in. We are here, stuck on a train together. What harm can there be in striking up a bit of a conversation?

'My dad's got dementia,' I say. 'Well, Alzheimer's actually.'

'Is there a difference?' she asks. 'I thought one was just the posh name for the other.'

'Yes,' I say, reluctant to get into too many details and already wondering whether I'd have been better keeping my mouth shut. 'Dementia is like an umbrella term. It covers lots of different kinds of illness. Alzheimer's is just one of those.'

She nods as if she's processing what I've said.

'I never knew that,' she says. 'And is he bad, your dad?'

I've never really thought of Dad's illness in terms of good or bad. It just is.

'Well,' I say. 'There are others who are worse, I suppose, but we've got to the stage when he can't be left on his own.'

'Is he in a nursing home then?' she asks, her head tipped to one side sympathetically.

'No. He's still at home with me.'

She looks confused and even looks around to see if there is any sign of Dad elsewhere in the carriage.

'I have some help,' I add. 'A nurse who comes in. She's with him today.'

'You see, that's great, that is,' says the lady, breaking off a piece of the pastry from the bottom of the Eccles cake and popping it into her mouth. 'That's how it should be. Children looking after their parents. That's how they do it on the Continent. They've got the right idea, those Italians. My daughter'll put me in a home as fast as look at me if she thinks there's any chance of me not coping by myself.'

I nod and try to ignore the fact that I've had the same discussion with myself many a time.

'And where's your mum?' the lady asks.

'My mum died when I was a little girl,' I reply.

The answer just trips out of me as it has done hundreds of times over my life. As the woman nods at me kindly, it occurs to me that this might be the last time that I ever say it.

'That's a shame,' the woman says. 'You poor little mite. A child needs its mother, make no mistake. A man is all well and good but there's some things when it just has to be a mum. No wonder you're taking such good care of him, your dad. There must be a real bond between the two of you.'

And that is when it hits me. There, in the train full of strangers, talking to this woman with her Eccles cake and her puzzle book. If my mother is not dead then where the hell is she? How could she possibly have left Michael and me to fend for ourselves when we were so tiny? And where has she been since? Did she think that a few postcards were enough to discharge her maternal duties? If so, then she was wrong.

The Eccles cake woman is looking at me, her eyes searching out mine, her head cocked to one side again, and I realise that she is expecting me to speak.

'Your dad,' she prompts. 'You must have a really special bond. Are you all right, duck?' she adds, as concern spreads across her round face.

I try to close my mind to the new ideas that are rampaging around.

'Sorry,' I say to her. 'Yes. We are quite close. If you don't mind, I just need to . . .'

I stand up and slide myself out from behind the table and set off towards the electric doors that separate this carriage from the next.

'Is everything all right, dear?' I hear her call out behind me.

I ignore her. I need to get away. I need fresh air. I need space to clear my head of this alien idea that has infiltrated my thoughts. It's like a virus. Now that it is in there, I can feel it spreading, corrupting everything that it touches. I want it to stop. I want to hold tight to the excitement that I felt when I was sitting at my computer, that I felt when I boarded the train, but it's too late. It's already tainted. Now, I can barely believe that it has taken so long for the thought to occur to me. How dare she leave us? Where did she go? Where has she been for thirty years?

I lean against the wall in between carriages, close my eyes and take deep breaths. I feel my body being gently jolted by the train and it calms me, like a baby being rocked. I don't know how long I stay there, but when I head back to my seat Eccles cake woman has gone.

CHAPTER FIFTEEN

I arrive at Michael's place feeling grubby and somehow violated by the busy tube journey. Their house, a semi with pointed gables and big bay windows, is built in tawny London brick. The gentle light of evening dances over it, pulling me in like a beacon to a ship lost at sea. It couldn't be more different from the blackened millstone grit of our house in Yorkshire. The front garden, now gravelled over for ease of maintenance, is dotted with pots that I assume once contained summer bedding but which are now stripped to bare compost. An encircling flower bed is home to various nondescript shrubs, which, in keeping with their anonymity, are neatly clipped. The garden is the embodiment of my brother – practical, efficient and understated – and it makes me smile.

I knock on the door and almost at once hear little feet running to open it.

'Auntie Cara's here!' my nieces shout through the wood, their voices far more excited than my appearance on their doorstep can possibly merit.

There is the clicking of bolts being pulled and then the door opens to reveal two small, dark-haired girls. Their initial excitement seems to desert them as soon as the door opens. They shuffle close to one other and eye me shyly.

'Hello, girls,' I say. 'Can I come in?'

They step aside in unison to let me enter and as I pass them, I feel a small hand being gently slipped into mine.

Marianne comes through from the kitchen at the back of the house. She is wearing an apron, which immediately makes me think of her as a mother. Her dark hair is pulled away from her face with a padded Alice band of the sort that you rarely see these days. She has flour on her hands and forearms.

'Cara. How lovely to see you. Did you have a good journey? Girls! Girls! Let your aunt get over the threshold.'

Her voice still harbours the sing-songy cadences of her Welsh roots despite her years in London. She bustles towards me, looks as if she is going to kiss me and then holds back at the last moment. We have never been very demonstrative, Michael and I, and I am grateful to Marianne for remembering this.

'Thanks for having me at such short notice,' I say. 'I needed stuff in town and, as usual, left it all too late to get it delivered. I could just have gone back home this evening but . . .'

'Of course you couldn't,' Marianne interrupts. 'Coming all this way and not calling in. We'd never forgive you, would we, girls?'

The girls, Zara and Esmé, shake their heads. They are like little miniatures of their mother. I can see no trace of my genes in their upturned faces.

'Michael isn't back from work yet but he said to tell you that he won't be late. Come in, come in.'

She motions towards the front room with her floury arm.

'Can I get you a drink?'

'A cup of tea would be great,' I say.

'Well, you go in there and make yourself comfortable while I put the kettle on. Girls, give Auntie Cara a bit of space.'

The girls have got over their initial shyness and are now clinging to a hip each, making it almost impossible for me to walk. They seem very small but I don't really have much to compare them with. I can't even quite remember how old they are – six, maybe, or seven?

'Yes, you come with me, girls, and I'll see if there might be something hidden in my bag for you.'

The girls bounce up and down, jostling my elbows.

'Oh, there was no need for that,' says Marianne, but she is smiling in a way that tells me that the gifts had been anticipated and I am relieved that I thought of it. I produce two striped paper bags and hand one to each niece. They look at each other with wide eyes before opening the bags and peering in and then in moments they're on the floor comparing the spoils. Each bag contains a selection of silk ribbons in bright, rainbow colours, a twist of paper holding tiny buttons in the shape of baby animals and a retractable tape measure with a case that looks like a ladybird. They are afterthoughts, hastily gathered at the haberdashery I was in earlier, but the girls seem delighted and Marianne, who has been loitering in the doorway, mouths a silent 'Thank you' over their heads.

I watch the girls barter over their buttons while Marianne makes my cup of tea. Obviously, I don't have any children. To have children you usually need a partner and I can't see that happening any time soon, but I can't help marvelling at what a great job Michael and Marianne are doing of bringing up theirs. It must be Marianne's influence. What experience does Michael have of creating a happy home life? When Michael proposed to Marianne, I was surprised by his choice. She's a plain woman, which immediately stood her out from his other girlfriends. She is quiet, too, though not in a shrinking-violet kind of way. It's more that she doesn't speak unless she has something worth saying and there's a kind of inner calm about her, an element of self-possession that is very comforting. As I get to know her better, I begin to understand exactly why Michael has chosen her to spend his life with. I'm not entirely sure why she has chosen Michael.

The button-and-ribbon redistribution seems to have been completed without fuss and the girls slink off to another part of the house, taking their treasure with them. Marianne comes in with a tray laden with the necessaries for a perfect cup of tea. She sets it down on the coffee table and pours me a cup, adding milk and one sugar without having to be asked. She passes it to me and I take it gratefully and sink a little deeper into the sofa.

'So,' says Marianne once she has her own drink. 'How's your dad? Is it working out well with the nurse?'

'It's good so far,' I reply. 'I think. Dad likes her and she's kind and treats him with dignity, which isn't always easy, given how he behaves a lot of the time.' I think I see Marianne wince a little at this but I am not pulling any punches. Life with Dad is hard and they need to understand that. 'I think it's going to work out fine,' I add and realise as I say it that it's true.

'Michael is incredibly grateful for all that you're doing,' Marianne says in her gentle voice. She looks straight into my eyes as she says this and I understand that she is trying to convey something more than just the words. I don't want to get into this kind of discussion; there's too much in my head already. I bat her away with a smile and a nod.

'I know that, Marianne,' I say, and hope that I don't sound too dismissive.

Michael should be bloody grateful. He runs away at the first chance he gets and never comes back, leaving me with the father he was escaping from and then later with the broken man that he's become. I hope his conscience does trouble him. It's no more than he deserves. I suppose he did the best he could, given the animosity between the pair of them, but sometimes your best just isn't enough.

'The girls have grown,' I say, neatly changing the subject.

Marianne smiles warmly at the mention of her daughters.

'Oh, they're little monkeys but we are proud of them. Zara is doing really well with her violin and Esmé seems to have inherited her Dad's love of maths. It's early days, I know, but so far so good.'

As she speaks, I hear a key sliding into the front door. Marianne hears it too and starts to straighten her hair, almost a Pavlovian response.

'Ah,' she says, with a greater sense of relief than seems necessary. She must find this one-to-one stuff difficult. Or maybe it is just me that's a challenge?

'Here he is. The man of the house. We're in here, Michael,' she shouts out to the hallway.

I get the impression that this is as much to remind Michael that they have a visitor as it is to direct him to where we are. There is the sound of keys being put down on a table and the rustling of a mackintosh and then my big brother appears at the door. He looks just like he did when we were kids but for the flecks of grey in his strong, dark hair. His tie is loose and his shirt sleeves are rolled to the elbow but they are both expensive-looking and his suit trousers hang neatly from his slim hips to just the right height above his polished shoes.

'Ca. Hi. How are you? Good trip? Got all your sewing supplies?'

Even though I haven't seen him for well over a year, there's no expectation that we will embrace; but I can hear the sincerity in his voice.

I nod a reply to all his questions, adding, 'You don't mind me landing on you like this, do you?'

He shakes his head.

'Of course not. It's great to see you.'

I notice that he does not follow this with the usual pleasantries about how long it has been since we saw each other last. We both know exactly how long it's been.

'We were just catching up,' says Marianne. 'Cara has bought some lovely things for the girls, which was really kind.'

I shrug to suggest that it's the least I can do.

'Anyway,' she continues. 'I'll just go and check on the dinner. It won't be long now.'

She stands up, lifts the tea tray and heads out of the room, leaving me alone with my brother.

'Well?' he says, seeing straight through my thin haberdashery excuse.

'Not here,' I say. 'Not now. Can we get away after dinner? Just the two of us. Go to the pub or something?'

Michael looks at me, clearly thinking about what could be so important that I don't want Marianne to hear. I think he might object but then he just says, 'Okay. I'll sort it. There'll be questions, though, and I'm not saying that I won't tell Marianne whatever it is later.'

'That's fine,' I say. 'I'd just rather discuss it with you in private first.'

He nods, happy with this, and then Marianne calls out from the kitchen that dinner is ready. The sound of the girls thundering down the stairs follows quickly after.

'I'm looking forward to this,' I say as I push myself to my feet.

One of Marianne's many talents is an ability to cook delicious food, which is something I can't do. Michael doesn't reply and I wonder, not for the first time, what goes on in his head.

CHAPTER SIXTEEN

Annie, 1984

Annie turns the oven down again. The chops that she has grilled for Joe's dinner are starting to crisp at the edges, the fat charred almost to the point of burning. The peas, once a vibrant green, are now a sludgy, processed khaki and there is a skin on the gravy that she won't be able to lift without making a mess of the once-perfect plate. It can't be helped. If he'd been home on time, his meal would have been there to greet him as he walked through the door. He doesn't like to wait. She can understand that. He works hard and wants things to be just so when he gets home. Her father was the same. She thinks now of her mother, who always spent the last twenty minutes of their day tidying the house and then touching up her face in the hall mirror. Annie loved watching her trace the contours of her mouth with the edge of the lipstick, pinching at her cheeks to bring up their colour. Now Annie tries to do the same for Joe. Each day, she aims to make their home a scene of tranquil, domestic bliss for when he gets back; but somehow she always falls short. Tonight, Michael and Cara have had their baths, and Cara is in bed, but the makings of a Lego fort are still scattered across the kitchen floor and their discarded clothes strewn over the landing. Try as she might, she can never seem to get dinner, the children and the house all sorted at the same time. Something is always out of place.

Joe is late and his meal is most definitely past its best. The pork is beyond help but she could perhaps do some more peas. She opens the oven door and reaches for the plate, remembering too late that it will be hot. The skin on the pads of her fingers contracts as she grasps the china. She grabs for a tea towel and tries again to retrieve the plate. The heat sears through the thin cotton and into her already-burned fingers. She knows she should put her hand under the cold tap but there's no time. She'll do it later, once the dinner has been rescued. She drops the plate on the table, refolds the tea towel into a thicker wedge and picks it up once again, her fingers crying out against the heat even through the padding. Propping the bin lid open with her elbow she tries to scrape the faded peas off the plate without losing anything else. The chop in its lake of congealed gravy begins to slide towards the waiting mouth of the bin. Gathering momentum, the mashed potatoes follow. Before she can stop it, the chop skates off the plate and lands on top of the remains of the children's spaghetti hoops.

For a second Annie freezes, not sure what to do to. Panic grips her but it is okay. She can fix it. Then she puts her hand into the bin and extracts the chop. It looks all right. There is a bit of tomato sauce on it but she can disguise that. She's just thinking that she might need to wipe the rim of the plate with a bit of kitchen roll when she hears Joe's key in the front door. Now there are no peas, the gravy looks like a dirty protest across the plate and the chop has ketchup on it. She had tried to make everything so perfect for him and she has messed it all up. Again. Then, right on cue, a howl of anguish rings out upstairs. Cara is awake.

Annie sits down heavily at the table, the remains of Joe's dinner before her, and puts her head in her hands. Tears sting her eyes but she bites her lip in an effort to keep control and takes deep, solid breaths.

'Hello,' Joe shouts. 'I'm home.'

'I'm in here,' Annie replies, her voice not much above a whisper. The door opens and in strolls Joe. Annie does not look up. 'I'm sorry,' she says quietly. 'I've ruined your dinner.' She can hear Joe cross the room towards her and feels his arm across her back. He gives her a gentle squeeze.

'You really can't be trusted on your own, can you, baby?' he says, laughing warmly. 'Only you could manage to ruin chops and mash.'

She can hear the smile in his words but she still doesn't raise her head. 'I'm sorry,' she says again. 'It was fine but then you were late and . . .' She stops speaking abruptly. She doesn't want Joe to think that she blames him for the spoiled dinner. She should have left it warming in a cooler oven. There's no one else to blame.

'It doesn't matter, pumpkin,' says Joe, and takes his arm from around her shoulder, which makes her feel suddenly cold and exposed. 'I had something to eat after work anyway. We'll just get rid of this . . .'

He takes the plate over to the bin, lifts the lid and lets the meal slip unceremoniously inside.

'There,' he says. 'Problem solved.'

As Annie watches the meat disappear, she thinks of the baked beans that she and the children regularly eat to make her housekeeping money stretch.

From upstairs, there comes another howl.

'I think she must be teething,' says Annie. 'She wouldn't settle all day. It's been exhausting, actually, trying to make her happy. I just haven't managed to get anything done.'

'Don't worry,' says Joe. 'You just keep sitting there and have a little rest and I'll go and sort her out.'

Annie knows that she should leap up and settle their daughter, that it's Joe who ought to be putting his feet up and relaxing after his hard day at work, but she just doesn't have the strength. 'Thank you,' she murmurs, but she doubts that he hears her as he bounds up the stairs to placate his grizzly little girl. She can just catch his sing-songy voice as it floats accusingly down the stairs.

'Now then, my little princess,' he sings. 'What's all this? Are those new teeth giving you some trouble? Mummy is too tired to come and help you but Daddy's here so everything is going to be all right. There, there.'

Annie pictures him pacing up and down the nursery, Cara pressing her tiny body into his shoulder, her perfect little head nestled into the space beneath his chin. Already the crying has stopped. He has done, in less than a minute, what she has failed to do in a whole day. She couldn't settle her own baby. She couldn't even make dinner without creating carnage. She is no good at being married. She is a terrible mother and a worse wife. The thought crosses her mind, and not for the first time, that they would all be so much better off without her.

CHAPTER SEVENTEEN

Cara, 2017

As anticipated, Marianne's dinner is delicious. I eat far more than is good for me but it's such a rare treat to be cooked for that I get carried away.

'Coffee anyone?' asks Marianne when dessert has been duly dispatched.

I throw a glance at Michael but he is already pushing his chair away from the table.

'That would be lovely, darling, but Cara and I have some things to talk through. About Dad,' he adds to clarify.

I don't correct him.

'I thought we might nip out to the pub.'

Marianne's eyebrows shoot up.

'There's no need for that,' she says, as if Michael has suggested that we sit out in the shed. 'I'll put the girls to bed and do the clearing up.' She glances round the kitchen in which barely a spoon is out of place. 'You two can sit in the lounge.'

'Thanks but I think we'll go out,' Michael replies in a tone that grazes harshness. He reminds me of Dad. 'There's a place that's not too bad at the end of the road, Ca. Grab your coat. Let's go.'

The pub really is just at the end of the road. It's painted white with numerous hanging baskets dangling along the frontage above low, dark windows. Michael leads the way and we easily find a table tucked away down one side. I make myself comfortable, with my back to the wall, as Michael asks what I'd like to drink.

'Brandy, please,' I say.

He looks at me quizzically. 'Am I going to need one as well?' he asks.

'Quite possibly.'

Not asking anything further, he heads to the bar, leaving me to think, yet again, about how I'm going to address the issue.

He returns in almost no time with two brandy glasses containing what look like double measures. He hands one to me and then drops into his seat.

'Are you going to tell me what this is all about?'

I take a deep breath and begin. 'It started with Mrs P,' I say.

Michael looks confused already.

'Mrs P. That's the nurse. I call her that because . . . well, it doesn't matter. Anyway, we got talking about Mum . . .'

I sense him bristle. Talking about Mum would not be something he'd do with a stranger. I ignore his reaction and plough on.

'Anyway, she's incredibly organised, is Mrs P – you'll like her. She's sorting the whole house out. You wouldn't recognise the place . . .'

Michael is radiating impatience. My 'all round the houses' delivery style is starting to irritate him. He raises an eyebrow but I refuse to let him fluster me.

'So, I went up to the attic to look for stuff that Dad might recognise, to help him feel settled and . . .'

'You went in the attic!' he says with mock horror.

The mood is immediately lightened.

'I know. It was very naughty. I kept thinking that I was going to get caught, which is obviously ridiculous. He's not like he used to be,

Michael. I doubt he even remembers we have an attic, let alone that we weren't allowed up there.'

Michael has the good grace to look at least a little sad before he moves me on.

'So, what did you find on this little expedition of yours?'

'Well, that's the thing,' I say and take a mouthful of brandy.

Over near the bar someone drops a glass. The chime of it smashing on the tiles is immediately followed by a cheer and a round of applause. I look over to see what is going on but when I look back Michael is still staring at me, as if nothing has interrupted my story. I continue.

'So, right at the back there was this box. It wasn't labelled like all the others. It just said "A" on it and when I opened it . . .'

'Bats flew out and a ghostly apparition floated . . .'

'If you're not going to take this seriously . . .'

'Sorry,' Michael says and bows his head in faux shame.

'Anyway,' I say with pointed emphasis. 'The box was full of post-cards. Like these.'

I scrabble in my bag, take out the envelope containing a sample of the postcards and push it across the table towards him.

Michael hesitates for a moment before reaching out to pick them up. He slides them out of the envelope, takes a cursory glance at the pictures and then turns them over. I scrutinise his face as he reads the message on one of them. He flicks through the others and clearly registers that all the messages are exactly the same; a deep line appears between his eyebrows.

'What's this supposed to mean?' he says. His tone is curt. '"My darling babies. I love you more than you will ever know. Please forgive me",' he reads flatly. There is a bitter, sarcastic tone to his voice that makes me uncomfortable. It's as if he is speaking to some trainee who's failed to do a piece of research to his satisfaction. 'Where have they come from?' he asks and drops the cards on to the table, pushing them back towards me. I hesitate. I need to take him with me on this but I'm in danger of losing him before I get to the important part.

'Look at the postmarks,' I say quickly. 'This is just a few of them but they start in March 1987 . . .' I pause to let the significance of the date dawn on him. I can tell from his face that he's with me. 'And they keep going until I turn eighteen and then they stop.'

'Okay,' he says slowly. 'You found some old postcards from a nutter with a screw loose. And?'

I take another drink, the brandy burning first my throat and then my stomach. 'So, this is where it gets really weird,' I say. 'I started wondering what if – and it's just a left-field idea – but what if Mum sent these postcards?'

'Well, she couldn't have,' says Michael dismissively. 'You've already said that the first one was sent after she was dead.'

I don't speak for a moment and just wait for the significance of what I'm saying to sink in.

'Oh, I get it,' he says, leaning back in his chair and putting his hands behind his head. 'I get it. Please tell me that you're not about to say you don't think Mum died.'

It is like we have gone back in time. Me, the stupid baby sister with nothing worthwhile to say, and him, my know-it-all big brother.

'Well,' I say as I rub at the lumpen skin on my damaged hand. 'What other explanation can there be? Who else would write postcards like that? And keep it up for our entire childhoods?'

Michael opens his mouth to speak but I talk across him.

'And anyway, that's not it. That's not the main thing.'

'Come on then,' he says. 'Let's have it.'

He's still trying to look like he isn't interested but now he leans forward in his seat again so that his head is close to mine. I take a deep breath. I knew that this was never going to be easy but everything will turn on how he reacts to my next sentence. I need to keep calm and just tell him the facts without any emotional angle so that he can't mock me and miss my point.

'I got to thinking. Suppose, just suppose, that they are from Mum, that she didn't actually die . . .'

Michael's eyebrows shoot up and he is about to tell me that I am being ridiculous but I keep talking.

'So, I did a search on the internet on one of those family-tree sites. I thought I'd see if I could find her death certificate.'

I'm talking really quickly now, my words all tumbling over one another in my rush to get them out before I lose him completely.

'And there's no death certificate, Michael. I searched over and over again and there is no death certificate for our mother. What if she didn't die? She sent us those postcards and she didn't die? And if that's true then that means that Dad has been lying to us for years and I don't know what to do next.'

The stress of the last twenty-four hours suddenly hits me. Hot tears build up behind my eyes, waiting to escape. My breathing becomes jagged and I begin to sob, loud and convulsing, like a little girl. Michael doesn't move.

'What if I'm right, Michael?' I splutter through my tears. 'What if she's been out there, somewhere, all these years and . . .'

I can't talk anymore. My head drops and I just shake, silently.

'That's bollocks,' says Michael loudly enough that I wince. 'Our mother died when we were small and that's all there is to it. I don't know who sent these but it must have been someone playing a sick joke on Dad. And as for this rubbish about the birth certificate, you probably just got the search wrong.'

Of course he resorts to assuming that I've made a mistake. Sometimes he can be so like Dad. I ignore the slight, determined to stick to my guns.

'I didn't, Michael. I didn't. There is no death certificate at the central registry for Anne Ferensby in 1987 or at any time. Unless that wasn't her real name then our mother is not dead. And what about the postcards? Surely they point to her being alive too? She left but she wanted us to know that she loved us so she sent the postcards. There are hundreds of them, Michael, Hundreds.'

'Like sending a bunch of postcards can ever make up for abandoning us.'

I smell the concession and seize on it.

'So you agree that she might not be dead?' I ask desperately.

'I don't know. I don't want to know. As far as I'm concerned, she died when she died or walked out on us or whatever she did back then. None of this . . .' He flicks at the postcards with his fingers and sends them flying off the table. 'None of this makes any difference. I have no mother.'

'But Michael. Don't you want to know why, what happened? Aren't you just the tiniest bit curious?'

'Nope,' he says with a finality that I recognise. 'I'm not interested. I couldn't care less. I don't want to hear anything else about it. Our mother is dead and that's the end of it.' He picks up his glass and drains it in one gulp. 'Come on. We're going home. And don't mention any of this to Marianne either. I don't want her and the girls caught up in your little fantasies.'

I look up at the face of my big brother and somewhere, deep behind the anger and the bravado, I see the little boy that he once was: hurt, confused and lost. But the impression is fleeting and then he's gone, striding towards the door and leaving me scrabbling around trying to retrieve my bag and the postcards.

We don't speak as he marches along the pavement, me taking two steps to his one to keep up. When we get to the house, he stops at the gate and turns to face me. He puts a hand gently on my shoulder. His expression has mellowed and his voice is calmer.

'Let it go, Ca,' he says. 'No good can come of it. If she abandoned us then she might as well have died. What kind of mother leaves her own children? This whole thing needs putting back in the attic where you found it and forgetting about.'

To my surprise, he puts his arm around me and gives me a quick, awkward squeeze. Then he turns and heads up to the front door. I follow, numbed by what just happened, but I can't put the genie back in the bottle, forget what I have discovered. I won't. It's out and there's nothing I can do about it now. And even if I could, I don't want to.

CHAPTER EIGHTEEN

Thankfully, Marianne has gone to bed when we get in. I am relieved. I am not sure that either of us could deal with her questioning looks just now. Michael checks doors and windows and pulls out plugs ready for the house to sleep. Who still does that?

I climb into bed and let the duvet smother my body. The room smells lightly of something floral, rose maybe, and the sheets are cool and crisp against my skin. My limbs are exhausted but my mind cannot sleep, not yet. I lie on my back and listen to the sounds of the city, so much more intrusive at night than during the day. At home, I'm more likely to be kept awake by an owl than a siren but I suppose what you're used to becomes the norm pretty quickly. I would miss the dark, though, if I lived in a city. It is never dark in London, not really dark like it is on the moors. I remember discovering the stars when we moved to Ilkley. I saw them in the winter sky for the first time when all I'd known before was the orange glow of the city and suddenly the nursery rhymes made sense. 'Twinkle, Twinkle Little Star' and 'The Man in the Moon' were real after all. I told Michael what I had found, pointing up at the sky with a sense of triumph, but he just shrugged, like he'd known about the stars all the while, and I felt cheated of my big discovery.

My eyes spring open. Something has just occurred to me. I know that it's important but, having drifted across my mind like a waft of smoke, it's now dissipated into the darkness. Suddenly the need to recapture it becomes all-consuming but the harder I search, the further away it seems to drift. I try retracing my mental steps. The siren, the sky, the dark, the stars, Michael. There's nothing there, nothing that feels significant anyway. I force myself to close my eyes again and then it comes to me. If I remember discovering the stars in Yorkshire then surely that means that I must remember what they were like in London – and that is a memory. A memory from before Mum died. And if there's one, then there must be more, somewhere. I just have to find where to look for them. I lie there, the rose scent drifting in and out of my nostrils, but nothing else comes. Perhaps that was it, the one memory that I have, triggered by being back here in the city. But I can't believe that's true. Memory is complicated, isn't it? It won't just have stored that one, random thing. Others must come, given time. I just have to be patient and wait. I'm not that good at being patient.

I don't think I'll ever get to sleep but of course I do. Around seven o'clock I start to hear people moving about the house, and I get up and dressed without bothering to shower. I just want to leave now, to get home, check on Dad, consider my next move. I must speak to Michael first, though. Does he really want nothing to do with this? What if I find her? Then what? Am I supposed to just not mention it to him? I am on this journey and he has to come with me. He has no choice this time. I can't let him go to work without checking where he's got to in his thoughts, to make sure that he is all right, that he's softening. I'll be able to tell just by looking at him. I always know.

But I'm too late. When I come down the stairs, Marianne is making sandwiches in the kitchen.

'Morning,' she says, her smile as bright as usual. 'You look tired, Cara. Did you not sleep well? It's always hard in a strange bed. You've just missed Michael. He had an early meeting. He says to say goodbye and that you mustn't worry. I imagine it must be really difficult for you, having the responsibility of your dad all by yourself. We're always here for you, though. All you have to do is ask.' She slices the sandwiches deftly into triangles. 'Coffee?'

'I think I'll just get off,' I say. 'I still have some bits and pieces to buy.'

'You can't do that. There's no point going without any breakfast inside you. And you haven't said goodbye to the girls. Sit down and I'll make a fresh pot. Toast?'

And so I am looked after by my capable sister-in-law, who apparently has no idea that her husband's carefully constructed world has just collapsed in on itself.

When I get home, I hurry up the drive, aware that my heart is beating a little faster. Empty milk bottles sit on the front step together with a terracotta plant pot, newly filled with winter-flowering pansies that Mrs P must have planted while I was away. I let myself in, shouting out before the door is closed behind me.

'Hello. It's me! I'm back.' Silence. The back of my neck prickles. 'Hello,' I call again. 'Dad! Mrs P! Is there anyone here?'

I drop my bags and open doors looking for signs of life but the house is tidy and very, very empty. I'm reaching for my mobile phone when it hits me. Why would I expect them to be here? Dad will be at the day centre and Mrs P doesn't hang around here when there's no one to look after. I look up at the clock in the hall to confirm my realisation but of course I'm right.

When I go into the kitchen, there is a note from Mrs P on the kitchen table written in neat, block capitals.

DEAR CARA. HOPE YOU HAD A SUCCESSFUL TRIP. ALL WELL HERE. YOUR FATHER WAS FINE. SEE YOU THIS EVENING.

REGARDS,
ANGELA PARTINGTON (MRS P)

As I flick the kettle on, I feel a little foolish. I assume that my guilt stems from not really doing a proper risk assessment of the situation before I raced off to see Michael. As it turned out, it was fine – but what if it hadn't been? Even as this thought crosses my mind, I dismiss it. All is well. I have no reason to worry about what ifs, which is good because I have far bigger things to worry about.

I'm just unpacking my purchases and putting them away in my workroom when the phone rings.

'Hi. You'll never guess what!' says a bubbly voice that I recognise immediately as Beth's.

'They've recreated the Taj Mahal in sugar cubes on the Grove.'

'What?! No! We've set a date.'

'That's exciting,' I say. 'May I ask when?'

'Christmas Eve! Isn't it just the most romantic thing you've ever heard? I'm thinking furs and candles and holly berries.'

I am a bit taken aback. 'What? Next Christmas Eve?'

'No, silly. This Christmas Eve.'

I do a quick mental calculation. 'The Christmas Eve that's in, what? Eight weeks?' Even as I work out how long it is away, I am already thinking of what I have on my books and how I can possibly get Beth's dress designed and made within such a short timescale.

'Eight weeks and five days, to be precise,' says Beth, and she sounds so delighted that I can't help but get caught up in it.

'Beth, that's fantastic! Congratulations,' I say eventually. 'But it's not long. How will you get a venue booked in that time, especially at Christmas? Isn't everywhere full?'

'That's the romantic part,' she says. 'You know that hotel that Greg took me to when he proposed?'

I nod down the telephone.

'Well, it's going to be there. Greg booked it in secret. Won't it be just perfect?'

'But he only proposed a few weeks ago,' I object. 'Surely . . .'

'Ah. But he'd already pencilled the date in for the wedding before he proposed. So when I said yes, all he had to do was confirm.'

I'm so taken aback by this that, for a moment, I can't respond.

'Cara?' I hear Beth say. 'Are you still there?'

'Yes,' I manage. My mind races with how to deal with this sensitively and without spoiling the moment for Beth, who couldn't be more pleased with the way things with Greg seem to be turning out. 'Don't you think it's a little bit odd that he booked the reception before he had even asked you to marry him?' I ask as gently as I can.

'No,' she laughs. 'That's Greg all over. He's just so well organised and he was certain that I'd love a Christmas wedding. We'll be able to fly off on honeymoon on Christmas Day. It'll be perfect. And he knew that I'd say yes. I mean, you knew that I'd say yes and you're only my best friend so of course the man who's going to be my husband knew.'

Of course he did, I think.

'So,' Beth continues. 'That means we're going to have to get our skates on with the dress. I know it's not long. Do you think we can do it in that time or is it too much to ask?'

I can hear in her voice how badly she wants me to say yes. I think of my existing commitments, admittedly not as bad as they would be in the spring. I think of what I have on my plate with Dad and what he needs from me. I think about the box of postcards and Michael.

'No problem,' I hear myself say. 'We may need to choose something that's not too complicated but I'm sure we can get it done in time. And I'm just back from London with silk in the prettiest ivory you've ever seen. I had you in mind when I bought it. If you like it, then I think it would be perfect.'

'I love you, Cara Ferensby,' she says. I can hear the smile in her voice.

'I know. I am totally wonderful and you could not possibly live without me,' I reply. 'Right. You need to get your bones down here

PDQ with some pictures and a head full of ideas so that we can get some drawings started.'

'I knew you wouldn't let me down,' says Beth. 'Greg said he thought there wouldn't be time and that we should go and get a dress from London but I told him that you could do it.'

That decides it. I will have the dress made in time and it will be the most beautiful dress that I have ever created. Even as I think this, it crosses my mind that Greg might have waited before telling Beth about the date precisely so that I wouldn't have enough time left, leaving her with no option than to do what he wants, but I keep that thought to myself.

CHAPTER NINETEEN

The next day, Beth arrives with her arms full of bridal magazines and her head full of ideas. I can't help but smile as I see her struggling up the path, the magazines threatening to slither from her grip. By the time I open the door to her, she is almost bent double as she tries to hold on to them all.

'Quick!' she squeals. 'Help!' and then pushes past me and into the front room, where she finally lets them slide into a heap on the floor.

'Did you did leave any in the shop?' I ask.

'I had them all in order when I left home, with my favourites at the top. Now I'll have to start again.'

She doesn't look like this should be too much of a hardship as she sets to, flicking though each one and stopping at the pages with turned-down corners. I feel a stab of envy. Isn't planning her wedding supposed to be every girl's dream? I have been involved in so many but never my own. What is it that they say? Always the bridesmaid, never the bride. That's me.

'There are so many to choose from,' Beth says and I wonder if eking a design out of her is going to be a long job. 'But I'm pretty clear on what I want now,' she adds.

'That's great,' I say, dismissing my darker thoughts. 'Once we've got the basic outline sorted, the rest of it should fall into place without too much difficulty. I'll go and put the kettle on.'

Dad is in the kitchen, where I left him, still sitting at the table. He's been looking at a coffee-table book about the Hebrides, poring over the images as if he's searching for clues to some mystery that only he can solve. He looks up hopefully when I walk in but then, when he sees it's me, he goes back to his book.

'Beth's here,' I say. 'She's in the front room. She's getting married soon. I'm going to make her dress.' Dad shows no flicker of recognition at her name. 'I'm making a cup of tea, Dad. Would you like one?'

He nods enthusiastically then he seems to smile broadly at the space behind me; and when I turn round, Beth is standing there, a magazine in hand.

'Hello, Mr Ferensby,' she says. 'How are you doing?'

Dad nods. 'Good,' he says.

'Has Cara told you that she's going to make my wedding dress? This is the one that I like the best,' she adds, handing me the magazine over Dad's head.

He reaches up to grab it but he's not fast enough. I bend down to show it to Dad. It's a beautiful dress, elegant and simple in a twenties style that wouldn't have looked out of place in *The Great Gatsby*. Beth will look stunning in it and it won't be too challenging to make – which is a bonus, bearing in mind how little time we have.

Dad nods his head in approval. 'Nice,' he says.

'No Mrs P today?' asks Beth.

'Day off,' I say. 'Just us today, isn't it, Dad?'

Dad nods at me and I wonder, not for the first time, just how much of what is said around him he actually follows these days. Maybe more than I give him credit for.

'So,' I say to Beth. 'Is this dress the starting point or *the* dress?' I'm hoping that it is the former. There's no fun for me in just copying someone else's design, setting aside any legal issues that that might raise.

'Well,' says Beth. 'I like the idea of this kind of thing but I want the waist to be lower and the skirt needs to be drapey-er somehow. And I'm not sure Greg would like a dress with no sleeves. He always says that a wedding is supposed to be a wedding and not a party.' She must see something change in my face because she adds, 'But it's my dress and I love how elegant this one is. Just look at the way the back falls.'

'It's gorgeous,' I agree. 'We'll go through to my workroom and I'll do some sketches of the kind of thing that I think might work. I need to show you that silk, too, see if you like it. I think it would be perfect but it might not be what you want.'

We leave Dad to his book and head to my workroom. Beth is like a kid in a sweetshop as she swoops on my boxes of beads and trims.

'This is it,' I say, passing her the fabric. It shimmers in the light. Beth actually gasps.

'Oh, Cara. It's absolutely the perfect colour,' she says and I allow myself a brief moment of smug self-congratulation for anticipating my friend's needs so accurately.

'If we cut it on the bias and drape it like this . . .' I take the bolt from her, unroll a couple of metres and hold it against her body. 'Then it will fall beautifully. What kind of train were you thinking about?' I can tell from her face that she has not given this any thought at all. 'No worries,' I say. 'Let me sketch a couple of ideas.' Reaching for my pad and a pencil, I start to trace the lines in long, sure strokes. I love this part of my job, how the brides gradually see what is in my head as it is transferred to the paper. I am creating their dream right in front of their eyes. It doesn't always come together straightaway. Sometimes it's hard for the bride to translate what she wants into words that I can interpret. With Beth, though, it's almost like translating my own thoughts to pictures. I know exactly what she likes and, while we've never discussed wedding dresses in detail, I feel pretty confident that it won't take me long to get it right. As I sketch, Beth looks at the photos on my pinboard.

'You're so clever, Cara.' Her compliment courses through me straight to my core and makes me glow from the inside. Praise has always been a bit thin on the ground around here.

'I'm just so delighted that you want me to make your dress,' I say. 'Despite the objections.' It is a barbed comment and I don't really mean anything by it but Beth pulls a face.

'I think he just wants to make sure that I have everything I want – and, to be fair, he's never seen your work. For all he knows, you might be sewing sacks.'

'Fair enough,' I say. 'Well, let's hope I don't disappoint him.' Again, I can hear the sharpness in my response. Beth can too.

'You do like him, don't you, Ca? I know he can be a bit pompous but his heart's in the right place and I know he loves me.'

It's a thin line between looking out for your friend and bursting their bubble. I remain unconvinced by Greg, but then I'm not marrying him and just because I don't like him doesn't mean he's flawed.

'I know that too,' I say. It's a compromise answer but it seems to satisfy Beth.

'What did you get up to in London?' she asks, sliding us neatly away from potential conflict. 'Apart from buying my perfect silk.'

I have been waiting for this question, pondered on how I might respond. The easy reply would be to say that it was nice to see Michael and Marianne and leave it at that; before I made the trip, this is what I imagined I'd say. Even though I always tell Beth everything, the news about my mother had seemed too precious to share even with her. It was almost as though if I told anyone, it would destroy it, like popping a soap bubble.

But Michael's reaction has changed everything. If he maintains his position and does not want anything to do with my discovery, then it would be great to have Beth to talk to. In fact, if I don't talk to Beth then I really won't have anyone at all.

In the blink of an eye, I make a decision and act on it before I can give myself time to change my mind. And so, I tell her all of it: the finding of the postcards, the internet discovery and finally my discussion with Michael and his response.

Despite the obvious shock of what I am saying, Beth waits until I have finished before she speaks. 'Oh, Ca. My poor baby,' she says and puts her hand gently on my damaged one, which is still sketching lines on the pad, as if this can somehow protect me from what I am saying. 'What are you going to do?' she asks. 'I assume you can't ask your dad.'

I shake my head. 'You've seen him,' I say. 'He barely knows who he is, let alone has the ability to deal with something like this. No. I have to do this by myself. Whatever "this" is.'

'So you really think she might still be alive? Will you look for her?' Beth studies my face, not missing anything.

'I don't know,' I say. 'I'm not sure how I would anyway. There was nothing on the internet. And I can't help thinking that if she wanted to be found she would have left more clues than a box of postcards. If she is alive, though, I really want to know why she left. Well . . .' I hesitate. 'I think I do.'

Beth nods. 'I can see why you'd want to know that. It's an odd thing for a mother to do, to leave her children.'

I am grateful to her for not speculating further. I have not got to that point myself yet.

'Is there anyone you could ask? Did she have any family?'

I have realised over the last few days just how little I know about my mother's family. I was so small when she stopped being in my life that I have never really thought about who else there was around her. 'I don't know,' I say. 'I suppose her parents might be dead by now. They would be in their eighties.'

'Maybe Michael knows a bit more.' Beth twists her dark hair around her finger as she thinks. 'You could ask him. I know that he doesn't want anything to do with her himself but surely he won't do anything to stop you looking?'

I think about this. Beth is probably right but I cannot be entirely sure.

The sketch is finished. I turn the pad round and show it to her. The gown on the page is elegant, simply cut with draping lines, a halter-neck, a low back-line and no sleeves. It is Beth to a T, even if I do say so myself. Her eyes sparkle when she looks at it and she bites her bottom lip like she always does when she's excited.

'That is completely perfect,' she says. 'Do you really think you can make it in time?'

I look at the sketch, doing calculations as to the work involved, add-ing margins for error, alterations, finishing touches. 'Yes,' I say slowly. 'If you like this fabric and I get started straightaway then I think we can just about get it done. There can be no changing your mind, though,' I warn. 'Once I start to cut, then that will be it.'

'It's perfect, Ca. Why would I want to change my mind?'

'Well, take it away with you and think it over for a couple of days. We have that at least. I want you to be absolutely sure.'

'Okay,' she agrees. 'And there's something else.'

'You don't want much, do you?' I laugh.

'I think you'll like this bit,' she says. 'Would you please be my bridesmaid?'

What with everything, I can genuinely say that I had not given this part of the wedding a moment's thought. Now that I do, the emotions that have been bubbling under the surface choose this moment to explode. Tears roll down my cheeks. 'I would be honoured,' I manage. Then a terrible thought crosses my mind. 'You don't want me to make my dress as well, do you?'

Beth laughs. 'No,' she says. 'You concentrate all your efforts on mine. If you don't mind, we'll buy yours.'

Outside I can hear Dad moving about. 'I need to go and check on Dad,' I say.

'And I need to be going,' says Beth. 'Greg will be home soon.'

I try not to take umbrage at playing second fiddle. 'Okay,' I say. 'Let me know if you want to make any changes to the design. Shall we say by the day after tomorrow?'

'Yes. That's fine.' She picks up the sketch, folds it neatly in two and then slides it into her bag. 'You should ask Michael about your family,' she says. 'You need to know, even if he doesn't.' And as she says it, I know that she's right.

Later that evening, I sit Dad in front of the television and ring Michael's number. Marianne answers. I listen carefully as she chats, trying to hear if there's any change in her voice, if she might know anything of my discussion with Michael, but there's nothing to suggest that she does. When Michael takes the phone his tone is guarded. I dive straight in.

'I know what you said the other day but I need to find out more. I can't just forget about it. I'm not sure I want to find her, necessarily – I'm still thinking that over – but I need to make sense of it all in my head. Does Mum have any other family?' Using the present tense in relation to Mum feels awkward, unnatural almost, but I'm determined to do it.

There is a silence at the other end of the phone. A long silence.

'She had a sister,' he says eventually. 'Ursula. I think she's an artist of some kind. She lives in the States. San Francisco maybe? We never saw her but Mum used to talk about her.' He uses the past tense. That's his choice. I fight hard to bury the jealousy that I feel because Michael has real memories of our mother. He can recall conversations, the sound of her voice, her smell. I have nothing.

'Do you know what Mum's maiden name was?' I ask.

'Kemp,' he says straightaway.

'How come I didn't know that?' I ask.

'There's a lot you don't know, Ca,' he says.

I wonder what he is trying to say but then he adds, 'You were only two when she . . .' He does not finish the sentence. When she left? Is that what he was going to say? Not when she died but when she left. I wonder if this is progress but I decide to let it lie. Softly, softly has to be the best approach here. At least he is talking to me about it all. I don't want to scare him off.

'Mum had a friend, too,' he continues, his voice less certain now. 'She was always at the house during the day when Dad was at work. I didn't like her.'

If Mum was still alive then surely she'd have told someone where she was. A best friend could be exactly what I need. I feel my heart beating fast in my chest.

'I don't suppose you can remember her name?'

There's another pause. 'No,' he says doubtfully. 'It was all such a long time ago.'

'What was she like?' I ask, desperate for anything that might help.

'Can't remember much. She had long, black hair. I used to find it all over the house. And she had a tattoo of a unicorn on her arm. No one had tattoos then. It was unusual.'

There's a shout at Michael's end of the line, Marianne wanting to know how long he will be. 'I'm sorry, Ca,' he says 'but I have to go. Zara has a concert at school and if we don't leave now, we'll be late.'

'No worries,' I say. 'Tell Zara good luck from me. I'll speak to you soon.'

'Will do. Take care,' he adds as he puts the receiver down.

I pop my head round the door to check on Dad but he's asleep in his chair so I head straight back to my computer and load up the search site. Now I know Mum's surname I search against Anne Kemp and 1959, when she was born. There should be a birth certificate. The familiar red words bounce back. 'Sorry, we could not find any results matching your search criteria.'

How can that be right? First no death certificate and now no birth certificate.

CHAPTER TWENTY

Annie, 1984

Annie unplugs the vacuum cleaner and wraps the cord neatly around the handle as she casts her eyes around for the final time. She tries to imagine how the room will appear to an outsider. The carpet is worn but not threadbare; the stain where Michael stepped on an ink cartridge is now hidden from view under the strategically positioned coffee table. She knows it is there and so does Joe but Babs will never spot it unless she is crawling around on her hands and knees. Annie thinks it is a shame she doesn't have any scatter cushions. They are all the rage, apparently. She saw an article in a magazine at the doctor's surgery. The magazine had been almost a year out of date, so she can only assume that every home in the country now has a full set. She'd mentioned the article to Joe in a light, understated way. He had scoffed, questioned what was wrong with the cushions that came with the sofa and then made a comment about unnecessary extravagance. Annie had been going to suggest that she make the cushions herself with remnant fabric from the market, but when she saw his face she decided not to mention cushions again. They would look nice, though, in a sunny yellow maybe.

Satisfied that everything is in its place, Annie hurries through to the kitchen, where a tray is ready-laid with the accoutrements for tea for two. Teapot, mugs, milk jug, sugar bowl, a plate with four Rich Tea biscuits. Did it look odd to have the tray out ready? And four biscuits? Might that come across as a bit mean? She gets the packet from the biscuit tin and adds an extra two. Now the plate looks overfull. She puts one back. An odd number looks less calculated and of course it is fine to have the tray ready. She is definitely over-thinking this.

Annie cocks her head to one side and listens but everything is quiet upstairs. She kept Cara up a little longer after lunch so that she might sleep through. It will make her harder to put down later but it's Joe's night to go to the snooker club after work so he'll never know. As long as Babs arrives on time, Annie reckons they will have a good hour and a half before she has to go and collect Michael from playgroup. Babs has a little boy at playgroup too, although he's younger than Michael and much more boisterous. She also has Martin, who is in the second year of school. The pair of them are a handful, especially next to Michael and Cara, but whenever her children are noisy or unruly, Babs rolls her eyes and says 'Boys will be boys' as if this excuses everything. Annie isn't sure that boys do have to be loud and badly behaved as a prerequisite of their gender. Michael never bounces on sofas or draws on walls or traipses mud and biscuit crumbs through the house – heaven forbid! – but a part of Annie admires her friend's approach. It shows a defiant, devil-may-care attitude that Annie just cannot replicate. She imagines what it must be like to stroll through life not worrying about stains on the carpet, not being constantly aware of how her children's behaviour is impacting on those around them. It must feel so liberating, thinks Annie, although perhaps that would just be how it would feel for her. For Babs it must be different. You can't be liberated if you've never been hemmed in.

A loud rap of the door knocker breaks Annie's train of thought and makes her jump. She stands for a moment, taking a couple of deep breaths before smoothing down her skirt and going to answer it. Babs waits on the doorstep, smiling broadly and holding a striped cardboard box tied up with curling ribbon.

'I brought treats!' she says as she pushes past Annie into the hall. Annie thinks of the sad-looking Rich Teas on the plate in the kitchen. She wonders if she can put them away before Babs sees them but Babs has gone straight through and is already running water for the kettle. She follows Babs into the kitchen.

'You sit down,' says Babs as she comes in. 'You look done in, Annie darling. Cara still not sleeping through? You have to let her cry, you know. She'll never learn to settle herself if you keep rushing in to comfort her.'

'I know,' says Annie, grateful to Babs for taking charge so effortlessly. 'But if she cries it wakes Joe and you know how he needs his sleep. He says he can't work out the odds properly at work if he hasn't had a decent night, and that costs us money. She'll manage it on her own eventually.'

'Not if you keep pandering to her she won't,' says Babs. 'Shall I use these cups?' Babs dismantles Annie's carefully arranged tray. 'I brought custard tarts. I hope you like them.'

Annie prefers doughnuts but anything is better than the Rich Tea that Joe likes. 'Perfect,' she says with a smile.

'I was just talking about you, actually,' continues Babs as she tips the water from the kettle straight into the cups, bypassing the teapot entirely. 'A group of mums from Martin's class are organising a night out. I didn't know if you might fancy it. I know that you won't know anyone except me but they're a lovely bunch – and you can pick up some tips on how it's going to be in September, when Michael starts.'

Babs has her back to her as she tugs at the ribbon around the cake box, giving Annie a bit of breathing space as she considers how to reply. It isn't enough, though. While she's still working out what to say, Babs has turned round and is staring at her. 'Well?' she asks as she puts the box on the table. 'What do you reckon?'

Annie still doesn't speak. There are too many problems. Can she ask Joe to mind the children? What will she do for money to buy the drinks? What on earth would she wear? The questions fly round her head and then are replaced with possible excuses. 'I'm not sure I'm free,' she says as a kind of holding response.

'I haven't told you when it is yet!' laughs Babs and Annie immediately feels stupid.

'No, but I'm not sure I can come on a night out. There's the children . . .' She lets the sentence hang, half-finished, in the air, hoping that this will do the trick.

'We've all got children,' says Babs. 'That's why we need a night out. And you've got a husband, which is more than some of them have. I'm sure he wouldn't mind sitting in for a couple of hours. Give you a break.'

'I'm not sure,' says Annie. She can feel her insides squirming. Is she blushing? Annie wants to distract her somehow but she knows it's hopeless. If only she'd listened more carefully to the plan instead of panicking, then she could have come up with a plausible excuse. As it is, Babs will think that she's either antisocial or not very fond of her or possibly both.

This isn't the first time that Babs has invited her out. The last time it was a proposed trip to the cinema to see a film that Annie had mentioned. Cara had been on a bottle and Annie had been sure it would be fine. She would only be out of the house for a couple of hours, three at the absolute tops. If she timed it right, Cara would be asleep and Michael would go to bed with no bother. Joe had had other ideas. She had mentioned the idea casually while she finished the washing up. They hadn't been out much since the children had been born, as Joe was uncomfortable having someone in to sit. She'd suggested her own mother at one point but he had crinkled his brow and shaken his head slowly as if he were considering the idea and then rejecting it. She had thought that perhaps if they did things separately it might get over this problem. After all, no babysitter would be required and Joe already went out at least once each week. When she had suggested the idea, his brow had crinkled again.

'That would be a really nice thing to do,' he had said, his voice gentle and filled with concern. 'But don't you think that Cara is a little bit young to be left just yet? You know how she clings to you. Maybe if you'd been a bit tougher with her from the beginning . . . but as it is she can hardly bear to be apart from you if you go to the loo, let alone a little jaunt to the cinema.'

And that had been it. He had dropped his head back into his *Racing Post*, leaving Annie feeling ashamed that she'd ever brought it up. Since then, Annie has not asked to be released from her domestic duties.

She realises that Babs is still looking at her expectantly. She needs to say that she doesn't fancy it or come up with a decent excuse quickly or the whole situation is going to become even more awkward. 'To be honest,' she begins, twisting her wedding ring round her finger. 'To be honest, I'm not a big drinker. I'm not sure that a night out is quite my thing.' Annie can feel her cheeks burning as the lie trips from her lips. She feels sure that Babs can see that she is talking rubbish and will be offended but Babs just says, 'That's okay. You should have said before. It was just a thought. Now pass me one of them custard tarts. I'm starving here.'

As Babs tucks into her custard tart and chats about children, Annie is only partly listening. Has she been hasty? Joe isn't an ogre. If she explains what the night out is about then surely he'd look after the children, just for an hour or two?

'I could maybe ask Joe?' Annie blurts out, cutting right across what Babs was saying.

Babs looks confused for a moment. 'Oh. About the night out?' she clarifies. 'Well, you're welcome to come along whatever.'

'I mean, I could just drink Coke or something,' Annie continues, although she isn't really talking to Babs. She deserves a night out. She hasn't had any fun for ages. Joe will see that. He goes out every week and she never complains. She'll have to ask him for some cash but if she only has a couple of Cokes that's hardly going to break the bank. She feels excited about the plan. She has no idea what she'd wear but she will cross that bridge when she comes to it. Babs chatters on but Annie isn't really listening anymore. When the time comes to wake Cara and go to collect Michael from playgroup, she has the whole evening mapped out in her head.

CHAPTER TWENTY-ONE

Cara, 2017

So, what is the form when you discover an undead parent? There are no help pages for that.

I need to clear my head so I go for a walk along the river. The last few leaves are clinging petulantly to the trees. The first hard frost will bring them tumbling down but for now they sway in the breeze that always blows along the bottom of the valley. A proud heron stands on one leg in the shallows, poised to spear his unsuspecting dinner.

I can't decide what I should do next. Everything that I think I know is spinning around inside my head and I can't get any of it to lie still. I'm not sure that I'm strong enough to take on any more. Or at least not yet. The implications are too huge. Having a mother who is not dead is a big enough thing to deal with on its own but what about the rest of it? She said we were precious in the postcards but then she left us behind like a finished-with paperback novel. Was there something new in her life that seemed so much more appealing to her than we did, something so tempting that she couldn't resist? Maybe she turned out not to be the maternal type after all. I mean, there's no guarantee that you will be mother material just because you manage to get yourself pregnant. If that was it, though, you'd have thought that she might have stopped at just Michael rather than going on to have me as well. I wonder if the pair of us were too difficult to manage or just plain disappointing, not the golden children of her dreams. Perhaps it was a mixture of both. Whichever way I look at it, there seem to be two possibilities. Either something happened to her to lure her away or, more likely, she just didn't want us anymore. This is the nub of it to me. Was she dazzled or just disappointed? Neither solution is particularly encouraging.

A dog walker with headphones jammed into his ears passes by me shoulder to shoulder on the narrow path. I smile but I get no response. When did the world become so unfriendly?

It's not just my mother's motives that I need to worry about. What about Dad? He has continued this ludicrous fabrication for my whole life, stringing me along, piling lie on top of lie. I am struggling to process what this says about him – was he trying to protect us or himself? And if he has lied to me about something so fundamental then how can I trust all the other things he's told me? Have I really had chicken pox? Was the scar on my chin actually a result of falling off my bike? Do I have any other siblings that no one has thought to mention? When I think about this then my whole life begins to wobble off-kilter. I am left untethered, like an escaping helium balloon just floating up and away.

This problem aside, life beyond the question of my dead mother is pretty steady because I now have the magnificent Mrs P to help me. I can't imagine how I used to cope without her. Her presence in our lives just makes everything feel so much calmer. Also, the house is transformed. My terrible attempts at window cleaning are a thing of the past. The cornices are no longer home to enormous spiders and the chequered tiles in the hall have never looked so shiny.

One day I find her on her hands and knees in the bathroom scrubbing the mould out of the grouting in the floor tiles.

'You shouldn't be doing that,' I say.

She looks at me, her eyes wide.

'I'm so sorry,' she says. 'I didn't mean to interfere. She struggles to her feet and starts peeling off her rubber gloves.

'No,' I say, anxious to correct the misunderstanding. 'I mean, we don't pay you to clean. When Dad's at The Limes you're free to go home. Cleaning up my mess really isn't part of your job.'

She looks relieved and smiles her gap-toothed smile. 'I don't mind, honestly,' she says.

'But haven't you got things you need to be doing?' I ask. 'Don't you work for other families when you're not here?'

She shakes her head. 'I told the agency that I didn't want any more hours. It's good to have the flexibility in case you need me. And there's not much going on at home.'

I wonder briefly about her family. I'd assumed there was a Mr Partington but maybe not. I don't ask, though, in case she thinks I'm being nosey but in any case I find that I'm pleased that she wants to spend time here, with me.

'Well, knock yourself out with the cleaning,' I say. 'If you really don't mind, that is.'

She smiles again and returns her attention to the floor. I have noticed that she seems to feel more and more at home here. She no longer asks permission before making herself a drink and she lets herself in without feeling obliged to ring the doorbell first. I suppose I could see these things as infringing on my privacy but instead it makes the house feel more lived in, like a real family home. It also leaves me with more time to get on with the tasks in hand, the main one being the creation, against all the odds, of Beth's perfect wedding dress.

Beth rings me the next morning. As soon as I answer, I can hear that there's reservation in her voice and some of her usual exuberance is being kept under control.

'Hi, Beth,' I say and wait to hear whatever it is.

'Hi.'

There is a pause.

'What's up?' I ask, although I can have a pretty good guess. 'Have you changed your mind? That's fine. I won't be offended if you go somewhere else.' In my heart, I know that I would be devastated if she did that but I can always pretend not to be for the sake of our friendship.

'No, no, it's nothing like that,' she says quickly. 'Well, it is a bit. I've had a few thoughts about the design . . .'

'I should hope so too,' I reply. 'It's the most important dress of your life. We can't just go with the first thing that I scribble down, no matter how artistically brilliant it is.' I can almost hear the tension seep out of her. 'So, is it a particular part that you don't like or shall we scrap the whole design and start again? You wouldn't be the first bride to do that.' I'm hoping to show her that it's perfectly all right to criticise the design and that I'm not going to take it personally.

'No. It's not the whole thing,' she says hurriedly. 'Not at all. I just wonder whether I might not be better with a bit more fabric in the back, add some sleeves maybe?'

'Okay,' I say, already picturing the alterations in my mind's eye. 'We can lose that drape so that your back is covered, which will allow me to set in some sleeves. Are we talking caps or three quarters or the full monty?'

'I'm not sure,' she says. 'What do you think?'

'I think you should have exactly what you want,' I say. I'm starting to smell a rat.

'Well, I thought a capped sleeve would be lovely but Greg said . . .' The words are out. There can be no retrieving them.

'You didn't show your dress design to Greg?' I say before I can stop myself. 'You do know that it's bad luck for the groom to see the dress before the big day?'

'I didn't show him,' she says indignantly. 'He found it by accident.'

'What do you mean, he found it? Did you leave it out on the breakfast table or something?' The line goes quiet. I can feel Beth struggling between confessing all to me and staying loyal to Greg. I am gratified when I appear to win.

'He found it in my bag,' she said quietly.

'What was he doing in your bag?' I ask. 'Does he often go snooping through your stuff?'

'He wasn't snooping. He was looking for my car key and it was just there.'

'Just there, folded in two and not looking anything like a car key,' I say.

'Well,' she says sharply. 'He found it. And now that he has found it, he obviously has a view.'

'But he's not entitled to a view,' I say, finding it hard to keep the irritation out of my voice. 'The dress is all about you. He should love it because you love it and because it will make you happy.'

'Well, he doesn't.'

I can hear her voice starting to break and so I make my tone gentler. 'Okay . . .'

'And if I know that he doesn't like it then that spoils it for me. You can see that, can't you, Ca?'

'Of course I can,' I say. 'But you have to have what you want. It's your dress and it's you he loves.'

Beth takes a deep breath at the other end of the line. 'It is a wedding and not a party,' she says, her voice regaining its strength. 'I know we're not getting married in church but I still need to look like a bride. And the back is very low.'

It is as if yesterday never happened. I want to remind her how blown away by my design she was when she first saw it, how perfectly it would suit the curve of her spine, but what would that achieve? The magic has been spoiled. We need to work with what we now have and move on. 'Well,' I say, thinking as I talk. 'As I see it, we have two options. We either alter this dress so that it has sleeves and a less plunging back, but that will maybe be a bit of a compromise on this design and might not work out quite as well.' I pause to give her a chance to think. 'Or,' I continue, 'we just start again and design something that has sleeves and a high back right from the outset. I think that might be the better path,' I add, daring my own opinion.

The dress as I visualised it has been damaged beyond repair. No amount of altering will turn it into something that I will be happy with. But it's Beth's wedding – she must decide.

'Have we got time to start again?' she asks.

'Of course!' I say. Absolutely not! I think. 'But we'll need to get a wiggle on. Which shift are you working today? Can you come round so that we can nail it? Your mags are all still here and I've got lots of other ideas that would work well.'

We agree that she will come later that afternoon and we'll begin again.

'And this time,' I say cautiously, 'I think we'll keep the sketches here. Just in case.'

I'm laughing but it's not funny. It's not funny at all.

CHAPTER TWENTY-TWO

I redesign Beth's dress and I keep my concerns about Greg's need to control everything and everyone to myself. Beth isn't stupid. She knows what she's getting into. Again, she is delighted with the results and this time we go ahead and cut out a calico for fitting and I get started without losing any more precious time.

I might have expected that my best friend getting married would require endless discussions about which florist to use and what would be the best hors d'oeuvres to serve with the champagne. There is almost none of that. Greg's ludicrously short timescale puts paid to any gentle deliberation. Instead we both seem to be running a solo race to our own goals. More than once I regret that the whole wedding-preparation thing is not turning out the way I had imagined, but it can't be helped. There is just no time to waste chatting.

Apart from making the dress, the main event as far as I am concerned is the shopping trip to buy the bridesmaid dresses. There will be three of us: me and Greg's two nieces, who are to be flower girls. Beth instructs by text as to where I need to be and when, and I turn up, ready to wear whatever she tells me. I really don't mind what my dress is like; I will wear a hessian sack if that's what Beth wants. But of course the dress she picks out for me is stylish and sophisticated, in a soft, sage-green satin with a sweetheart neckline and a nipped-in waist. The sleeves are cut off just beneath the elbow and the hem sits on the calf. I stand in front of the mirror in the little shop with Beth, her mother and the shop assistant, all cooing at how beautiful it is and how the colour suits my hair and skin tone. They are right. Even I can see that the dress looks perfect. Except for one thing.

I don't think about it anymore and I don't think Beth does either but I catch Beth's mother looking at my hand. She is discreet about it – she doesn't stare outright – but I see her eyes drawn to the silvery, puckered skin. I want to snatch my hand away but there's nowhere to hide. Beth sees her mother looking and in the mirror behind me I watch a silent exchange take place between them: Beth's mother raising her eyebrows; Beth furrowing her forehead and shaking her head.

I have found over the years that the easiest way to deal with other people's embarrassment is to approach it head on. 'What about gloves?' I say. 'I mean, it is December. Some long, satin gloves might be perfect.'

I see Beth's mum relax as this potentially awkward moment is so easily averted but Beth is shaking her head.

'I don't think that would look right with the sleeve length,' she says. 'I like it just the way it is.'

Beth's mother goes to contradict her but is stopped by the social awkwardness of the situation. She can hardly say out loud that the chief bridesmaid's hideously disfigured hand will spoil the photographs.

'I don't mind,' I say, anxious not to make things any worse. 'I'll do whatever you want, Beth.'

'And I want no gloves,' says Beth and it is clear that this discussion is over. 'You look beautiful,' she adds. 'Really beautiful.'

The smile she offers me is wide and open and I take it deep into my heart. Thank you, Beth, I try to smile back.

Less easy to please are Greg's nieces – or, to be more precise, their mother, Greg's sister, Xanthe. The girls, Evangeline and Phoebe, are pretty little things with huge blue eyes and blonde hair that hangs, poker-straight, down their backs. When they are asked to try the dresses on, they do so without complaint and then twirl endlessly in front of the mirror, desperate to catch a glimpse of the back view as well as the front.

'Can we have high heels, Auntie Beth?' they chant. 'Can we? Please?' They draw the word out to its full length, adding endless vowels. Beth winks at them, which sends them into another frenzy of jumping and spinning on the spot. Their dresses are as lovely as mine. Beth has chosen an ivory organza with the sage of my dress picked out in satin sashes around their waists. They suit the girls perfectly but Xanthe, standing a little bit away from us, is shaking her head. When neither Beth nor I ask what is troubling her, she sighs loudly.

'They look gorgeous,' she says, pulling a face that suggests the complete opposite. 'I mean, of course they do. They're stunning, my girls.' She pauses so that we can acknowledge how beautiful her daughters are. Beth nods enthusiastically. I don't react. 'But I have to say,' Xanthe continues, 'that I'm a bit disappointed with the dresses.'

I cannot quite believe what I am hearing and I am about to object on Beth's behalf but Beth throws Xanthe her best concerned face and engages.

'Why, Xanthe? What's the matter? The girls look absolutely delightful, don't they, Mum?'

Beth's mother pulls her shoulders back and sets her jaw, her lips pursed into a narrow, bloodless line. She nods her head but Xanthe pays her no attention.

'Of course they do,' Xanthe agrees, without a hint of modesty. 'But green?' She elongates the vowel, sounding it out exactly the way her daughters had done moments earlier. 'It's not really a colour for little girls, is it?'

I am lost for words, which is a good job as it really isn't for me to get involved.

'Well, green is kind of the theme,' says Beth. 'The flowers are all ivory and green and it all ties in with Greg's waistcoat and the buttonholes,' she says.

I hate to hear Beth talk as if she needs to justify her choices. What possible business is it of Xanthe's which colour Beth chooses for her own wedding? Xanthe, however, has other ideas.

'When you said it was going to a Christmas wedding,' she continues, 'I thought you'd go for red or at the very least gold. But green? It's not very festive.'

To be fair to the woman, I'd thought we'd be pushing the whole jolly Christmas thing far more than we are doing.

'Well, I did think about red . . .' says Beth cagily. 'But it's not really my colour.'

This is not true. Beth looks fantastic in red, in most colours in fact. Then it hits me what is really going on here. This is the hand of Greg again. Beth meets Xanthe's gaze defiantly but I see her twisting her engagement ring round her finger so quickly that I fear for the skin underneath.

'But you look fantastic in red,' objects Xanthe. 'And it would be so pretty for the girls to wear red sashes and little red shoes.'

'I think it's a bit late to change everything now,' I say, trying to support Beth just as she supported me over the gloves. 'And the green does look very pretty on them.'

'Hmmm,' says Xanthe, and I could slap her.

Beth stands a little taller and swallows hard. 'Greg and I chose the green together. He thinks that red is a bit tacky, especially at Christmas, and that the green is much classier, and I agree.' She stands with her hands on her hips, defying Xanthe to disagree with her. Xanthe cocks her head on one side as she decides whether or not to be insulted. For one minute, I think she is going to challenge Beth but then she says, 'Well, maybe . . . Red might be a bit hackneyed for a Christmas wedding.' She pauses. 'You and Greg must have what you want, of course. And the dresses are just too cute.'

Beth nods. 'The girls look lovely. And so do you, Cara,' she says, as if to signal the end of the discussion. 'Now, let's see about those shoes,' she says to the girls, who start to squeal all over again.

I try to catch her eye but she's focusing all her attention on her little bridesmaids. She looks slightly bruised by the whole exchange.

Later, when the dresses are paid for and Xanthe and the girls have twirled out of the shop and away, I suggest that we go for a drink on the way home. Beth looks at her watch and bites her lip but then she says, 'Okay. Just a quick one but then I have to get back.' She fiddles with her phone, sending a quick text to Greg, I assume, although she doesn't say so. I wonder if this is starting to be a sensitive subject between us.

We make our way to the wine bar a couple of doors down. It is remarkably busy, given that it is still mid-afternoon.

'You grab a table,' I say, 'And I'll go to the bar. What would you like? If you say Diet Coke, you can consider our friendship over.'

Beth smiles weakly. 'A glass of white wine? Something dry-ish?'

I get a bottle, carrying it to the table in a chiller, two glasses caught up in one hand.

'Cara!' she says when she sees me. 'You said a drink, not a session.'

'I know but I haven't seen you for a proper catch-up in ages. One glass or three? What difference will it make?'

Beth looks like she's going to object but then she doesn't, and when I have poured the wine, she takes a long drink.

'That's good,' she says and then pushes herself back into the chair.

'So that went well,' I say. 'The dresses are lovely. Especially mine,' I add. 'Thank you.'

'Do you really think so?' she asks, as she bites at her already-bitten nails. 'I thought they were but . . . well, after what Xanthe said . . .'

'Take no notice of her,' I say. 'The girls will look adorable. The colour is perfect and whose wedding is it anyway?'

'Exactly!' Beth says, fortified, and takes another drink. 'Xanthe's lucky that she's even invited to the wedding,' she adds mischievously.

'How come?'

'She and Greg have had a falling out about her dog.'

I can't disguise a smirk.

'Oh, don't laugh!' Beth says and laughs herself. 'It really was touch and go for a bit. Xanthe has this dog. Greg calls it the rat on a string.'

I stifle a giggle.

'It's a Shih Tzu,' she adds, and I laugh out loud. 'Coco. It's quite sweet I suppose. Anyway, you know how much Greg hates dogs . . .'

I don't but I just nod.

'Well, he hates Coco even more than most. She nipped him on the leg when she was a puppy and she makes this really annoying yapping that gets on his nerves. Anyway, Xanthe takes the dog almost everywhere with her so she just assumed that it could come to the wedding. She was even talking about some matching ribbon for its hair, a little ribbon lead, that kind of rubbish. Greg went ballistic, said there was no way that a dog was coming to his wedding and that Xanthe would have to arrange to leave it at home. Xanthe had a prima-donna hissy fit and said if Coco couldn't come then neither would she. Honestly, it was absolutely ridiculous.'

'But they sorted it out, right? I mean, the girls are still bridesmaids.'

'Oh yes. In the end, Xanthe agreed that the dog could stay in her car with the windows open and plenty of water and she'll just nip out from time to time to take it for walks.'

'And Greg is happy with that?'

'He's compromised,' she says, and I can tell from her face that this is rare.

'Beth?' I say carefully. 'You are okay, aren't you? I mean, you are happy?'

She looks at me, her face confused.

'What do you mean? Of course I'm happy. I'm about to marry the man of my dreams. Why wouldn't I be happy?'

I pause but only for a nanosecond. This is my moment and if I don't grasp it, it might not come again. As her best friend, it's my duty just to check. 'And is he?' I ask, looking straight into her eyes. 'Is he really the man of your dreams?'

She thinks about this but she doesn't seem angry with me and I'm relieved. 'I know he's not everybody's cup of tea,' she says. 'He likes things done in a particular way. He has an opinion on everything and he'd choose my socks for me if I let him but I love him. I know he's a bit controlling but that's part of what I love about him. And he wouldn't hurt me, Ca. When we're alone he treats me like a princess, he really does.'

I decide to believe her.

When I get home, I have another glass of wine with my dinner and then one after that. It slips down so easily and I like feeling not quite in control. It makes the other things in my life seem more stable. Instead of pushing my unwelcome thoughts away, the alcohol gives me permission to think about things, albeit foggily.

After Mrs P has left and Dad is safely tucked up in bed, I wander into my workroom. I have no particular plan, some idea about checking stock levels, I don't know. Anyway, before I've thought it through, I've logged on to the internet. Without really thinking about it, I type 'How do I find my mother?' into Google. I click on the first site on the list.

The home page is covered with pictures of smiling faces. There is a little YouTube clip that shows a woman being reunited with a son she had placed for adoption when he was newborn. I scroll down to see what you have to do. It is a free service. You simply fill in the details, write a personal message and click 'Send'. Then, if my mother is on the site looking, she'll see the message and reply. It all seems very straightforward in my slightly muddled brain. Outside a tawny owl hoots in the tall, dark trees, calling to its mate. Or its children?

This is madness. As if some random, late-night internet search is going to turn up a woman who has been missing/dead for thirty years! I'm clutching at straws here and in any event, what am I trying to achieve? There are two sides to this conundrum but as they have sprouted in my mind they have twisted together, like the stems of an ancient vine. I force my mind to focus. First, I need to find out whether my mother is actually alive. Every cell in my body is screaming out to me that she is but that hardly counts as empirical proof. But even assuming I can establish that she isn't dead, then what? Do I want to find her, meet her, build some sort of relationship, even? Here, I draw a blank.

CHAPTER TWENTY-THREE

Annie, 1984

Annie's heart bangs so hard in her chest that she can't hear herself think. She mustn't panic. She has one shot at this. She can't mess it up like she does everything else. She must stay calm and just carry out the plan just like she's been practising it in her head.

She looks at her watch. Two thirty. There's half an hour until she has to go and collect Michael from school. If she wakes Cara as normal at quarter to, then she'll be just coming round from her grumpiness and shouldn't cry. The last thing she needs is for Cara to be difficult.

She tries to calm her breathing but the air rushes from her mouth in ragged shivers. Her body is pulled as tight as a bow, ready to propel her when she lets go. This is the right thing to do. It's not as if she hasn't tried . . . God knows she has tried, with all her might, but she can't do it. She can't make it work. It is never going to be all right.

In the cupboard under the sink, behind the bleach where Joe would never look, nestles her lifeline. It's not much, just what she's managed to siphon off the barely adequate housekeeping, but at least it's something and it will give her a chance. Quickly, quietly, she takes the tin and tips the contents out into her hand. She stuffs the money into her purse, which she then plunges deep inside her handbag. Her bag is already full, not with the usual things that a woman carries but with underwear and favourite toys, nappies and toothbrushes. It's just full enough that it won't attract attention.

The pram is in the hallway and she goes to check, for the hundredth time, that she has everything. She can only take what she can carry and even then she can't be drawing attention to herself. She has to stand in the playground with all those wagging tongues. If there is even a hint of a story then it will be out before Michael has come running from his classroom.

It will work, though, she tells herself as she climbs the stairs to Cara's room. She has a plan and everything will be all right once the dust has settled. A bit of nastiness and then everyone will see that this is for the best.

Cara is lying on her front in the semidarkness of the nursery, her bottom high in the air and her head turned to one side. Her fine, blonde hair sticks to the side of her head with sleepy sweat and her cheek is furiously pink. The next tooth will be through soon. Annie touches her head, tries to straighten the damp hair, and Cara stirs, her little face angry at being disturbed even in her sleep. Annie picks her up, quickly swinging her round until she lies against her breastbone. Gently pressing her daughter's head into her chest, she makes soothing sounds to prevent Cara exploding. It works. Cara roots into her and Annie sighs. This is going to be all right.

Downstairs, she lays Cara down in the pram gently and pulls the string of the musical toy that hangs over her head. Cara doesn't open her eyes.

It is not easy to manoeuvre the pram down the front steps when its basket is so full but Annie manages it without losing anything and sets off up the street towards the school just as she usually does. She doesn't look back.

The playground is already full of groups of mothers, all standing in their little cliques. Annie would usually make a beeline for Babs, her only friend, but today she holds back. She doesn't want to get drawn into conversation. She just has to collect Michael and leave. She keeps her head low so that she doesn't make eye contact with anyone and pretends to talk to the sleeping Cara, leaning into the pram, entirely focused on her.

'You been shopping?' asks a voice behind her.

It's Babs; Annie recognises her voice before she sees her. 'Jumble,' she says quickly. 'Dropping it off on our way home.'

She has pre-planned this answer, knowing that Babs isn't the kind to know the precise details of any forthcoming jumble sales. Annie would like to have talked through her plan with Babs but she decided against it. They'll be able to unpick it all over a cup of tea afterwards but for now it's best that no one knows.

Babs nods but, as predicted, doesn't question and Annie keeps quiet, not inviting further conversation. After a few moments, Babs drifts off to talk to someone else and then the bell rings and Michael appears. He is almost always first out of school, his coat on and his bag neatly fastened. Annie smiles proudly at him but doesn't kiss him, as instructed. He's told her that he's too old for a kiss – well, not in front of the others anyway.

'Spit spot,' says Annie. 'Let's get going.'

Michael looks at the pram with its unusual burden and seems about to ask but then doesn't and starts to tell Annie about his day, interrupting himself only when they turn right not left at the pelican crossing.

'We're going to Gran's for tea,' Annie says, but in a tone that doesn't invite further comment.

The bus is difficult. So many bags mean that the pram won't fold and it takes up more space than is available. The driver looks about to complain but he takes one look at Annie and seems to change his mind. She smiles at him gratefully and stands in the aisle, holding on to the pram tightly so that it doesn't roll about.

Cara, disturbed by the bumping, begins to howl. Annie squeezes her eyes shut tight, trying to silence her child with the power of thought alone. What is she doing? This is ridiculous. Why did she ever think it was a good plan? Then Cara stops screaming and when Annie opens her eyes she sees Michael leaning over the side of the pram, blowing raspberries on his sister's cheeks. Cara giggles.

Her mother's house is not far from the bus stop. They'll be there in less than five minutes. Annie pushes the bell for the next stop and when the bus draws to a halt she bounces the pram down the steps backwards, kicking an escaping bag back into the basket with her foot.

The bus pulls away and the three of them stand alone on the pavement. It is three fifty. She takes a deep breath, letting the air reach the very bottom of her lungs. Then she starts to walk.

There is no sense of coming home when she reaches the house, no fond memories, no warmth. Even though it is a year since her father passed away – a massive heart attack that snatched him on his solitary stumble home from the pub – his presence still casts a shadow over the place for Annie. She feels her heart beating harder as she approaches, though there is no longer any threat behind the flaking front door. Of course, Ursula is long gone as well, but nothing else has changed. The same tired nets hang at the windows, the old wire milk-bottle basket, slightly bent out of shape where Ursula once kicked it, still sits on the step.

Annie rings the doorbell.

Her mother answers the door. Her apron is stained; gravy maybe. She looks thinner than she did the last time Annie saw her. When would that have been? Just after Cara was born, so maybe six months ago. Her eyes are dark, with shadows like bruises encircling them. They are still sharp, though. Annie sees her mother take in the scene and understand its consequences immediately. She does not smile.

'I've left him, Mum,' Annie says, even though Michael is there, listening, taking it all in. 'It was a mistake to marry him. Ursula always said it was and she's right. I did it for all the wrong reasons. I think I'll be better off just me and the kids. So can we come and stay here for a bit? I've got some money saved up so I can pay our way and it won't be for long, just until I get something else sorted out.'

Her mother doesn't move, doesn't stand aside to welcome her in, doesn't even speak. She just shakes her head.

Annie starts to panic. It never occurred to her, in all the versions of the plan that she's run through in her mind, that her mother might not take them in. She thinks for a moment that her mother is joking, just pretending to reject her, that she will open her arms wide any second now and usher them into safety, or relative safety, but her mother stays stony-faced and shakes her head again.

Then she speaks. 'No.'

Annie looks at her, confused. Did she really just refuse? She tries to push the pram past her and into the hall but her mother bars the way with her foot.

'No,' she says again.

'But, Mum, don't you understand? I've left him. We need to come in,' says Annie, pleading now.

Michael takes a step back from the doorstep and reaches for Annie's hand, despite his new reluctance to hold it.

'You are married, Anneliese,' says her mother. 'You took vows. For better or worse, that's what you said. You have a duty to make things work. You can't just up sticks when the going gets tough. Being married is hard work. It's not all hearts and flowers, you know? Men can be a challenge. Your father certainly was but did I give up? No. I knew my duty to my husband and my children and I made the best of it. Joseph is nothing like your father was. He's a lovely man and if you can't make your marriage work, then that's just because you're not trying hard enough. Turn round right now, go back home and get on with Joe's supper. If you're lucky he need never know anything about any of this silliness.'

Annie feels the tears that she has been beating away start to choke her. 'But, Mum,' she tries again, but she knows it is hopeless.

She takes a deep breath and turns the pram around.

'Okay,' she says. 'If that's what you want. Say goodbye, Michael.'

Michael squeezes her hand so tightly that her fingers hurt.

'Goodbye, Gran,' he says. He lifts his chin and speaks loudly as if, for all that he is only five, he understands completely what is going on here.

Then she walks away from the house and her mother and goes back the way she came.

CHAPTER TWENTY-FOUR

Cara, 2017

Beth's wedding dress is ready. It hangs in my workroom with a good three weeks to go before the deadline and I can't help but feel smug. When she came for the final fitting and was standing staring at herself in the mirror, not quite able to take in what she saw, I felt a buzz of pride fizzing through me that I had finished the dress in time and against all the odds that Greg had piled up in my way.

So, if the wedding is almost upon us then Christmas must be just around the corner as well. The festive season has never been a big event in the Ferensby household. When we were small, the lack of uncles, aunts or family friends meant that there was never a bulging sack of presents for Michael and me. Dad never felt the need to compensate for our meagre stash of gifts either, and bought us one present each and a bag of chocolate coins for the end of our beds. Then he would cook a variation on Sunday lunch and retire to his study, leaving us to watch whatever was on the television. I knew what a family Christmas was supposed to look like from the endless sitcoms and soap operas that I watched, but visitors, noise and party games never featured in our reality.

Dad and I have sometimes been invited to Michael's for Christmas, although I suspect that was Marianne's doing. Dad always refused to go so I went on my own and that's where I got a taste of what other people's Christmases are like. Marianne must spend most of December cooking and wrapping presents, judging by the incredible bounty that there always is. I once caught Michael shaking his head and rolling his eyes in my direction, mock disbelief at his family's extravagance written all over his face. All the same, he couldn't disguise his pride at the Christmas that Marianne had created and his joy at providing for his children. The contrast with what we'd had couldn't have been starker.

I spend some time pondering over what to do with regard to Mrs P and Christmas presents. I am not sure we have reached the personal gift stage in our relationship but I want to get her something to show her how grateful I am. She is becoming such a large part of my life and I hope, but am not sure, that she feels the same. I find her in the kitchen with Dad. She is wiping his mouth with a flannel and he holds his face up to her like a puppy waiting to be tickled.

'Here's Cara,' she says to Dad as I walk in. 'Have you seen the beautiful dress that she's made for Beth? It's quite a work of art.'

'I wouldn't go that far,' I say, brushing off the praise. 'But I am very relieved that it's finished. The wedding's on Christmas Eve, Dad.'

Dad isn't listening but Mrs P ploughs on.

'It's so romantic,' she says. 'And Cara's a bridesmaid. Do you hear that, Joe? Your little girl is going to be a bridesmaid.'

I like to hear her chat like this to Dad. There seems to be an easy, if one-sided, banter passing between them. Every so often, Dad will cock his head to one side and look at her as if he has something to say but the words he needs are no longer within his grasp.

'What are you doing for Christmas, Mrs P?' I ask.

'Oh, nothing special,' she says. 'I'll get myself a little bird to cook and some mince pies and then settle down for the Queen and a good film.'

'Will it just be you this year?' I ask delicately.

'Yes,' she replies. 'Just me.'

I invite her before I have time to think about it. It just seems the natural thing to do. As soon as the words are out of my mouth, I worry that she might think I am trying to get help with Dad, but actually it's more about me having some company. If she is suspicious of any less than altruistic motives, she doesn't show it. She beams at me, a proper wide smile that makes her hazel eyes twinkle and shows the gap between her teeth.

'Are you sure that I wouldn't be interrupting?'

I nod at Dad and wink at her. 'Interrupting what exactly? I know that there are two of us but Dad's not much of a conversationalist these days. Michael is having Marianne's tribe and Beth and Greg will be on honeymoon. You'll be doing me a favour by coming. Otherwise I'll just talk to myself all day and eat too many chocolates. You wouldn't be working, of course,' I add quickly, just in case she thinks otherwise. 'You'd come as our guest. And bring someone with you if you'd like.'

'That's very kind of you,' she says, still beaming. 'But it'll just be me.'

'Well, that's settled then. I'll order a turkey!'

Guests for Christmas. Or, rather, guest. I surprise myself by how excited I feel at the prospect until I realise that I have no real idea where to start. Christmas has never been much to write home about around here. I buy myself a glossy magazine on how to deliver 'the perfect Christmas' and waste time thinking about table settings and holly garlands and hope that Mrs P isn't expecting too much.

CHAPTER TWENTY-FIVE

Michael, 1986

This is his favourite time of day. With the detritus of their lunch still on the floor, his mother unfastens Cara's pelican bib, clicks open the highchair straps expertly with one hand and carefully slides his sister out and on to her hip. Michael watches as his mother takes a flannel from the drawer, runs it for a moment under the tap and squeezes the excess water from it while all the time chatting to Cara about the mess she has got herself into. Carefully, she pats at Cara's face to remove the remains of the strawberry yoghurt that didn't quite make it into her mouth. Cara screws up her nose and shakes her head, trying to make the task more difficult, but his mother perseveres and soon Cara is clean again.

'Right then, my little pixie,' his mother says. 'It's time for your nap.'

Cara's objecting body goes stiff, her arms and legs jutting out like lollipop sticks, and she hurls her head back in readiness to protest, but before she can scream, his mother pushes her nose into the space beneath Cara's chin and rubs her head backwards and forwards. Cara starts to giggle. Michael watches as his mother places a gentle hand on Cara's head and pulls her in close to her shoulder. That was Michael's favourite place, the hollow above his mother's collarbone, and for a moment he feels a stab of jealousy that his sister is still small enough to snuggle into it. He probably could do too but he has learned, now that he is seven and at school, that he is too grown up for that kind of baby-ness.

He wonders what they will do today while his baby sister has her nap. He has been looking forward to these special times, the parts of each day when Cara is asleep and he gets his mother to himself. He hopes that they might get out the Play-Doh and make spiders and ladybirds, cupcakes and worms. It is important, he knows, that each creature be fashioned from a single colour. His father is very particular about the Play-Doh. He knows this because he has seen his father lose his temper when a tiny piece of the yellow accidentally got mixed in with the green. After that, he and Cara were only allowed to make things using one colour at a time so that there could be no danger of cross-contamination. Michael remembers his surprise and disappointment when he started going to playgroup and learned that not everyone kept the different Play-Doh colours separated in their own pots. Playgroup Play-Doh was all a dull orangey-brown, like the dead leaves that lay in the gutters on the way to school. Michael thinks, slightly regretfully, that he is probably too big for Play-Doh now.

The shrill siren of Cara's wailing snakes down the stairs and he knows that this must mean that his mother has put her down in her cot. The complaining will continue for a minute or two before Cara stops objecting and resigns herself to sleep. Then Michael will get a delicious two hours of his mother to himself. That's one of the problems with going to school. He is forced to be away for the precious time each afternoon when Cara is asleep. It is such a waste. Michael is not sure what his mother does with the time when he isn't here but it cannot possibly be as good as spending it with him.

He hears his mother tiptoeing across the hall and then she appears at the door. Or rather, her hands do. The rest of her remains hidden.

She is holding something up, roundish, a pale-orange colour, some kind of vegetable. He is confused.

'Look what I've got!' she says as she appears around the door.

He tries hard to remember the name for the thing that she is holding. 'A turnip?' he tries but he feels that that is the wrong answer.

'Nearly,' she says. 'It's a swede.'

He is too old for Guess the Vegetable.

'And do you know what day it is tomorrow?' she asks.

'Friday,' he says impatiently.

'No!' his mother says and then, 'Well, yes, but that's not it. It's Halloween! So I thought we could have a little Halloween party, the three of us and Daddy. With apple bobbing and some toffee apples and . . .' She holds the vegetable above her head as if it is a silver cup that she has won in a race. 'A jack-o'-lantern. We'll chop the top off, hollow the middle out and cut out a face. Then we can put a candle inside.'

Michael can see that this idea has potential. He has noticed these lanterns in shop windows and likes the way the carved heads leer out of the gloom at him as he walks past. He nods enthusiastically and seats himself at the table while his mother bustles about retrieving a wooden chopping board, a knife and two spoons from various drawers.

'So, first we chop off the top,' she says and offers him the knife, handle first. It is the long knife with the wooden handle and this is the first time that he has been permitted to touch it. He takes it gingerly, as if it might explode in his hands. His mother stands close behind him. He can feel the warmth of her through his sweater. She holds the swede still with one hand and guides the knife with the other.

'I think we need to chop just about . . .' She moves the knife across the surface of the swede until she judges that the ratio of lantern to lid is about right. 'Here.'

He pushes the knife into the swede but it won't sink into the flesh and just slides to the right.

'Careful!' says his mother quickly. 'Try again.'

He does but the swede is much harder than the apples that he has been allowed to chop before.

'Shall I help?' she asks and wraps her hand around his so that they can push down together. The force of her hand digging into his hurts his fingers but he mustn't show her this in case it upsets her so he bites his lip and lets her push harder. The knife makes a jagged path through the first third of the swede and then stops in the middle.

'Oh,' says his mother. 'Well that's no good. Let me just . . .' She takes the knife from him, swede still attached, and presses down. The knife slides another inch. His mother leans into the task, pushing all her weight down on to the board, and finally the knife slices through, coming out at the bottom at an odd angle. She lifts what will be the lid and examines it. One side is much thicker than the other. 'That'll do,' she laughs. 'Now, we have to gouge out the insides so we have space for the candle.' She passes him the swede and a spoon. Having seen how much difficulty the knife had, Michael is not holding out much hope for the spoon, but he jabs at the yellowy flesh with as much force as he can muster. A little piece about the size of a penny flies out and his mother claps her hands. 'That's it!' she says, in a way that makes Michael think that cutting this one tiny piece will somehow magically signal the rest of the flesh to come away easily. It does not.

When he has hacked away five or six little slivers and the surface of the swede is barely dented, he gives up. He puts the spoon down on the chopping board and rubs at his finger where the pressure of the metal has made a dent in the flesh.

'Can you do some now?' he asks, not wanting to disappoint her but at the same time not relishing the prospect of digging at the swede any longer.

She smiles at him. 'I'd forgotten how tough it is,' she says, taking the spoon from him. 'When I was a girl, Auntie Ursula used to carve the lantern. She was really good at drawing. Her face shapes were fantastic. Mine were always kind of wobbly.'

Michael listens, enjoying hearing his mother talk. He has never met his Aunt Ursula because she lives a long way away. In America, he thinks. Or was it Australia? Or Africa? All these places sound the same to Michael, who has never been far out of London. His mother stabs at the swede as she talks, the little pieces of flesh flying all over the floor. 'We need to clear up before Daddy comes home. He's not going to be very pleased with us when he sees all this mess,' she says, laughing and biting her lip at the naughtiness of it all.

Michael is torn between wanting to spend time with his mother in the kitchen and dragging her off to play with his Lego. The lantern is making very slow progress and there is such a short period of time before Cara will wake up and career, like a walking bomb, through his delicate models. 'Can I just go and play while you finish that?' he chances, hoping that she won't be too disappointed.

She is concentrating on the swede. Michael notices that her tongue is sticking out of the corner of her mouth, like his does when he is working on sums at school. She doesn't seem to hear him so he slides down from his chair and slips quietly away. As he leaves the kitchen, an angry cry comes from upstairs and he holds his breath but then silence is restored.

He is just getting his Lego down from the shelf where it lives, out of Cara's reach, when he hears a knock at the door. It is too late for the postman and so there is only one person it can be. Michael feels his mood changing like lights going off all around him. He puts the Lego down and goes to look out into the hallway. His mother is there before him, almost running towards the front door, the spoon still in her hand. He watches as she lifts the latch. The woman, Tilly, is on the front step. She's all hair, Michael thinks. He is irritated. Does she not know that this is his time with his mother?

'Oh, hello,' says his mother. 'How nice to see you. I wasn't expecting you today.' She says this in a way that makes Michael think she means the exact opposite.

'Oh, I was just passing,' says Tilly and winks at his mother.

When she winks she sticks her head forward, her long neck straining and one side of her face creases up. She looks like a tortoise, thinks Michael.

'Well, do come in. I'm not doing anything special,' says his mother to the woman, Tilly. Michael resents calling her by her name and it's worse when his mother makes him call her 'Auntie Tilly'. He only has one Auntie and she is called Ursula. Yes you are doing something special, he wants to shout. You are spending time with me while Cara is asleep, and we are making a lantern for Halloween. He wishes now that he had not deserted the kitchen for his Lego. It would have been much easier to stake his claim for his mother's attention if they had been together when the doorbell rang.

'Have you got time for a cup of tea?' his mother asks.

The woman, Tilly, doesn't answer. She just follows his mother towards the kitchen.

'You're all right with your Lego, aren't you, Michael?' his mother asks.

He can feel her slipping away from him. She is going to go in the kitchen with this woman where they will sit and drink tea and laugh loudly at things that aren't funny. Panicked, he says, 'Actually, Mummy, I think I might get a bit stuck and need some help. And we're making the lantern, aren't we?'

'We can finish that later,' she says, without making eye contact, and then disappears into the kitchen.

The woman, Tilly, looks back at him as she follows his mother. She twists her face into what others might call a smile but Michael knows that it is isn't real. It does not stretch as far as her eyes. Nice try, child, she seems to say, but you can't compete with me and my tales of the world outside this house.

'You play nicely, Mikey boy,' she says and then she pulls the door shut behind her.

Michael goes back into the lounge. The castle that he has been building all holiday is sitting on the carpet. He has used only yellow and red bricks and has worked out how to join the walls at the corners so that they hold each other up. He is inordinately proud of it. Even his father has commented on how excellent it is. He picks the castle up and throws it at the floor. The tiny pieces scatter in all directions.

CHAPTER TWENTY-SIX

Cara, 2017

Now that we have a guest for Christmas, I feel the need to make more of a festive effort than usual. I buy a real tree, something I've never done before. The cleansing scent of pine fills the house but the needles begin to shed the minute I bring it inside. I also get new lights and some garish pink baubles from the supermarket. They look out of place in our shabby sitting room, like a glitter ball in a library, but I like them and keep watching them twist and turn on the branches, casting rectangles of light across the walls. I even buy a cut-price advent calendar, reduced because December is halfway through already. I open all the little cardboard doors up to date in one go. The pictures are unsurprising. Toys and parcels and snowflakes and a little elf. Behind the door for the fourteenth I discover a tiny picture of an angel. She has blonde curls and a dress the colour of periwinkle flowers. Two little half-circles suggest that her eyes are closed and another that she is smiling. The image seems familiar and I stare at her for a moment or two trying to place what it is that I recognise, but nothing springs to mind.

The gifts for Michael and his family sit, unwrapped and accusing, on the table. I'm pretty sure I haven't missed the last day for posting yet but I really must get them sent. There are no excuses other than my bad organisation. It is not like I'm inundated with Christmas presents to send. I've bought one of those fancy wrapping-paper sets: red tree-spotted paper, gold curling ribbon, tasteful gift tags. I set to with Marianne's gift first because it is pleasingly rectangular. I am just cutting the paper to size when, out of nowhere, it comes to me why the angel in the advent calendar is so familiar. We had one just like it that used to sit on the top of the tree. She was made from a clothes peg and had a tiny china head that wobbled from side to side if you shook her, not that we were permitted to shake her. Somewhere inside me I hear a voice.

'Be gentle, Cara. She's very precious. If you wobble her head like that you'll break her and Mummy will be very sad.'

Mummy?

I try to concentrate but the memory drifts away like the scent of a lilac blossom on a breeze. Whose voice was it? I claw at my memory, desperately trying to retrieve the sound, but the more I struggle, the further it retreats. Surely, it must have been my mother? Who else would be worried about the fate of a Christmas-tree angel? Not Dad, for sure, nor Michael, and there was no one else. It must have been her.

But that's all. No images play in my head other than the angel in her pale-blue dress. It is just a soundtrack, not a film, but it is something. A memory.

This feels like walking on scree. Small stones of recollection are becoming dislodged and rolling away from me down an invisible hill. There've been two memories now: the angel, and the stars (or lack of them) in London. There must be more hidden in the depths of my subconscious. Who knows what else may escape?

I can't wait any longer for them to reveal themselves. The need to dig deeper grabs me and won't let go. What do they do in television dramas to retrieve memory? Hypnotherapy, maybe, or some sort of counselling? My head spins with ideas and I have to rein myself back to try to think logically. I go back to the trigger. The angel. Would we still have it? Might it be lurking in one of those millions of boxes in the attic? Perhaps the angel is the key to unlocking more of the details that have always been hidden from me.

Leaving Marianne's present half-wrapped, I run up the stairs towards the attic. I pass Mrs P and Dad on the landing. They are making faltering progress, him leaning heavily into her, her capable arms having to take almost his entire weight. We'll need a stair-lift soon, I think as I fly past.

'Is everything all right?' asks Mrs P.

'Yes,' I call out as I bound up the creaking steps. 'Just had an idea about something, that's all.'

'In a hurry,' says Dad.

'She is in a hurry,' Mrs P replies.

I leave them behind, reach the box room and flick on the lights. Then I stop, the wind robbed from my sails by the sheer size of the task ahead of me. Where to begin? There are just so many boxes.

It makes sense that the angel, if it is here at all, will be at the back of the attic. I am almost certain that I haven't seen it since we moved to this house, so if it had come from our house in London it would be with the things that were first stored away. I make my way carefully through the stacks to the back wall. Again, I'm squinting at labels, but I can't see anything that says 'Christmas Decorations'. 'Bank Statements 1983–88', 'Cassette Tapes (Classical)' . . . I lift a few lids but the contents match the labels. There are no blue angels.

I see a box labelled 'Correspondence'. I nearly ignore it, as it's clearly nothing to do with Christmas, but curiosity gets the better of me. The label is incongruous in its lack of specifics. Correspondence with whom and which period? I'm expecting buff, foolscap envelopes but the piles of letters, despite being neatly stacked on their sides, are all of different sizes and colours.

I pull a letter out and open it up. It is a single sheet of paper, decorated up the side with hand-drawn hearts. It is obvious at once that it must be a love letter and that it's been written by a woman. I smile to myself. These must be letters that Mum sent Dad before they were married. I have never thought of my father as the romantic type but I suppose he might have been back then – and to have kept them for all these years says something too. I scan to the top of the sheet, with the intention of reading down, but then something stops me.

Ought I to read them? I debate with myself about the validity of invading Dad's privacy for less than a second. That he might have lied to me my entire life cancels out any argument against snooping and so I start to read.

Baby

You have no idea how tough it is to see you and not grab hold of you. I swear it's killing me. Thought we'd been spotted today. Bit risky to touch your bum like that but I couldn't resist. It's just so squeezable. xxxxx Think we got away with it. My heart was going like the clappers though. Won't be forever. One day very soon we'll be together.

Can't wait.
Xxxxxxx

I read the letter twice, trying to piece the story together from what I can glean. It cannot be from Mum to Dad. They were together. There would be no need for all this clandestine stuff unless they were indulging in some kind of role-playing, which seems highly unlikely. Set on trying to work out what was going on, I pull out another letter. This one is written on a piece of lined A4. There is no envelope. It is just a note, folded neatly into eighths. When I open it out, the deep creases make it hard to read but I see that the paper is entirely covered in sketches of love hearts, arrows skewering their centres.

The pictures is a great plan. We can make for the back row. Who needs to watch the film!!!!!! See you at the Odeon at 7.30.

Time for a quick bite afterwards? And then we can maybe get some food! (Ha ha!)

Love you T x

T? I realise at once that the letters can't be from Mum. And then the implication of what that must mean hits me hard in the chest. Someone else was writing these letters. Dad has kept them. There is only one conclusion for me to draw. Dad was having an affair. He was unfaithful to Mum and so she left us. In effect, he drove her away from us. It was all his fault.

My world lurches again and I have to hold on to the boxes for support. Is there no part of my childhood that is going to remain intact after this juggernaut has torn through it? In the film version of my life, the actor faced with this realisation would lash out at the nearest wall, venting their anger dramatically, but I'm not sure that what I'm feeling is anger. It's more like betrayal.

Dad told us that our mother was dead for all those years when the truth was that his unfaithful philandering had forced her to leave. Since I discovered that she didn't die, I've been worrying that it was our fault that she left – that Michael and I did something to drive her away. Now it appears that we were blameless all along. She left because of Dad's behaviour, not ours.

Suddenly everything seems to make a kind of sense and yet . . . I grapple with the facts, such as I know them. They had family courts in the 1980s. It wasn't the Dark Ages. If Dad had an affair then why didn't Mum fight for us? As our mother and the wronged party, she would surely have got custody without too much difficulty. Then Dad would have moved out and gone to live with his fancy piece and we would have stayed with Mum in London. There would have been no need for us to run the length of the country and make a clean start. Actually, now I think about it more clearly, none of it makes any sense at all.

CHAPTER TWENTY-SEVEN

Christmas Eve arrives. My lifelong best friend is getting married today. I know I should be delighted for her. I mean, that's what best friends do, isn't it? I'm supposed to run with her excitement, share her dreams for her bright new future with Greg. But, as I dry myself off after my shower, all I feel is a dull sense of loss. Right now, I'm not sure that I can even pretend to be happy. I have never felt more alone.

A single tear trickles down my cheek and I brush it away with the back of my hand. I've never been the kind of woman that weeps openly. You need a true depth of emotion for that kind of display and that's not something that comes naturally to me. Love is a learned behaviour, I understand. If you're not shown it then you struggle to demonstrate it to others. I suppose Dad, Michael, maybe even Mum all love me in their own ways but I'm not sure that I've absorbed enough to teach me any empathy. Their love feels like it's a feather on a beach, leaving no imprint of where it has touched the sand.

Beth has always been there, though, no matter what. She looked out for me at school, when Dad's unusual parenting style branded me as a bit weird. She asks me the important but difficult questions that I don't like to ask myself and makes sure that I always have an answer. She understands how my thoughts order themselves, and can finish my sentences for me. She anticipates what I need next before I know it myself. If there is any love in my narrow little life then it all emanates from Beth.

Now she is leaving me too.

I rub hard at the pale skin of my shoulder with the towel, so hard that my nerve endings shout out in protest. I know I should stop. It will leave marks that might show in my bridesmaid's dress, but the pain of the towel dragging across my skin takes my mind away from the pain inside my heart. There's a pleasure in the sensation even though it cannot last, like scratching an insect bite. I think of Beth and what she needs from me today and force myself to stop. When I move the towel away there is a small patch of skin missing, the flesh beneath freshly pink. As I watch, pinpricks of blood appear across the damaged surface. I observe them bloom, fascinated by the perfection of the tiny spheres. I've not done much damage. I have done worse before.

The bleeding stops almost as quickly as it started. I dab at the graze with some toilet paper and soon there is nothing to see but a blotchy red patch, which should be covered by the dress. Given the state of my burned hand, I doubt anyone will be distracted by a slightly discoloured shoulder.

I take a deep breath and stand up straight. I stare at myself in the steamy mirror, thankful that the woman staring back is a little blurred, her sharp edges indistinct.

'Enough,' I say sternly to the woman. 'Pull yourself together, Cara. Today is not about you.'

I meet Beth at the hairdresser's and am blow-dried into shape and soon we are back at her cottage, perching on the sofa with a plate of delicately cut smoked-salmon sandwiches. We eat them in small, mouse-like nibbles as if taking big bites will spoil our hair. In the corner of the room, the Christmas tree twinkles.

'I can't believe you bothered to put a tree up,' I say. 'You won't be here on the day and then it'll still be here when you get back from honeymoon.'

'But I won't be coming back,' says Beth grandly. 'Last night was my very last night here.'

'Of course,' I say, swallowing hard as it hits me again how much is about to change. No more will we curl up together on this old sofa and put the world to rights. I'm going to lose more than I can bear. 'I hadn't really thought beyond today,' I lie. 'What will you do with the old place?'

'Greg thinks we should sell but I don't want to. I'm going to stay firm and hold on to it. I'll probably let it out to some student nurses or something.'

'Is that wise?' I laugh. 'Remember when you were a student nurse?'

'I'll choose nice, responsible ones . . .' She breaks off and casts a gaze around the familiar room. 'I can't quite believe it, Ca. I'm leaving here. I'm getting married. Everything is going to be so different.'

I reach across and touch her cheek. 'Not quite everything,' I say and I know that she understands.

The day runs like clockwork. Beth looks beautiful in her dress. I hear the murmurs of appreciation as I follow her up the aisle, and feel quietly smug. After the ceremony Greg takes me to one side. 'Thank you for all that you've done, Cara,' he says solemnly. 'You know I had my doubts at the beginning, but I have to hand it to you. You pulled it off. Beth looks stunning in your dress. I had no idea how talented you are. I'm sorry for not quite trusting you.'

I don't believe him. There's something off about his smile, something just out of kilter. Maybe it's the pressure of the day that makes it feel fake, or the champagne, but, almost out of habit, I interpret his motives with suspicion. I wonder whether he knows how much I resent him. I'm certain that he thinks I'm an unwelcome influence on his new wife. And, to be fair, he's probably right to be wary of me.

'I'm just glad I could help,' I say sweetly, matching his counterfeit smile with one of my own. It's on the tip of my tongue to make a comment about my achievement being doubly remarkable because of his ludicrously short deadline but I decide against it. He knows that he tried to sabotage my chances and failed. If this were a war, then this battle would be mine. Of course, though, it's not a war and I remind myself of this as he prattles on about the provenance of one the grooms-men, who is apparently a member of the minor aristocracy. Greg is now married to my best friend. I have to get used to it. But, I also remind myself, I don't have to like it.

By the time we get to the first dance, the evening has taken on a distinctly mellow feel, everyone conscious that Father Christmas will be sliding down their chimneys in a few hours' time. One by one people begin to slope off. There are rooms in the hotel, of course, but very few of the wedding guests have taken them up. By midnight there are just a handful of us left in the bar.

Beth, her hair now back to its habitually chaotic state and her dress hitched up so that she can perch on the bar stool, gives a very wide yawn.

'That's me beat,' she says. 'I think I shall retire.'

'Not too beat, I trust, my darling,' purrs Greg, licking his lips and winking at his best man.

I roll my eyes and Beth catches sight and winks at me.

'Oh, there'll be plenty of time for all that on the honeymoon,' says Beth, wriggling herself down from the stool and pulling Greg by the arm.

'Good night all,' she says. 'Thank you for coming. And a special thank you to Cara, the best friend a girl could have.'

She blows a kiss at me and then heads towards the lifts with Greg in tow.

'This is how it's going to be from now on. Under the thumb!' he jokes as he follows his new wife out.

I do hope so, I think.

CHAPTER TWENTY-EIGHT

Michael, 1987

Michael wakes up with a start. He is confused. What day is it? Should he be putting his school uniform on? Is it his day for a bath? As his eyes become adjusted to the light, he realises that there is something that isn't quite right. It's far too dark to be morning. Either that or it's still very early.

He reaches for the clock that his father bought him two and a half years ago, when he started school. It has a small round face and folds away into a leather case for travel. Michael has not yet had the opportunity to make use of this feature. His father had said that, now Michael was at school, it was up to him to make sure he never overslept; his mother couldn't do everything for him and Michael had to start taking responsibility for himself. His mother had picked up the clock, running her fingers over the grainy leather.

'He's far too small for a clock, Joe. He can barely even tell the time yet,' she said. She reached out to Michael, pushing his knotted hair away from his forehead.

'Well, it's about time he learned,' his father said crossly, as if the fact that he couldn't tell the time was somehow Michael's fault.

Michael wanted to say that they had not done time-telling at play-group but that he knew when it was the hour and the half hour and which hand was which. His mother smiled at him, the special, secret smile that she used when she didn't really agree with what his father was saying but didn't want to contradict him.

'We'll learn to tell the time, won't we Michael?' she said gently. 'And in the meantime, I will wake you up.' She winked at him. 'Just in case.'

The clock face has stripes of luminous paint on the numbers and the hands but it shows up in the dark only if you hold the clock in the light before you go to sleep. Michael peers at it now but he can't see it with any certainty. He flicks on his bedside light and looks again. His time-telling skills are still a bit wobbly but he is sure that the clock says ten thirty. That's before midnight. It's not even tomorrow yet. So why is he awake?

Then he hears the sound again and he realises what has woken him. His father is shouting, loudly and with scant regard for the noise levels. Sometimes his parents are so irresponsible. He needs to make him stop or he will wake Cara and then all hell will break loose.

Michael slides out of bed, feeling cross. His parents are supposed to be adults. Do they not know that people are trying to sleep? He stomps across the bedroom. He will go and tell them to be quiet, to stop arguing and to go to bed. Surely it must be their bedtime by now.

On the landing, he is about to go downstairs when something makes him stop. The voices sound different. His father is yelling. This is nothing new. His father yells at his mother all the time, criticising her, telling what she has done wrong, how she can improve things. Sometimes Michael wants to step in and defend her and will take a deep breath in readiness for all the words he will have to use, but his mother, as if she can read his mind, always puts a finger to her lips to silence him before he has begun. When his father shouts, she just says that she is sorry, that she will try harder, do better. This is how it usually works.

Tonight, though, the arguing is different. His father is shouting as usual but his mother is shouting back. No. Not exactly shouting. Her voice is low and calm but there is no mistaking her anger. Michael holds back on the top stair, torn between wanting to move closer so he can hear what is being said and staying out of sight where he will not get into trouble. His father is shouting again. His tone is familiar.

'I don't know where you're getting these ludicrous ideas,' he shouts. 'What am I saying? Of course I know. That bloody woman. Well, I won't have it. Not in my house. Not under my roof.'

Again Michael hears the low rumble of his mother's voice, her words inaudible but her rage coming across loud and clear.

'I said no,' his father shouts. 'No wife of mine is going out to work. What I say goes around here and I am saying no so you can tell your new friend . . .' His father spits this word out so that it sounds anything but friendly. 'That she can take her ridiculous ideas and stick them where the sun don't shine.'

They move out of the kitchen and into the hallway. Michael slinks back against the wall so that the shadows engulf him.

'I don't know why you're being so unreasonable,' his mother is saying. 'It's just part-time. Michael is at school and Cara can go to a childminder for a few hours a week.'

'There is no way on God's earth that you are fobbing my child off on some stranger while you go off and indulge your petty little fantasies.'

Michael does not know what 'petty' means but it sounds like a nice thing, gentle and playful.

The front door opens. Michael recognises the creak that the hinges make.

'I'm going out,' snarls his father. 'And when I get back I don't want to hear another word about it.'

Then the door slams.

Michael winces and holds his breath. That will surely have woken Cara. He is right. Her wail starts up like an air-raid siren. His mother will come now to soothe her. For a moment, he thinks he should stay where he is, show solidarity to his mother, but then he remembers her menacing tone and he changes his mind, turning on his heel and scampering back into his room before she can see him. His light is still on. If he turns it off, she will know that he was awake. He decides to leave it. She can think that he awoke earlier in the night, turned it on and then drifted back to sleep.

He hops into his bed and arranges the covers on top of him, closing his eyes and feigning sleep. Seconds later, the bedroom door moves gently over the carpet and he senses rather than hears his mother's presence. He lies as still as he can. She lingers by the door rather than coming over to him. Cara's cries are getting louder still so his mother leaves his room and goes to her. Michael hears her gentle shushing and the sound of her footsteps pacing backwards and forwards in Cara's room. Gradually the screaming diminishes, is replaced by the odd sob, and then nothing. Cara has gone back to sleep.

He hears his mother cross the landing and come into his room to turn off the light. He tries to breathe as evenly as he can. He can sense her standing over him and he squeezes his eyes tightly.

'Did she wake you up?' asks his mother gently.

For a second, Michael thinks that he should continue to pretend but there is no point. She can always tell when he is not asleep. He opens his eyes. She is crouching at the bedside, her head level with his.

'It was Daddy,' he says. 'The shouting.'

His mother nods. She understands. She runs the pad of her forefinger down his face, following its contours.

'You go back to sleep now,' she says. 'It's all finished. There's nothing to worry about.'

Michael is not sure that she is telling him the truth. It is true that there is often shouting but, as he remembers the calm, controlled anger in his mother's voice, some level of childhood intuition tells him that

CHAPTER TWENTY-NINE

Cara, 2017

Even though Christmas has always been a low-key affair around here, I still wake up early on Christmas morning, my insides buzzing with anticipation. Years of social conditioning from marketing and television have ingrained themselves into my expectations, despite my lack of personal experience. This initial excitement never materialises into much but why shouldn't I get a bit of the Christmas buzz just like everyone else?

I have the beginnings of a headache – too much wedding champagne and not enough sleep – but it's not bad and certainly nothing that a couple of paracetamol and a cup of tea won't shift. I lie still, listening for sounds of Dad moving about, but the house is quiet. There are no cars on the road outside either. The world is silent as it wakes up to Christmas.

Unbidden, my mind flicks to the complicated time schedule that I have drawn up for today, with the assistance of my *Best Christmas Ever* magazine. The excitement of a moment ago morphs into a sinking feeling of dread deep in the pit of my stomach. What on earth had I been thinking when I decided to do Christmas from scratch? How did I imagine I could replicate, in the course of one day, what it has taken generations of other women, passing knowledge lovingly from mother to daughter, decades to perfect? It would have been so much less stressful to buy the whole meal ready-prepared and then just heat it up. When I mess this up, as I'm bound to do, I am going to end up looking stupid and feeling worse.

It's too late now, though. The raw materials are in the fridge and the shops are shut for the duration. I am just going to have to grit my teeth and get on with it. From memory, the first requirement is to turn the oven on at eight forty-five. I turn and look at my alarm clock. It's eight fifty-seven.

'Cara! Cara!'

I can hear Dad's confused cry from across the landing. I leap out of bed, tussling with the duvet as I go. I have to get to him before he realises, a little too late, that he needs the loo. As I burst into his room, he is struggling to stand up. Just pushing himself to a sitting position is beginning to seem too much for him. I wonder if the plateau that we have been teetering along for a while is about to reach a sheer drop.

'Come on then, Dad,' I say. 'Let's get you to the bathroom, shall we?'

He smiles at me and I can tell that he's with me, that today I am his daughter and not some stranger who has conned their way into his house to rob him blind.

'Guess what day it is?' I say as I guide him across the landing to the bathroom. I don't give him time to make a guess. His inability to find the words upsets us both. 'It's Christmas Day!' I can't tell whether this means anything to him or not but I reach over and give him a kiss on his cheek anyway. 'Merry Christmas, Dad. And guess who's coming to dinner. Mrs P! So that'll be fun, won't it, the three of us. I'm even going to have a bash at doing Christmas dinner with all the trimmings. Can you believe that? Not sure how good it'll be but I can try, can't I?'

I work hard at keeping my voice cheerful, my comments positive. It would be so easy to slip into accusation and anger. I remember once watching a dog-training film on television. Apparently, the words you use are unimportant. It is the tone of voice that they respond to. I could try it, I think.

'Hi, Dad. Season's greetings to you – and, while we're bathing in the spirit of goodwill, could you please explain precisely why you told me that my mother was dead when in fact you appear to have driven her away with your extramarital affair?'

I don't actually voice this out loud. There's still a chance that he might understand what I'm saying, but he could never respond. Not now. And certainly not with reasoned argument. This frail and vulnerable man who needs so much care and love is not my father. There's no point hurling accusations at him. Whatever my dad chose to do all those years ago has nothing to do with the man who needs me to help him to the bathroom.

I get him dressed in a jacket and tie in honour of the occasion and when he is downstairs, and mesmerised by the Christmas cartoons on the television, I turn my attention to my schedule. I am almost an hour behind already so I just scribble out all the timings and rewrite them, adding one hour as I go. With renewed, if slightly shaky, confidence, I turn on the oven.

I am feeling kind of in control of the kitchen when the doorbell rings. It's spot on one o'clock. As soon as I open the door, I see that Mrs P has made an effort with her appearance. She is dressed in a boxy, Chanel-style jacket in a coral pink with smart black trousers and a pair of black patent heels. There is a hint of colour on her eyelids and her lips are skimmed with a delicate shade of peach. I'm aware of the briefest of pauses as I take in her new look and she immediately looks uncomfortable, pulling at the bottom of her jacket and dropping her eyes. Anxious to undo what I have inadvertently done to unbalance her, I overcompensate.

'Come in! Come in,' I gush. 'You look fabulous. I love that jacket.'

I whip off the apron to show her that I too have dressed up, albeit not quite so formally. She gives me a tight little smile and nods a thank you.

'I'm afraid I've got a bit behind with the dinner,' I say as I show her through to the lounge.

I don't want her in the kitchen with me, watching me flounder around.

'We shouldn't be eating too much later than planned, though. Can I get you a drink?' I see her struggle with the decision. 'It's okay,' I add, when it dawns on me what's causing her reluctance. 'You're absolutely not here to look after Dad. That's my job today. You are off duty. Please have a glass of champagne with me. I've chilled some specially.'

It comes across like a plea. I'm going to need a drink or two to get through today and I don't want to go it alone.

'That would be lovely,' she says.

In the lounge, Dad is still facing the television screen but his eyes seem to be focused somewhere above it. The tree lights twinkle prettily. I try to ignore the paltry offering of presents beneath. I see Mrs P take it in but she doesn't comment. After all, what can you expect in a house with no children and only one functioning adult?

'May I?' she asks, gesturing towards the tree. She opens her hand-bag and takes out two presents, each exquisitely wrapped in gold tissue paper with white curled ribbons. She places them gently on top of the others.

'Oh, there was no need . . .' I begin but she silences me with a wave of her hand.

'Can I do anything to help?' she asks.

'No. You sit there and relax and I'll go get you that drink. Dad, Mrs P is here to spend Christmas with us. That's lovely, isn't it?'

At the sound of my voice, Dad turns his head. He sees Mrs P and something like recognition skates across his face but then it's gone and he turns back to the television.

I know I should invite her to come with me to the kitchen but I really can't face it so I say, 'I'll be right back with your drink,' and I disappear.

I stand in front of the oven and take a couple of deep breaths. There's so much that can go wrong with this meal, so many component parts that might fail and bring the rest of it crashing down around me. The smidgen of control that I thought I had earlier is slipping away. I take the champagne from the fridge, struggling to prise off the foiled cage and pour it into three flutes. They don't match; two are what are left of Dad's lead crystal, which we were forbidden to touch as children. The third is a glass that came free with petrol sometime in the eighties and has proved indestructible over the years. I pour slightly less champagne into this one, earmarking it for Dad. I feel a twinge of guilt that he should have to slum it with pre-pressed glass while Mrs P and I enjoy our drinks from his crystal, but I reconcile this by reminding myself that he'll never notice.

My hands shake as I transfer the glasses to a tray. It is silly. I'm a grown woman, and this is just one meal, but I want to show that I'm up to the task even though there's never been anyone there to teach me how. This meal is an elaborate and self-imposed test. What makes my nerves worse is the almost-certain knowledge that Mrs P could knock up a delicious Christmas dinner for ten without even batting an eyelid.

With clammy palms, I check my schedule. The turkey is nestled in its silver-foil cave in the oven. According to my timings, it'll be ready to come out and rest in just under an hour. The vegetables are peeled and ready to go. Pigs-in-blankets wait snugly in the fridge. Everything appears to be in hand.

I add a bowl of pistachio nuts and some hand-cut crisps to the drinks tray and carry it through to the lounge. Dad hasn't moved and is still sitting and staring, open-mouthed, at the TV screen. Mrs P's attention is fixed on the Christmas tree.

'Here we are,' I say. 'Champagne and some nibbly things to keep us going.'

I pass her a flute. 'Thank you,' she says. She takes the glass, holding it carefully by the stem. 'What are we drinking to?'

I think it over for a moment. 'To getting dinner before Boxing Day?' I suggest.

She smiles, a broad, open smile that makes her eyes almost disappear in the crinkles of skin.

'To timely meals,' she says, raising her glass. 'The tree looks nice,' she adds.

'Thanks.'

I am about to tell her about the missing little blue angel, but that might lead me on to the letters and I don't want to stray into that minefield. My life is turning into one long secret. Instead I take another sip and soon my champagne is all gone. Mrs P has barely started hers. Dad's glass remains untouched. It was pointless to pour it for him really. I pick it up from the table and drink that one too and immediately feel the alcohol coursing into my bloodstream. My head feels deliciously light and suddenly the ever-increasing time lag in my schedule seems much less important.

'I'd better go and check on that turkey,' I say.

'Do you need any help?' Mrs P asks again.

'No thanks,' I say brightly and flee to the kitchen.

Things are not really going as well in the food department as I'd hoped. When I open the door, the bird is sizzling nicely. I peep under its silver cloak and see that the bacon cross that I placed there so carefully this morning has slipped to a rakish angle and is starting to blacken. I pinch it between the tips of my finger and thumb and slide it out. The hot fat burns my skin and I drop the burned bacon on the floor and then curse. Quickly I scoop it up and on to the work surface (five-second rule).

Of course, one turkey a Christmas dinner does not make. I'm starting to regret the champagne and I can feel the vestiges of the post-wedding hangover start to creep back. I've prepped the vegetables already but I have forgotten the roast potatoes, which are still soaking in a pan of salted water. I also need to cook the pigs-in-blankets and the parsnips, not to mention the gravy and the sauces that I thought I'd do as finishing touches.

My heart starts to race but I tell myself that there's nothing panic-inducing about a pan of uncooked potatoes. I'll serve them boiled instead. The parsnips were always an added bonus anyway. I feel better for a moment but as I catch sight of my carefully written schedule, now spattered with bacon fat and hopelessly diverted from, I feel hot, angry tears pricking at my eyes. I so wanted to make everything perfect and now it's all going wrong. What was I playing at anyway, thinking that I could have a Christmas Day like everyone else?

'Are you sure you couldn't use a sous-chef?'

The voice at my shoulder makes me jump. Mrs P is standing in the doorway, empty champagne glass in hand. She goes to wash it up at the sink, reminding me, as if I could forget, that she is more than just a guest.

'No thank you. It's all under control,' I lie, blinking away the tears and hoping that she doesn't see them. Then something inside me just snaps and I give up the pretence. 'Actually, yes!' I say. 'My timings are miles out. The turkey will be ready and nothing else is. I think I'm going to have to jettison the roasties because they aren't even parboiled yet and the parsnips are just a step too far!'

Mrs P takes off her little jacket, hanging it on the back of a chair, and rolls up the sleeves of her blouse.

'There's no rush,' she says calmly. 'Your father is asleep and I'm sure we can find something to nibble on if we get peckish. When the turkey's done we can just keep it warm under some tea towels while we finish everything else off.' Her voice is so calm and reassuring. It's like being wrapped in a warm duvet. She takes an apron from the back of the door and sets to with the goose fat that I was intimidated into buying, cutting off small slices and dotting them around a roasting tin. Relief washes over me.

'Glass of wine?' I say, grateful to be back in familiar territory.

She nods and smiles and then suddenly we are a team in the kitchen, two women pulling together Christmas dinner for their men folk just like millions of others around the world.

The meal is a success, when eventually I serve it on the long-forgotten best china. Of course, there's far too much food for the three of us.

'I'll be eating leftovers into January,' I joke and Dad smiles as if pureed turkey is his absolute favourite.

Mrs P and I chat about this year's batch of Christmas Day films and tell each other gentle and insignificant anecdotes. We both seem to steer clear of Christmases past, as if those ghosts are as daunting for each of us. Dad, who has at least been trying to follow the conversation, eventually falls asleep at the table and we lift him between us to his chair in the lounge. He barely weighs anything these days, like his bones have been hollowed out. The thinness of his neck is exaggerated by his shirt collar, which stands proud like a tall fence some distance from his flesh.

'He hasn't opened his presents,' I say as we head back to the kitchen to clear up. 'I'm not sure why I bothered to buy him anything. You definitely shouldn't have,' I add.

'Oh, it's only a little token,' she says.

'Well, you needn't have worried on his account,' I say as I run the hot tap to fill a washing-up bowl.

My voice comes out sharper than I mean it to be. Mrs P takes a clean tea towel from the drawer and waits for me to start stacking plates on the draining rack.

'Say if I'm speaking out of turn,' she says carefully. 'But have you and your father had a falling out?'

'No,' I reply. 'What makes you ask that?'

But I know what has made her ask. There's been a shift. I was trying to ignore it but first the postcards and now the love letters have made the ground between me and my father unstable. I'm struggling to prevent my anger at him seeping out into my feelings for the broken old man who has usurped his place. Part of it is pure frustration because I can't ask him all the questions that are now flooding my mind. There's more to it than that, though.

'I've found some things out,' I say, my tongue loosened by the wine. 'About Dad. Recently. It's led to a lot of questions that I can't find answers for.'

'Is that why you went to London to see Michael?' she asks.

We don't look at each other, both focusing on the job in hand. Not being able to see her expression makes it easier to speak more freely.

'Partly,' I say. 'I suppose I'm just cross because I'm never going to know the answers. And also . . .'

I pause. I should probably keep this to myself but I'm tired of dealing with it all on my own.

'Dad was no saint,' I continue. 'I mean, before . . .' I don't finish the sentence but there's no need to. 'He loved us in his way but he was a difficult man to live with. He had very fixed ideas about how things should be. And so, when I discovered that . . .'

Another pause. I take the roasting tray that I have been scrubbing out of the bowl and balance it on the plate rack. Water drips on to the stainless-steel sink top with a regular rhythm, like a heartbeat.

'. . . That he didn't always act in line with the high standards that he imposed on us, then that makes it a bit difficult to accept. The fact that I can't ask him about it is causing me a bit of a problem.'

She picks up the roasting tray and starts to dry it. I see that I've done a terrible job of washing it up. Dark grease smears the tea towel but she ignores this and just wipes it away.

'Whatever he's done,' she says quietly, 'or whatever you think he's done, it's not going to be improved by you getting angry. That'll just bring resentment and bitterness. And for what? You can't change the situation and you're never going to be able to talk to him about it.'

I put the last tray on the draining rack and tip the dirty water down the sink. Some of it splashes up at my dress.

'For your own sanity, you need to let it go,' she says.

'But it's a really big thing that I think he's done,' I say. 'I mean, really big. It's affected my entire life.'

'That may well be so, but it doesn't alter the fact that the father you think did this thing has gone. If you let it eat away at your insides then you'll never move on. What did your brother say?'

'He doesn't want anything to do with it. He thinks I should ignore it,' I say.

'Well, maybe you don't need to ignore it,' she says. 'I mean, you might need to find out more for your own peace of mind.'

I find myself nodding. She is right and Michael is wrong.

'But, as far as your father is concerned, there's nothing you can do. He's never going to be able to tell you anything. You have to accept that.'

'That's the problem,' I say. 'I'm not sure I can.'

'I'm not sure you have much option,' she replies. 'In the long run, it'll cause far less pain if you find a way to deal with whatever you think he's done and move on.'

'You mean forgive him?'

'Not necessarily. But you do have to find a way of living with not knowing. We can't all just forget our past like your father has done.'

She starts taking her apron off, yanking at the strings so that the bow releases. She pulls it over the head.

'Would you like some help getting him into bed?' she asks.

The way I feel at the moment, I would happily leave him in the chair to sleep all night, but I know that's not really an option and I'll only end up having to move him myself later.

'Yes please.'

We work in silence, waking Dad gently and manoeuvring him up the stairs while he's still groggy and then stripping him out of his best clothes and into his nightshirt. We take him to the bathroom, moving as a team until finally he is lying tucked up in his bed. I bend down to turn on his night light and his eyes open. He sees me and smiles. I don't smile back.

When we get back downstairs I suggest a cup of tea but she shakes her head.

'It's been a lovely day,' she says. 'Thank you so much for inviting me. But now I really should be going.'

She collects her things and I see her out. It's only when she's gone that I realise that we've not opened the presents. A little buzz of excitement tingles in me as I kneel on the floor by the Christmas tree and reach underneath for my gift. I take the little gold box in both hands. The tag reads 'Merry Christmas Cara', written in neat block lettering. I pull the ribbon and remove the gold paper to reveal a square, black box. Inside is a delicate necklace, a tiny butterfly on a silver chain. It's exquisite and makes me feel slightly ashamed of the wholly inadequate jar of hand cream that I've bought for her. I put the necklace on. The butterfly sits perfectly flat against my skin. Then I open the present for Dad – with slightly less care this time, although it is just as beautifully wrapped. It's a framed photograph of the oak tree in the garden, the one that loses its leaves over the grass.

CHAPTER THIRTY

The period between Christmas and New Year is generally a time for contemplation and consolidation and this year is no different, especially with Beth away on her honeymoon. Boxing Day passes in a haze of old films and tray meals concocted with very little effort from the enormous quantities of leftovers that my fantasy Christmas Day produced. If Dad is still aware that it's Christmas then he shows very little sign of it. He sits silently staring at the lights twinkling on the tree.

'I love Christmas lights, don't you?' I ask him, dropping down to my knees by his chair and pointing towards the tree.

There is no response. It's as if he hasn't even heard me speak. He's no longer engaged with the world around him. I don't know whether it's because of my changed attitude towards him or whether he really is deteriorating before my eyes but I fear the latter. I wouldn't want to leave him in the house on his own anymore, not even for a few minutes. As I watch him sit and stare, this shell that was once my father, the realisation that the time has come for full-time care drenches me like a rainstorm in June. This is a new stage, one that I knew would arrive eventually. But, what with the wedding and Christmas occupying my thoughts recently, I hadn't noticed that it had crept up on us quite as far as it has done. It's perfectly obvious that Mrs P can't do it all by herself. I need a new plan.

I ring the agency, assuming that I'll speak to an answerphone, but my call is answered on the second ring. By the time I put the phone down, we have agreed around-the-clock help, with Mrs P doing most of the care and other, rota staff filling in when she has time off. It'll cost a fortune but Dad has the money sitting in the bank just waiting for Michael and me to inherit. We don't need his money, though. We've both made our own way in the world, in spite of everything. I don't need Dad's money and I don't want it.

Later, in some kind of pre-New Year frenzy, I decide to tidy out my workroom and carry out an inventory of what I have and what needs replenishing. I start with gusto, pulling out fabrics and files of patterns to dust behind them, but pretty quickly my motivation begins to wane. I'm hopeless at this stuff. I am tempted to just put everything back the way it was but who am I kidding? The mess is made. I might as well try to do a decent job.

As I flick fabric fluff off the shelves, my mind drifts to my mother. The wedding and then Christmas have given me the excuses that I needed to keep my mind closed to the endless possibilities and when I have had time to think, it has been Dad's letters that have been troubling me. Mrs P was right in what she said on Christmas Day, though. I won't uncover anything else about my Dad's past unless I discover who 'T' is or was – but how do I go about finding a woman who wrote some letters thirty-odd years ago? Without Dad to ask, there's no solution to that particular problem. The only way forward is to find my mother as soon as possible and ask her. And with the country at a standstill unless you fancy shopping or a pantomime, I have very little else to distract me.

I make two decisions as I stand in the kitchen, having shut the door on the chaos I have created in my workroom. First, I can't face cold turkey for lunch again and second, internet searching to trace my mother is not the way to go. As I stand in front of the fridge, systematically removing items from inside and sniffing beneath their cling-film covers, I contemplate how best to proceed. I have to start with what I know for sure. This, when I turn it over and inspect it, is decidedly thin. I know that I had a mother at some point, even though there's no trace of either her birth or death certificate. We're not talking immaculate conception here. Somebody gave birth to me. After that, the knowns become very shady. The only thing that seems certain about my mother is that she had a sister.

This, therefore, is where I must begin.

My aunt's name is, or was – I'm learning not to treat these things as black and white – Ursula Kemp. She is, or was, an artist. She may or may not live in San Francisco – and that is it: the sum total of what I know about my aunt and indeed my entire maternal family. It's not much to go on but it is all I have.

I head to my workroom, steadfastly ignoring the mid-reorganisation devastation, sit down at the computer and type her name into Google. Ursula Kemp . . . and up it all pops. There is a whole page of results for an artist called Ursula Kemp. It's so surprising that I delete what I've typed and re-enter it, even though I can see that my search has no spelling errors. Is this my aunt? Really? She even has the honour of a page on Wikipedia. As I sit and look at the words on the screen, the now-familiar mixture of excitement and nausea floods my body. If this really is her then she appears to be well known, famous even. I should be able to trace her and suddenly it all feels very real.

I start with the Wiki page, which tells me that she was born in 1956 in London, England. I do a quick calculation. This tallies with what little I know about Mum's background. Feeling more confident that I have the right Ursula Kemp, I read on.

Following school, she was accepted at Goldsmiths where she studied Fine Art. After graduating, she went to San Francisco, California, where she still lives.

My eyes dart to the top of the page to see when it was posted. The entry was originally written a few years ago but has been recently updated. There is a pretty good chance that the information is accurate and Ursula is only sixty-one. It's not very likely that she'll have died in the short time since the page was last redone.

There are a couple of links on the page. One to Goldsmiths and another to a simple website displaying some of her work but not giving much information about the woman herself. Returning to the Wiki page, my eyes scan the words, trying to squeeze out the smallest splinter of knowledge. At the bottom of the page, there is a single sentence.

Very little is known about Ursula Kemp's private life.

I almost laugh out loud. This is starting to feel like a conspiracy. Leaving the Wiki page, I return to my Google search and click on 'Images'. Mostly what pops up are pictures taken from exhibition catalogues, but towards the bottom of the page there is one photograph with people in it. I click it open. It's a woman with closely cropped hair staring out defiantly at the camera. She is standing by a white wall on which is mounted a single canvas: dark petrol colours with a red mass pulsing at its heart. Another woman stands slightly back, her arms crossed tightly across her body. The caption reads: 'Ursula Kemp with woman believed to be her sister, San Francisco, 1990.'

Her sister? I zoom in on the image looking for anything familiar, but the larger I make it the less defined it becomes. I reach for the one photo I have of Mum, my eyes flicking from one face to the other. Is this the same woman? I scan the features, searching for anything definitive. It certainly looks like it might be her and she's with her sister, which makes perfect sense. Surely if she'd run from Dad she would've gone to someone she knew and trusted? I search her face for echoes of mine and think that I can see myself reflected there but it's hard to tell when the picture I have of her is so small. Then I notice something dangling from her jacket pocket. I zoom in closer. It's a yellow and blue scarf – the same yellow and blue scarf that ties back her hair in my photo. It is her. It has to be. I think I knew, really, from just looking at her, but this confirms it. So that means that this Ursula Kemp is definitely my aunt. And that my mother was indeed alive in 1990. My breath comes quick and fast.

Urgently, I click on to the website from where the image was taken but it is an old WordPress site about the San Francisco art scene that hasn't been touched in years. There are no other pictures of Ursula. I go back to the picture of the two of them and sit staring at it. Surely this is proof that Mum didn't die when Dad said she did. I feel sick.

When I start to feel a bit calmer, I return to my search and follow another link to a gallery in San Francisco that displays and sells Ursula's work. It is hard to get a true impression of the pictures on a small screen, but even without the dimensions I can tell that she paints on a large scale. From what I remember from my art-school days, I think you'd call her style 'lyrical abstraction'. It's all about intuition and spontaneity. If there's any figurative element to her work then it escapes me. It's all dark, sludgy colours with the occasional flash of harsh red; not my thing at all but, if the number of search results is anything to go by, it's brought her some success.

I scan the sides of the page to see if there's anywhere to contact the artist direct but I'm not surprised when the only links seem to be to the gallery itself. I click on the 'Contact Us' page and start to compose a message in my head but I don't get very far. What am I trying to say?

'I am the artist's long-lost niece from England who has just discovered that her mother, your client's sister, didn't die as was previously believed, but is alive and well and living Lord-only-knows where. Please can you give me your client's email address?'

Well, that isn't going to work. If she's as private as they say, they are hardly going to just pass on her email address to a complete stranger.

The gallery might be able to give me some information but it's not likely to be the details that I need. Maybe they would forward an email to her?

Or I could just go to San Francisco and track her down myself.

This is a ludicrous idea. Even as I consider it, I can hear Michael laughing at me.

'You want to travel halfway round the world to find some woman who may or may not be there and is highly unlikely to want to talk to you anyway? Are you mad?'

Strangely, though, whereas in the past I would have listened to Michael's voice in my head, valued his opinion and let it form the major part of my decision-making process, this time he holds no sway. He's been wholeheartedly unenthusiastic from the outset and so has waived any right he might have had to be involved. I haven't told him about the love letters and I shan't tell him about this either, not until I have something concrete to report. I can go to California for a few days on holiday. I need a break. I deserve one. I can keep the purpose of my mission secret and if there's no trace of Ursula then, well, I can think of worse places to visit.

Even as my mouse clicks its way through to a cheap-flights site, I'm planning what I'll say to Mrs P – but I know it won't be a problem. Between her and the other care staff, Dad'll be more than adequately cared for, spoiled even, and it is not like he'll miss me. I shake my head and backtrack my thinking. That's not fair. He might miss me but I will never know.

But then I have a slight wobble. Irritating though it is for the voice of Michael in my head to be right, it would be madness just to fly halfway round the world on a hunch. But now I have the photograph. This isn't just a hunch anymore. It's more than that. I click to the gallery site and compose a short email explaining that I will be visiting from England with a view to making a purchase in the next seven days and would like the opportunity to meet the artist if at all possible.

It's just going dark outside as I leave my workroom, having decided that the rest of the reorganisation will just have to wait until tomorrow. Just as I'm flicking off the light, my laptop pings – an email. I spring back to my desk and click it open. It is from the gallery.

Dear Ms Ferensby,

Thank you for your enquiry. We are delighted that you are interested in Ursula Kemp's work and would be very happy to discuss this with you. While Ms Kemp generally does her business through us, we can confirm that she will be in town over the next seven days and there may be an opportunity for you to meet with her in person. Please reach out when you arrive so we can make the necessary arrangements.

We look forward to doing business with you.

Kind regards,
Skyler T. Murphy
Gallery Director

So it is decided. I will fly to San Francisco, see the Golden Gate Bridge, ride the cable car and find the key to my family's mysterious history. Just like that.

CHAPTER THIRTY-ONE

It's no good. I can't face any more meals scavenged from what remains of the turkey. I must finally venture out and buy fresh food. Even though it's not yet five o'clock, the sky over the moor is an inky blue and the pavement dotted with puddles of yellow from the streetlights. I head towards the shops, trying to think of things that I fancy to eat. Definitely no meat or cheese. Fruit maybe? Something fishy? I'm lost in thought when I hear a tapping on glass somewhere close.

'Cara! Cara!' A muffled voice is calling me. 'In here.'

Looking up, I see Laura Cross sitting in the window of a bar. Laura is a former client. I made her the most beautifully extravagant gown in gold organza for her wedding two winters back. The dress was exquisite, the marriage less so, not surviving to see its first anniversary. I stop walking and go to talk to her through the window.

'Hi. Merry Christmas,' I say, mouthing my words clearly but not speaking loudly enough to be heard either through the plate glass or in the street.

'Come in,' she shouts. 'I haven't seen you for ages. Come and have a drink with us.'

She is with a mixed group of seven or eight people. I don't know any of them. I shake my head but I can see her struggling to her feet and sidestepping her way towards me. She sticks her head around the door of the bar, her body remaining inside.

'Oh, come on,' she says. 'Just one drink. What else have you got to do?' She looks at my bag-for-life. 'Oh my God! You're not going to the supermarket? How excruciatingly dull. Come and tell me things. I heard your friend Beth got hitched. I assume you made the dress?'

She comes out of the bar now and links her arm through mine, pulling me gently towards the door. I protest a little at first but then I give in. Dad is being looked after. I have nowhere I need to be. I go in.

Inside, the bar looks like it should be in a village in rural France rather than Yorkshire. The floor, bar and tables, all fashioned from reclaimed wood, shine as if they have been rubbed smooth by generations of farmers. Open shelving scampers up the walls, making the place feel as if you have accidentally stepped into someone's pantry.

'There's wine,' says Laura as she clambers over several laps to get back into her seat, but when she takes the bottle from the cooler it's empty. She tips it upside down just to make sure. 'Soz,' she says with a shrug.

I order myself a gin and tonic, which arrives in a glass that could comfortably house a goldfish, then head over to join Laura and her friends.

'This is Cara,' Laura tells the group as I approach. 'Designer of exquisite wedding dresses, including mine, which I still have, despite the early demise of my marriage. So, if any of you are thinking of getting married, which I really cannot recommend, and want the most beautiful dress available, then look no further. Cara is a genius.'

They look up at me briefly and I smile, trying not to look as awkward as I feel. I don't know any of them, although I recognise one of the girls as Laura's chief bridesmaid. I pull a spare chair over from another table but there's not a space big enough for me to squeeze into, and none of the others move up, so I am forced to sit slightly away from the table. I wonder how long I will have to stick it out before I can politely leave. I take a slug of gin.

The conversation is fast and furious, but with the murmur of other voices behind me it's hard to catch everything. I sit a little forward in my seat and smile, trying to make sense of the snatches that I can hear. In the end, I give up and sit back again, sipping at my drink quickly and smiling inanely as I count the minutes. The gin has a sprig of rosemary floating in it, which keeps going up my nose.

'Did you really make her wedding dress?' asks a voice to my left.

I turn and see a man in a chunky-knit navy sweater sitting in the next chair, which is also positioned just out of the larger group. He has tufty dark hair, slightly longer than it should be to be tidy, and a thick beard. He reminds me of Captain Haddock from the Tintin books that Michael loved when we were children. His eyes are a startling blue.

I finish my gin in one surprising gulp and nod.

'It was beautiful,' he says. 'Best bit of that terrible wedding. Did you know that Laura's mum and Nick's grandma had the most spectacular row just after the speeches? The auspices for a long and successful marriage were not good. The dress was pretty special, though. Even I remember the dress.'

I notice how he says 'even I', like he is totally insignificant.

'Thanks,' I say.

I'm aware that if I'm going to carry on a conversation with the only person who's bothered to speak to me since I arrived, then I'll have to come up with something to say, but my mind is blank. I resort to the old faithfuls.

'So how do you know Laura?' I ask, cringing inwardly at my lack of originality.

'I don't,' he says. 'I came in for a quiet pint but she's chained my ankles to this chair and she won't let me go until . . .' He shakes his head and blows his lips out in defeat. 'I like to pretend that I'm one of those men who's always ready with a slightly surreal joke at the drop of the hat,' he says. 'But actually, I'm just not sharp enough. I get so far in and then my mind goes blank and I end up looking like an idiot. The truth is, Laura works with my ex-girlfriend. The girlfriend came and went but somehow Laura and I stayed friends. Just friends,' he adds quickly as my eyebrows stray upwards.

'And do you have a name, oh quiet-pint-drinking-captive friend of Laura's?'

I try to adopt the same flirty style as him but I'm afraid I sound a bit pompous.

'Simeon,' he says. 'I know. Don't laugh,' he adds before I even have chance to smirk. 'My mother was a huge fan of French detective novels.'

I struggle to make the connections but eventually a name appears out of the fog.

'Oh! Maigret!' I say. 'But wasn't that . . . ?'

'Simenon? Yes. I am named after the misspelling of a French detective-story writer. Could it be any more humiliating? Mum just liked the name. By the time she'd worked out that she'd spelled it wrong, it was too late. I was Simeon and there was nothing anyone could do about it. My granddad nearly had a fit, apparently.'

'Simeon's a nice name,' I say, rolling it round in my mouth. 'I think I like Simenon even better but there's not much you can do about that.'

'You're not helping,' he says and I notice again how very blue his eyes are.

He picks up a wine bottle from the floor by his chair and then, plucking the rosemary sprig from my empty glass, he tips some wine into it without asking me if I want any. I might have objected but I'm so surprised that I let him pour.

'Cara,' he says. 'Now that's a beautiful name. It's Italian, right?'

'I think so,' I reply. 'How do you know?'

'Italian ex-girlfriend.'

'You've left quite a trail,' I say, and he shrugs.

'What can I say? I'm hard to love. It means "beloved" doesn't it?'

'Apparently. Ironic, really.' He looks at me, waiting for me to fill him in, but I'm not about to tell my life story to a stranger in a bar, no matter how blue his eyes. 'I really should be going,' I say, getting to my feet. 'I was on my way to the supermarket when Laura accosted me.'

I leave the unrequested wine untouched.

'Want some company?' he asks. 'I'm sure there must be something that I need.'

'I thought you were chained to the seat.'

He stands up with a flourish.

'Houdini is my middle name,' he says.

'Suit yourself.' I say my goodbyes to Laura. She makes a bit of a show of asking me to stay. 'But we haven't had a chance to catch up yet . . .' Then she sees the man, Simeon, leaving with me and gives me an enormous and very unsubtle wink. I don't look to see if he has noticed as my stomach squirms with mortification.

We walk along the dark streets side by side, his shoes clicking on the stone pavement. A dog barks loudly not far away and then is rudely reprimanded by its owner.

'So, what is ironic about your name?' he asks, as if no time at all has passed since I made the comment.

I toy with ignoring the question, batting it away with a light-hearted joke. I surprise myself when I say, 'I think my mother abandoned me when I was two. I'm not sure I can have been all that beloved.'

'What do you mean?' he asks. 'Surely you know whether she left or not.'

'You'd think.' I know that this isn't an answer to his question. I can feel him turning to look at me as we walk along but he doesn't press me when I don't explain. I keep my focus on the pavement in front of me. 'I thought she was dead,' I say without raising my gaze. 'That's what my dad told me. Now it turns out that she might not be. Hence the abandoning theory.'

'That's tough,' he says. 'What will you do?' His voice is a mixture of curiosity and something that sounds like genuine concern. It throws me a little. This is the last thing I was expecting when I went out to buy some fruit.

'I'm going to find her sister,' I say. 'And ask.'

'Seems fair enough,' he says and doesn't delve any deeper.

I like that he's let it drop. I'm not sure why I even told him but I appreciate that he is allowing me to control the pace at which information flows. I don't mention it again.

The supermarket is quiet. I pick up some unripe bananas and a bag of shiny satsumas, and then lose interest. Simeon has disappeared and I catch myself feeling disappointed. I assume that he's bored of trying to prise information out of me or bumped into someone else and decided to just slip away. When he reappears with a bottle in either hand I'm remarkably pleased to see him. Warning bells start to ring in my head but I throw a metaphorical blanket over them so I can't hear.

'Red or white?' he says, brandishing the bottles at me in turn. 'Call me presumptuous,' he continues. 'But I think this conversation needs continuing over a glass of wine. My flat isn't far away. Or we could sit outside if you'd rather. Or you could just pay for your . . .' He looks at my basket. 'Your frankly pathetic selection of groceries and go home on your own.'

I don't even think about it. 'Either,' I say. 'And your flat sounds nice.'

'You haven't seen it yet,' he warns and he smiles, a broad open smile that makes me respond in kind. 'I'll get both just in case,' he says.

As we walk up the hill to his place, I get my phone out to ring home.

'Hi,' I say when the rota nurse answers. 'It's me, Cara. I'm going to be a little bit later than I said. Just thought I should let you know.'

He doesn't ask but I feel the need to explain.

'My dad,' I say when I finish the call to home. 'He's not well.'

He just nods.

His flat is at the top of the road where the town ends and the moor begins and the dark hills loom up behind us like a shadow. The building looks square and tall with lots of windows, although it's difficult to make out any details in the dark. There is a blue tourist plaque on the wall.

'It used to be a maternity hospital,' says Simeon, seeing me trying to read the sign in the gloom. 'And Charles Darwin stayed here when it was a hotel. He was here waiting for *On the Origin of Species* to be published, apparently. He won't have slept in my bit, though. I'm up in the eaves, where the servants hung out.' He winks at me. He's quite handsome, I suppose, in a scruffy kind of way.

He turns the key in the front door, which swings open on to a wide entrance hall, and leads the way to the lift. It crosses my mind that I'm playing fast and loose with my personal safety but my instincts tell me I have nothing to worry about here.

As we get out of the lift he stops in his tracks. 'Damn,' he says, hitting himself on his forehead with the heel of his hand.

'What?'

'I just remembered what state I left the place in when I went to meet the others in the pub. If you don't want to see the single man in his natural environment then I suggest you leave now.'

'I'm sure I'll cope,' I say. Now that I'm here, I find that I really do want to spend some time with him, no matter what state his flat is in.

'Well, don't say I didn't warn you,' he says and opens the door.

The flat is cut into the eaves of the house. The ceiling slants on every side and there is only true standing headroom in the centre of the room. There is a kitchen and a small dining table at one end and a battered-looking leather sofa and a TV at the other. It looks tidy too. There are no dirty dishes in the sink and the sofa is clear of clothing. I'm just thinking that maybe he's a neat freak when I notice the floor. Laid out on various pieces of newspaper across the carpet is a bike, completely dismantled with all its component parts spread neatly around the frame. The room smells subtly of WD-40.

He looks at the bike and then back at me, his nose crinkled.

'Sorry. I was just cleaning it when Laura rang. I wasn't expecting visitors.'

A pair of Lycra cycling tights hang on a radiator together with a lurid, fluorescent-green jersey and some ankle socks. He follows my gaze.

'They're clean,' he assures me. 'But I can't tumble dry them in case they shrink. Just pretend they're not there. Now, make yourself at home. Red or white?'

I pick my way over the bike bits and sit right at the very end of the sofa.

'White please,' I say. 'Nice flat.'

And it is a nice flat. Though it's small, it's clutter-free and everything looks to have been carefully chosen rather than just thrown together. I quickly scan the space for signs of a girlfriend. He said he was single but don't men always say that when it suits them? Not that I know much about the subject of male behaviour, but I watch a lot of television. However, there are no photographs or anything else that might be a clue. I assume that he was telling the truth and find, somewhat surprisingly, that I'm pleased.

'Thanks,' he says as he pours the wine into stemless glasses. 'I can be a bit clumsy,' he adds when he sees me looking curiously. 'These are harder to knock over.'

He brings the glasses over and sits down next to me but not so close that I might feel uncomfortable. I actually catch myself feeling a little disappointed that he's sat so far away. If only Beth could see me now.

'So,' I say, after I've taken a courage-enhancing swig of the wine. 'What else do you do, apart from pull bikes to pieces?'

He tells me that he's a primary-school teacher, that he's lived here for two years, that he's from Grantham originally and came to Yorkshire for a job. He moves his hands a lot when he talks, gesticulating enthusiastically and running his fingers through his hair when he's trying to think of something. Every part of him buzzes with energy, as if he's got nowhere to store it and the excess is about to crackle out of his fingertips. He talks quickly and confidently about films and bikes and his work and I'm happy to listen to him. Every so often he'll ask me a question, which I answer succinctly. He doesn't ask me anything else about my mother and I'm grateful. When I look up at the clock on the wall it's almost midnight.

'I should go,' I say. 'They'll be wondering where I've got to.' But I know this isn't true.

'That's a shame,' he says. 'I'm enjoying myself. Shall I walk you home?'

I nod and stand but I've been sitting on my foot, which is now refusing to cooperate. I stumble and before I realise he has caught me. He holds me by my shoulders and it feels a bit like something out of a film. It's one of those moments, when you think you might kiss – but then he lets his arms drop to his sides and I right myself. Whatever might be happening here, it isn't happening tonight.

CHAPTER THIRTY-TWO

It is New Year's Eve and I have no plans. Again. In years gone by, the lack of a social engagement on what might be considered the biggest night of the year would have sent me into a spiral of fretting about my lack of friends. I'd have convinced myself that everyone was having a much better life than me. Now, though, I know that most of it is hype. So many fabulous-looking lives are fake. People only share the good parts and skip over the bad. Perfect, eye-sparkling, snow-dusted, heart-stoppingly romantic New Year's Eves only happen in the movies.

Unbidden, my mind skips to my evening with Simeon and I wonder idly how he might be spending his New Year's Eve. No doubt he's got a string of parties already lined up, jam-packed with interesting and beautiful people. I'm pretty certain that he won't have given me a second's thought since we said goodbye on my doorstep. Surprisingly, I find that this thought makes me feel a bit disappointed. Most of the time, my single status doesn't worry me. I don't really have time for a relationship, what with work and looking after Dad, and I almost never meet anyone that might fit the bill. But Simeon is a bit different. I really enjoyed the time we spent together and I think he did too, although my rusty radar might be a bit off-kilter. So, having parted company with him with no plans to meet again and not even a goodnight kiss, I can't help but feel a bit let down. I torture myself by playing through various 'what if' scenarios in my head, but conclude that he obviously isn't that interested.

Mrs P arrives bright and early. Dad and I are trying to build a jigsaw of the Eiffel Tower. Dad's contribution is minimal. His deteriorating fine motor skills prevent him from being able to reliably pick up a piece and the lattice pattern of ironwork making up the legs of the tower is challenging enough for me, let alone him. Instead, I offer him a running commentary of my progress and he seems happy enough just to watch, locked in his own near-silent world.

'Would it be all right with you,' I say as Mrs P comes into the room, 'if I go away for a few days next week? I'll tell the agency and get the cover sorted but I wondered if you might move in here while I'm gone, for a bit of continuity for Dad.'

Her reply comes quickly. 'Yes. No problem. Going anywhere nice?'

'San Francisco,' I say lightly, like I've said Blackpool or somewhere else that's not halfway across the planet.

Her expression changes slightly. I cannot tell whether she is working out the feasibility of this or is concerned, but then she nods her head slowly.

'Fine. How long will you be away?'

'I'll be gone four days,' I say, trying not to make it sound like a question.

'That's a long way to go for such a short break.'

As she says this, I am trying to work out whether she is reluctant to be left or just pointing out the obvious; I can't tell which.

'Yes, but that's all the time I need. I'm trying to track someone down. An aunt,' I add. 'My mother's sister.'

'You never mentioned any relatives before – apart from your brother, that is,' she says. Her tone is almost accusatory but she corrects herself before I have chance to take offence. 'Not that it's any of my business, of course.'

For a moment, I think I'm going to tell her everything, about Mum and Ursula and Dad's affair. I'm still longing to find someone to talk to about it all and I know, after our conversation on Christmas Day, that she'll be understanding. But then I see Dad sitting there. I'm almost certain that he can no longer follow what is happening around him but what if some part of his mind is still working? How would he feel to hear that discussion and yet not be able to tell his side of things? If I am going to tell her, then I need to pick a better moment.

'I've only just found out about her,' I say. 'Well, I think I always knew that I had an aunt but I'd forgotten. Something Michael said made me remember. Anyway, she lives in San Francisco so I thought I'd track her down.'

'Lovely,' she says to me as she disappears from view. 'Let me know when you're going and I'll bring some of my things over. I'll use the spare room next to the bathroom if that suits.'

If only everything was so simple.

Later, I am trying to research January weather conditions in San Francisco when there is a knock at the door. I open it and Simeon is standing on the doorstep. He's wearing a waxed jacket, a pair of leather walking boots and a deerstalker hat. I bite back a giggle.

'I'm going for a stroll on the moor,' he says. 'Fancy coming?' He looks at me expectantly, like a dog hoping for a tasty snack. I have a list a mile long of things to do but without even thinking about it I nod enthusiastically.

'Nice idea. Just let me get a coat.'

'And some footwear,' he says, looking at my pink pom-pom slippers, which were a present from Beth and are very warm but make my feet look like small islands.

I don't own any walking boots and my wellies rub my heels if I have to walk any distance in them. I make do with a pair of leather biker boots that, from memory, don't leak too badly. I can't match him on a coat either but at least my down jacket is warm. I grab a hat and some mittens and shout to Mrs P that I'm just popping out.

'You look quite the country gent,' I say to him as we head up the hill towards the moor.

I mean it as a joke but he looks slightly affronted and I have to backtrack a little.

'I've never really got myself kitted out for walking,' I add, trying to suggest that this is my failing rather than his, although the expression 'All the gear, no idea' is on the tip of my tongue.

'If you have the right kit then you never get caught out by the weather,' he says. 'I learned that on my bike. This must be the greyest, wettest place I've ever lived.'

'Doesn't it rain in Lincolnshire?' I ask.

'Not like it does here, for days on end. And the grey skies . . .' He shakes his head. 'They kill me.'

'I like the grey,' I say. 'It makes me feel safe, cosseted. You can keep your picture-book blue heavens. Give me clouds any day of the week.'

He turns his head as he walks so that he can look at me.

'You are a strange and complicated creature, Cara Ferensby,' he says and I'm not sure whether to be pleased or offended.

We head upwards for half an hour or so, eventually getting to the top of the moor, where we follow a path parallel to the valley bottom. There's no one else up this high. Any tourists wanting to blow away the cobwebs tend not to stray out of sight of the iconic Cow and Calf rocks. Every so often, a grouse rises out of the bracken noisily at our sides, its odd guttural call sounding more like a trumpet than a bird. In places the ground beneath our feet is springy and then boggy. I can feel the cold water seeping in through the stitches of my boots but I don't let on. Below us, Ilkley nestles in the valley, lights just starting to flicker as households begin to prepare for the evening's celebrations. We press on, the silences punctuated by the wind whipping through the bracken and Simeon's boots stomping on the stone path.

'Going to a party tonight?' he asks me.

For a moment, I consider lying, making up some extravagant invitation. He misinterprets my hesitation.

'I'm not fishing for an invite,' he adds. 'I'm not that keen on New Year's Eve, to be honest. I'd rather stay home with Jools Holland and a nice bottle.'

Now I feel awkward. If I say that I have no plans either will he think that I'm trying to muscle in on his evening? I take a deep breath. In for a penny . . .

'You could come and watch Jools at my place,' I say. 'I mean, if you fancy some company. Or not,' I add. 'I have no particular plans. My friends are still away and I didn't get round to sorting anything out. But if you'd rather do the Jools thing by yourself then that's fine. I know some people choose to spend . . .'

He leans across, places his hands on my shoulders and kisses me firmly, forcing me to stop talking. To start with, I am so taken aback that I don't respond but then I lean into him and we kiss, like Cathy and Heathcliff, high up on the moor above the town.

'I've been wanting to do that since last night,' he says, like someone out of a chick flick. It's so long since anyone has kissed me that I think I must be slightly in shock. It is not like I hadn't considered the possibility. It's just that I wasn't expecting it any time soon. 'And Jools at your place would be great,' he adds.

Even as he says this, I am thinking about what there is in the house to eat, who is on the rota to help with Dad tonight, whether I have any wine . . .

'I've got no food,' I blurt out.

'Still?!'

'Well, I got distracted yesterday, remember?'

'I'll cook,' he says. 'I'll bring everything with me. You just provide the kitchen.'

I envy him his easy manner. I would no more offer to cook at his flat than fly to the moon, but the idea of cooking somewhere strange seems to hold no terror for him.

'Perfect,' I say and suddenly I'm buzzing like a teenager. I have a plan for New Year's Eve and it involves a man. Wait until Beth hears.

'There's some stuff I need to explain first,' I say as we head back down towards the town. I tell him a little bit about Dad and the arrangements with Mrs P, but that doesn't seem to put him off. We arrange for him to come around eight. Just thinking about this makes my stomach flip over. In the gap between our walk and our date, if that is what it is, I find myself in the supermarket looking at croissants and wonder about changing the sheets.

I wish Beth were here.

'I've got a friend coming over tonight,' I say to Mrs P as I unpack the shopping and finally throw out the remains of the leftovers. 'A man.'

I make my voice go up at the end to suggest that this is unusual although, as she's been here for a few months now, she surely knows this already. She is cutting Dad's hair for him. He sits on a kitchen chair surrounded by a sea of newspaper, a towel tucked round his shoulders. When I try to do this, he fidgets like a toddler and I have to abandon the job half-finished, but for her he sits tall and still.

'Well, don't mind me,' she says, scissors poised. 'I'll get your dad into bed and then make myself scarce.'

She doesn't ask any questions but I want to talk.

'I only met him yesterday. He's a friend of a friend. He seems very nice. He's a teacher, at a primary school near Leeds.'

'Was that him who called earlier?' she asks, snipping carefully around Dad's large ears. 'He's a bit of a looker,' she adds and winks at me over the top of Dad's head.

Normally only Beth would tease me like this and I prepare to bristle at her over-familiarity but then I realise that I quite like it. What's wrong with dropping my guard from time to time? This woman is virtually living in my house and performing no end of intimate tasks for my father. It'd be ridiculous of me to take offence when she shows some interest in my life.

'Isn't he?' I agree and twist my face into an expression of mock shock. 'His name's Simeon. He lives up near the moor. I think I might quite like him, although it's obviously very early days.'

She brushes the snipped ends off Dad's shoulders and on to the waiting newspaper.

'It's about time you had some fun,' she says. 'For what it's worth, I think you take life far too seriously for someone so young. Live a little, Cara. Life is short. You should grasp it with both hands and shake it hard.'

She's right, of course. I don't suppose it'll go anywhere with Simeon but it's good to have someone new to talk to.

The doorbell rings a little after eight and there he stands, his hair still refusing to lie flat. He has changed out of his moor walking clothes and is now wearing some jeans and a boxy leather jacket, a pair of suede Chelsea boots on his feet. I look at him and at once feel dowdy. I should never have invited him. It was a stupid idea and now, because he's here rather than at his place, I can't escape. He'll come in out of politeness and watch the clock tick round until he can leave without causing offence. I should just tell him that I have made a mistake, changed my mind. I'll have an early night with my book.

'Are you going to invite me in or what?' he says and takes a step towards the door.

'Sorry,' I say and step aside.

He doesn't hesitate. In the hallway, Mrs P is just helping Dad towards the stairs. They make slow progress, Dad more shuffling than walking.

'Hello,' Simeon says with a wide smile and I feel absurdly proud that he has come to visit me. 'I'm Simeon.'

'Oh, hello,' replies Mrs P. 'I've been hearing all about you.'

I freeze. God, how embarrassing if he thinks that I've been rattling on about him to Mrs P but hasn't given me a second thought. This must occur to Mrs P too, because she shoots me a glance to make sure that she hasn't said the wrong thing, but what can she do? The words are out.

'All good, I hope,' says Simeon, seemingly oblivious to the awkwardness that I have conjured up for myself. 'And this must be your father?' he asks. 'Good evening, Mr Ferensby.' He holds his hand out for Dad to shake but Dad just stares at it. This is a social convention that has clearly left him.

'It is indeed,' says Mrs P. 'And we're just going upstairs out of the way, aren't we, Joe?'

Dad doesn't seem to have noticed that Simeon is even here. His eyes are focused on a spot on the wall in front of him.

'Well, it's nice to meet you both,' says Simeon.

His manner is open, genuine, and he's not at all thrown by Dad's lack of interest in him.

'Enjoy your evening,' says Mrs P and they begin to climb the stairs slowly, one step at a time. I show him into the sitting room.

'I didn't know what you liked to eat so I've gone for pasta with chicken in a creamy tarragon sauce. Oh, God. You're not vegetarian, are you?' he adds, his blue eyes suddenly wide. His worried expression makes me laugh and that reminds me why I invited him in the first place.

'No. Fully signed-up meat-eater. Shall we have a drink first?'

A couple of hours later we have made it on to a second bottle of wine and there's no sign of the pasta. We are sitting on the sofa, me cross-legged, him lounging backwards, his long legs sticking out in front of him. We're not quite close enough to touch.

'Can I ask you a personal question?' he says.

I nod. My mind races with what it might be. Why are you still living at home with your father? How come you've never married? Is your life really as dull as you make out?

'What happened to your hand?' he asks.

Instinctively I go to pull down my sleeve in an attempt to cover the worst of the scars but he stops me and gently takes my hand between both of his, stroking the puckered skin with his thumb. The urge to pull it back to safety is almost overwhelming but somehow I let it rest where it is.

'It was an accident,' I say. 'When I was very small. I can't remember much about it. Dad had made a fire in the garden and I put my hand in it to pull something out. I was too little to realise how hot it would be. The doctors did the best they could but it never fully recovered. I was lucky, really. It could have been much worse.'

'Does it hurt?' he asks, lifting my hand to his lips and kissing its ridged surface lightly.

Inside I wince but I try to stay calm.

'No. Not really. It's just part of who I am now. I don't think about it much.' This is a lie but he doesn't need to know that. I'm desperate to change the subject, to steer him away from focusing on my flaws. 'I'm going to San Francisco the day after tomorrow,' I say without much thought.

'Are you coming back?' he asks, and it throws me for a moment.

I punch him lightly on the arm and realise that I must have moved a little closer to him.

'I'm only going for a few days,' I say. 'I have a mystery to solve.'

'Sounds intriguing.'

'It's about my mother.'

'She who may or may not be missing?' he asks and I'm touched that he remembers.

'Yes. She has a sister, an artist who lives there. I've decided to track her down so I can ask her, face to face, about what happened to my mum.'

'Wow!' he says and for a moment I can't work out if he is being serious or sarcastic, but then he looks straight at me, holding my eyes with his. 'You've got balls, Cara Ferensby.'

Have I? I'm not sure that he is right. Making this trip is more of a compulsion than an act of bravery. As the clock ticks ever closer to midnight, I tell him everything that I have discovered so far. When I've finished, I realise that this is the first time I've shown all the individual jigsaw pieces to anyone. There still isn't enough to make the whole picture but at least I can see what it might look like now.

I don't know if it's the sharing or the wine but I can feel myself start to shake. A tiny tremor shivers right through me. Simeon sees and without saying anything he just leans in closer and wraps his arms around me. I let him. His aftershave smells of cloves and lemons. I focus on the individual scents to stop myself from crying. I'm determined not to cry.

Gently he lifts my head from its burrow on his shoulder and then we kiss again.

CHAPTER THIRTY-THREE

Michael, 1998

Michael looks at the clock by his bed. In three hours, he will be free. Outside it is light and the birds are working hard to muster a decent orchestra but he can tell by the shade of his curtains that there is no sign of the sun. The sky is always grey in this godforsaken town. Something to do with the moor, apparently. The hills mess with the weather, casting leaden light over the town when just a few miles away the sky is blue. He doesn't care anymore, though, because after today he will be gone from Yorkshire. He will leave and never look back. The mere thought makes his heart beat faster. He lies on his bed, staring at the clock and watching the digital numbers flick over: 6.10 . . . 6.11 . . . 6.12 . . .

The only blot on his horizon, the only dark patch in his heart, is Cara. He thinks of her now with her quirky, homemade clothes and that waif-like look that she cultivates and which makes her seem even more vulnerable. Guilt tugs deep inside him but he cuts it free. Cara is not his problem. It sounds harsh but it's the truth. What she chooses to do when she finishes school is up to her. She can leave too if she wants. There will be virtually nothing tying her here.

And anyway, he thinks, it not like he's leaving Cara entirely on her own. She has Beth. When he thinks of Beth, Michael's mind starts to go to places that he'd rather it didn't. He can't put his finger on exactly when Beth stopped being his sister's toothy little mate and became the object of his teenage desire but the whole thing is really weird. Obviously, he's never said anything, let alone done anything about it. She's only fourteen, for God's sake, and she's Cara's best friend. He lies back and indulges his fantasy for a few minutes. It will kill a bit more time.

6.37 . . .

Less than three hours now. He will walk up to school, be there when the huge, wooden door opens to admit him. The results will be in the hall, sitting in their brown envelopes in neat, alphabetical rows just waiting to be claimed. Michael hasn't the slightest doubt that he'll get what he needs. With his outstanding GCSE results, the top universities were falling over themselves to make him an offer. He is aware that he is exactly the kind of student they wish to encourage. Intelligent, conscientious, ambitious. The reference from his form tutor was unambiguous:

> *You would have to go a long way to find a pupil as focused and driven as Michael Ferensby. Becoming a solicitor has been Michael's ambition from the youngest age and he has been working with determination towards this end ever since.*

No one has ever questioned his motives, asked him what it is that pushes him on towards his goal with such surefooted certainty. Maybe they thought it was just something that he saw on TV and then clung to for want of a better idea? Michael is a private person and has never felt the need to share exactly why he wants to work as a solicitor. His motivation is a personal matter: his secret, if you like. He hasn't faltered at any point since he found his father's legal papers and knew that he had to understand them in order to understand everything. His place to read law at King's College, London is as good as in the bag. He knows that the A Level results that he will collect today are just a necessary formality.

His father has shown almost no interest in the university application process but then Michael has hardly encouraged him. The invitation to the parents' information evening never made it beyond the bin in the sixth-form centre. His father, not having been to university himself, can't see the point of it.

'What you need is a good, honest job,' he'd said. 'That'll stand you in much better stead than three years of debt and some letters after your name. You should get ahead of the pack, Michael. Get your foot in the door at a decent firm while your mates are busy drinking away their grants. It's just a waste of time when you should be out there earning.'

Michael could have explained that he wanted to be a solicitor, and that that required a law degree and a professional qualification, but what would have been the point? Instead he had filled in the form at school, carefully forging his father's signature, and sent it off without mentioning it at home. And now, in two hours' time, he will pick up his results and will finally begin the process of leaving home.

Unable to lie still any longer, he gets up and goes to take a shower. How many more showers will he take in this bathroom, he wonders, as the droplets rain down, plastering his dark hair to his head like seaweed. Twenty, maybe. Twenty-five at the outside. Barely worth counting. He turns the taps up high so the hot water sears his skin and then, when he can bear the heat no longer, he flicks it back down to cold so that his body screams out from shock.

'What are you doing in that shower? I'm not made of money, you know.'

Michael hears his father shouting and ignores him. He turns the water back to a normal temperature and stands under the jets, not moving. He watches the wasted water gush down the plughole. Steam billows up around him and soon he can barely see his hand in front of his face.

'If you don't turn that shower off,' comes the voice from behind the door, 'then so help me God . . .'

Leisurely, Michael turns the water off and steps out of the shower. He wraps himself in his towel and opens the door. His father is standing so close that he almost falls into the bathroom.

'Then so help me God what?' asks Michael, pushing past his father and strolling across the landing to his bedroom.

'You're not too big to take over my knee,' warns his father.

'Oh, but I am,' says Michael. 'You touch me, old man, and I'll break your neck. I'll snap you like a twig.'

Michael is enjoying himself. His freedom is so close that he can almost taste it. It is making him reckless.

A door opens and Cara appears on the landing. She has clearly only just woken up. Her blonde hair fizzes out around her in a halo. She seems about to complain about the noise but then picks up the tension and changes tack.

'Michael, don't,' she says, her eyes imploring him to rein his behaviour in, but Michael is invincible today. Even just wearing a towel he knows that nothing can touch him.

'You watch your mouth,' says his father.

'Or what?'

'Or you'll be out in the street as fast you can say "Jack Robinson".'

'Suits me just fine,' says Michael. 'If you think I am going to spend a second longer than I have to under this roof then you're badly mistaken.'

With that, he saunters into his room, closing the door with a satisfying slam.

'This is my house,' his father is shouting through the door. 'And you will abide by my rules.'

Michael pulls on pants, tracksuit bottoms, a T-shirt. Outside he can hear Cara doing her best to placate their father. He opens the door and strides over to where his father is still standing and shouting the odds.

Imogen Clark

He is taller than his father – not by much, but it is enough. He stands closer to him than he feels comfortable with but he needs to make sure that his point is made.

'Your days of telling me what to do are over,' he says, his breath bouncing off his father's face and back to his own nostrils.

He doesn't shout like his father. He speaks quietly, calmly, each word carefully enunciated so there can be no misunderstanding.

'I have put up with your shouting and your bullying for twelve long years. I can't understand why you think you have the right to speak to me the way you do. Especially after what you did. Any power that you think you had over me was forfeited years ago. You may technically be my father but it's just a title. You're not fit for purpose. Not since then. Probably not ever.'

When he'd pictured this moment in his head, Michael had wondered whether he would need to be more explicit, but it seems not. His father's face, puce just a moment ago, blanches. He looks suddenly diminished.

'Oh, what's the matter, Daddy?' continues Michael. 'Did you think I didn't know? I'm not stupid. I pieced it all together a long time ago. I've just been biding my time until I was ready to leave.'

For a moment, it crosses his mind that he should just let it all come out, here and now. Those beans are surely ready to be spilled. He has dragged the burden of them around with him for long enough. But then he looks at Cara. She is standing there on the landing in her checked pyjamas, her narrow feet bare on the well-worn carpet, her forehead wrinkled because she hates that they are arguing again. She puts a hand on his arm and shushes him, trying, as ever, to keep the peace.

He must not do it. He must not say anything else. Once it is spoken, it cannot be taken back and Cara doesn't need to shoulder the burden as well. He knows what happened. His father now knows that he knows, but Cara never can.

She looks at him, questions written all over her face.

'What are you talking about, Michael?' she asks him. 'What do you know?'

'I know that I have a ticket out of here,' Michael says, diverting her question. 'I am going to university in London as soon as I can and there is nothing you can do to stop me.'

Cara keeps her gaze fixed on him, her hazel eyes filling with tears. She looks so much like their mother. More so with each year that passes, he thinks. Their father must see it too, although he never passes comment.

'What?' she says. 'What do you mean, you're going? You can't go.'

Michael steps away from his father and puts his arms round his little sister, not so little anymore. She melts into him and he feels her start to shake.

'I'm sorry, Ca, but I can't stay here. You never expected that I would, did you? You must have known that as soon as I got my results I'd leave.'

'But how . . . ?' Cara whispers.

'It's today. I'm going to get my results now and then I start in London in three weeks. It's all arranged.'

'You can't go,' she says again. And then, 'Take me with you.'

He shakes his head slowly.

'I would if I could. You know I would.'

His father, recovering his voice, starts up again.

'Well, if you think I'm paying for any pretentious university crap then . . .'

Michael lets go of Cara and turns to look at his father. He sees a man, broken beyond repair, entrenched, through years of lies and hurt, in a hole from which there is no escape. Michael doesn't care. He turns and heads down the stairs and out of the front door into the grey day outside.

When the main door at the school opens at nine o'clock, Michael is first in the queue. He strides through to the hall, ignoring the headmaster, who is standing in the foyer with a clipboard. He scans the table for the envelope bearing his name. He picks it up and slips it into his tracksuit pocket.

'Aren't you going to open that, Ferensby?' asks Mrs Glaser, the deputy head.

'No need,' Michael says. 'I know what it says.'

He turns and leaves the hall, stalking back down the corridor and out of the door. There is a gap in the clouds and the smallest sliver of blue sky peeps out. Michael turns left and heads up towards the moor. The strip of paper nestles in its envelope in his pocket. It reads 'A A A A'.

CHAPTER THIRTY-FOUR

Cara, 2018

When I wake up, it takes me a moment to identify the regular pace of Simeon's breathing next to me. The duvet rises and falls gently on my shoulders as his chest expands and contracts. I change position as gently as I can. I don't want to wake him, not yet. I'm happy to lie here for a while, replaying the evening in my head. Gratefully, I find that I haven't lost any of it. This was not a drunken mistake. Our progress from sofa to bed was swift but not rushed and we definitely didn't end up here accidentally.

I check my alarm clock. It is seven fifteen. Under the duvet my stomach growls. The pasta and chicken never made it as far as a pan. I suck my tummy muscles in, trying to make it stop, and hope he doesn't hear.

And then it happens, as it always does. My mind takes me from the present moment, in bed with a man I like, to a darker place occupied by 'what if's and 'maybe's. The confidence with which I led him to my room last night drains away until I am left, a nervous thirty-three-year-old, lying next to a total stranger who will see the parts of me of which I am less proud and smell my morning-after breath.

And, as if the gods are toying with me, it is at this exact moment that he stirs and then opens his eyes. My cheeks flush at having been caught staring at him in his sleep.

'Happy New Year,' he says, rubbing an eye with the heel of his hand and stretching luxuriously. He does not touch me, as if sensing that, despite our current location, I need some space.

'Happy New Year,' I reply. 'Are you okay?' My voice sounds distant, aloof even. He lifts the duvet and looks down at his naked body.

'All seems to be in working order,' he says, but he drops the duvet back down so that I retain my dignity.

I think I might really fall for this man in time but already I can feel myself retreating. Keep yourself safe, Cara. Don't let anyone penetrate that steely shell, says the voice in my head. It's a bit late for that, I tell myself, but still I feel my natural defences rising into formation.

'I have to get up,' I say. My voice is abrupt and I'm aware that he must be thinking I want him to leave. This is not what I want. 'My Dad,' I add, a genuine explanation but which sounds like an excuse. 'He gets a bit confused when he wakes up. I like to be around to give Mrs P a hand.'

Simeon is pushing himself to a sitting position. I reach for my robe and slip out of the bed.

'I completely understand,' he says. 'I'll get out of your hair. Just give me two minutes to get dressed.'

This is not panning out the way it ought to. I want to tell him to stay where he is, that I'll just check that everything is all right with Dad and then come back. I bought croissants, for goodness' sake. But what I say is, 'Okay.'

Just that. I do not even look at him so I can't see if he's at all disappointed.

'Pass my kecks,' he says. His clothes are on a chair in a neat pile. I scoop them up and pass them over.

'I . . .' I try but he interrupts.

'No worries,' he says, raising a hand to silence me. 'I understand.' But he doesn't. He can't possibly. I don't understand myself.

He pulls his pants on under the duvet with a show of modesty that belies our recent intimacy and then stands up to put the rest of his clothes on. I drop my eyes but not before I catch a glimpse of his torso, the trail of dark hair that leads down from his chest. I know that I need to do something to make this right before he slips out of my reach.

'I had a lovely evening,' I manage. Is it my imagination or does his smile look sad?

'Me too,' he says as he buttons his shirt. 'I really enjoyed it, Cara Beloved. Can I see you again or is this the brush off?'

I wince. I don't want him to think that he's being brushed off but something in the way I hesitate before I speak makes it seem like that is my intention. When I go to contradict him, my words sound hollow, even to me.

'No. Not all. That would be lovely. It's just that I'm going away and there's Dad and . . .'

Why can't I just tell him how I feel, that he's the best thing to happen to me for as long as I can remember? Somehow the words just don't come. He shrugs.

'I'll leave my number,' he says. 'Just in case.' He takes an old receipt out of his wallet, scans around for a pen and scribbles his number down. He places the paper gently on my pillow.

'Cara! Cara!' Dad is shouting for me from his room. I look to the door and then back to Simeon.

'I have to go. I'm really sorry.'

He nods. 'You go,' he says. 'It's okay, Cara. I get it.' But he doesn't. He doesn't get it at all.

As I cross the corridor to Dad's room he follows me. I turn to say goodbye but he's gone down the stairs. A moment later, I hear the front door open and then gently close behind him.

Dad is lying in bed. He stares at the ceiling. He doesn't turn to look at me as I approach his bed.

'Let's get you up,' I say.

My voice has none of the softness of tone that I usually adopt when I'm talking to him. Right now, I have no affection for this man, my father, who has turned my life upside down and is still managing to spoil things for me even now.

'Happy New Year, Dad,' I add without a smile.

I put my arms around him to haul him up. The sodden pyjamas stick to his spindle legs.

Later, after we have got through breakfast and I've put Dad's bedding on to wash, I go to get dressed. Simeon's number is still resting on my pillow. I pick it up. I should just ring him, explain that I'm an idiot and that the last thing I want is to drive him away, that I'm not much good with people being nice to me through a lack of practice. That's what I should do, but I know that I won't. I do pick the paper up, though, and slip it carefully between the pages of my book.

CHAPTER THIRTY-FIVE

I leave for America on January 2nd. As the train pulls out of the station, bound for the airport, I don't allow myself to think about leaving Dad or Mrs P living in my house or what Michael will say when he finds out where I've gone. Or Simeon. I particularly don't let myself think about Simeon.

While I'm waiting in the airport, I accidentally google Captain Haddock, just to see if he looks like I remember, with his unruly black hair and piercing blue eyes. Sadly, Hergé's drawings don't have any eyes at all, just flesh-coloured circles where eyes would be. My comparison of man and cartoon seems to have been misplaced. I decide to close my mind to blue eyes.

The flight is uneventful and the queue to clear Immigration long. Eventually I find myself a taxi and as we crawl into San Francisco I sit back in my seat to enjoy my first view of the city. A thin mist rises like steam from the water to my left and the tops of the skyscrapers are hidden by clouds. Through the fog, I spot the iconic Golden Gate Bridge. It's smaller than I expect and while I'm processing this information, I realise that it's also white and not red. Wrong bridge – I'm such a tourist. My cheeks burn and I'm thankful that I hadn't passed comment to the taxi driver. A few blocks further on, the red bridge appears, the tips of its towers lost to the mist. As we pass the neatly numbered piers, I realise that what little I know of San Francisco has mainly been gleaned from reading *Tales of the City*. Isn't there a supermarket with a singles' night somewhere?

This thought sends my mind skipping off in search of Simeon again. I tell myself that I don't have room in my life for any more complications just now, although I'm not really sure why I think he would prove to be one. He seems quite straightforward so far.

For just one moment, I allow his ready smile to infiltrate my defences – but then I pull the drawbridge of my mind back up and lock him out. I've probably blown any chance I had with him anyway but, rather than tearing his number into small pieces and putting it in the kitchen bin where soggy teabags would render it illegible before I could change my mind, I have kept it. Right now it's safe in my purse, nestling between a book of first-class stamps and a money-off voucher that I've saved but will probably never use. Of course, he won't be interested in me anymore, but I take the number out and add it to the contacts in my phone. Just in case.

When I look up again, we are passing Pier 33 and I notice the signs for the ferry to Alcatraz. I try to catch a glimpse of the island but the buildings are in the way. It doesn't matter. There'll be time enough for sightseeing, particularly if I can't track Ursula down.

The taxi pulls off the road that follows the bay round and turns left, into the city, and soon we're pulling up outside the hotel. I tip the driver and wheel my little case up the ramp into the reception, where I am greeted with the enthusiasm that only the Americans can make sound genuine.

My room is an anonymous, corporate cell. When I walk in, the TV is already on, displaying pictures of the bay. The Englishness in me balks at the waste of power. I try to turn it off but can only find a standby option. I drop my bag on one of the huge beds. Disappointingly, the view through the muslin curtains is of the street outside. That's probably what the TV images are all about. It occurs to me that I've been allocated a room without a view because I'm a young woman travelling on her own and unlikely to make a fuss. I suppose I could object but what would be the point?

I remove the detritus of a long-haul flight from my handbag, rip off the luggage tag and take a quick glance at the street map that I picked up in the reception to get my bearings. Ursula's gallery is very close and so, ignoring my need for coffee, I set off in search of it.

I find it, as I knew I would, just around the corner from the hotel. It's small and discreet, the signage quiet, a classy font on a deep-blue background. The window display is simple, just three easels, each holding a small, abstract canvas. None of them look as if they might be Ursula's. From the street, there are few clues about what is inside. The doorway, like the opening to a cave, is dark, deep and slightly threatening.

I spot a café across the road, Coffee Bean and Tea Leaf. It looks nice enough, the signs written in friendly white chalk. I could just go and get myself a cup of coffee while I work out the lay of the land. Or, I could gird my loins, go in and ask about my aunt. I give myself a little pep talk. I haven't come halfway round the world to go and drink coffee. I'm here right now, so what's stopping me? Whatever I discover here will help me to work out what happened to my mother. Reluctantly, and with my heart banging in my chest, I step across the threshold.

Inside, the gallery is dark. The air smells lightly of vanilla and it reminds me that I haven't eaten since the plane. The pictures are displayed on wires, spotlights throwing sharp circles of light that highlight parts but not the whole of each one. It's an odd way to display art. The urge to flick a switch and throw light into the space comes over me. This darkness feels smothering, claustrophobic even.

The gallery goes a long way back, its depth emphasised by its narrowness. Because of the strange lighting effects, I can't actually see all the way to the back wall and I feel exposed and vulnerable as I peer into the dimness.

To settle my nerves, I glance at the pictures hanging in the first section and then move a little further back, hoping to find a style that I can recognise as Ursula's. About halfway in, a huge canvas catches my eye, smears of mud-coloured oil paint slashed by a scar of vivid red. I can't look at it for long. It's too disturbing and makes me feel uncomfortable and unsettled.

'Awesome, isn't it?' says a voice at my elbow.

I turn to see a woman with a shock of ginger hair. It's the kind of colour that's just too bright to be natural: woman tampering with nature's work. She wears it tied up in a twist on her head that looks like it might tumble down at any second, releasing the fiery tendrils to burn her shoulders. Her hair is the biggest thing about her. She is a good six inches shorter than me and her frame is tiny. Her delicate collarbone looks more like a pencil than a structural part of her body. As she talks, her hands flutter like little birds, her many rings catching the spotlights and making what little light there is dance around her.

'It's one of her early pieces, obviously. We are lucky to have it. It's not for sale, I'm afraid. Just on loan for a while.'

'On loan from the artist?' I ask.

'God no!' she says, inadvertently dashing my sprouting hope. 'Ms Kemp never keeps her own work. She creates pieces and then sends them straight to us to sell. She doesn't want to see them again once they're finished. I heard her talking about it once. She said it was like cutting out a cancer, painting, for her.'

My disgust at this image must have shown on my face because she added, 'I know. Gross. Are you interested in her work?'

Her eyes flick up and down, taking in my flight-tired clothing and scruffy sneakers, making me feel very provincial.

'In a way,' I say evasively. 'I emailed a few days back . . . ?'

My voice goes up questioningly as my sentence trails off. I should just ask her but something is pulling me back. I have so much to lose here that I hardly dare begin. She looks at me expectantly, her hands uncharacteristically still, as if frozen in this moment.

'Actually,' I try again. 'I was hoping to track Ms Kemp down. She lives here in San Francisco, doesn't she?'

The woman's smile slips and she takes a tiny step backwards.

'Are you a journalist? She is a very private person and never talks to the press. We guard her privacy very carefully.'

She gives a little sniff and folds her arms over her chest.

'Oh no!' I say quickly. 'It's nothing like that. I'm not a journalist. I design wedding dresses for a living. That's not why I want to meet her, though.'

Words skitter out of my mouth and the woman looks at me as if I could actually be slightly unhinged.

'No. I'm trying to find Ms Kemp because I think we might be related.'

One eyebrow shoots up towards her ginger topknot and her mouth twists into a curl. She has clearly heard this before. I can sense that I have one shot and that the target is getting further and further away. If I don't tell her now, she will think that I've used the time to cook the story up.

'I've just discovered that my mother, who I've always been told was dead, might actually be alive,' I begin. 'She left me and my brother when we were little and I'm trying to find out why. The only lead I have is that my mother's sister is an artist called Ursula Kemp. I'm pretty sure your Ursula Kemp is the same person and, as far as I know, she's my only living blood relative – apart from my brother, that is.'

I don't mention Dad. This is complicated enough.

'I'd like to talk to her to see what she can tell me about my mother. I've just arrived from the UK . . .' I look at my watch. 'About thirty minutes ago. Please could you help me?'

The woman is looking sceptical but she unfolds her arms.

'Are you Cara Ferensby? The one who emailed about a potential purchase?'

I nod sheepishly.

'That was a bit of a fib,' I say. I try to look shamefaced. 'I was actually hoping that you could get this letter to Ms Kemp. I'm only here until Friday and then I have to fly home.'

I scrabble in my bag for the letter that I wrote at my desk back in England and offer it to her. My hand is shaking. She looks at the letter and then at me. She bites her bottom lip with tiny, pearly white teeth.

'I don't know,' she says. 'Ms Kemp is very strict about who we put in touch with her.'

I'm still holding the letter out. I nudge it gently against her arm.

'Please,' I say.

She looks at it again and then takes it.

'I suppose I could take it with me tonight. But I can't guarantee that she'll accept delivery of it, let alone read it.'

I am so relieved I could kiss her but I restrain myself.

'That would be so kind,' I say. 'The name of my hotel is in the letter. I can't find her address by myself. I have tried but . . .'

'Well, you wouldn't be able to,' says the woman. 'Like I say, she's really private. She only trusts me.'

She beams at me, pride radiating from her.

'You really are my last hope then,' I say and give her my widest smile. I hold my hand out towards her.

'I'm Skyler,' she says as she takes my hand in both of hers.

This is probably nothing more than American over-familiarity but I feel grateful nonetheless.

'I'll do my best, Cara,' Skyler says. 'Why don't you call back here at noon tomorrow and I'll let you know if there's any news.'

'Thank you,' I say, the relief making my voice sound breathy. 'I'll see you here tomorrow.'

And so I leave the letter and set off into San Francisco to wait. My hunger, now impossible to ignore, forces me over the road to the coffee shop to get myself an espresso and a sourdough sandwich, which turns out to look better than it tastes. My body clock is telling me that it is now early evening, although the sun is still high in the sky in California. I need to keep going until at least dinner time or I'll be counting sheep in the wee small hours.

Feeling a little revived, I set off to see what San Francisco has to offer the tourist about town. I follow the crowds to Lombard Street and marvel at the kind of mind that thought snaking streets like this one were the future of traffic calming. It does work though. The cars creep down the twisting hill, nose to tail. Next, I catch a rickety wooden cable car to Union Square and stand armpit to nostril with some French tourists.

Looking at the chattering groups, I consider how I must appear to them, but then again, who is going to notice me, a single woman, unaccompanied, unloved? I am, to all intents and purposes, invisible to the wider world. If the cable snapped and the car plunged us to our deaths at the bottom of the hill, would anyone even remember the blondish English woman who stood towards the back of the carriage in a list of its occupants? It seems unlikely.

Still, I don't mind. When you pass through life single, as I have, you learn to travel alone or not at all. Of course, there have been plenty of trips with Beth over the years, us laughing our way around Europe's major destinations, sunning ourselves on various beaches. Those precious times will be fewer and further between from now on, I suppose. She and Greg will be back from their honeymoon any day now and I smile to myself as I picture her trying to work out what's sent me skipping halfway round the world on next to no notice.

The thought of honeymoons makes me, rather prematurely, think of Simeon. Despite my determination to forget all about him, I just can't seem to shake the idea of him out of my head. I wonder what he's up to right now, whether he's thought about me since he virtually ran from my bed, but there's no point. I pretty much drove him away and he made it pretty clear that he didn't want to stick around.

There is a couple standing just to my right. He is taller than she is and he wraps his arms around her from behind to stop her from toppling over in the wobbly cable car. She laughs and then spins on the spot to face him and they kiss. I turn away. I can't bear to look at them, knowing that I've probably blown the best chance I've had in as long as I can remember. Other people's romances are just too painful right now.

When we reach Union Square, I hop off the cable car and look around me. No doubt in summer these wide-open steps will be filled with people basking in the sunshine. Today, though, the air is chilly, a biting wind twisting round the tall buildings. No one is loitering for long. As I stand and stare at the world bustling by, I wonder what will happen next. Skyler seems the empathetic type. I'm sure she'll do as she says and not just put my letter in the nearest bin. She might even speak up for me, tell Ursula that I seem genuine and am not some dirt-seeking journalist with an ulterior motive. I can't help thinking that, even if she does, it might not make any difference. If Ursula has made a decision to cut herself off from her family, and indeed most of the world, then why would she want to speak to me, a stranger from a time that she has left behind? Although surely she'll be just a tiny bit curious. I am a new niece after all.

Soon, I can barely stifle my yawns. I need sleep. Even though it is only six o'clock here, I skip dinner and crawl into my bed, letting the fresh, white bedding engulf me. I don't even dream.

CHAPTER THIRTY-SIX

As penance for going to bed before dinner, I wake ludicrously early. The street below my window is quiet and the little patch of sky that I can see is made chocolatey brown by the city lights. I go back to bed for a while but I am too fidgety to stay there for long. Up, showered and dressed in clean and slightly smarter clothes, I head to the lobby where the night staff are unsurprised to see a jet-lagged tourist wandering around. They point me in the direction of a twenty-four-hour diner, tacitly accepting that I won't want to pay what the hotel charges for breakfast.

I find it and see that it's obviously part of a chain. I'm a bit disappointed that I'm not going to get that authentic American experience you see in the movies, but its lights are welcoming enough and there are already a few people drinking coffee and eating. I go in and am shown to a table. I order pancakes with crispy bacon and maple syrup, which, when they arrive, would feed me for an entire week, and my coffee cup is topped up without me asking for refills. I love America.

'You here in town on vacation?' asks Charlize, my waitress. I nod. 'I thought so. We get a lot of tourists in here early in the morning. It's jet-lag, right?' I nod again. 'Well,' Charlize says as she refills my coffee cup with one hand while sweeping up what remains of my pancakes with the other, 'you need to go to Alcatraz. It don't matter what else you do when you're in town but you have to go there. I tell all my guests that,' she adds, her chest swelling with pride at her self-appointed second job as tour guide.

'Thanks,' I say. 'I'll try.'

'You need to get down there early, mind,' she adds. 'It gets busy fast. But early's no problem, right?' She smiles at me and I see that one of her front teeth is gold.

'Can I have the bill, please? The check, I mean.'

'Coming right up,' and then she is gone.

There are still seven hours to go until I am due back at the gallery so I decide to at least go and check out the Alcatraz ferry. The first trip leaves at eight forty-five. When I ask to buy a ticket, the man in the kiosk shakes his head and sucks his teeth but he puts me on the standby list and I end up on the boat. As we pull away from the pier and into the bay, the wind whips the water up into choppy white horses and I pull my scarf closer round me. It looks like I'm the only one making the trip alone. I imagine, briefly, what it might be like to travel with Simeon and then dismiss the thought. I need to get him out of my head. It's doing me no good, thinking about him all the time, but I just can't help it. Gaggles of schoolchildren and a few families fill the seats inside the ferry while us hardier souls brave the outside, peering over the waves for that first clear photo of the island.

Sheer cliff faces greet us as we pull into the harbour, the butter-milk prison building standing erect on the top of the rock. Gulls call overhead. It's such a plaintive sound that it's almost as if they too are imprisoned on this forbidding lump of rock. The island had looked just a mere hop and skip away from the shore but we've been sailing for a good fifteen minutes before we tie up at the dock. Not an easy swim for those dreaming of escape.

The tour comprises a soundtrack made by former inmates, which is evocative and quite moving in parts. I peer into the cramped cells but can't begin to imagine what life here must have been like. Some of the doors have been left open for the visitors to wander in and get a better feel for the cells' dimensions but somehow it feels like I am intruding on private space. By the time I reach the recreational area, with its high walls and watchtowers looming ominously overhead, I'm starting to understand how confining the island really is. I stand and look out across the choppy water to San Francisco, so close and yet tantalisingly out of reach. The tour said that the prisoners could hear the music and laughter of partygoers across the water. The only sounds now are the low hum of tourist chatter and the cries of the reeling seagulls.

By the time the ferry pulls into the little harbour to take me back to the mainland, I'm desperate to escape. It's only as we nudge back into Pier 33 and I look at my watch that the nausea of claustrophobia is replaced by the nausea of fear and anticipation. Skyler had told me to be back at the gallery by twelve. It's eleven thirty. I decide to walk to the gallery. Even though it's still chilly, the early-morning mist has burned away and the sky above the city is a crisp, fresh blue. I cast a final backwards glance at Alcatraz. It almost sparkles in the sunlight. How deceiving appearances can be.

The gallery looks dark as I approach and for a mad moment I convince myself that Skyler's shut up shop just to avoid me. I picture her hiding behind the door until I go away but then she appears in the doorway, her fiery hair calling out to me like a beacon. When she sees me she starts jumping up and down like a little girl waiting for her best friend to arrive. I'm quite touched.

'Woohoo! Cara!' she shouts to me, although I'm still not quite close enough to speak to.

People turn to see what all the fuss is about but then lose interest when there's no drama.

'Hurry up,' she urges as I get nearer. 'I've got a message for you.' She sounds genuinely excited, her smile broad and open. I resist the temptation to break into a run. My heart is now beating so hard that just breathing is an effort. I feel very sick. My fear must be written all over my face.

'Don't worry,' she says as I reach the door. 'It's good news!'

I just stare at her, waiting for her to tell me more. The power of speech seems to have deserted me and my mouth hangs open slackly as I suck air in.

'So,' says Skyler, threading her arm through mine and leading me into the gallery. 'I gave your letter to Ms Kemp yesterday and sent her an email to warn her that it was coming. I was kinda thinking she was going to ignore it and I didn't dare chase her in case I made it worse. But then when I came in this morning there's a reply. She says she'll meet you tonight. I've got the address. Wait! What am I doing? Here. You gotta read it for yourself.'

She pulls me to her desk at the back of the gallery, brings the laptop to life and clicks on an email. It says:

Got letter. Okay. 6.30 p.m. Capo's. U. Kemp.

That is it. My first-ever communication from my aunt is composed of seven words. I look at Skyler for an explanation.

'Her emails are always like that,' she says, screwing her tiny nose up. 'But isn't it fabulous? She wants to meet up. I'm so excited for you.'

What was I expecting? Something more effusive? A touch of curiosity, maybe? An outright refusal? Whatever it was, it wasn't this flat instruction barked at me as if I were a recalcitrant employee. I try not to feel slighted. After all, I have what I want – a meeting with my aunt. I should be over the moon but, somehow, I'm not. My confusion must show on my face because Skyler puts her arm around my shoulder. Instinctively I flinch at this unexpected venture into my personal space but then I'm glad that she's there to talk to. I suddenly feel very alone in this strange city.

'Don't worry, honey,' she says as she rubs my upper arm gently. 'Social skills are not her thing. She's out of practice. But she barks worse than she bites.'

'You've met her?' I ask, snatching at any information that I can gather.

A pretty blush spreads across Skyler's cheeks.

'Yes. She can be quite chatty if she's in the right mood.'

I wonder what happens if she's not but there's no point worrying about that now.

'So what's Capo's? Is it a club?'

Skyler smiles at me indulgently.

'It's a restaurant, an Italian. It's actually very popular. I'm surprised she's chosen there. She's bound to be seen.'

'Maybe that's the plan?' I muse. 'Meet me in public and then if I turn out to be one sandwich short of a picnic she can shake me off without too much difficulty.' And, I suppose but don't say, there'll be plenty of witnesses in case I try to sell an embellished story to the press. Smart lady.

'Is it easy to find?' I ask, and Skyler nods. She digs a street map out of her desk drawer, locates the restaurant and shows me. It's not far from the hotel. I can probably walk.

'It's just a quick cab ride,' Skyler says. 'The driver will know it.' She cocks her head to one side and looks at me through her dishevelled fringe.

'Will you come back tomorrow and tell me how you get on?'

I think about this for a moment.

'Yes,' I say decisively. 'I will. Thank you so much for all your help, Skyler. I'm really grateful. If I don't come back tomorrow then you'll know that she ate me alive.' I am joking but Skyler's expression suggests that this might actually be a possibility.

I have six hours to kill. There are things that I could go and visit but I decide to go back to the hotel and try to get some rest. As I am here for such a short period, there seems little point in trying to align my body clock with the local time, but when I get up to my room, I find that the buzz in my head is too loud to sleep through. I lie and stare up at the ceiling. Someone is having a disagreement in a neighbouring room, speaking in strained, hushed tones that actually travel as far as if they were shouting. I wish Beth were here. I long for someone to talk to.

My bag is lying on the bed next to me. I reach into it and fish out my phone. I find Simeon's number and before I have time to talk myself out of it, I am tapping out a message.

> About the other day. We got our wires crossed. Am in San Fran. Aunt agreed to meet me later. My nerve appears to be lost in transit. x

Then it occurs to me that he doesn't have my number so he will not know who it is from. I send another message.

> It's me. Cara x

When a reply pings back, which it does very quickly, it makes me jump.

> Cara Beloved!! Meeting Ursula eh? Do you think she'll be a scary shape-shifter like in The Little Mermaid? S x

He makes me laugh. He's thousands of miles away, I have been downright rude to him and it would serve me right if he never wanted to hear from me ever again and yet here he is, still making me laugh. I visualise Ursula the sea witch with her vampish rictus and her blue skin, but it doesn't make me feel any less scared about the impending meeting. I remember something that a teacher once told me before a school debate: if you're nervous, think of your audience stark naked. I am not sure it really helps but then it crosses my mind that I can turn Ursula into the Disney sea witch in my head and that makes me smile again.

Quickly I type a reply.

I shall take my trident with me just in case!

Rather than getting some rest, I pass a few hours in this silly game of text ping-pong back and forth across the Atlantic, all the time wondering why I am letting it happen. But then again, I cannot seem to stop.

CHAPTER THIRTY-SEVEN

It is six o'clock and I am ready to leave. I look at myself in the mirror by the room door. The hotel lighting is so dim that it's hard to get a true idea of what I look like but the impression that I am left with will do. In between increasingly ludicrous texts to Simeon, I managed to have a shower, wash and dry my hair and put some make-up on. I find a travel iron in the wardrobe while hunting for the hairdryer and I have a stab at removing some of the deeper creases from my blouse. I'm not sure that I've made much difference but it killed another fifteen minutes of the interminable wait.

I recheck the location of the restaurant yet again, although I already have the route straight in my head.

It takes me about twenty minutes to walk there. The pavements are still busy but instead of having to steer round irritating tourists who take a couple of steps then stand and stare, I'm now jostled by office workers trying to get home. I push against the tide as I make my way through the grid of streets towards the restaurant. When I'm little more than five minutes away, a giant thunderclap reverberates around me and then the heavens open, huge drops of rain falling so fast that it's hard to see through the sheets of water. I have a coat but no umbrella and almost within seconds am soaked through. I can feel my carefully dried hair hanging flat against my head as if I've stepped out of the shower.

I'm just wondering how well my make-up is standing up to the storm when a van drives past too close and a newly fallen puddle splashes up from the curb and covers me in icy water. At first, I'm too shocked to speak and stand open-mouthed like a fish, but when I look down and see the state I'm now in, outrage takes over and I scream after the van driver, who zooms off, oblivious to the devastation that he leaves in his wake. I look around me, expecting sympathy from my fellow pedestrians, but nobody cares. They're just glad the tsunami missed them. I try to undo the damage. The worst of the water brushes away. At least it is all over my coat and not my blouse, but there are telltale black splatters covering my trousers. There is nothing I can do. It's too late to go back to the hotel and change. I can't run the risk of Ursula getting impatient and leaving before I get back. I'll just have to brazen it out. I can go straight to the ladies' when I arrive, do my best with my hair under the hand dryer, rescue my make-up. It's not the start I was hoping for but it's not the end of the world.

The restaurant is just around the next corner. The frontage is bathed in light from its red neon sign and the place looks warm and inviting. I try to peer inside but the lighting is too dim. There's nothing for it but to go in. My heart is racing so fast that I'm struggling to catch my breath. I make one last, futile rub at my smudged mascara and cross the threshold.

As soon as I walk in a man is there to greet me. So much for tidying myself up.

'Hi. Can I help you?' he asks.

'I'm meeting someone. Ursula Kemp?'

I don't know if she's well known or whether her name will ring a bell. It clearly does.

'Ah, Signora Kemp,' he says and raises an eyebrow. 'She's already here. Please. Follow me.'

With no time to check how I look, I trail after him, trying to revitalise my limp hair as I walk. The restaurant feels relaxed and welcoming.

The walls are exposed brick, the ceiling dotted with fairy lights. Even though it's early, most of the tables are already full with couples and groups chatting and laughing. Enormous pizzas balance precariously on terracotta stands. It's clearly the kind of place where people share the food, which surprises me. I didn't have Ursula pegged as the food-sharing type.

Beyond the bar there are one or two booths, upholstered in buttoned red leather, and it's to one of these that I'm shown.

'Here you are, signorina,' he says.

In normal circumstances I'd scoff at this feeble flattery, but right now I have other things on my mind. Pushed to the back of the booth with her arm resting languidly across the table is my aunt. Before her stands a wine bottle and a half-empty glass.

She looks older than I imagined. Her hair is white and cropped in a pixie cut. I couldn't wear my hair as short as that but it really suits her. Her face is gaunt and criss-crossed with deep wrinkles. One runs straight down her forehead like a battle scar and she has the puckered lips and wrinkled eyes of a perpetual smoker. She looks me up and down and, without thinking, I find myself folding my arms across my chest.

'It's raining,' I say, thrown by her stare and feeling the need to explain my appearance.

'So I see.' Her accent is pure East London, with barely a trace to show that she has lived here for thirty years.

'Bring us another, Enzo,' she says, nodding at the bottle, and I wonder quite how long she has been here. The waiter nods and bustles off. I just stand there, dishevelled, and stare at my new aunt. 'Don't gawk at me like that,' she says, her voice bordering on aggressive. 'And sit down, for God's sake. You're drawing attention to me.'

I snap out of whatever has been holding me and slide into the bench seat opposite her. Her aggressive tone is gone when she speaks again but there's no warmth in her voice.

'Well, just look at you,' she says, taking a drag of her drink. 'Annie's little baby, all grown up.'

My jaw feels like it is wired shut. Even if I could open my mouth, I can't think of a single sensible thing to say and so I don't speak. I wish the waiter would hurry up with a drink for me so that I'd at least have something to do with my hands.

'Why are you here, Cara? What do you want from me?' Her bluntness does nothing to help my frozen state but I know that if I don't speak soon she will think I'm a half-wit.

'Hello, Aunt Ursula,' I manage.

'We'll have less of that,' she says. 'I may be your aunt by birth but I lay no claim to the title. Just plain Ursula will do fine.'

Enzo arrives with the bottle, which he opens in front of us and then pours without waiting for us to taste it. That is fine by me. I do not care what I drink. I just need one. I lift the glass and put it to my lips.

'What? No toast?' asks Ursula. 'How about, To absent friends?' She waves her glass in the air at me but I do not respond. I don't think I'm going to like Ursula Kemp.

'So,' I begin. 'As I said in my letter, I wanted to ask you some questions about my mother, Anne.'

'Darling little Annie,' she says, her words dripping with something cold that I can't quite identify. It is not exactly malice but there's no tenderness there.

This is not going at all to plan. I had hoped she might be pleased to see me, her long-lost niece, but there's none of that kind of warmth here. Her animosity sits between us like the bars in a prison. There is nothing else for it. If I want to get what I have come for, I will have to be as blunt and direct as she is being. I start to feel bolder. I can do this. If she wants cold and aloof then she's got it.

I'm about to speak when Enzo arrives with menus. Ursula bats him away like an irritating fly. She's clearly intent on just drinking but I'm hungry and accept the proffered menu with thanks. I order a jug of water and the smallest margherita they offer, which it says will feed two to three people. I think Ursula is watching me but her eyes are so narrowed that it is hard to tell whether they are even open.

'So,' she says when Enzo has retreated again. Her voice is dripping with indifference. 'I ask yet again. What, exactly, is it that you want to know?' She lingers over the word 'exactly', giving it prominence by enunciating each syllable individually. I pick up my glass, more to give myself breathing space than anything. My shaking hand disturbs the surface of the wine, making little red ripples, but if Ursula notices then she chooses not to comment.

'Until very recently,' I say, 'I thought my mother had died when I was two but now I think she might still be alive. I was wondering if you could shed any light on this.' I speak in a calm, matter-of-fact tone as if I have nothing invested in whatever she might tell me.

'His conscience finally pricking him then?' she says.

'Whose conscience?'

'That arrogant, cocksure idiot that calls himself your father.'

This knocks me sideways. I want to leap in and defend Dad but I can tell that if I do, Ursula will build even higher barriers between us.

'You mean, did Dad tell me?' I reply, keeping my voice as flat as I can manage. 'No. He didn't. I found something that made me ask questions.'

'And he wouldn't answer them so you fly all the way here and pester me like a spoiled child?'

'No,' I say, stung by her accusation. 'I haven't talked to Dad about it at all.'

'You should have saved yourself the airfare and me the effort. Or is he still playing the self-righteous prat and telling his little lies?'

'I can't ask him. He isn't well. He has Alzheimer's. He barely knows who he is, let alone is able to answer questions about something that happened thirty years ago.'

Ursula takes up her glass and swirls the wine around in the bowl before downing the lot in one mouthful.

'Oh, I am sorry to hear that,' she says, although she sounds anything but. 'Couldn't have happened to a nicer bloke. So he's completely gaga then?'

This pushes buttons that I can't ignore.

'Don't talk about him like that,' I snap. 'He's really not well.'

'Ooh,' she says. 'Quick to defend him, aren't you. I find that surprising. I really do. In the circumstances.' She's clearly enjoying this game of cat and mouse but it's making me increasingly angry.

'Look,' I say through gritted teeth to keep my voice low. 'I've come a long way to see you. You agreed to meet me. No one made you come. If you have nothing constructive to tell me then I can just leave now and forget all about it. But I'm not prepared to sit here and be the subject of your sad little mind games.'

Even before the words have left my lips, I know that I've blown it. Ursula is gathering her things and pushes herself, slightly unsteadily, to her feet.

'Then we have nothing else to say to each other,' she says. She opens her bag and tosses a $50 note on the table and then storms towards the door, oblivious to the heads that are turning to watch her.

I just sit there, not quite able to take in what has just happened, and then the pizza made for sharing arrives. Enzo looks at her empty seat.

'She had to leave,' I say.

He shrugs as though customers flouncing out before their food has even arrived is only to be expected.

'Enjoy,' he says and leaves me to it.

My hunger has completely gone. The mere smell of the pizza is making me feel nauseous. I push it away and reach for my glass instead.

CHAPTER THIRTY-EIGHT

I'm back at the hotel by 8 p.m. Nothing has changed. The lobby still hums with guests coming and going. Suitcase wheels trundle over the tiled floor. The concierge shouts out at passing cabs. Guests huddle in corners taking advantage of the Wi-Fi, their faces up-lit by the eerie blue light of their screens. For them, it's just another night on their travels. For me, the world has just imploded.

I think about heading straight for the bar, downing a couple of swift gin and tonics to numb whatever it is that I'm feeling, but I don't want to be among people and run the risk of someone trying to strike up a conversation with me.

Instead, I turn left and make for the lifts. One arrives almost at once and I leap in and push the 'Close Door' button as quickly as I can to prevent anyone sharing it with me. As the lift rises, so does the lump in my throat. Tears prick at my eyes. I bite the inside of my mouth until it hurts to take my mind off the hurt in my heart. As the lift stops at my floor, I can taste the sharp, metallic tang of my own blood.

I fumble for my key card as I walk along the corridor to save precious seconds when I reach my door. I let myself in and push the door closed behind me as if someone has been chasing me. Then my legs give way and I sink to the corporately carpeted floor. I don't even try to hold the tears back. I cry until snot and tears mingle like snail-trail over my chin.

After a while, the tears stop flowing and dry tightly on my cheeks. I sit there with my back against the door, clutching my bag like a teddy bear for a while longer. There seems no point in getting up and moving myself over towards the bed. I am spent.

Over the next hour or two, my confused emotions fling me back and forth. First, I'm embarrassed, mortified that I have managed to provoke a row with almost my only living relative and in such a devastating fashion. Did I have to be so rude to her? I replay the conversation, such as it was, in my head to see if there were other ways in which I could have handled her antagonism. I'm usually so calm, not easily riled, my emotional response to situations safely buried deep where no one can hurt it. What provoked me were the cruel things she said about Dad. Even after everything he's done, my gut reaction is still to take his side when the chips are down. Clearly Ursula knows something of what happened. Not that that matters anymore. She's not about to share it with me now.

Then I start to feel angry with her. Who the hell does she think she is, arranging to meet her long-lost niece and then turning up half-drunk, shouting the odds and being unforgivably rude? It doesn't matter how insular your life: there's no excuse for rudeness, especially to strangers, which is in effect what I am.

This anger is enough to get me up from my slump. I pace the room, looking out at the lights in the streets below. In this phase of my emotional journey I almost raid the mini-bar, but then I decide that another drink or two won't help me with my thinking process – and this does need thinking about carefully.

When the anger burns itself out, I'm left just feeling sad. Incredibly, deeply sad. I mourn an opportunity lost. Gone is my chance to find out about my mother but also to get to know my aunt, who, for all her charged personality, might have been someone I could have got along with. One ill-judged spat and it is all lost – and this thought makes me cry again.

I curl up in a ball on the bed. I don't even bother pulling the curtains against the neon glow of the sky outside. I should get undressed, try to sleep, but there I lie, nipping at the skin on my damaged arm with my finger nails, making little red ridges among the silvery white ones.

Then my phone buzzes. With no real interest, I give it a cursory glance. It is the wee small hours in England and who would be contacting me anyway? If there was a problem with Dad then Mrs P would ring, not text. It will no doubt be some irritating marketing message.

It is from Simeon.

I flip myself over as if the bed were hot and read the message. It is short and sweet.

How did it go?

Bless him. What is he doing up at this time? It must be about 5 a.m. at home. Suddenly I wish with all my heart that he were here with me to tell me that everything is okay, that it doesn't matter that my aunt is a mean-spirited, bitter and twisted, drunken old witch, and to hold me while I cry it all out all over again. Then he could take me out to the Golden Gate Bridge to watch the sunrise and off to breakfast in a lovely little café. If he were here, he could shield me in his arms and protect me against all evils and I would no longer feel isolated and scared in a country where I know no one. He could listen to me cry and rage at the injustice of it all and then we could make lingering, tender love until we both fall asleep, safe and secure in each other's arms.

But that kind of thing does not happen in my life. I hit reply and type an equally short message back to him.

Fine thanks.

CHAPTER THIRTY-NINE

Annie, 1986

'Have you collected the Child Benefit yet this week?' Joe asks her, and Annie feels her heart sink.

She had meant to do it yesterday on her way back from the supermarket but it had been raining cats and dogs and she couldn't get the rain cover for the pushchair to sit right. Soaked to the skin in minutes, she'd run home with Cara, intending to go and get the money when the weather cleared up.

'No, sorry,' she says. 'I forgot. I'll get it on Monday.'

Joe looks up from his paper.

'Well, that's no good,' he says, smiling at her.

It is the smile that he saves for when she's been particularly hopeless, the one that makes her feel like a stupid child.

'I need that money today,' he adds. 'Can't you nip and get it?'

Annie looks at her watch. It's eleven forty-five. The post office closes at twelve. By the time she has got coats and shoes on the children, cajoled Cara into the pushchair and got there it'll be shut.

'Well,' she says, chewing on her thumb as she speaks. 'If you could mind the children for a few minutes, I could run down. I should just get there before they close.'

The children are happy. Michael is watching cartoons on the telly and Cara is in her playpen posting shapes into a wooden post box.

'Fine,' says Joe. 'You go and get it and then you can get on with the lunch when you get back.'

Annie finds her bag, slips her coat on, plants a kiss on the crown of each child's head and leaves the house.

It's a glorious day outside, the sun high in the sky, the light golden and full of promise. Kids play on bikes or kick balls up and down the street. A group of teenagers is hanging about on the corner listening to Grace Jones playing on a huge tape player. Annie drops her head as she squeezes past and hurries along to the post office. Her watch says eleven fifty-five when she gets there and, feeling relieved, she goes inside and joins the small queue.

Moments behind her, someone else comes in. Annie smells them before she sees them, the heady, floral notes of Giorgio Beverly Hills. Annie recognises it because Babs had some for Christmas and wore it every day until it ran out. The queue moves forward one place.

'Annie, isn't it?' says the person wearing the perfume.

Annie turns round.

'I thought so. Annie Kemp. How the devil are you? You look well. What have you been up to for all this time?'

The woman snatches up Annie's left hand, admires the ring and then drops it back down.

'Got yourself hitched, I see. Shame. All the best ones get snaffled up too soon.'

Annie would know this woman anywhere, although she was little more than a girl last time they met. She was a friend of Katrina's, Annie's erstwhile workmate from her days at Selfridges, and they went on many a night out back in the day, before Annie married Joe. Even then she was intriguing, set aside from the crowd. Annie remembers platform boots higher, bell bottoms wider, make-up bolder than anyone else's around her.

'Tilly!' says Annie, smiling widely at the woman, who returns her smile.

'Sure is!'

'Hi. It's been so long. You look just the same.'

And she does. Long, dark hair contrasting sharply with her pale skin, dark make-up, lots of jewellery.

'What are you doing round here?' asks Annie.

'I was flying through in a taxi on my way back from delivering a contract. I saw the post office and remembered that I hadn't posted my mum's birthday card. Bad girl!' She slaps herself playfully on the wrist. She has a tattoo, Annie sees, and feels at first shocked and then delighted by the riskiness of it. It's a unicorn inked skilfully on to her forearm. In Annie's very narrow experience only sailors and prostitutes have tattoos. And Tilly. 'It probably won't get there in time now anyway but at least she'll see the postmark and know that I tried. Come for a drink with me,' she adds. 'Let's have a proper catch-up.'

Annie's heart sinks. 'Oh, I can't,' she says. 'I only popped out for a minute. Joe's got the kids and I've got to make the lunch.'

'Who says? Surely Joe can make his own lunch and they're his kids too. They are his, aren't they?' she adds, her eyes sparkling with mischief. 'He can look after them while you have a quick drink with an old friend. Come on.'

'Next.'

The man at the counter calls Annie forward and she digs in her bag for her Child Benefit book.

'Well . . . I'm not sure . . .' she says to Tilly.

'Next!' says the man again.

Annie waits outside the post office, the Child Benefit money tucked carefully in her purse out of sight. Seconds later, Tilly skips out into the street, grabs hold of Annie's arm and starts to pull her along the pavement.

'Come on. Just a quick one. I won't take no for an answer.'

239

And she won't. Annie can see that and what harm will it do? She could have a quick drink and then rush back. She could tell Joe that she called to buy some bits for lunch. He might not even notice how long she's gone. Her heart is in her mouth as she tries to decide what to do but she can feel a tiny spark of rebellion firing in her veins.

'What's the worst that can happen?' asks Tilly. She is laughing and Annie remembers why she liked her so much when Katrina first introduced them. She decides to go for the drink and feels immediately liberated by her decision.

'Are you still working at Selfridges?' she asks, allowing herself to be propelled along the street in the opposite direction from home.

'God no! That was just while I was a student, to keep the parents happy. I'm working for the BBC now. Researcher on *Wogan*.'

Annie gasps.

'Really? Do you meet all the stars then? Do you know Terry Wogan?'

Tilly waves her hand dismissively. 'Yes, but most of them aren't worth knowing. Except Terry. He's a real gentleman.'

They reach a pub, The Coach and Horses, and Tilly pushes the door open. Annie hesitates for a moment and then follows her.

Inside it feels very dark after the bright sunshine and Annie's eyes struggle to adjust.

'What'll you have?' asks Tilly. 'My treat.'

Annie dithers. She can't have a proper drink. Joe will smell it on her. She's already wondering how she's going to explain the cigarette smoke on her clothes.

'I'll just have a lemonade,' she says.

Tilly pulls a face, scoffing. 'You are joking!'

'No, really. I have stuff to do and I can't stay long.'

'Okay,' says Tilly over her shoulder. She returns a moment later with a pint of lemonade and something tall in a highball glass. 'So,' she says, putting the drinks down and dropping on to the stool. 'Tell me everything.'

Tilly generates an energy about her, just as she had done back when Katrina first introduced them. It's like static electricity and Annie imagines that her skin will spark if they touch.

'There's not much to tell. I married Joe. Remember him?'

Tilly nods appreciatively. 'Nice.'

'And we have two children. Michael is six and Cara is two.'

Tilly yawns theatrically. 'You done too much, much too young,' she sings. 'Children. Really? I'm sorry but I'm just not ready for settling down any time soon. Too much living to do first. I have to travel some more and I get invited to some amazing parties you know, through work.'

Annie nods but really she can't imagine how Tilly's life must be. As Tilly chatters on, mentioning film stars and musicians as if they are people she knows from school, Annie listens and tries to stop her jaw from crashing on to the table. Tilly isn't namedropping or showing off, though. It seems rather that the rich and famous have become such a part of her lifestyle that she's forgotten that it's not the same for everyone else. Annie tries to absorb it all, as if there is nothing unusual about hearing Tina Turner dropped into conversation, but inside she's fizzing with vicarious excitement.

'And what about you?' asks Tilly after a while. 'Do you still see Katrina and the old crowd?'

Annie shakes her head. How can she explain that she doesn't see anyone anymore without making her life sound horribly dull next to the glamour that Tilly carries with her? 'No. We kind of drifted apart after I got married. I don't really have much time to see people anymore, not with the children and everything.'

She is so proud of her beautiful children but now, talking to Tilly, she can already see that her old friend won't understand the choices she's made, will think she has thrown her opportunities away, grown up too fast. Thinking of the children now makes Annie realise, with a start, that she has been gone far longer than she said and she looks at her watch. It's almost one o'clock. She has to leave. Now.

She stands up so quickly that her stool clatters to the floor behind her and everyone turns to stare. As she bends to pick it up, embarrassed, Tilly salutes in the air to acknowledge the attention.

'I must go,' says Annie, gathering her bag close to her. 'Joe will be wondering where I've got to. Thanks for the drink.'

'No problem,' says Tilly and Annie notices that she doesn't try to persuade her to stay. But then she adds, 'Let's do this again sometime.'

Annie assumes she is being polite but Tilly scrabbles round in her bag and pulls out a business card. She hands it to Annie. 'Ring me,' she says, drawing dialling in the air with her finger. 'I mean it,' she adds, holding Annie with her dark eyes. 'Ring me.'

Annie nods her goodbyes and rushes out into the street, where her eyes have to readjust again as she quietly slips from one world to another. Anxiety races through her system and she almost runs back to the house, thinking through excuses for her lateness as she goes.

At the front door, she straightens her hair and tries to slow her breathing. Then she puts her key in the lock and goes inside.

'I'm back,' she calls out, her voice artificially bright.

No one calls back. Joe must be angry with her. He is just waiting until she appears and then she will catch it for being gone too long. She braces herself for what is to come and then pushes open the door to the lounge.

Michael is sitting exactly where she left him in front of the television.

'Hello, Mummy,' he says without looking away from the screen.

Annie looks into Cara's playpen but it's empty. Panicked, she scans the room and finds her little girl on the couch, lying propped on Joe's chest. They are both sound asleep.

CHAPTER FORTY

Cara, 2018

My body clock must be righting itself or I'm just exhausted, because by the time I turn my head to find the neon numbers of the radio alarm it's already well past nine. Even before I look in the mirror I can tell that my eyes are a mess. The skin around them feels wrong, pulled too tight by the puffiness that my tears have left behind. It'll be dark glasses for me this morning, I think. Not that it matters, as no one I know will see me in this state. No one here knows me or cares why I went to sleep with swollen eyes.

No one except Skyler. She flits across my mind with a shiver of guilt. I picture her sitting cross-legged at her tidy desk in the dark gallery waiting for news of the grand reunion with the introverted Ursula Kemp. Some reunion. I tussle briefly with my conscience. I should really report back, let her know that the meeting was not a resounding success. It's the least I can do, given the part that she played in setting it up in the first place. Right now, though, I can't face the idea of recounting it to her, explaining my own part in the shoddy little tale. I push Skyler out of my mind.

Thoughts of her are replaced by pangs of hunger as I remember that, for reasons that I'd rather not dwell on, I didn't have any dinner last night. Ideas of breakfast are enough to drag me from the bed and into the shower, where I stand for longer than I would have had Dad been paying for the water in an attempt to steam my eyes back open. I almost miss the ringing phone and even when the unfamiliar tone wafts through the billowing steam to me, it still takes me a while to recognise it for what it is. I grab a towel as I drip on the carpet to answer it.

'Hello?' I say.

'Miss Ferensby?'

'Yes.'

'We have a lady waiting for you in reception. She says she's your aunt. Should I ask her to take a seat?'

I don't speak as I try to process what I've just been told. I wonder how Ursula has found me until I remember that I put the hotel details in my letter. Then I wonder what she wants. I don't speak for so long that the receptionist on the other end asks whether I am still there.

'Sorry. Yes. Could you ask her to wait there and I'll be down as quickly as I can,' I manage.

I put the phone down and stare at the handset. My feet are making damp prints on the carpet. What is this? Has she come back for round two? Initially, my still-raw anger makes me think that she can whistle. It would probably serve her right if I crept out through a back entrance, leaving her there to stew, but I know that I need to speak to her if I ever want to discover what happened to my mother. With heart pounding, I pad back to the bathroom and start to get ready.

Ten minutes later I'm heading down to reception in the lift. My hair is wet again, just as it was last night, but this time I don't care about how I look. Ursula is no longer worth making the effort for.

When I reach the lobby I hold back a little, casting my eyes around for her. At first there's no sign but then I spot her sitting half-hidden by a potted palm. She is worrying the skin around her thumbnail with her teeth and biting away the hangnails. I watch her for a moment, enjoying the knowledge that she is unaware of my presence. As I watch, I wonder if I can see something of myself in her; in the fall of her shoulders, the shape of the chin, maybe. We aren't obviously alike, though. I'm probably imagining a similarity because I'm half hoping to see something familiar when I look at her. Perhaps she looks like her sister? Could I see my mother's face staring out at me from my aunt's cragged features, if only I knew what to look for?

She must sense me staring because she raises her eyes in my direction and then sees me. For a moment neither of us moves. We just stare at each other. I am very conscious of my swollen eyes, but as I look into hers I see that she too looks like she might have passed at least part of the previous evening crying. Is this atonement then, this unannounced appearance?

Then she raises her hand: not high – a little movement that suggests a degree of contrition. I don't respond straightaway. Her half-smile slips slightly and she raises her eyebrows questioningly, imploringly. Still I don't move. I feel like I'm standing on a train station. I have two choices. I can stay where I am and let the doors of the train close in front of me or I can climb aboard and see where the journey takes me. Ursula's hand drops into her lap. She looks down. I take a step towards her.

She is no longer the woman of the night before. The languid self-confidence is gone and she seems to be occupying much less space. Even her sharp, pixie haircut looks as if she is just coming through a health scare rather than making a fashion statement. Despite the anguished night that I have just spent, the hurt that she caused me, my bruised sense of self, I find that I'm still drawn to her.

I forgive her in a heartbeat. I know that this is dangerous. Who's to say that she won't do exactly the same to me again? Yet as she sits partly obscured by the potted palm, I see in her a vulnerability that something buried deep inside me recognises. She is protecting herself from harm and I know all about that.

As I approach her, she stands up. I stop a couple of feet from her, too far away for any awkward physical contact. We are definitely not at the kiss-and-make-up stage. There's not even a whiff of an air kiss. It's apparent that Ursula is as uncomfortable with that kind of casual contact as I am.

Neither of us speaks. We look into each other's eyes. Hers are perhaps puffier than mine but that might be how she always looks this early in the morning. Then, at the corner of her mouth, the glimpse of a crooked smile. I don't respond. Not yet.

'I think we might have got off on the wrong foot,' she says. I hold her gaze. 'Shall we start again?'

I note, with slight irritation, that there's not even a hint of an apology, but that's okay. We've given each other a second chance; I can overlook the social niceties. She must feel sorry, otherwise why would she be here? Maybe saying it out loud is more than she can manage?

So I smile. I give her a real Bobby Dazzler just to show her that I can forgive her, even without an apology. 'Yes,' I say. 'Let's start again.'

She nods her head but there's clearly going to be no excuses, no post mortem, no blaming of the red wine. Nothing. 'There's a bakery down in Fisherman's Wharf,' she says. 'They do great sourdough and the coffee's not bad. Shall we go for breakfast?'

I agree.

We leave the hotel. Outside the air is cold but crisp, with a deep-blue sky and no sign today of San Francisco's habitual morning clouds. A beautiful day for new beginnings. We walk side by side but the pavements are already filled with sightseers and any conversation is too stilted to be worth having so we don't even try. The bakery stands right on the waterfront. Its huge glass windows are filled with piles of loaves in different shapes and colours. A woman in white overalls and a hairnet stands in the window making tiny dough hedgehogs. They stand in rows like a little army.

Ursula guides me in and points at a mezzanine.

'You find us a table and I'll get breakfast. What do you want?'

She speaks as if she is issuing orders but I'm beginning to think that this is just her manner so I try not to let it rile me.

'Cappuccino to drink but I'll leave the food up to you. Just get whatever looks nice.'

It all looks lovely and she looks at me as if I am a simpleton, the arch of her eyebrow giving a hint of the high-handed woman I met last night, but she doesn't say anything and heads off towards the queue.

The café is filled with a mixture of tourists and people in business-wear who are presumably on their way to work. One wall is all glass and behind it the bakery is in full swing, with people in white aprons emptying ovens and pushing trolleys piled high with bread. They remind me of Oompa-Loompas even though they are neither tiny nor orange. All around the perimeter there is an overhead track that carries wire baskets filled with bread from the bakery to the shop, although when I settle on one basket and watch its slow progress around the building no one stops it at either destination to empty or refill it. Maybe they are just for the tourists.

I climb the few steps to the mezzanine and find an empty table that looks out over a service yard and then on to the bay. I can just glimpse the bridge.

Ursula approaches carrying a tray with two white cups and two pastries, which she puts down in front of me without a word.

'Thank you,' I say, reaching to take a cup. The pastry doesn't look big enough to make even a dint in my hunger but it will do for now. 'Nice place,' I say, not quite sure how to begin.

Ursula nods. She takes one of the pastries and cuts it into tiny little cubes, which she begins popping into her mouth like sweets. I just cut mine neatly down the middle and tackle a half at a time.

'So,' she says after she has eaten about a third of the pastry. 'To recap. You thought your mother, my sister, was dead. You have recently learned that this is not . . .' She pauses as she considers her sentence and then continues. 'Or at least might not be the case. Your father has some form of dementia and is unable to answer your questions and so you have sought me out. Is that about it? Did I leave anything out?'

There's no emotional engagement. To her this is simply a list of facts rather than the complicated and very sad story of her own family history. However, I suppose in many ways her distanced, offhand approach might make the situation easier to deal with. This emotionless summing-up does manage to capture the essence of it all. I nod, not quite trusting my voice to work. My stomach knots tighter and tighter and my chest constricts as I sit and wait for her to tell me the truth about my entire life.

'Well,' says Ursula, searching out my wide-open eyes with hers and locking her gaze on to them. 'She didn't die. She's still with us, God bless her.'

Her tone is scornful, derisory almost, like she has no time for her sister. But I can't focus on that. I am working too hard to process what she just told me. My mother is definitely alive. She did not die like they all said. She left us. Of course, I have considered this possibility endlessly since I first found the postcards but it is only now that I know the truth. I find that I have only one word.

'Why?'

Ursula picks up her coffee cup and starts to swirl the contents around. The dark liquid gets higher up the side of the cup, closer to the edge. Just as I think she is going to send it out over the table, she stops.

'You do realise, don't you, Cara, that when I tell you what it is that you think you want to know, then that'll be it. There's nothing that you can do to un-know it, no matter how hard you wish that you could. Are you sure that you're ready for that?'

This is something that I've thought about a lot. Ever since I found the postcards, I've been tossing the problem of what to do next around in my mind like a toy boat caught in a typhoon. Sometimes I think that it would be better to forget all about it and just carry on with things as they were before, but really, in my heart of hearts, I know that's not an option. I have to understand. There is no way back now.

I nod my head decisively. 'Believe me,' I say, 'I know that. But now I've got this far, I really don't know what else to do. I've barely let myself think about what I might do next, not until I knew for sure that she left us. And until I understand why she did that I can't get any further with it. Please just tell me it all. Everything.'

I fight to keep the frustration out of my voice. If this is going to work then I need to stay calm. Even though this morning's Ursula seems much less volatile than the one who stormed out of the restaurant, I mustn't say anything that'll make her bolt again. She eyes me up carefully as if deciding what to do and then she starts to nod slowly.

'Okay,' she says. 'If you're sure. You remind me of her, you know. She was a pretty determined kind of person too.'

So determined that she walked out on her tiny children, I want to say, but I swallow my words back into my throat. Ursula sits back in her chair and closes her eyes for a moment. Then she speaks.

'Your mum and I grew up in a tiny two-bedroom terraced house in Tottenham. There were just the four of us. Our mother, your grandma, worked in the rag trade, sewing tatty clothes for market stalls. Dad was a locksmith. He didn't have a shop of his own. He worked for someone who I suspect probably had some kind of gangland connections, but he was a long way down the food chain. Me and Annie, we did all right. Mum tried hard to keep us looking nice. She sewed our clothes and made sure our shoes didn't have holes in and cooked us decent food. She was a good woman, really, despite everything. She mostly did her best by us. But Dad . . . Now he was a completely different kettle of fish.'

She gazes up at the wire bread baskets on their little track as they pass over our heads and she doesn't say anything for a while. I can't decide whether she is getting her memories in order or if she's trying to find the right words. I pick at my pastry and wait.

'Basically, my father was a bully. He bullied Mum and then, when we got big enough, he bullied us.'

'How do you mean?' I ask before I have time to stop myself.

Ursula looks irritated by my interruption. She's clearly going to tell me the story at her own pace.

'Sorry,' I say and I don't stop her again.

'He was handy with his fists. Nothing unusual in that. Lots of men are. He'd go to the pub after work, especially if he'd had a good day on the horses, have a skinful and then come back and try to knock the life out of Mum. She was good at managing him, on the whole. She'd had to learn. She'd make sure there was food for him when he got back and that we were either in bed or at least quiet. If she thought he was going to be really bad, she'd take herself off. Not out of the house – she wouldn't have left us on our own – but she'd make herself scarce upstairs or be in bed when he got back. Sometimes, though, there was no avoiding his fists. Annie and I shared a bed and we'd lie there, quiet as little mice, hoping that he'd forget we existed. We'd hear him come in and then Mum talking to him. She had this odd, bright voice that she used when she thought there might be bother. And then sometimes we'd hear him shout and then her sob. It was grim. Often it was unbearable.'

She stops talking again. Her skin looks grey, more deeply lined than before. Recounting this for me is clearly painful and I almost feel sorry for her.

'I need more coffee,' she says abruptly. 'Want one?' I can see that she needs a break, to regroup before she continues, so I nod and watch as she takes small, slow steps back downstairs to the counter.

When she returns, she sits the cups down on the table carefully and then she drops her head and runs her hands through her cropped hair. She has hands a bit like mine, slender-fingered with prominent veins snaking across their backs. She doesn't look up but carries on speaking.

'Anyway, that was how it was at home, with the three of us creeping about the house trying not to attract his attention, making sure there was nothing out of place that might set him off. I sometimes wished we could just leave him – me, Mum and Annie. Pack our stuff and go and live somewhere he couldn't find us, but this was the seventies. There was nowhere for us to go. And Mum didn't make enough at the factory to keep us even if we could find somewhere. Annie and I used to whisper in corners about what we'd do when we left school. We were going to get jobs and share a flat, just the two of us . . .'

For a moment she looks almost wistful, but then her eyes narrow and her mouth hardens again. 'Not that that's how things turned out.'

Ursula spits the words out but then she takes a deep breath and pulls herself back from the anger that is just bubbling beneath the surface. 'I don't remember worrying about Mum much, just me and Annie. I thought that Mum'd made her bed by marrying Dad in the first place. It wasn't our fault that she was such a bad judge of character, but we were being made to suffer the consequences. I remember the first time he really hurt me,' she says.

As she talks, it's almost as if I'm not even there. She speaks into the middle distance without making eye contact with anyone. I sit so still that I'm barely even breathing.

'He threw me against the kitchen wall and broke my collarbone. Mum just watched. Annie, she was younger than me, she tried to pull him off and got a black eye for her trouble, but Mum . . . She just stood there and waited until it was all over. I never really forgave her for that.'

A steady stream of people snakes into the café but the tables around us stay empty, as if it's somehow obvious that we need some space. Ursula continues.

'It wasn't just the violence. The man was basically a controlling, manipulative bastard. He was always telling us how useless we were. He bandied insults about like someone else might tell jokes. We were never good enough. We were ugly or fat or a waste of air or costing him a fortune or whatever it happened to be that day. Annie and I, we had each other. We'd tell each other that he was talking trash, that we shouldn't

251

take any notice, but I think Mum got really ground down by it. Every year she seemed smaller, less able to deal with him. She stopped hiding when he came in, like she was challenging him to hit her; as if, in some twisted way, she deserved it.

'Then Anneliese met your father.'

Something in Ursula's voice changes. Her mouth tightens, the lines around her lips becoming more prominent. She's called Mum 'Anneliese'. I've never heard this name before. I want to question it but I daren't interrupt in case she stops talking.

'He was quite a catch,' she continues, her voice still low, 'your father. He was older than Annie by eight or nine years. He seemed so sophisticated. What a joke that turned out to be, but I'm not surprised she fell for his charms. He had a good job and he used to flash his cash around. He'd take Annie out dancing and when he arrived at the house to pick her up he'd flirt with Mum. She'd smile and tell him not to be so silly but it was obvious that she really liked it. He even seemed to get on well with Dad. They'd often go for a pint together after work.'

It sounds a bit like a fairytale romance, Prince Charming arriving on a white charger to rescue my mum from peril, but I can tell by the way Ursula's expression hasn't changed that she doesn't think so. I scan her face closely as she talks. The words spill out of her mouth. She barely pauses for breath. It's like she needs to get this over and done with as quickly as possible. I sit motionless and listen hard, trying to remember every last word. I get the impression that there will be no repetition.

'Then he proposed,' Ursula says. 'It felt all wrong. She was nineteen by then but I was twenty-two. It should have been me flying the nest and yet here was my baby sister with a ticket out of there. I was furious. It felt like she was abandoning me, like she was kicking me and all our plans in the teeth. Looking back, I should've done things differently. She was young. She didn't know any better. I should have cut her some slack, looked after her, but I couldn't. I just couldn't forgive her for leaving me with him. I was vile.'

I think about how little I know about my Aunt Ursula. Her name just never came up at home. It's only because Michael has dim memories of her that I even got to know she existed. My mind races ahead now as she talks, trying to match what she is telling me with what I already know. I have to pull myself back to the present so I don't miss anything.

'Anyway,' Ursula continues. 'She got married and had your brother and at first everything seemed rosy for her, not that I was taking much notice. Then you came along. I'd left by then but Mum told me that one day Annie just turned up on her doorstep. She had you all bundled up in her arms and a bag stuffed with as much as she could carry. She said she'd left your father, that he was treating her badly and that she wasn't going back. Mum was furious. She wouldn't let Annie in, made her stand on the doorstep. She wouldn't even take the baby from her. Mum told her to turn round and go right back home. A married woman stands by her man no matter what, according to Mum. I suppose she thought that if she'd put up with our father for all those years then Annie could too.

'And that was it. Annie had to turn round and go back to Joe. I don't think Mum saw her again after that.'

Ursula chews on her lip and takes a couple of deep breaths. Things are starting to fall into place in my head but it still isn't making much sense.

'Well,' I say slowly. 'That explains why we never saw you or our grandparents but not why Mum left me and Michael. Did she leave after the affair?'

I don't really know for sure that Dad had an affair but it is worth a shot. All I have is one side of some correspondence found hidden in a box, but it's the only explanation for the break-up that makes any sense so far.

'Ah,' says Ursula as she stirs her coffee round and round the cup. 'The delightful Tilly.'

Tilly? 'T'? The 'T' of the love letters? My heart is beating so fast as I wait for Ursula to explain that I have to take one deep breath, right to the very bottom of my lungs, to stop me from fainting.

'Was Tilly Mum's friend? Is she the one with long, black hair? And a tattoo of a unicorn?' I ask, trying to remember what Michael told me about her.

Could this be the same woman? Did Dad have an affair with Mum's best friend?

'That's her. And I suppose she was your mother's friend. In a manner of speaking,' says Ursula with a sniff.

I can tell at once that there is no love lost between her and whoever this Tilly is.

'And she had the affair?' I ask.

Understanding floods through me. Poor Mum. Living with two small children in an abusive marriage and with only one friend in the world, who then has an affair with her husband. She must have felt completely alone. Her own family had already rejected her and then her best friend goes off with her husband. No wonder she left him. What else could she do?

My mind is making connections so fast that I can barely keep up. That must be why she left and then maybe Dad was so angry that he lied about her being dead to get back at her. His thing with Tilly can't have lasted long. I would have remembered if there had been someone to replace Mum; and if I didn't then Michael definitely would have. But that still doesn't explain why Mum left us behind. Surely if she was running from an unfaithful husband she'd have taken her children with her? She wouldn't have left them with him and the new woman. None of it adds up.

'Yup,' says Ursula, draining the end of her coffee and putting the cup down hard so that it clatters in the saucer.

'But why would Mum leave if Dad was having an affair? Wouldn't she just have kicked him out, made him go and live with his new woman?'

Ursula looks at me, her sharp eyes narrowed, and then she shakes her head slowly.

'It wasn't your father that was having an affair with Tilly. It was your mother.'

CHAPTER FORTY-ONE

I do not know what to do. It feels like my whole world has suddenly stopped turning and yet all around me life continues. Crockery chinks, orders are shouted at the counter, the wire baskets hum along their track . . . But the sounds all deaden to nothing as I try to process what Ursula has just told me. It was my mother who was having an affair. My mother left me. Not because she was abused by my father and it was the only way that she could see to make her pain stop. No, she left me behind while she indulged herself in some kind of self-centred flight of fancy. It is so clichéd that I almost laugh. My mother went off to find herself with some woman, some silk-scarf-wearing, crystal-fondling woman. Where did they run to? A remote Greek island? Goa, maybe? What a shallow, selfish person she must be. I mean, you read about women like that, who complain that having children means that they lose touch with the 'real' them, that their own essence gets swamped in the deluge of dirty nappies and night feeds. But to have one as your own mother . . . ? Maybe she had intended to come back and pick us up once her journey of discovery was at an end. Well, that never worked out, did it? Clearly the draw of freedom was stronger, more appealing than the pull of her maternal instinct.

I'm beginning to understand why Ursula warned me about the power of what she was about to say. Any little fantasy that I might have invented for myself as to why my mother left me, a vulnerable two-year-old girl, is about to smash to pieces on the rocks.

Suddenly I feel very sick. I have to get out of here, out into the fresh air. Away. I lurch from the table, almost falling down the steps, and push my way through the queue to the door. The air outside is tainted by exhaust fumes and the faint scent of fish but at least it's cold. It bites into my cheeks and, as I gasp it down in big, desperate lungfuls, it cools me from the inside out. I lean against the plate-glass window of the bakery while I gather myself. The woman in the white apron has moved on from making hedgehogs to little sourdough teddies, a tray full of pasty, uncooked bears at her side.

I set off at a run, desperate now to get away from the crowds, to find some space where I can breathe. The pavements are busy, people walking calmly towards their destinations, but I jostle my way through and then find myself running along in the gutter where the route is clearer. The occasional car honks its horn at me, a mad woman running down the street without a care for her personal safety. I bear right, heading towards the bridge, drawn to the calming powers of the water, and soon the landscape breaks up into an urban park. There are grass banks and a path for runners and cyclists that snakes its way through the space. I make my way to an empty bench and drop down to it, my legs no longer having the power to carry me.

It's only when I stop, my breath coming in short, ragged bursts, that I realise that I have left Ursula sitting in the bakery. She and I probably can't come back from the brink a second time. That will no doubt be the last I ever see of her, my aunt. I have no way of contacting her other than through Skyler at the gallery. It'll be up to Ursula whether she responds to my messages or not and once I leave here and head back home, that link will be broken.

Suddenly, I feel very, very alone. My father has disappeared into a place where I will never reach him again, the mother of my imagination turns out to be more of a nightmare, and my brother has washed his hands of the whole sorry mess that is our family. I have no one. I should cry. That's what's expected in tragic circumstances like these. But I find that there are no more tears, just a dull pain in my heart that I will have to carry with me forever.

I look out across the bay. The water is a dark indigo, its surface broken by strong, criss-crossing waves that push towards the shore. I see the bridge, its two red pillars standing tall against the speedwell sky. I could just walk across it and disappear. No one would know where I'd gone. Barely anyone would even miss me. I could just go . . .

Someone sits down heavily on the end of my bench and breaks my chain of thought. I am irritated. There are countless other unoccupied benches and no need to crowd me right now, in my darkest moment. I'm about to stand up and move when I realise that it's Ursula.

'I need to get to the gym more,' she wheezes. 'Or give up the fags.'

She chose to follow me. I ran but she ran behind. Maybe I'm not alone after all.

'Listen, Cara,' she says, her breath coming in sharp bursts. 'I don't know what's going on in that pretty little head of yours but I think you might have got this all wrong.'

I pull my gaze away from the ocean and turn to look at her. Her cheeks are flushed and there are beads of sweat on her forehead despite the chilly air temperature, but her eyes flash. They remind me of mine.

'God knows why I've just chased you halfway across San Francisco. It's like dealing with a toddler.'

I should probably take offence but I just don't have the strength.

'I suppose,' she continues, 'that that little display of petulance was because I told you about Anneliese and Tilly. So, your mother had an affair with a woman. So what? Women are generally far more successful human beings than men,' she says. 'Although I might make an exception in this particular case.'

I'm about to explain why I'm so upset but then I stop, hooking into what she just said. 'Which case? Tilly? What was wrong with her?' I ask.

'What wasn't wrong with her is a better question. She was loaded to start with. Not that there's anything wrong with money. But she'd always had it. A trust fund from Daddy, expensive school, horses. All that. She was used to getting everything her own way. If she wanted something, she just tossed her hair and someone gave it to her. It made her impulsive, which your mother seemed to like. We never had the chance to be impulsive, you see. We were too busy looking over our shoulders to see where the next blow was coming from. And I suppose it might be fun, acting without fear of the consequences. I don't know. I've never done it. But there's a downside too. Basically, Tilly was spoiled. If things didn't go her way she'd sulk until they did. By the end, that was what she was doing most of the time – sulking.'

My anger for my flighty mother is evaporating as I get sucked into Ursula's story again. 'How do you know?' I ask. 'Did they come here then, after they left us?'

'Not straightaway. First they went on a grand tour, burning their way through Tilly's trust fund.'

I think of the early postcards, how they'd been sent from tourist hotspots in Europe.

'They weren't in touch with me. Tilly made sure of that. She wanted your mother to herself, got her to drop all links with her family. But eventually they landed up here. San Francisco was the centre of the gay world in the 1980s so of course Tilly fancied being part of that scene, although they weren't really lesbians. For Tilly, it was just a passing phase because she wanted people to talk about her, and for your mother . . .' She rubs her hands to get some heat into them. 'Well, for Annie it was all about a way out. So, they rocked up here for the vibe. They weren't interested in me, although I did see a bit of them once my work started to take off. Tilly could see that I might open doors for them in the kinds of circles that she wanted to move in.'

Ursula is looking out across the water as she speaks, half a smile playing across her lips. It's almost as if she is finally enjoying telling her tale. 'It wasn't going so well between them, though,' she continues. 'They'd been travelling for a few years by then without really putting down any roots. I think Tilly's money was starting to run a bit low. Annie wanted to work, pay her way a bit, but Tilly wouldn't have it. That meant that Annie was stuck. Again. She was completely dependent on Tilly for everything. Turns out she'd just swapped one controlling influence for another. And when Tilly got bored of her, she was left high and dry. She had nothing. I heard that they'd split up on the grapevine but I didn't see either of them again. I assume they went back to England.'

I try to imagine my mother racing round the globe after this woman. Maybe she did see Tilly as her only means of escape. If she'd married Dad young to try to get away from an abusive father, like Ursula said, then perhaps she realised later that she'd made a massive mistake. I think of how Dad was when we were children – domineering, uncompromising, frightening sometimes. But we were children. It's hard to believe that Mum would have been frightened of him. Trapped, though? Now, that I can understand; and if Mum wanted more from her life than Dad could offer, then who knows? Maybe Tilly offered her a way out that was too tempting to refuse?

This brings me right back to the same problem. I have come full circle. What about us, Michael and me? She was our mother. She had responsibilities. Just because her life wasn't turning out quite the way she had hoped, she should never have just abandoned us. This thought translates itself to an angry outburst before I have time to rein it in.

'But she left us. I was two years old and she abandoned me with a man who she knew was less than perfect even if he was my dad. How could she have just have gone and then made no effort whatsoever to see us? A box of postcards. Is that supposed to be a substitute for a life of parenting?'

Ursula reaches out and puts her vein-tracked hand on my coat and I see, for the first time, something approaching concern in her face. 'But she couldn't take you,' she says. 'She couldn't even see you.'

My head is spinning. 'What do you mean? Of course she could. She just chose not to. She swanned off to find a better life and didn't look back.'

'No, Cara. You've got it all wrong. As soon as she told your father about Tilly, he went to his solicitors. He got an injunction against her. Your mother was forbidden from coming near you by the court.'

This is too much. I cannot bear it. I don't know what to think anymore. I feel my breakfast rising in my throat and I swallow it back down. Ursula speaks more gently now.

'Your mother didn't abandon you. Yes, she had an affair and, yes, she left your father, but she fully intended to take you with her. But don't forget, this was the eighties. I know it doesn't seem that long ago but culturally it was like a different planet. AIDS was just starting to be understood. People were scared. Homophobia was rife and not just against gay men. Two mothers in a family? You have to be joking. You can't imagine now how shocking that seemed back then. People really believed that you needed a male role model to bring up kids, especially boys. Not everyone thought like that, of course, but enough people did. All your father had to do was find an old-school male judge and convince him that his philandering, lesbian wife was an unfit mother. It wasn't that difficult.'

'But surely she could have fought the decision?'

'What with? She had no money and Tilly wanted your mother, not you and Michael. She wasn't about to bankroll Annie through an expensive court case. And Annie was worried about the impact that it would have on the pair of you. Yes, these things are supposed to be held in private, but a woman running off with another woman and leaving her children? The papers wouldn't have been able to resist. She was desperate not to do anything that would make things worse. She decided that the best thing to do would be to obey the injunction and leave your father to bring you up. She knew you were safe and well cared for. She felt like she had no choice, but it broke her heart.'

My head is spinning. So it was Dad. He drove her away and then made sure that she could never come back.

'So where is she now?' I hear myself shout.

Ursula shakes her head. 'Honestly? I have no idea. We drifted apart after she married your dad and when she turned up here I made it pretty clear what I thought of Tilly. When they left we lost touch. I haven't heard from her since.'

'And you didn't think to get in touch with me and Michael?' I spit, my anger suddenly directed at the only person I can find to aim it at.

'And do what?' says Ursula coldly. 'What could I have done? It wasn't my battle to fight.'

'But didn't you care whether we were all right?'

'Your father isn't a monster, Cara. Not like mine. He did what he thought was best for the three of you. And I think he really did love Annie. Things just got away from him in the heat of the moment. Maybe he was too proud to go back? Who knows? In any case, he made it pretty clear that he wanted to go it alone. I did write to him to tell him when our mother died but he didn't reply. I figured you were better off without me.'

I cannot process any of this. I am totally bombarded by information and emotion and I don't seem to have any resources to deal with it. I just sit there and say nothing.

'Let's walk,' says Ursula, standing up and rubbing at her thin frame through her coat. 'It's freezing.'

I can't just sit here so I follow her. She's limping slightly after her chase to find me. I suppose at her age she isn't used to running through the streets. We drop down to the water's edge just at the foot of the bridge. Something catches my eye and as I scan the breakers I see it again. It looks at first like a small brown ball bobbing on the surface, but when I look harder I see its slick back as it dives under the waves.

'Was that a seal?' I ask.

Ursula glances in the direction that I have pointed but gives up looking pretty quickly. 'It'll be a sea lion,' she says. 'The bay is overrun with them.'

I have only ever seen sea lions at water parks doing tricks for rewards of dull-eyed fish. Seeing one here, in the wild, alters my perspective. I keep staring at the water for ages but he doesn't show himself again. By the time I look away, Ursula has turned round and is heading back along the path in the direction that we came. I have to run to catch up with her.

'I'm sorry we got off on the wrong foot yesterday,' she says, keeping her gaze fixed on the horizon ahead. 'I'm glad that you came all this way to find me. I truly am. I maybe should have got in touch . . .' Her voice drifts off. She turns to look at me, her eyes lingering over parts of my face. 'I can see bits of me in you,' she says.

I think about our hands, about the way she holds her neck, but then something else crosses my mind.

'I went to art school,' I say. 'Just like you. I studied textiles, not fine art, but it must be something in the Kemp genes. Dad can't even hold a paintbrush the right way up.'

'And now you design wedding dresses?' she asks. 'Tell me about how that happened.'

And so we wander slowly back towards the city, with me chatting away about my business. I ask her about her art, when she first found success, what she is working on now.

'And how long have you been using the gallery?' I ask.

'Oh, forever,' she says. 'They know me well in there, know how I work, make allowances for my . . .' She half smiles at me. 'For my antisocial tendencies.'

'That email you sent me was something else,' I say. 'I almost ran away right there and then. Actually, you're not that bad once you get to know you a bit.'

She taps me lightly on the shoulder. 'Oi!' she says. 'I have a reputation to maintain, you know. They are very good to me. Skyler's a good kid. She always makes room for my work and they put on an exhibition whenever I have enough new work to justify it.'

Her face changes. She looks wistful for a moment.

'Which is less and less often,' she adds. 'I don't work like I used to. I'm not driven in the same way. The anger that fuelled my earlier painting, well, it's kind of mellowing.'

She looks at me, suddenly earnest.

'Don't tell anyone, will you?'

I think she is serious for a moment and then she smiles at me and I know that she's joking.

'Seriously though, I am producing less work at the moment but that's because I'm working on something new and it's taking time to bed itself in properly. I don't want to go off in a new direction half-cocked. Can't go upsetting my public.'

The wind whips across the water and tunnels its way through my clothing. I shiver.

'I can't believe that I have to go home tomorrow,' I say.

'I can't believe you came all this way for just a couple of days,' Ursula replies.

'Well, I felt bad leaving Dad. I don't like to be gone too long in case something happens.'

'He's not home alone, though, right?'

'God no! That would be interesting. We have a nurse who helps me look after him. She's good with him, very calm, and they seem to get along okay, to the extent that he can get along with anyone these days.'

'And does your brother help out too?'

It is a reasonable question but I have the impression that she's fishing for information. Normally I would avoid answering such direct questions about our private life but she has been honest with me and I feel I should reciprocate.

'Michael and Dad don't really get along. They never have done. They just don't see eye to eye.'

'Too alike?' asks Ursula slyly.

'No. Not at all. Michael's not a bit like Dad.'

I think of Michael and Marianne and their beautiful home filled to the brim with their lively daughters. Then I think of how Michael has been with me over all this: how dismissive, unhelpful, unsupportive. Maybe Ursula is closer to the truth than I've ever admitted to myself.

'Well, maybe a bit,' I concede. 'There's always been an atmosphere between them, though, ever since we were kids.'

'Maybe he remembers more than he's letting on?' she says.

This has never occurred to me. I have always envied Michael and his memories, assuming, because I had none, that they were something that he could treasure. But perhaps that's wrong. I remember what he said when I asked him about Ursula. 'There's a lot you don't know, Cara.' What was he talking about? He had remembered Tilly. Did he know about the injunction? That might explain a lot.

'Michael left home as soon as he finished school,' I continue. 'He went off to university and he never came back. He lives in London, a lawyer in the city. He's married with twin girls. He's happy.'

Ursula looks at me and pulls a face.

'And you don't mind? That you have to do all the caring, I mean.'

I think about her question for a moment.

'No,' I answer. 'I don't mind. Someone has to do it. I'm single and I still live in the house. Well, to all intents and purposes it's my house now I suppose. I have my workroom and everything I need there. It's convenient. It works for us. I suppose it might be different if I met someone, but for now . . .'

An image of Simeon comes, unbidden, into my head. I bat it away.

'How about you?' I ask, happy to divert attention away from my life. 'Are you single?'

Ursula nods.

'There was someone once but it didn't work out. He was an artist too. Declan Murphy. You might have heard of him?' She looks at me expectantly but I shake my head. She shrugs. 'It was a long time ago now. I met him when I first came over here, we fell in love then we fell out of love. The usual story. He had fiery Celtic blood and a quick temper. You should have heard the fights! Boy! We could have sold tickets. Anyway, my art was starting to sell and so I moved on and never looked back.'

The story is too tidy, even for her. I can tell that she is holding something back. Something is sparking at the back of my mind but I cannot quite grasp it.

'And you've been on your own ever since?' I ask.

'Not on my own. I have a child.'

She's smirking at me. And then it clicks. Celtic blood. Red hair. Murphy.

'Skyler!' I virtually shout. 'So she's . . .'

'My daughter.'

Now she says it, I can see the similarities between the two women. Of course, I would not have seen it before. When I met Skyler, I had no idea what Ursula looked like.

'So that makes her . . .'

My mind struggles to work out the genealogy.

'Your cousin,' she says.

I can't quite take this in. I arrived here with next to no family and now I have an aunt and a cousin.

The sun disappears behind a cloud and the temperature drops rapidly. I pull my coat more tightly across my chest.

'My cousin,' I repeat. 'I have a cousin.' I can feel my throat tightening and I clench my jaw tight to stop myself crying. I blink hard.

'So,' Ursula continues, 'I thought for your last night in San Francisco you should both come over to my place for dinner. It won't be anything fancy,' she adds quickly. 'I'm no cook. I'll probably order in. Do you eat Chinese? The Chinese food here is incredible.'

I seem to have lost the power of speech. I just nod at her and hope that she can pick up from my face how grateful I am.

'Good God, it's Arctic in this wind,' she says, choosing to ignore the struggle that I am obviously having to maintain my composure. 'I'm sorry but I have to get back. I've got some stuff I have to deal with this afternoon. But here's my address.' She fishes in her bag for a notebook and quickly scribbles it down. 'Shall we say around six?'

I take the paper from her without looking at it and nod, accepting the instruction like a small child.

'Have you got plans for this afternoon? You could do worse than visit the Museum of Modern Art. If you keep your eyes open you might see something by yours truly,' she adds with a wink. 'Get yourself a postcard. I'll see you at six.'

Then she heads off, leaving me alone. Seagulls circle overhead in their endless pursuit of food. I really am cold now. I need to get moving again but instead I just stand there and watch the waves break on the shore.

CHAPTER FORTY-TWO

Annie, 1989

Annie sits next to the window and watches as the train pulls slowly into Rome. She's the only one awake so far and she relishes the peace while it lasts. Rome has been sprawling, neither city nor country, for miles. The tall apartment buildings springing up from either side of the tracks are scruffy and unloved, each smeared with ugly graffiti in greys and reds. It reminds her of Ursula's artwork from the old days: angry, defiant, refusing to toe the line. Do the people who live here mind that their homes are defaced with such discontentment? Do they even know?

Though it's not yet eight, the temperature in the compartment is beyond what Annie feels comfortable with. She takes big, gasping breaths to cleanse her lungs but the stale air is not fit for purpose. As the train raced through the night, she'd wanted to fling the windows open, but apparently that would have been too noisy, with all the stopping and starting at the various stations along the line. Annie barely got any sleep anyhow because of the heat. Chicken and egg. Leaning over their luggage, which is piled up on the floor, she reaches up to open the window now. The air that rushes in is not exactly refreshing but it is better than what is rushing out.

How long they will stay in Rome? They have been zigzagging across Europe on a Grand Tour like a pair of wealthy Victorians. She has liked everywhere that she has been shown so far, except St Petersburg, where the open aggression of the authorities coupled with the terrible food shrouded their visit with a shadowy hue. Tilly kept telling her how daring they were to be behind the Iron Curtain, that it was a privilege to be where so few tourists ever went, but Annie didn't get it and felt only relief when the train trundled back over the border into West Germany. Even though Germany was unfamiliar too, it felt more safely unfamiliar.

Now they are working their way down Italy. First Venice, then Pisa, then Florence and now Rome, flitting from place to place, following Tilly's plan. Annie tags along after her, ready to look delighted on cue when she is shown yet another building or painting. Rome is a treasure trove of ancient history and stolen wealth, according to Tilly. When Annie thinks of England, she has to bite her lip to maintain control. She tries not to think of it at all.

A guard walks down the corridor outside, shouting something in Italian that Annie doesn't understand but assumes is a suggestion that the travellers rouse themselves and get ready to disembark. The train goes on to Naples so there'll not be much time on the platform. She leans over and touches Tilly's arm gently. She stirs and then is awake almost at once. She scrunches up her eyes tightly, pings them back open and is then fully present. There are no in-betweens with Tilly, no grey areas.

'We're here,' whispers Annie, instinctively careful not to wake their fellow passengers, despite the guard's instruction.

Tilly shuffles in her seat, testing her back, her legs, to see how they have survived the journey. Rubbing at her thighs to bring some life back into them, she smiles at Annie.

'Wait until you see the Colosseum,' she says, eyes shining. 'You're going to love it. It's incredible. Everything here is incredible. Thousands of years of history just sitting there. Honestly, atmosphere radiates out of the walls. Can you imagine how many people have walked on the pavements?'

Annie cannot imagine. In fact, she has no idea what Tilly is talking about, but she's learned just to listen when she is being evangelical about something, as now. History seems to mean so much more to her than it does to Annie. Perhaps she listened harder at school? Tilly has seemed genuinely moved by some of the places that they have seen. Annie has tried to match her excitement but to her they are just buildings – and dilapidated buildings at that. It's nice to keep in touch with the past but do they really need to keep everything?

'The Romans are so blasé about what they have on their doorstep,' Tilly continues as she folds the sweater that she has been using as a blanket and slots it back into her rucksack. 'I mean, just take the Via dei Fori Imperiali.'

The Italian words roll off Tilly's tongue as if she were born pronouncing them.

'It runs right through the centre of Ancient Rome. You can virtually touch the Colosseum from a bus window. It's ridiculous. Can you imagine us having lorries running right next to Windsor Castle? Not that it's the same. I mean, Windsor has only been there five minutes next to the Colosseum.'

And then she is off again, dazzling Annie with what she knows.

The train comes to a juddering stop, which wakes the other woman in their compartment. She opens her eyes, takes in the sign for Rome on that platform and then closes them again. Tilly picks up her rucksack and steps over the woman's outstretched legs, rolling her eyes at the inconvenience. She slides open the compartment door and they step out into the hustle and bustle of the station, which seems to begin in the train's corridor. Travellers are pushing and shoving to get off, the guard is shouting and gesticulating wildly, and beyond, a tannoy calls out unrecognisable messages to all and sundry.

Annie drags her battered faux-leather suitcase out after Tilly, banging it down the steps and on to the platform. Tilly, whose smart rucksack presents her with none of the same logistical difficulties that Annie faces, does not notice. When they left England, Tilly promised to buy Annie a rucksack like hers. 'Can't have you looking like a gypsy,' she said, but the rucksack has never appeared and Annie doesn't like to ask. Tilly is paying for everything as it is. This doesn't seem to bother her, but it makes Annie feel uncomfortable and she is reluctant to draw more attention to it than necessary. Annie finds it easier to ignore the fact that, yet again, she is financially dependent on someone else.

Tilly sets off, striding purposefully towards the end of the platform, waving at fellow passengers and calling out '*Buon giorno*' as if they are all friends of hers. Tilly has friends the world over, or so it seems to Annie.

Annie struggles after her, using both hands to lug her heavy suitcase. Sweat patches are already forming on her back and they haven't even had breakfast yet.

'Do you think there might be a Left Luggage office?' she calls out after Tilly, who either does not or chooses not to hear.

Out on the street, Rome is going about its business noisily. Horns pap and Vespas buzz up and down like angry wasps. There is much shouting and waving of arms, and everywhere Annie looks there are people looking busy but doing little. Tilly steers them off the main road and they stop at a little café and buy a slice of pizza, which they eat as they walk. When they started on this adventure they ate inside the cafés, not in the street.

A raggedy bunch of small, nut-brown children starts to gather around them and Tilly brushes them away with a flick of her wrist. In Pisa, Annie caught a gypsy woman slipping her hand inside Tilly's handbag. She shouted at the woman in English and the woman screamed back in Italian but then left them alone to go and try her luck on another tourist. Annie was pleased that she had managed to avert disaster with her quick thinking but Tilly just shrugged, as if being pick-pocketed was the price one paid for foreign travel. She seems more cautious now, though, her confidence slightly dented.

It's so hot that Annie can barely breathe. Never having left England before, her only experience of real heat is the summer of 1976, but this is much hotter than she remembers that being. At least they have left the bags at the *pensione*. The thought of pushing through the crowds dragging her case behind her makes her feel faint.

'I'm taking you to the Trevi Fountain,' says Tilly, looking triumphant, and when Annie shows no sign of recognition, she frowns at her. 'You know. The film? *Three Coins in the Fountain?*'

Annie looks at her blankly. Tilly shakes her head and smiles fondly.

'Frank Sinatra? No? How did you spend your childhood, darling? Well, tradition says that we have to throw a coin in the fountain to make sure that we come back to Rome.'

Right now, Annie is not sure that she ever wants to come back here. It's dirty and smelly and far too hot but she won't tell Tilly that. She trails after her friend, who is striding down the street like she's on home turf. Then she sees a small shop cut into the wall. There are postcards displayed on rickety racks attached to its wooden shutters. She hesitates. Tilly will be cross but she doesn't care.

'Could I just have some money to buy a postcard and a stamp?' she asks. 'Please.'

Tilly sighs loudly.

'What? Again?' she asks, but she digs into her money belt, newly purchased after the near miss in Pisa, and pulls out a couple of 1,000 Lire notes. She waves them at Annie as if she is summoning a waitress in a strip joint.

Annie takes the money and makes her way across the narrow street to the shop. She runs a grubby finger up the rack, stopping at a painting that looks kind of familiar. In it, a naked man is almost touching fingers with an old man in a toga.

'Ah,' says Tilly coming up and standing behind her. '*The Creation of Adam*. I'll take you there tomorrow. We can't leave Rome without seeing the Sistine Chapel.'

Annie has seen inside enough churches to last her a lifetime and has no interest in another. Also, she's not sure that a postcard of an entirely naked man is appropriate. Her hand moves on and she chooses a picture of an ornate white building with naked statues in front of it. Does no one wear any clothes here?

'That's it,' breathes Tilly excitedly into her neck. 'That's the Trevi Fountain.'

Now that Annie looks a bit harder she can see a bit of water at the front. Not much of a fountain, though. She takes the card to the till and is served by a tiny and very wrinkled woman dressed entirely in black. Annie signals that she wants a stamp and the woman sells her one, which she sticks on to the postcard for safekeeping.

Back out in the street, Tilly links arms with Annie, pulls her into her and places a kiss gently on her cheek.

'Are you happy, darling?' she asks.

Annie hesitates for only a second but it's long enough. Tilly pulls away and scowls.

'Sometimes I wonder why you bothered coming. If you're having such a bloody miserable time then you can always go back, you know. I'm not stopping you.'

'I'm not,' says Annie. 'I'm having a great time. You know I am. It's just hard . . .'

She feels the tears, the lump in her throat, which she swallows back down. There's no point trying to explain how she feels to Tilly. She has tried before and got nowhere. She stuffs the postcard deep inside her bag so that Tilly won't catch a stray glimpse of it and start again. She takes a deep breath and smiles brightly.

'So: where's this fountain then?'

Tilly's anger is immediately appeased and she skips along next to Annie.

'Well, if memory serves . . .' she says and leads her along the street.

Annie follows obediently. Tilly is wrong, of course. She can't go back. Joe has seen to that. She can never go back.

CHAPTER FORTY-THREE

Cara, 2018

When I get back to the hotel, I check my phone. There is a message from Beth and I click on it urgently.

> Hi. Mrs Jackson here! (How weird does that look?) I'm back!!!
>
> Honeymoon was fab. Hotel to die for. Perfect beach. Delicious food etc etc . . . Feeling jealous yet?! But enough of me and my perfect life ;-) How was your Christmas and New Year? Any news? Can't wait to see you. How are you fixed for a catch up? B xxx

'Any news?' I don't really know where to start. I type out a quick reply.

> Hi. Glad you had a great time. Really missed you. Am in San Francisco! Long story. Back day after tomorrow. Will tell all then. Bit of romance too! It's all happening. Can't wait to see you. C xxx

I smile to myself as I picture Beth reading my message and trying to work out what has been going on while she's been away. Not knowing will kill her.

I scroll down the rest of the new messages. Nestled in amongst the others is one that makes my heart lurch. Simeon. My finger hovers momentarily over the button before I open it but then I click.

Cara Beloved. Just wondering how it's working out with the new aunt. Maybe you can tell me all over a drink or maybe dinner? S.

He is persistent, I'll give him that. For a moment, I let him linger in my mind's eye but then I close him down. There's no free space in my head right now and anyway I know that I'm no good for him. A lovely bloke like Simeon deserves so much more than I can give. I should just ignore him and let whatever we have going on fizzle out. History shows that my relationships never turn out well. I'm not great at letting people close and, sooner or later, they always discover the hole where my heart should be. It'll be better for everyone if I just walk away before either of us gets hurt. A little pain now is better than being ripped apart when it all goes wrong later.

Reluctantly, I tap out a short reply promising to get in touch when I get home and wonder if he can read the goodbye between the lines.

A little later, when my taxi pulls up outside Ursula's place, I have buried any thoughts of Simeon again. Ursula's house is industrial-looking, boxy and flat-roofed with huge square windows. It's painted an uncompromising gunmetal grey, or that's how it looks in the semi-darkness. I knock on the door, realising, just too late, that I should have brought a bottle of wine or some flowers with me. I hear the sound of someone clattering down metal stairs inside, then the door flies open and there stands Skyler. Before she has even invited me in, she throws her arms around my neck and squeezes hard.

'Cara!' she screeches into my hair. 'We're cousins! Can you believe it? It's going to be great! We're going to be, like, best friends. I just know we are.'

After what feels like an age, she finally releases me.

'Come in, come in,' she says.

The house seems to be upside down, with the living rooms upstairs – to catch the views, I presume. Skyler leads the way up the steel staircase and I follow, my footsteps ringing out in the echoing space. There are paintings hanging on the walls but I don't see any of Ursula's characteristic red. These are also abstracts but softer and brighter with no dark corners or violent slashes of colour. I wonder if this is the new work she was talking about. The air smells faintly of turps.

At the landing, Skyler shows me into a lounge. It is a double-height room with a huge window that takes up the whole of one wall and very little furniture, just a couple of sofas and a chrome coffee table. Ursula is reclining on one of the sofas, glass of wine in hand. She nods at me as I enter but makes no effort to stand. Skyler, slightly breathless from the speed at which she took the stairs, buzzes around near me, offering to take my coat, get me a drink, show me the apartment.

'For God's sake, Skyler,' Ursula says. 'Will you calm down. You're like a puppy. Give Cara some space. Go get her a drink. Come in, Cara. Sit down.'

She doesn't pull her legs in to make space for me so I opt for the other sofa and perch on the edge. There's not much sign of the warmth generated by our meeting this morning and all of a sudden I feel my guard rising, ready to protect myself should the need arise again.

I can hear Skyler opening a bottle in the kitchen. Ursula does not speak, just watches me with narrowed eyes, and it is a relief when Skyler comes bustling back in with a tray stacked high with bottles, glasses and a bowl of pistachios.

Imogen Clark

'I didn't know what you'd like so I brought red and white but we have beer or soda as well. Just say the word. And I've brought us some snacks. Oh, you don't have a nut allergy, do you? I can just as easily take them away.'

I shake my head and smile at Skyler. 'No. No allergies. White wine would be lovely, thank you.'

'I just adore your British accent,' she says as she pours a large glass for each of us. 'You sound so regal. Does everyone in Britain sound like you?'

'Don't be so ridiculous, Skyler,' says Ursula. Her voice is impatient but not angry. 'And anyway, you should be used to British accents.'

'Oh, yours doesn't count, Mom,' says Skyler dismissively. 'I just knew there was something about you,' she continues, ignoring her mother and addressing me. 'The minute you walked into the gallery, I could just tell. I didn't know that we were cousins, of course,' she adds. 'Not straightaway. But I just felt like there was something between us, some kind of bond.'

'Oh, sweet Jesus,' says Ursula. 'Will you shut up!'

But I ignore Ursula too.

'I know what you mean,' I say. 'I felt that we would be friends, well, given half a chance.'

'See!' says Skyler, looking at her mother triumphantly. 'Cara felt it too. We're not all miserable, antisocial hermits like you, Mom.'

Ursula just waves a dismissive hand at Skyler. 'You think whatever pleases you,' she says with a roll of her eyes, but I think I see the shadow of a smile flit across her lips.

'And she . . .' Skyler nods at her mother. 'She banned me from telling you who I was even though I knew from the moment you said she was your aunt.'

I look at Ursula quizzically. 'Why? Were you ashamed of me?'

'No,' she replies, but so slowly that I am not convinced that that was not the reason. 'It was more that I needed to get things straight in my head before we all started playing happy families. You've met Skyler. You must understand what I'm saying. I'd never have heard the last of it.'

I want to ask what would be wrong with that, with talking about me and where I came from, but already I can feel that there is no point. From the little I've learned about Ursula so far, I know that she'll do things in her own time, in her own way.

And so the evening passes. We order in Chinese food and chat about nothing important but it feels good, like an easy evening spent with old friends. Around midnight, I cannot stifle my yawns anymore. I look at my watch.

'I ought to go,' I say. 'I can barely stay awake.'

'Don't bother with sleep,' says Skyler. 'You can sleep on the plane.'

But Ursula is nodding her head.

'Let her go. She'll be back, won't you, Cara?'

'I hope so,' I reply. 'And of course you two are welcome in England any time you want to come.'

I stand up and from nowhere I feel like I am going to cry. I need to hold that back so I focus on practicalities.

'Can we call me a taxi?'

'I'll do it,' says Skyler and disappears, leaving me alone with Ursula. She eyes me quizzically and I realise that she doesn't miss much.

'You okay?' she asks.

I nod.

'I'm glad you came,' she says.

'Me too.'

As I take the short ride back to the hotel, I run over the last three days in my head. I have an aunt and a cousin, which is lovely, but more importantly I have a greater sense of who I am. I feel more grounded somehow. This part feels nice but the rest of what I have learned is more difficult to process. It's obvious now that this whole sorry mess can be dropped firmly at Dad's door. My growing up without a mother is entirely his doing and on top of that, because he told me that she was dead, I've also wasted the years since I became an adult. I could have hunted for her so much earlier but his lies have stolen that chance from me.

And what about Michael? How much of all this did he already know? I have always assumed that he ran at the first chance he got because he couldn't get along with Dad, but what if there was more to it than that?

I have to speak to Michael and suddenly this becomes the most compelling issue in my confused world. I can't ring him now – he'll be asleep – but I have to talk to him as soon as possible. Face to face.

When I get back to the hotel, any suggestion of tiredness has left me. I get on to my laptop and change my flight so that I land at Heathrow rather than Manchester. Then I email Mrs P to tell her that I will be a few hours later than originally planned and Michael to tell him to meet me when I get to London. I ponder for a moment over where to suggest. It needs to be somewhere central, easy for him to get to from his office but where we can talk without having a row, and if we can keep walking as we talk then there's less chance of him walking out on me.

I choose Tate Modern.

CHAPTER FORTY-FOUR

The journey back to the UK is straightforward but long. I try to sleep on the plane, knowing that I will need as much energy as I can muster for the day ahead, but my brain will not quieten. The air stewards turn down the lights and hand out fleece blankets and tiny pillows but I stare out of the little oval porthole at the blackness of the night sky. Why has this all come out now, when my father is too ill to explain himself? I could have stumbled across the postcards at any time. The key to unlocking these awful secrets has been sitting in the attic – but it never occurred to me to look because I didn't know there was a secret to find. My life was just my life. Small, quiet, as it had always been. How could I have known that it was based on lies?

And now, when my head is exploding with questions, I have nowhere to turn. Dad's lies, his twisted reasoning, any doubts or regrets that he might have had are all lost in the chaos of his shrinking mind. I will never know what he thought and that is something that I'm going to have to learn to come to terms with, somehow.

As we fly towards the dawn, the sky slips silently from velvety ink, through violet, to a startling crimson. The beauty of a sunrise never fails to lift me. Although it happens every day, and has happened every day since the dawn of time, I never tire of watching the colours seep into one another. It soothes my jagged mind. For a few moments, I let myself think of Simeon. Despite the mixed messages that he must have been getting from me, he keeps coming back. That must mean that he likes me a little bit. Am I being over-cautious? Maybe I should just relax into the whole thing and let it take me where it wants to go? With the disaster that the rest of my life is becoming, would it really be so bad if I just had a little corner of something good to retreat into? I decide that, if he gets in touch again, I will let myself enjoy whatever it is that we have without guilt or fear. As I watch the sunrise, I feel a tingle of excitement deep inside me, in spite of everything else.

Tate Modern stands on the edge of the Thames, majestic, its former life forgotten. My world is all about reinvention today.

I see Michael before he sees me. He strides, his head held high, his coat tails flying out behind. He looks so much like our father did. As he approaches, I see that he is talking into his phone, though when he sees me he ends the call abruptly. I thought I was angry with him for whatever his part is in this mess, but now that he is standing in front of me I can't seem to retrieve that fury to use against him. He's still my big brother, my protector, my port in a storm.

'Cara,' he snaps, starting to talk before he has reached me. 'What is this all about? I'm incredibly busy. I can't just drop everything to meet you. Well, I can, as it turns out, but it better be important.'

'Did you know?' I say without any preliminaries. 'Did you know that not only is Mum not dead but that Dad took out an injunction to prevent her from seeing us?'

I see instantly from his face that he does.

'Why didn't you tell me?'

Michael seems to age twenty years in five seconds. The frown lines in his forehead deepen as his skin blanches and then blushes. I can see tears glistening in the corners of his eyes but not a drop escapes on to his cheek. He clenches his jaw, takes a deep breath and says, as I knew he would, 'Let's walk.'

We turn into the gallery and walk down the central concourse. The huge, grey space of the building towers above us, with echoing footsteps and voices blending together to make a low rumble of dull sound. It feels almost like a cathedral. The air is still and I half expect to see people with their heads bowed in prayer. Halfway down the slope Michael stops abruptly and turns to face me.

'It's not like you think,' he says. 'I don't remember much and what I know I've pieced together myself over the years. Dad would never talk about it. The row, the last row, the one before I left for uni. That's what that was about.'

'What did you know?' I ask, impatient to hear it all now.

'Like I said before, I can remember the woman, Mum's friend.'

'Tilly?' I say.

He nods.

'I didn't like her. She was never interested in us. If you tried to talk to her or show her something you'd made, she'd just dismiss it as rubbish. It used to annoy me, the way she brushed you off, even though you were just a baby.'

So he was protecting me, even then, aware of how I felt when I was only two. My heart swells.

'But Mum liked her,' he continues. 'Mum didn't see her the way I did. Tilly became the centre of her world – more so than us, it felt like. She was like the cuckoo in the nest, pushing us away. And she was always there. To start with, she'd disappear before Dad got home, but gradually it felt like she never left. Mum and Dad argued about her a lot. I was in bed but I could hear them shouting. I didn't understand but I could see why Dad didn't like her. I was kind of on his side.'

Michael sets off again, striding down the slope, and I scamper after him like a little girl. 'Then one night there was an almighty row. Mum was screaming at Dad but I couldn't hear what she said. There was a lot of door slamming. I snuck out of bed and sat on the stairs. There was a suitcase in the hall. I thought we were going on holiday.' He takes a deep breath, running his hand through his greying hair. 'I couldn't work out how Mum had packed stuff for all four of us in one bag,' he says, shaking his head. 'Then Tilly arrived and Mum left with her and that was it. I never saw her again.'

Michael looks defeated and I can see that maintaining his composure is taking every ounce of strength that he has. I don't care. I need to know it all.

'Didn't she say goodbye or anything?' I ask. 'She just left?'

'She didn't realise she wasn't coming back. That's what I think anyway. They rowed. She left with Tilly and she assumed that she'd be back the next day to get us. But Dad changed the locks and went to the lawyers and that was that. Well, I didn't understand that at the time, but I pieced it all together later.'

'But no access at all? How could that be? She was our mother, for God's sake.'

'I'm not sure that that was what Dad was aiming for, but he just got lucky. The judge allocated to the case was a real "hang 'em, flog 'em" sort. He thought that lesbians were the spawn of the devil and absolutely could not be trusted with the care of delicate little minds. I've read the court papers: I looked them up in the National Archives. Dad couldn't have had a more sympathetic hearing if he'd designed the judge himself and built him out of Plasticine.'

I can't believe what I'm hearing. Michael has read the court papers? I have only just found out that there was a case and he's read the bloody papers! I can't unpick this now, though. We have to keep moving forward.

'Ursula said that Mum had no money to fight the court case and that Tilly refused to bankroll her,' I say.

'That makes sense. Tilly was a selfish cow. I think she was just having fun. I don't think it crossed her mind how much damage she was doing to us. You were only two, Cara. You had no idea what had happened. All you knew what that your Mummy wasn't there anymore. You cried for weeks and weeks. We moved to Yorkshire and you still cried. Dad couldn't stand it. That's when he started retreating to his study. He didn't even get any help. I suppose he was worried that someone might somehow find out the truth and spoil his widower cover story. So I looked after you, to the extent that I could, and I held you when you cried. And, eventually, you stopped.'

I can't get my breath. How could Dad have done this to us? A mother forms the entire world of a two-year-old child. If she disappeared overnight then what damage would that do to you? And what if you were the big brother trying to make things right for his little sister? Oh my God, poor Michael. A tidal wave of pure hatred for my father washes over me. How could he put us both through that?

Then something else occurs to me.

'So you knew she wasn't dead. You've always known.'

He nods and I see in his eyes how great a burden this has been on him. They are imploring me to understand.

'But why didn't you tell me?'

'I couldn't,' he says, his voice catching. 'You'd been hurt so badly already but you'd made something of your life, despite everything. I was trying to protect you from any more harm, Ca. You'd been damaged enough.'

His eyes drop to my hand. I grasp it with my good hand, rubbing my fingers across the puckered skin.

'What do you mean?'

Michael takes another deep breath and I can see how much it is costing him to tell me everything. He lets the breath out and his body shudders.

'It was about six months after Mum had gone. Dad was in the garden in Ilkley. He was having a bonfire in an old steel bin, burning bits of paper, I don't know. You had gone to bed but you wanted a drink so you'd climbed out of your cot and wandered downstairs. You must have spotted Dad in the garden and gone out to see him. I remember you were wearing a little pink nightdress. I could see the outline of your bedtime nappy. You had nothing on your feet.'

He swallows hard, determined to keep going.

'Dad didn't hear you coming. He was too intent on putting things into the fire. You arrived just as he threw Mum's sketchbook into the flames. She was always drawing. Do you remember that, how she drew stuff? You put your hand into the fire to save it . . .'

Michael can't hold it back any longer. His shoulders start to shake and his breath comes in ragged sobs.

'I couldn't stop you,' he says. 'I was too late.'

He throws his arms around me and buries his head into my shoulder. People turn to stare at us as his whole body heaves with the release of decades of buried emotion. I just hold him as tightly as I can and let it flood out of him. I can't be angry with him, with Mum, with Dad, even. They each, in their own twisted way, thought they were doing the right thing. Everyone has been trying to protect me. I was the baby and each of them was trying to keep me safe.

'It's all right,' I whisper into Michael's hair. 'I understand. It wasn't your fault. None of it was your fault. I don't blame you. How could I?'

He lifts his head from my shoulder and looks deep into my eyes. I can't remember the last time we were this close.

'Do you mean it?' he asks, his eyes pleading, desperate. He needs forgiveness. He has carried this with him since we were children. All the anger I felt on the plane has evaporated. So much about him – his distance, his running to London, his lack of involvement with Dad, with me – suddenly it all makes sense. For the first time, I am finally grateful that I was so young. For all those years, I thought that Michael was the lucky one because he had been old enough to remember. I didn't realise that he has spent his whole life trying to forget.

'Of course I mean it,' I say.

'What will you do now?' he asks.

Honestly, I have no idea. I have to get home and think through everything that I have learned over the last few days. At the moment I cannot see further than that.

'Nothing,' I say. 'Nothing.'

I leave him at Blackfriars Station and make my way up to King's Cross, where I catch a train back home. I am exhausted from lack of sleep and wrung out by everything that I have learned over the last few days. Now all I want is to get home.

CHAPTER FORTY-FIVE

I can tell as soon as I approach the house that something is wrong. It's late and I would expect the street to be quiet anyway, but somehow, like some eerie premonition, I know that all is not well at home.

I'm all fingers and thumbs as I try to find my purse and pay the taxi driver, scrabbling about for some English change, finding only quarters. As he pulls away, I hunt for my house key, which I put somewhere safe but now can't lay my hands on. It seems like I have been gone forever, though it's been just a few days. This is a wholly different Cara Ferensby returning home.

Finally, I find the key and let myself in. Silence sits on the house as heavy as a shroud but then I hear the soft sounds of someone moving about upstairs, gently, calmly. I call out as quietly as I can while still hoping to be heard.

'Mrs P. Is that you? I'm back. Is everything okay?'

Mrs P appears at the top of the stairs. She is fully dressed in her uniform, a white, plastic apron tied neatly at her waist.

'Hello, Cara,' she says. 'Have you had a good trip?'

'Yes,' I reply, abruptly dismissing her question. 'What's the matter? Is something wrong with Dad?'

'I'm afraid he's not very well,' she says baldly and then starts down the stairs towards me but I'm already bounding up to meet her.

'We've had the doctor in. They think it's pneumonia. It's quite common, given his other conditions.'

I squeeze past her and run straight to Dad's room. She calls after me.

'I didn't want to worry you, seeing as you couldn't have got back any sooner.'

But I could have been back sooner. If I hadn't changed my flight, if I hadn't been to see Michael . . .

It's dark in Dad's room with just the bedside light casting a glow over the top half of his bed. The air is very still and it's stuffy, the sharp smell of disinfectant masking anything else. An open book and a pair of reading glasses lie on the chair by the bed. Mrs P must have been keeping watch. A drip stands sentinel over him too, the tubes snaking across his chest. I approach the bed with my heart in my mouth, as if something might jump out at me.

Dad is lying with his eyes closed but I can't tell if he's asleep or not. His breathing is laboured and every third breath or so just doesn't come at all. He seems to have shrunk in the four days I've been away. He looks no bigger than a child under the crisp, white sheet and his skin, translucent in the half-light, is milky pale. He coughs but it's a weary sound, as if even this is too much for him.

I look at Mrs P desperately, hoping for some kind of comfort. She comes and places an arm gently around my shoulders.

'How long has he been like this?'

'He started with it yesterday. He was right as rain up until then. I called the doctor out in the evening and she said that your father could stay here as I was on hand to nurse him. The antibiotics should start to kick in soon.'

I look at Dad. He is so diminished that it's hard to see the man I know in this aged, broken shell. 'Do you think he should be in hospital?' I ask quietly.

Mrs P straightens an invisible crease in his covers. 'That's up to you, Cara, but I don't think they will do anything that I'm not doing here and it's far less stressful to leave him be than move him. I think we just need to keep him comfortable and see how he is when it gets light. We can always call an ambulance if he takes a turn for the worse.'

Suddenly I feel like a child. I need someone to tell me what to do for the best so that I don't have to make any decisions myself.

'Do you think . . . this might be it?' I ask her. I feel unprepared. Of course, I knew he would die but it hadn't occurred to me that it would happen so soon. I look at Mrs P, waiting for her professional opinion. I don't know what I want her to say.

'Oh, we're not there yet,' she says in a tone that reminds me of matrons or Girl Guide leaders. 'Let's see how he goes.'

I sit myself down by the bed but then I shoot back up again.

'My case. I left it in the street.'

'I'll go and fetch it,' she says calmly. 'And do you think you should ring Michael?'

This hadn't even crossed my mind.

'Of course. What time is it?'

'It's half past one. Maybe you should wait until morning.'

'No. I'll ring now. What shall I say?'

Mrs P looks at me. She doesn't speak but what she's saying to me is clear. Why wake your brother now, when there's no news?

'No. I'll ring when it gets light,' I say. 'That'll be best. Dad will probably be a bit better when he wakes up and then there'll be no need to worry Michael.'

In light of what I've learned over the last few days, part of me thinks that Michael won't even care, but that's not the point. I can't unilaterally decide not to tell him but I will wait until morning. Anyway, a middle-of-the-night phone call might wake the twins and this might be hard enough without that on top.

Mrs P leaves me and I hear her tripping lightly down the stairs, opening and closing the front door and putting my bag down in the hall. I lean forward and stroke Dad's face. His eyes flicker, the eyelids paper-thin. Then they open and he smiles at me, a proper smile like he really knows who I am. This weak and broken man has caused so much hurt to so many people but now, when I touch his hollowed cheek, I find it hard to feel anger. The last few days of revelation cannot displace a lifetime of love because he has loved me, in his own, misguided way. All the lies were told to protect me and no matter how ill-judged his actions were, he believed that he was doing the right thing. Michael has taken one view but I don't have to share it. I'm not sure I will ever totally forgive or even understand what he did, but that man is gone. The old man lying in this bed is someone else entirely.

He opens his mouth but no words come and even the effort of that small movement seems too much for him.

'Don't talk, Dad,' I say. 'You need to save your strength. And anyway, I'm quite enjoying the peace and quiet.' I squeeze his hand and hope that he can't see the tears brimming in my eyes.

'Good girl,' he says, so quietly that I wouldn't catch his words if I couldn't see his mouth moving. 'Good girl.'

'You get some rest,' I say, and his eyes close again.

I'm so tired. I lean forward and rest my face on the sheets next to Dad's fragile hand. I can feel his ratchety breathing and I follow it with my own.

I wake up to Mrs P gently touching my arm. For a moment, I'm confused and then I remember where I am and why.

'I must have dropped off. What time is it?'

'It's almost five,' she says.

There is the briefest of pauses and then she says, 'I'm so sorry, Cara, but your father has gone.'

It takes a moment for her words to sink in.

'It was very peaceful,' she continues. 'He just passed away in his sleep.'

I look at Dad. For a moment, in the half-light, he looks just as he did before; but when I look more carefully, he is completely still. His face is already a mask. When I touch his cheek, it is cool.

'But I only closed my eyes for a moment. He can't be gone. He was fine. He spoke to me.'

There is so much to say and yet nothing. I wanted to tell Dad everything that I learned from Ursula and Michael, even though I knew he wouldn't be able to respond or even understand, but I'm too late.

'But he can't be gone,' I say again, though I can see the truth for myself.

Mrs P takes my elbow and begins to lead me away but I resist her. I don't even know why. It just feels wrong to leave Dad here by himself when he needs me.

'Come on, Cara,' she says gently. 'I need to ring for an ambulance and a doctor to register the death. And you should perhaps call Michael?'

Michael. He knows nothing. I didn't even warn him that there was a chance Dad might die and now it's too late. As if she can hear my thoughts, Mrs P adds, 'He could never have made it all the way from London in time. It was all so very quick.'

'Yes,' I say, searching out every crumb of comfort from her words. 'It was very quick. We had no idea, did we?'

I look to her, desperate for her to confirm my words and assuage this unidentified feeling that I fear is quickly becoming guilt.

'Of course not,' she says.

We both know this sentiment is not true but I grasp at it like a drowning man flails at a passing stick. I let her lead me from the room. Downstairs I pick up the phone and call my brother. For some reason that I don't quite understand, I feel that I should use a landline, as if that will make a real connection between us. I sit on the bottom step and tap in his number. Marianne answers almost at once.

'Hello?' she says, her voice made anxious by receiving a call so early in the morning.

'Marianne. It's Cara,' I say and in those three words the deed is done.

'Oh,' she says quietly.

'Is Michael there?'

'Yes,' she says. 'You've just caught him. Hang on.' She puts the receiver down and I hear her go off in search of Michael. I can't hear what she says to him but when the receiver is lifted up again, it is my brother's voice that speaks.

'Cara?' he says.

'Dad's gone,' I say.

The sentence is so resounding with euphemism that I for a moment I think he might not have fully grasped my meaning and that I'll have to be more explicit. However, when he speaks, I know that he has understood.

'When?'

'Just now. He was asleep and then . . .'

'What was it?'

'Pneumonia,' I say.

'Are you okay?'

I nod and I know that he has understood even though he can't see me.

'Do you need me to do anything?' he asks.

'I don't know. Mrs P is here. She knows what to do.'

'All right,' he says gently. 'Well, we can speak later in the day when you know more about the arrangements. I'll come up for the funeral. Do you need me there before then?'

Do I need him? Yes, of course I do. I need him to whisper to me that it will all be all right like he used to when we were children. I need him to hold me and tell me jokes until the tears dry up. I need him to reassure me that we are the only two people in the whole world who matter and that we don't care about anyone else. Except that isn't true anymore. He has Marianne and the girls. In fact, I am the only person in the whole wide world.

'No,' I reply. 'I'll be fine. I'll ring you later. I'm sorry, Michael,' I add.

'There's no need, Ca,' he says quietly. 'We'll speak later.'

Then he puts the receiver down and I am on my own.

CHAPTER FORTY-SIX

Time must be making its steady progress round the big, white clock in the kitchen but I don't notice. I make tea and then let it go cold on the kitchen table in front of me. I suppose it must be shock, this numbness, but shock at which part of the story I'm not sure. Mrs P makes some calls, dealing quietly and efficiently with all the practical matters that I should be attending to but can't face. People come to the house and eventually Dad leaves it. I do nothing. I just sit here, unable to balance the grief I feel for the passing of my only parent with the anger I feel about him depriving me of the other one. It hurts too much to examine which pain is the greater so I lock it all away and just breathe, slowly. In and out.

After what would have been lunch, if such things mattered, the doorbell rings again. I don't get up but I hear Mrs P go to answer it. There are hushed voices in the hall and a moment later Beth's tanned face appears around the door.

'Cara, sweetie,' she says quietly. 'I came as fast as I could.'

To begin with, it feels like the most natural thing in the world that Beth has arrived, but then my muddled brain realises that I haven't told her what's happened. I haven't told anyone except Michael.

'How . . . ?' I ask.

'Mrs P,' she explains. 'She rang me. I'm so sorry, Ca.'

Beth, who held my ruined hand tight when girls at school were cruel, who was there to examine, in microscopic detail, our first-ever party, who has always stuck by me no matter what happened to put her off, rushes across the room, throws her arms around my neck and holds me. That is all it takes to summon the tears that until this point have been missing. I feel my face crumple and a single sob escapes, like a lookout for an approaching army.

She sits down next to me, puts her arm across my shoulders and I lean into her. She smells clean and fresh, like washing on a line in spring. Her arms tighten around me, mother, sister and best friend all rolled into one person.

'There, there,' she says as she rubs my back. 'You let it all out.'

And I do.

Later, when my chest aches, my eyes are stinging and dry and I have no more tears to release, Beth makes more tea and we take it into the lounge for a change of scene.

'So, tell me about your honeymoon,' I say.

Beth half-smiles, a little ashamed at her own pleasure in the face of my pain. 'It was lovely,' she says quietly. 'The hotel was perfect and the beach was beautiful. I could go and live on a tropical beach, I really think I could. Imagine being somewhere where you don't have to think about the weather, where you can guarantee it'll be warm and sunny every day.'

'You'd get bored,' I say. 'That endless blue? I bet you'd be longing for a leaden sky before you ran out of knickers. And you'd hate a flat horizon.'

'I suppose I might miss the moor,' she says, and we both sit quietly for a moment, imagining how flawed a perfect life really is.

I should tell her about Simeon now but something holds me back. Partly it's because I don't have the strength for her excitement, but I'm also still not entirely sure where Simeon and I stand. I haven't been in touch with him since I got back. There's barely been time for one thing, given everything that's happened. That's not it, though. I've held off because, having decided on the plane that I don't want it to end, I am scared that Simeon might have changed his mind about me. As long as we haven't spoken, I can pretend to myself that he is still keen. Guiltily, I keep my news to myself.

Then, apropos of nothing, Beth says, 'I'm not sure that I want to sell the cottage.'

This comes so wide from the left field that I can't make any connection with the conversation we were having and Simeon slips quietly from my mind. My confusion must be showing on my face.

'Now that I'm married,' she clarifies. 'Greg says I should sell the cottage so that we can invest the money for the future, but I'm not sure I want to.'

'Well, it's your cottage,' I reason. 'Surely you can do what you like with it?'

'You'd think so, wouldn't you?'

Her words are barbed, their spikes poking out clearly enough for me to touch.

'What's this?' I say. 'Trouble in paradise?'

'No,' she says on an out breath so that even the word sounds like an effort to pronounce.

I cock my head to one side and look at her, eyebrows raised.

'It's just that . . .'

I wait. There's no point pushing her. She'll get there in her own good time.

'Well,' she continues. 'He can be quite controlling, you know?'

Really?! I think, but I keep my mouth firmly shut. For Beth to be criticising Greg is rare enough let alone to be doing it now, when they've been married for less than a month. I nod sympathetically.

'Don't get me wrong,' she continues. 'Sometimes it's lovely. He can sweep into a room and take control and I don't have to think about anything at all. Greg just makes things happen around him. It's quite impressive, actually. It's like a kind of presence that he has, an aura.' That's not what I would call it but I hold my tongue and let her continue to explain. 'But, well, my cottage is mine. I worked really hard to save for the deposit and cover the mortgage on my own. Well, you know I did.'

'Of course you did,' I agree.

'And I know it's nothing to him, with his surgeon's salary and what have you, but it's a lot to me. I don't think I'm ready to let it go. Not yet.'

'And have you told him how you feel?'

She holds her head high, defiant. 'He says I'm being ridiculous. He says the cottage will soon become a liability because it needs so much work doing on it and that we should sell it to a developer now and liquidise the asset.'

I can hear Greg speaking through her. I can't believe that the words 'liquidise the asset' have ever come from Beth's lips before. 'So, what are you going to do?' I ask.

Beth looks at me and raises an eyebrow. There is a sparkle in her eyes that I've missed these last few weeks. I welcome it like an old friend.

'You're not going to do what he says, are you?' I say with a wry smile. I feel like we are co-conspirators in some devilish plot, just like in the old days before Greg, before all of this.

'No,' she says decisively. 'I don't think I am. It's my cottage. Just because we got married doesn't mean I have to agree with everything he says. Hanging on to the cottage is a sound business decision too. It's an asset with an appreciating value. And I can rent it out, cover the mortgage.'

'Precisely,' I say. And you'll still have somewhere to run to if it all goes pear-shaped, I think, but I don't say that out loud either.

'Anyway,' says Beth, leaning forward and looking straight into my eyes, her head cocked to one side, her brows knitted. 'Less of me. How are you? I really am sorry about your Dad.'

In the few minutes that have passed since she arrived, I've almost forgotten that Dad has gone. Now that she says it out loud, it sounds wrong to me, like something someone might say for dramatic effect. 'I can't really take it in,' I manage.

'Of course you can't. It's not like it was expected, well not yet anyway. It's bound to have come as a shock. Mrs P said it was pneumonia?'

'That's what the doctors said. I should have been here.' It's not until I hear myself say it out loud that I know that this is how I'm feeling. I went away and abandoned him while I chased halfway round the planet after something that I might very well have been better leaving well alone, and look what has happened. My world has changed beyond recognition and my father is dead.

Beth is having none of it. 'You're being silly,' she says gently.

I can feel the burning heat of tears welling up in my eyes again.

'This could have happened at any time. He wasn't well, Cara. He hadn't been well for a long time. And he would have caught pneumonia whether you had been here or not. You can't blame yourself. Apart from anything else, I won't let you.'

I know she's right but that doesn't make the guilt any less sharp.

'Is he . . . ?' She inclines her head towards the ceiling. 'Is he still here?'

She looks so serious that it makes me laugh. The sound is wrong in this melancholy house and that makes me laugh again.

'No. They've taken him away. He wouldn't be very impressed to hear me laughing.'

I mean so soon after his demise but Beth says, 'No. He never did like us to have too much fun.' Her hand shoots to her mouth and her eyes grow wide. 'God, I'm so sorry. He's not been dead two minutes and here I am speaking ill of him.'

She's right, though. We did use to have to be quiet while we played for fear of disturbing him and bringing his wrath down on our heads.

'Do you remember that time he locked us out because he said he couldn't hear himself think over our shouting?' I ask.

'Yes,' says Beth, nodding enthusiastically. 'It was freezing and chucking it down. My mum was furious when I got home. I was totally soaked through and blue.'

'Was she? I didn't know that.'

'Yes. It's always stuck in my memory because she was so angry about it. She said that she didn't know what went on in this house but that your dad needed to get his priorities sorted. No!' she adds with a kind of gasp. 'I've done it again. I'm so sorry. What my mum thought twenty years ago is neither here nor there.'

'It doesn't matter,' I say. 'It was probably true.'

I'm interested in what Beth's mum said about Dad. I've never really had an alternative perspective on his parenting and I don't have anything to compare it with.

'What else did she say?'

Beth frowns. It's obvious that she's trying to decide what she should tell me and what she should hold back. 'Well,' she starts doubtfully. 'I think she just thought that he was doing his best in difficult circumstances.' Her gaze leaves my eyes and drops to the table between us. 'But that sometimes you and Michael were a little bit neglected.'

She looks at back up me earnestly, her teeth pushing into her bottom lip as she waits to see if she has overstepped the mark.

'I think that's fair comment,' I say and I see relief wash over her face. 'He wasn't exactly your average, hands-on father. He could be a difficult bugger and he made no allowances for visitors. At least he was consistent. What you saw was what you got.'

I suppose, when I think about it now, from an adult's perspective, that perhaps Dad just wasn't very good with kids. He'd found himself a single parent overnight and had to learn how to deal with two small children on his own with no support. And there was the shock and humiliation of my mother walking out with Tilly. Maybe it's not that surprising that he got angry with us. Mum probably would have done too if she'd been on her own. It was all bluster, though. He never really hurt us. Maybe he was just doing his best and it was just that his best wasn't that great.

'He did get cross with us, though, didn't he?' Beth says, her tongued loosened a little by my reaction to her criticism. 'I was scared stiff of him.'

'Were you?' I ask, but of course I already knew that. It was one of the reasons that there were so few visitors to the house. Once our friends encountered Dad on a bad day they were very reluctant to come back again. There was no friendly welcome chez Ferensby.

'I think I'd forgotten what he used to be like,' I muse. 'For so long he's been this pliant, confused shadow of how he was that that version of him has kind of replaced the original in my mind. Thinking about how he's been since he got ill, it's hard to imagine that he was ever that scary.'

'He was, though,' says Beth quietly. 'Look,' she continues. 'Tell me if you think this is a really stupid idea, but shall we go out for dinner tonight, just the two of us, so we can have a proper catch-up?'

'I'm absolutely shot,' I say, shaking my head.

She looks worried again and is on the verge of apologising for her suggestion. Quickly I rethink. What else have I got to do? Sit here on my own and cry? I cut across her apology.

'But I suppose if I went to bed this afternoon, I might get a bit of sleep. Yes. I think that would be exactly what I need, Beth. Thank you.'

'I'll book us a table,' she says. 'Eight o'clock?'

I nod, stifling a yawn. 'I'm looking forward to it already.'

I show Beth out and when I turn round, Mrs P is standing in the hall, her coat on, her suitcase in her hand. I wonder where she's going and then I remember that, with Dad gone, there's no reason for her to hang around.

'I'll be getting off then, Cara,' she says.

I don't know what to say. The fact that she has to leave hits me like a train. It had never crossed my mind that she would go, although it's obvious now that I think about it, but I want her to stay. I need her. I've got so used to having her here with us, with me. How normal it has felt to have someone to talk to when, in fact, that has never really been the norm for me. For her, though, we are just another job. She moves on all the time. If she gets on with the family for whom she's caring then that must be a bonus, but at the end of the day this is just the thing that pays her bills. She's a professional. No doubt she would have been just as kind to me and Dad had she hated everything about us.

I stumble over my words as I try, and fail, to express my gratitude.

'It's been so lovely . . .' I begin. 'I don't know what I'd have done without you. You've made such a difference; I know Dad appreciated it. I hope it goes well with the next . . .'

She opens her arms wide and I fall into them.

'I'm going to miss you so much,' I say, sobs rising in my throat again.

'Oh, don't be daft,' she says, but I think I can hear something in her voice, a fissure in the facade of calm that usually surrounds her. 'I'll keep in touch and I'll be back for the funeral. If you need anything then just ring me. I'll not be taking any more work on for a couple of weeks.'

She allows me to hold her for a few more seconds and then she delicately extracts herself from my grip. Then she opens the door and walks away down the path without looking back.

CHAPTER FORTY-SEVEN

When I wake to the grating rasp of the alarm on my phone, it is already dark outside. Automatically, I listen out for sounds of Dad and it is a moment or two before I remember. The house is completely silent. I am alone.

I flick the bedside light on and get up. I still feel groggy, almost hungover, and I wonder whether sleeping during the day was the best idea. It'll take me forever to get over the jet-lag if I go about it like this but suddenly that seems unimportant. I could totally switch my body clock if I wanted to. Who is there to care how I organise my life now?

When I'm showered and dressed, I head downstairs to go and meet Beth at the restaurant. Something makes me put my head round Dad's bedroom door. It's like picking at a scab. I know that it will hurt but I cannot help myself. The room is tidy, the bed stripped and remade with fresh linen. I can smell Dettol and furniture polish. Mrs P. Bless her.

When I arrive at the restaurant, Beth is already there. She has ordered a bottle of our favourite wine and is halfway through a bowl of plump, green olives.

'Am I late?' I ask as I sit down.

'No. I'm early. I didn't want you arriving and having to sit on your own and Greg was watching some football or rugby or something so he'll have barely registered that I've left. Olive?' she asks, passing me the bowl. She pours me a glass of wine. 'A toast?' she asks.

I raise my glass and chink it delicately against hers. 'To Dad,' I say and we both drink.

The restaurant is busy and slightly short-staffed. The waitress who appears to be responsible for us is steadfastly refusing to make eye contact with the diners and just getting on with the jobs in hand before she takes in any more requests. It's fine by us. We're in no rush.

'Right. Tell me why you went racing off to San Francisco,' says Beth.

So I tell her how I tracked Ursula down online and about the photograph I found with her and Mum.

'So, you knew for sure that your dad had lied about her dying, then?' she asks.

'Well, not for certain,' I say. 'But when I fitted all the bits together, it started to look more and more likely. That's why I needed to see Ursula, to ask her face to face.'

'That was so brave,' Beth says, her eyes wide. 'Weren't you scared of what you might find out? I'd have been terrified. You know, when part of you wants to know something and part of you really doesn't.'

I love that about Beth; that she always manages to hit my nails on their heads. And it all comes pouring out, about going to the gallery and meeting Skyler and waiting for the email and that first, disastrous meeting.

'What a bitch!' she says. 'I think I'd have run after her and told her exactly what I thought of her.' But we both know that she wouldn't have really. Then I explain how she came to find me the next day and how I forgave her. 'And what did she tell you? About your mum, I mean?'

The first bottle is almost empty and we have still had no menus let alone any food beyond the now-depleted olives, but neither of us really cares.

'It's kind of complicated,' I say. 'Turns out my mum ran off with another woman and Dad had her declared as an unfit mother and got a court order to prevent her seeing us. And Michael knew all the time and never said.'

And there it is. My whole, sorry life story in a small and slightly crushed nutshell. Beth just sits there with her mouth open. The waitress finally makes her way to our table but Beth waves her away impatiently.

'Oh my God,' she says, stunned. 'Oh my God! And where is she now, your mum? Is she still with this woman?'

'Lord only knows. Ursula thought she'd split up with Tilly but she's not heard from Mum since the nineties. I suppose she could actually be dead after all.'

'What a mess,' says Beth. 'But she sent all those postcards.'

'Yes, but they stopped when I turned eighteen. There's been no sign of her for fifteen years.'

'Will you keep looking for her?'

Air escapes from my lungs in a deep sigh. That and the wine make me feel lightheaded.

'I don't know. I don't know what to do. I can't think about it at the moment. There's too much else to deal with, with Dad and everything. One thing I did learn from Ursula, though, is that Mum was called Anneliese, not Anne, so that might explain why I couldn't find any record of her.'

'Anneliese. That's so pretty. Just like Cara.'

It doesn't matter how bad things get. Beth will always find the positive. The waitress arrives again and this time we give her our order, which she commits to memory rather than writing it down.

'Chances of that order making its way to the kitchen?' asks Beth and tops up our glasses.

'Thanks Beth,' I say. 'For always just being there.'

'What are best friends for?' she asks, her head cocked to one side as she looks at me, making sure that I'm okay.

Another wave of emotion hits me. Beth reaches across and takes my hands in hers. 'You cry, Cara. Just let it all out.'

There are no more tears, though. My eyes are dry. But my heart aches.

The food arrives and is as we ordered. I realise when it is in front of me how hungry I am and I eat quickly and with relish.

'I have news,' says Beth. I can tell from her smirk that it's something good and that she has been waiting for us to get the end of my troubles before she divulges it.

'Oh yes?' I say, through a mouthful of dauphinoise potato.

The smirk becomes a full smile, her eyes full of mischief. 'I've bought a puppy, a Cockapoo. He is absolutely adorable. He's chocolate brown with the cutest little button nose and the softest fur you've ever felt. He's only eight weeks old. He's coming at the weekend. I'm going to call him Samson.'

She gives a little squeak of excitement and then looks at me slyly from behind her eyelashes.

'But I thought . . .' I say slowly. 'Doesn't Greg hate dogs?'

'Yup. With a passion because they make a mess and they smell and they trample muddy footprints into the house. But I love dogs and he has married me. He'll just have to get used to it!'

I laugh, long and loud. People turn to look and then smile at us because we are clearly having such a lovely time. How wrong I was to worry about Beth with Greg. She knows exactly how to play him. He may want to keep her at his beck and call but he's going to have a fight like a fisherman landing a feisty swordfish. Who can say whether fisherman or fish will be the victor?

CHAPTER FORTY-EIGHT

The days running up to the funeral are very quiet. There are no visitors or well-wishers. While I am grateful for the solitude, a part of me can't help but think how small the space that Dad and I occupy in the world really is. One or two cards with well-meaning messages arrive as the news filters out but, really, who is there to grieve for him? Colleagues with whom he lost touch, friends from the day centre whom he wouldn't remember anyway, Mrs P?

I distract myself with work. I have deadlines for my spring brides and so there is plenty to do. Settling myself in my workroom, I put the radio on. Its low hum, blended with the sound of the sewing machine, is comfortingly familiar, but it's really only a mask over the silence that fills the house. I try not to think about Dad or Mum or even Simeon. I just function and am remarkably productive without interruptions and distractions. Despite everything, though, I find myself regularly checking my phone for texts. Once or twice, I even start typing out a message to Simeon but now that I'm home all my resolve to make a go of it seems to have deserted me and I delete rather than send them.

Michael, Marianne and the girls are due to arrive in the early evening the day before the funeral. They will have eaten by the time they get here, according to Marianne, to whom this kind of detail is important. There has been some debate as to whether the girls should come at all but I gather that Marianne has put her foot down, saying that it is important that they say their goodbyes to their grandfather. I rather uncharitably wonder whether she does this to set a precedent for future funerals, which will clearly have more to do with her side of the family, but ultimately it doesn't matter what her motives might be. I am just pleased that I won't be on my own anymore.

I busy myself changing sheets and arranging towels. I decide to leave Dad's room unoccupied and just pull the door closed without looking in. No one will want to sleep in a bed so recently tainted by death.

The fridge tells its own tale. On opening the door, I see a half-drunk bottle of wine, a plastic carton of milk and some cheese that has gone green at the edges. I have been surviving on toast and Quality Street. The replenishing of the larder brings with it a renewed sense of normality and by the time I hear Michael's car pulling up outside I have lit a fire in the grate and the house feels warm and welcoming.

I stand at the front door of what is now my house to greet them. The girls step out first, looking suitably sombre, having presumably just been briefed by Marianne on the appropriate etiquette.

'Hello, Auntie Cara,' they chorus. 'We are very sorry about Granddad.'

I open my arms and pull a child into each hip, where they stand, heads bowed. 'Thank you, girls,' I say. 'It's very sad but Granddad had been very poorly and so perhaps it was for the best that he died.'

They stand there until they judge a suitably respectful period has passed and then they look up at me, their eyes shining.

'Can we go and explore now?' they ask, jumping up and down on the spot, all funereal conduct forgotten.

'Girls! Girls! What did I just say?' Marianne's voice comes from the drive. 'Auntie Cara is very sad and she doesn't want you two behaving like a pair of puppies. Simmer down.'

I continue to hug each of the girls into me, talking over their heads to Marianne.

'It's fine, honestly. Actually, it's lovely. It's been so quiet around here. I'm just rattling around on my own. Please, come in. Have you had a good trip?'

The four of them decant from car to house, the girls chattering excitedly and Marianne giving details of the journey. Only Michael is quiet. He carries in the single suitcase, following behind his family like a porter. I just wait. He'll speak when he's ready. I nod and smile at Marianne but I'm not really listening to her. All my attention is focused on Michael. He holds back from the others, cautiously taking in his surroundings. As he crosses the threshold, I think I see him hesitate slightly, like an animal sniffing the air for signs of danger. I've never noticed this in him before. I wonder if I am imagining it, whether my altered perception of our family history is projecting itself on to his behaviour and making me reinterpret it. But if he is being cautious, his nervousness quickly evaporates, leaving me wondering if I've been oversensitive in imagining that it was ever there.

'The old place looks just the same,' he says, but with affection not scorn. 'What are your plans, Ca? Will you sell up or stay on?'

The bluntness of his question doesn't surprise me. I know my brother.

'I think I'll stay,' I reply. 'At least for the time being. There'll be all the clearing out to do if I move. If I stay, I can just close the door on it for a bit and forget about it. And I think the old place could use a bit of TLC.'

Marianne casts an appraising eye over the faded carpets, the yellowing paintwork. 'It just needs a bit of freshening up,' she says, charitably.

I hadn't noticed how tired the house was looking until now. With my focus on caring for Dad and keeping on top of my work, I've developed a blind spot for its failings, especially when there was Mrs P keeping things clean and tidy. Now that I look round with a more discerning eye, I see the house as others must see it and this realisation brings with it a wave of grief that comes from nowhere and knocks me off my feet.

Marianne puts a gentle arm around my shoulder and leads me into the kitchen, where she flicks the switch on the kettle before I have even worked out that tea is what is required.

'I'm sorry,' I say when the sobs subside. 'I don't know . . .'

'Don't apologise,' she says. 'It's natural. It's early days. It takes time.' Her voice is gentle, calm, like submerging yourself into a warm bath.

'But I didn't expect . . .'

She stops what she's doing with the tea things and looks straight at me. 'You didn't expect what?' she asks. 'Didn't expect to be so upset? Whatever happened, whatever he did or didn't do, whatever he had become, he was still your father.' Her hand rubs my back as she speaks. Even through my grief, I can tell that this is a speech that's been pre-prepared and I wonder how much Michael has told her. There is no sign of him.

As she pours the tea, I hear the girls thundering back down the stairs. They start to speak even before they enter the room.

'Can we sleep in the attic?' they ask.

'But I've made you a bedroom next to mine,' I say, looking as sincere as I can manage. I watch as their little smiles slip a little. 'But . . . if it's okay with Mum and Dad then I suppose we can move the mattresses up there.'

'Girls. I really don't think . . .' begins Marianne, shooting them a look.

'It's all right,' I say. 'We might need to do a bit of dusting, though,' I add, thinking of the state of the attic room, not the one with the boxes but the other, less cluttered one. 'And I hope you've brought your best muscles with you to help us shift the mattresses.'

I follow them back up the stairs, shouting for Michael as we go. He emerges silently from Dad's room but I can't see the expression on his face.

'Dad! Dad! We need you to come and help us carry the mattresses into the attic,' Esmé shouts, grabbing his arms as she and Zara pass him, and dragging him along behind them. He laughs, relinquishing himself to the relentless force of his daughters.

'How about we just take up one mattress and you sleep top-to-tail?' he suggests. The girls look at one another questioningly and then nod their agreement.

Between the four of us, we manage to manhandle the mattress up the creaking wooden stairs. At one point, Zara's iPod slips from her pocket and clatters down the steps. The moment reverberates with the haunting clamour of the past. I look at Michael. For one moment, I think he'll be angry. He scowls at his daughter but then his face cracks into a smile.

'Butterfingers!' he says. 'Good job it's got that case on it. Is it okay?'

Zara lets go of the mattress, picks the iPod up and examines the screen carefully.

'It's fine,' she announces. 'No need to panic.'

'Well, can you look after it a bit more carefully please,' Michael says. 'If it breaks, there won't be another one.'

We continue our struggle up the stairs and into the room that the twins have recently disturbed. Dust motes circle in the air.

'You don't really want to sleep in here, surely,' I protest. 'It's filthy.'

'We do! We do!' they chorus. 'We can, can't we, Auntie Cara?'

I let my eyes wander towards Michael, who nods almost imperceptibly.

'Well, if you're sure . . .' I say. 'But I think you're mad! Let's go get the duvet and see if we can't find a little light or something.'

The girls hurl themselves on to the bare mattress and feign sleep while Michael and I head back downstairs.

'It's good,' he says quietly. 'I like it. It helps.'

When the girls are quiet in their makeshift bedroom, Michael stokes the fire and the three of us settle down on the sofa, a loaded tea tray on the carpet in front of us. I've bought fat rascals, a kind of Yorkshire scone, from the smart bakery in town. Cherries shine like jewels in the top of each one. My eye is caught by something glinting and I see two or three shreds of tinsel still caught in the carpet. I hadn't even thought about the Christmas decorations. Mrs P must have cleared them all away when I was in San Francisco and it hits me how much I miss having her here.

And so the three of us chat about their London life, steadfastly avoiding any other topics, until the embers glow in the grate.

CHAPTER FORTY-NINE

I suppose that normal families are really busy before a funeral, with lots of rushing around cutting sandwiches, checking music and giving last-minute directions. Dad's funeral isn't like that. I've placed a notice in the local paper, recording the death and giving all the details. There's no mention of a wake. I buy a couple of extra loaves and a packet of wafer-thin ham, just in case. We have sherry left over from Christmas and there's wine. I have no beer but as Michael intends to drive home straight afterwards I don't suppose any will be needed. I tell myself that it's not that I don't want to give Dad a good send-off. It's just that there'll only be us there and we won't need much.

In my heart, though, I know that that's not entirely true. I'm sure I would have made more of an effort if Dad had died six months ago, back before I knew what he did. There would still have been no one at his funeral but perhaps I would have approached it with more grace. Or perhaps I wouldn't. There really is no way of telling.

We're ready to leave for the crematorium far too early. The girls, who could still be heard scampering around overhead long after we went to bed, are up before dawn. I'm already awake when I hear them padding down to the bathroom. I lie staring up at the ceiling and enjoy the sounds of life in the house. Living alone is going to take some getting used to.

'Is there nothing I can be doing?' asks Marianne after we've put away the breakfast things.

'I don't think so,' I reply, trying not to sound dismissive but at the same time not opening up a conversation.

I can tell that she wants to say something, is judging her moment carefully, but I don't make it easy for her. I don't want her to force me to examine my motives for this low-key send-off too closely. I'm frightened of what I might find if I start to unpick it. So I don't give her a chance. I flit around the house, moving things from one spot to another, creating non-existent tasks to do until there is a knock at the door.

'That'll be the undertakers,' I shout down the stairs. 'Can you let them in please? I won't be a minute.'

I hear the door open and then words spoken in deep, hushed voices but I can't tell what they're saying. I don't really want to know. I stay where I am, hiding upstairs, until I hear Michael calling me down and I can no longer avoid the inevitable.

'Cara. They're ready for us. Should we go?'

Of course we should go but still I falter.

'Just coming,' I shout down, but I don't move.

Marianne is marshalling the girls into their coats, keys are jangled, the front door squeaks as it opens wide. I would do anything to stay here, to hide until it's all over. The thought of exposing whatever I've buried over the last few days frightens me and I worry that if I start to cry, I might never stop.

And then Michael is by my side, even though I didn't hear him come up the stairs. He looks at me, his expression resigned, and holds out his arm to try and corral me in the appropriate direction.

'We have to go, Ca,' he says as he takes my hand and squeezes it gently. 'Come on. It'll be okay. You just have to get through this part and then things will start to get back to normal. Is Beth coming?'

I had forgotten all about Beth and the thought of her being there at my side cheers me.

'Yes. Yes, she is,' I say.

'Good. Come on then. They're waiting for us.'

I let my big brother lead me down the stairs and out to the car. The winter sun hangs like a silver coin in the pale-blue sky. Isn't it supposed to be raining or at the very least overcast for a funeral? It feels slightly obscene that it's such a nice day, the first for weeks. The funeral car is huge and very, very black. Marianne and the girls are already sitting in the row at the back. Michael and I slide into the middle and the undertaker waits patiently to close the door behind us. I notice, as I bend to climb in, that there's a stain on the cuff of his black overcoat. It looks like baby sick but the thought of this sombre man ever taking charge of a baby seems so unlikely that I almost laugh. He sees my eye catch sight of the stain and retracts his arm behind his back so that he looks like a policeman. This strikes me as even funnier. I bite my lip and try to remember where I am.

The crematorium is not far away. As we drive, the girls sit as quietly as they can, although I can hear them whispering twin talk to each other.

When we arrive, the tail-end Charlies of the previous service are just leaving. They look like a proper funeral party, top to tail in black, leaning on each other for support as they shuffle away, their heads bowed.

We get out of the car and file silently into the empty room. There are at least twenty rows of benches, pews I suppose you'd call them if this were a church. Sitting about halfway down is Brian, the bus driver from The Limes, and a couple of old men who I don't recognise but who presumably know Dad from there. It crosses my mind that they might only have come for the bun fight. I toy with telling them that there'll be no wake to avoid disappointing them but then they might leave before we've had the service. On the other side, closer to the front, is Beth. She is wearing her darkest clothes but her tan doesn't sit well with the solemn occasion and she looks a bit out of place. She sees us come in and smiles broadly and then moves to sit between me and Michael's family. We fill half a row.

And that is it. The sum total of the mourners for my father. There's some music playing. It sounds a bit like a hymn but it's not a tune that I recognise. Dad would probably have known it. I look for an organ or a piano but it must be a recording. I realise with another sharp stab of guilt that I should probably have chosen a piece that meant something to Dad. I dismiss the fact that I have no idea what that might have been.

The undertakers carry the coffin slowly down to the front and place it carefully in front of the pale-grey curtain behind which I assume the incinerator lies. A simple bunch of white lilies rests on its oak lid. Did I order those or did they just put them there out of pity for the lack of floral tribute? I have no idea.

When the celebrant comes out, he checks his watch to make sure that he has got the time right before starting. There are no prayers – Dad didn't do God, despite knowing all those hymns – and no readings. The absence of God at an occasion like this seems strange to me: as if, without some form of ritual, the funeral is somehow invalid. But this is how Dad would have wanted it. There is no eulogy either. Michael and I discussed whether one of us should speak and decided that there was no need. What would we have said? 'Here lies our father who banned our mother from our lives and told us she was dead.'

And so, faced with a lack of material, the celebrant hasn't much to do.

'We gather here today to say goodbye to Joseph Ferensby, father to Michael and Cara and grandfather to Esmé and Zara. May he rest in peace.'

He looks around to make sure that no one is taken by a sudden desire to speak and then nods and the curtains open and the coffin moves slowly out of sight. Esmé asks a question and Marianne quietens her. And that is it. He has gone. I feel numb rather than sad. I reach for Michael's gloved hand and take it in my own. He presses my fingers gently between his and that sets off a chain reaction. I feel the lump rising in my throat and then my face crumples and the tears fall. Michael passes me a freshly laundered handkerchief but I use one of the tissues that I have ready in my coat pocket. On my other side, Beth places her head gently on my shoulder. I feel safe, cocooned between the two of them.

We sit there for a long time. I hear Brian and the old men get up and leave. One of them is muttering something about it not being much of a do. I know that I should get up, go and thank them for making the effort to come, but I don't want to move. As if reading my thoughts, Marianne shuffles out of the pew and goes to speak to them. I hear them saying how sorry they are and then they are gone. The three of us just sit there. The girls whisper to each other.

'We should perhaps make a move,' says Michael after a few minutes. 'Do we need to sign anything before we leave?'

I laugh at him, a small sudden release of air that sounds more a sneeze than a laugh.

'That is so typically you,' I say, and he raises his eyebrows questioningly. 'It's all done,' I say. 'We can just go. The car is going to take us back to the house.'

We stand up and turn round to leave. The canned music has resumed and is floating down from speakers in the corner of the room. I listen but still don't recognise it; something bland without any connotations, presumably written for just this type of event. I wonder briefly if someone makes a living from writing bland, anonymous tunes.

The room is empty except for a figure sitting with her head bowed a couple of rows behind us. As we walk towards her, she looks up and I see the familiar face of Mrs P. I had forgotten all about her, although I was pretty certain that she would come. I want to invite her to the house with us so that she can meet Michael and so I can say thank you again and perhaps get an address for her so we can keep in touch.

'Oh, thank you for coming,' I say. 'You will come back to the house for . . .'

I stop speaking. Michael has stopped in his tracks. His face is suddenly deathly pale, his mouth open.

'Mum . . . ?' he says.

CHAPTER FIFTY

I look at Michael and then back at Mrs P.

'No, Michael. This is Angela Partington. She's the nurse I was telling you about, the one I hired to help with Dad. She's been fantastic. I really couldn't have coped . . .'

Michael is still staring and shaking his head.

'Mum,' he says again.

Mrs P looks as confused as I am. Michael strides down the aisle towards her. I am totally lost. Why does he think that Mrs P is our mother? I know her and I know that she would have said. She would never have lived in my house all this time and not told me. It makes no sense. She looks nothing like us either.

And then, for a horrible moment, it crosses my mind that he might be right. Maybe Mrs P has been lying to me as well, just like the rest of them? This thought leaves me as quickly as it came. I know Michael is wrong. I just know.

Michael continues to move down the aisle but he races straight past Mrs P, breaking into a run as a small figure in a dark coat disappears into the hallway outside.

I just stand there, mouth open.

'Go after him,' says Mrs P and she pushes me gently towards the door. When I still don't move, she shoves me harder. 'Go and find out what's going on.'

I follow Michael but when I get to the door of the chapel, there is no sign of either him or the woman. My head spins left and right, frantically searching, and then I catch sight of Michael standing near a small ante-room off to the left. His body, wrapped in his grey woollen overcoat, fills the whole doorway and I can't really see beyond him, but I assume that the woman is in there. He has her cornered, like a terrier with a rabbit.

'Michael, what's going on?' I ask as I approach him.

He doesn't move and I have to stand on my tiptoes to see over his broad shoulders. The room is full of flowers in various vases and display stands but when I get closer I can see that they are all fake, mainly silk, one or two in moulded plastic. They must be what they use if there are no family flowers. I wonder what kind of family doesn't even provide flowers for the coffin and then remember the unrequested lilies.

The woman has backed herself into the corner of the room and can go no further. She is wearing black clothes but they are a little too big for her, the fabrics over-washed to a muted grey. She is a similar height to me, although she is thinner. The gentle curve of her collarbones stands proud, leaving a little hollow around her neck. Her shoulders are hunched, her arms crossed firmly over her chest, one hand in front of her face. I search for something that is familiar but can see nothing.

Michael takes a step into the room and she seems to retreat even further back.

'Mum?' he says, so gently that I can barely hear him. 'It is you, isn't it?'

She lifts her eyes to Michael's and nods her head.

My world tilts.

Michael doesn't hesitate. He walks straight over to this stranger and throws his arms around her. I think she was expecting something different because she shrinks away from him, bowing her head still lower, but then she accepts Michael into her and embraces him, gingerly at first, as if he might evaporate. Then she stretches out her arms and wraps them around his waist. Michael's shoulders are shaking but she is still, her head buried into his chest.

I don't know what to do. The bond between the two of them is evidently secure, despite thirty years apart. I feel nothing. Nothing about this woman is familiar. She is as alien to me as any random person that I might pass in the street.

They pull apart from one another and she runs her fingers over his face, tracing the outline of his ear with the flat of her fingernail.

'You always used to do that when I was little,' says Michael, and she smiles. 'You loved it best when my ears were cold.'

Michael is no longer a man in his thirties but has regressed back to his seven-year-old self. If he could sit on her knee I think that he would. She strokes his hair, pushing it back from his hairline, her fingers halting over the grey strands. They are as one. It's as if I am not even there.

I can't bear it any longer. I feel sick. I need some air. I have to get away. I turn in the doorway and crash straight into Marianne, who has followed us out of the chapel.

'What's going on? Are you all right, Cara?' she calls out after me as I run from the building and into the gardens outside.

I stumble like a kitten that has just opened its eyes. The funeral car is waiting for us by the entrance, the driver leaning against the bonnet, a cigarette glowing in his hand. As he sees me he drops it smartly, stubbing it out with his toe and grabbing his hat from the roof of the car.

'Are you ready to go, miss?' he asks as I run past, but I don't reply.

I almost trip down some stone stairs and into a sunken garden. What remains of the summer planting stands stooped and broken, the flower beds dead and brown. In the centre of the lawn is a huge weeping willow, bare branches drooping across the grass. In summer, you would be able to hide at its centre, protected by the leafy boughs. How I would have loved that as a child. I make my way in through the branches and lean with my forehead against the rough bark of the trunk. I breathe slowly, in and out, until my heartbeat returns to normal. If I could be anywhere but here . . .

'Cara?'

I feel a hand on my shoulder, a gentle touch.

'Cara, are you all right?'

I recognise Mrs P's voice but I don't open my eyes.

'It must be a terrible shock,' she says. 'Really she should have got in touch beforehand rather than just turning up here unannounced. It's no wonder you're feeling out of sorts.'

Out of sorts. How I love her turn of phrase, the way that everything is so underplayed.

'Where is she?' I ask without turning round.

'She's still inside with Michael but she wants to see you. You don't have to go if you don't want. You don't have to do anything just now.'

'I want to go home,' I say.

'Then that's what we'll do. I can take you in my car if you'd rather not travel with the others.'

I nod my head. The thought of being bundled up with them all right now makes me feel sick.

'Come on, then,' she says and puts her arm around my shoulder. 'Let's go.'

She leads me back up the stairs and towards the car park. I hear Michael calling after me but I don't turn round. I feel Mrs P gesturing to him with her spare arm but I don't know what she says. I don't care. I just want to leave. Mrs P opens the door and lowers me into the seat carefully as if she fears I might break.

'Pop your seatbelt on,' she says and it's as if I too have regressed to my childhood.

I obey her, fumbling at first with the buckle and then clicking the belt into position around me. She drives slowly, with respect for our surroundings, but she doesn't slow down further as we pass the rest of our party and I'm grateful for that. I lower my head as we drive on but I see them all standing there. They make a sombre little group.

The house is cold and dark when we get back. The sky has clouded over and is now threatening rain. Even though it's not yet lunchtime, it feels like night can't be far away. Mrs P flicks on lights and trips the central-heating switch and the boiler rumbles into action.

'Let's get you sat down. I'll make us a nice cup of tea.'

She leads me into the lounge. I am completely numb, happy just to be steered about. I perch on the edge of the sofa as if I might leap up again at any minute. Dad's chair stands opposite me, empty. A wave of anger passes through me. How could he have done this to me, to us? What kind of sick mind could possibly think it was an appropriate lie to tell? He carried it for all those years and never once relented. Even if he might have thought it was justified when I was small, surely he could have told me the truth when I grew up? I suppose he was scared. Scared of what I might say or do. Scared that I might react just as Michael had done and run from him. When he started to get ill perhaps he worried that he could no longer trust himself to keep the facts straight in his head? Then, one day, he would just have forgotten. It would have become, to him, as if it had never happened. I might never have known. It's obvious that Michael had decided never to tell me. I would have gone through my entire life not knowing. How dare they do that to me? I feel my jaw tighten and my fists bunch with the fury that I have nowhere else to put.

And now, the not-dead mother has turned up. Judging by his reaction, I'm pretty certain that Michael didn't know she was going to be there, but then I'm no longer sure what I can be certain of. Everything that was once secure in my world has fallen away.

Mrs P comes in and presses a hot cup of tea into my hand.

'I've put plenty of sugar into it,' she says. 'For the shock. The others will be back in a moment, I'm sure. Is there anything I can do before they arrive?'

I shake my head.

'Well, maybe I'll go and see if I can sort things out in the kitchen,' she says and then disappears to do what she does best. Part of me wishes that she would stay with me. I don't want to talk. Right now, I have no words for what I'm feeling but I crave the sense of calm that she always brings me. The contrast between what I feel for her and what I feel for the woman who has just appeared at Dad's funeral couldn't be more marked. It strikes me that Mrs P, an agency nurse paid to live in my house and look after my father, has become so much more of a mother to me than I have ever known. Over the last few months she has been quietly compassionate, gentle and supportive, knowing instinctively what I needed and what should be said or not said. Her reassuring presence in my life is the closest thing I can remember to having an actual mother. And now, just as I finally understand that, she is going to leave me with a woman for whom I feel precisely nothing. It is the saddest thought.

I hear the front door open and close, whispering voices in the hall, before the lounge door swings and Michael comes in.

'Cara? Are you okay?'

He kneels at my feet and lifts my chin so that he can look into my face. His eyes are rimmed red.

'I've brought Mum back here,' he says, his voice almost a whisper. 'I think we need to talk.'

Before I have time to reply, the woman appears at the door. She is standing a little taller than she was before, her shoulders a little less rounded.

'Please give me chance to explain everything,' she says. 'Then I'll leave if you want me to.'

I look at Michael. He nods at me, eyebrows raised in expectation.

I hear Marianne in the hallway.

'Come on, girls. Let's go with Beth into the kitchen and see if we can find a drink.'

'Can we show Beth our den?' says Zara.

'I love dens,' I hear Beth say and then the voices are lost.

CHAPTER FIFTY-ONE

The woman, my mother, sits down in the chair that was Dad's. Part of me flinches at her audacity: the man was cremated less than an hour ago. But then I suppose that she doesn't know it's his chair. I let it pass. Michael stays where he is, next to me. We look like an interview panel, which I suppose is appropriate in a way.

The woman bites at her knuckle and my heart starts to soften a little. This must be really hard for her too, not that that excuses anything. Still . . .

Then she clears her throat, a small sound like a child's cough.

'The first thing I need you to understand,' she says, looking me straight in the eye, 'is how deeply, deeply sorry I am for what happened.'

My heart hardens again. Sorry? She's sorry. She, my mother, abandons me for thirty years and now she says she's sorry. And sorry not for what she did but for what happened. I dig my fingernails into my palms, feeling the distracting, comforting pain as they sink into my flesh, but somehow I manage to keep my mouth shut.

'I love you,' she says. 'I have never stopped loving you. I did what I did because I genuinely thought it would cause the least amount of pain for you.'

I can't believe what I'm hearing.

'Have you any idea . . .' I begin but Michael shakes his head.

'Shhhh, Cara,' he says. 'Let her tell her side.'

I sit back, my arms folded tightly across my chest.

'I did leave that night. It was Tilly's idea. It was supposed to be a gesture to show Joseph that I wasn't going to let him walk all over me anymore. I thought that he could stew overnight and then, when he'd calmed down, I'd go back in the morning and collect you and we could all leave together. I thought Tilly would help me find somewhere for us to live and then we'd work out visiting rights and what have you for your father. That was my idea. I'm not sure now that that was what Tilly had in mind . . .'

She looks down, her cheeks pink. From what I now understand of Tilly, it must have been blindingly obvious that we didn't feature in her plans. How could our mother not have seen that? But then, maybe, when times are desperate, people take leaps of faith without really considering how far they are going to have to jump to get to safety.

'But then everything went wrong,' she continues. 'Your father changed the locks that night and then he wouldn't let me in or answer the phone. I was hammering on the door for hours. I could hear you crying inside but he wouldn't open it. I tried calling to you through the letterbox but he just turned the radio up so loud that you couldn't hear me. The neighbours all came out to watch but no one came forward to help. I sat there all day, just shouting for you.'

Her breath is coming in gulps now but there are no tears. I listen but I can't imagine what she is describing, can hardly believe that she's talking about something that involved me. I look at Michael. There are tears trickling down his cheeks and I realise that he might remember this, or be allowing himself to remember it for the first time.

'Then the police got involved,' she says. 'Joseph called them and they came and took me to the cells for causing a disturbance. They didn't charge me but, by the time I got back to the house, your father had seen a solicitor and got the emergency injunction with the restriction order. You know about those?'

Michael nods.

'So then, on top of everything else, I had the threat of prison hang-ing over me if I came anywhere near you. Tilly said I would be no good to you if I was locked up. I agreed but it was so hard to keep away. Tilly really hated your father. She filled my head with hatred too, although it wasn't very hard. He had stolen my precious babies from me and there was nothing I could do to stop him.'

She pauses for a moment, collecting herself. I feel myself warming to her, part of me longing to forgive her for what she did. But part of me is still too angry. Then she begins to speak again.

'That's when Tilly suggested that we go on a trip, just a short one, until things calmed down. So we went to Europe, travelled around for a while. We ended up staying longer than I'd hoped,' she adds quietly.

I snort. I've seen the postcards. They were gone for years. I'm about to challenge her but Michael flicks my foot with his and I hold my com-ments back. My mother takes a deep breath and continues.

'You have to understand,' she says, in a voice so quiet that I can barely hear her, 'when you've spent your whole life being told that you're rubbish, that you'll never amount to anything, then you start to believe it. I tried so hard for him but nothing I did was ever good enough. If I cooked his favourite food, it was boring. If I experimented with something new, he'd complain that he didn't like it. If he came home from work and I hadn't managed to tidy up, he made me feel like I was a sloppy housewife who spent all day lounging around spending his money. Not that I had any money to spend. He gave me housekeeping for food but that was all. If I needed anything for you, shoes or new clothes, then I had to ask. I had next to nothing for myself because he didn't seem to realise that I needed it. I didn't even have money for . . . for personal things.'

Her cheeks burn as she says this. I think about the implications of what she's describing. I can't imagine being so dependent on someone that they could humiliate me by just withholding cash. I feel myself soften, just a little.

'He used to joke that I was taking advantage of him and, after a while, I started to believe it. He never wanted any of my friends round. I had plenty of friends when we first got married, but if they came to visit when he was at home, he'd be rude to them and make them feel uncomfortable. So, eventually, they made excuses and stopped coming.'

Her words chime with what Ursula told me about Dad: the control, the passive aggression that seems to have been his modus operandi. I think about what Beth said just last night as well, what her mum had thought about our home life, and then my mother's story starts to slot into the bigger picture. I try to put myself in her shoes but I still can't get beyond the fact that she left us with him.

'He kept going on at me, every day,' my mother continues. 'Drip-feeding me with how useless I was. My self-confidence had been all but destroyed by my father. It didn't take much for Joe to knock me down lower still. I don't think he even knew he was doing it half the time, but the spark at the heart of me was getting dimmer and dimmer. I was so frightened that it would go out altogether.'

She looks up at us, imploring us to understand. I think I can, maybe a little. Ursula told me stories of their life at home, of how their father treated them. I know that my mother was damaged long before she ever met Dad.

'I'm not making excuses,' she continues. 'That's just how it was. When someone tells you over and over again that you are pointless and no good, that's how you begin to see yourself. When he was cross, he'd tell me that I was a terrible mother, and gradually I began to feel that he was right. I knew I was hopeless, that I was no good for you. For either of you.'

Her bottom lip begins to quiver, showing emotion for the first time since she started to speak.

'That's when I met Tilly,' she says, and her tone changes. She almost smiles. 'Well, we'd met before I was married. She was a friend of a friend but we bumped into each other at the post office. I couldn't believe that someone like her would remember someone like me but she knew me straightaway. She dragged me for a drink. I was so nervous about being late back. But Tilly wouldn't take no for an answer. She was like that, Tilly. When she wanted something, she just made it happen. She just blew into my life like a hurricane. She had this fantastic job and loads of money. She made things seem exciting again. Of course, Joseph couldn't bear her – I suppose he could see how dangerous she was – but she didn't care. She wasn't scared of him like my other friends were. I loved that she could stand up to him. She made me feel brave. After all that time, I started to feel like I had choices.'

The door opens and Esmé comes running in, with Marianne right behind her. Esmé has a picture in her hand. It's of her family standing in front of a house that could be this one, with its high gable roof. Standing slightly apart from the four of them is a single figure in a long, white dress, which I assume is me.

'Auntie Cara,' she says. 'I drew you a picture.' She holds it out towards me. The pain that slices through me as I see myself standing alone snatches my breath away. There, in this child's drawing, is a clear depiction of who I am and all that I have lost.

'Esmé,' Marianne is saying. 'Come out please. Daddy and Auntie Cara . . .'

Marianne looks up and, seeing my stricken face asks, 'Is everything okay, Cara?'

I can't move but Michael nods and so Marianne takes an objecting Esmé by the hand and pulls her from the room.

'So,' I say, trying to reclaim the anger I'd felt a moment before. Anger somehow seems easier to deal with than pain. 'You abandoned us so that you could go and "find yourself" with Tilly.' My fingers flick air commas round my words.

I know from what Ursula told me that this is neither true nor fair. The woman, my mother, doesn't leap to defend herself and shame washes over me. I want to rage at what has been done to me but right now my heart is full of an incredibly deep sadness at all that the three of us have lost.

'That's not fair, Cara,' says Michael, but he doesn't need to stand up for her. I can see in her face how much what happened has cost her.

'I had no idea of what would happen,' she says. 'I thought I was taking a stand, showing your father that I had a mind of my own and could do things that he wasn't expecting. Yes, I was unhappy, and I really thought I loved Tilly, but I never dreamed that packing that suitcase would lead to me being pushed out of your lives completely. Leaving you that night was the biggest mistake of my life.'

And then she weeps: hard, silent tears that pour down her cheeks. She makes no move to wipe them. They just fall away.

CHAPTER FIFTY-TWO

Annie, 2018

What makes the perfect mother?

This is something that I've thought about a lot over the years. I'm certain all mothers do, as they try to process the crushing guilt they feel for the mistakes they believe they have made.

Is the perfect mother the one who stays with her children night and day, putting their needs before her own, sacrificing the life that she once had in order to focus all her attention on them?

What about the woman who juggles everything to try to forge a balance between work and home, providing a role model for her daughters while at the same time preserving a little of what she was before they were born?

Should the perfect mother let her children make mistakes or sweep in to protect them against every false step? Does she twist the truth to make the world seem more palatable or be brutally honest from the outset? Santa, the Tooth Fairy, the Easter Bunny . . . are these all legends that enrich childhood or lies that destroy trust?

You see, there are so many ways of parenting a child. Who can say which is the right path to take?

Every mother has to work this out for herself. She must decide what she thinks is best for her children at any given moment.

Yet this decision cannot help but be coloured by so many other factors: her own childhood, her financial position, her partner's views, her mental fortitude. And what she does may not be what she would choose to do in an ideal world; life is all about compromise, after all.

However, the one thing that drives each mother on is a visceral need to do her best for her offspring. She may make mistakes, have regrets, wish for another spin on the merry-go-round, but each mother truly believes that the decisions she makes about her children are the best that she is capable of making at the time that she makes them.

There is not a day goes by that I don't wish that things had turned out differently. I have played the 'what if' card in the poker game of life until my fingers are sore and bleeding. What if I hadn't married Joseph, if I hadn't let him bully me, if I hadn't left with Tilly, if I hadn't accepted the court's decision or continued to stay away after the children came of age? What if any one of these things had played out in another way . . . But if I hadn't married Joseph I would never have brought Michael and Cara into the world and it is always at that point that I stop this endless questioning. They are the pinnacle of what my life has been about. Even though I have not had the good fortune to play much of a part in their lives until now, they have always been in my heart.

So condemn me if you choose, criticise my decisions, compare how you would have played my hand if it had been yours. But remember, before you rush to judgement, that all mothers are ultimately driven by the same engine, despite their differing makes and models. We are all just doing what we think is best for our children.

CHAPTER FIFTY-THREE

Cara, 2018

Marianne has made some food. Of course she has. That's what Marianne does in a crisis. She nurtures.

I'm not hungry but I follow the others to the kitchen where I see no sign of the ham sandwiches that I had planned. Instead, there's a huge bowl of some kind of kedgeree and another of pasta drenched in a rich tomato sauce.

'I just used what I could find, Cara,' she says to me with an expression somewhere between concern and pride. 'I hope that's okay.'

'That's great, Marianne,' I mumble. 'Thanks.'

So we sit to eat like the family we have never been, with Beth and Mrs P hovering awkwardly at the edges. Mrs P suggests that they should leave us to it, but I am adamant that they must both stay. I need them with me. I'm not interested in touching family reunions, not yet.

As we eat, the girls chatter away and I'm grateful that their prattling fills the holes that thirty years of being apart has left. Michael is trying hard too, but I can't talk. Just being here is taking up every ounce of energy that I have.

Then suddenly I can't bear it any longer. I stand up quickly.

'I'm sorry,' I say. 'I just have to . . .'

I don't say what I have to do but I grab my coat from the hook in the hall and leave. I hear them asking each other whether someone should go after me, Michael telling them to leave me be.

As I close the front door behind me, there is no sign of a tail.

The sky is threatening trouble and yet failing to deliver anything but dark, flat light. Down to the river or up to the moor? I dither on the doorstep and then turn uphill. The valley, with its low-hanging trees and dark undergrowth, feels too small today, too confining and claustrophobic. I need space, a big horizon, room to breathe.

There must be something wrong with me. The others have just taken the news in their stride. Half an hour or so of devastating family history and then a nice light lunch. What's for afters? I don't understand how they can be so calm. And Michael? Why does this all seem simple to him when my heart is being torn apart?

I'm so focused on myself that I don't even notice that I'm walking right past Simeon's flat. I cross the cattle grid, not bothering to use the gate, and head straight up. There are a few cars parked – dog walkers, probably, and runners – but there's no one around so when I hear someone shouting, the sound cuts across the silence. It takes me a moment or two to register that they are calling my name.

'Cara! Cara. Wait.'

I turn round and there he is, striding up the hill after me, struggling with the sleeve of his outdoor coat, which flaps behind him like a broken wing, his bootlaces still undone.

'When did you get back?' he asks. 'Did you have a good trip?'

These questions have so little to do with my life now that I wonder if he is talking to me and I look over my shoulder, half-expecting there to be someone else there.

'San Francisco?' he says with a smirk. 'Remember?'

So much has happened since then that it seems like a lifetime ago. New Year's Eve and the morning after, the last time that I saw

Simeon . . . It feels as if that happened to a different person – which it did, I suppose.

He catches me up and bends down to tie his bootlaces.

'Hang on,' he says. 'My gran will be turning in her grave, me walking round with my laces undone.'

I barely know this man. We've spent a handful of hours and a night together and since then I have pushed him away, and yet there is no anger or bitterness in his clear blue eyes as he looks up at me. I throw my arms around his neck and press myself as close to him as I can get. He seems surprised at first and then leans into me and wraps me tightly in his arms. We don't speak for what feels like forever. When I finally pull myself free he looks at me with a quizzical grin. 'Well, hello there,' he says. 'Welcome back.' He looks so pleased to see me that it makes me want to cry. 'So, what's new with you, Cara Beloved?'

'It's complicated,' I reply, as I struggle to hold back the tears. 'And I can't guarantee that I'll get to the end without ending up a nasty, snotty mess.'

'Well, you'd better start at the beginning,' he says, slipping his hand into mine.

We set off up the hill towards the moor. I have surprised myself. For what has felt like forever, I've been locked in this vortex of confusion and self-doubt, and yet, when Simeon appears, there's a hint of a new me, the me I might become, given love and space. It's like the edge of the sun peeping out through clouds. I try to hang on to it.

As we walk, I tell him it all and he listens, interrupting only to clarify things.

'And now they are all back at my house having lunch,' I say. 'Like it's the most normal thing in the world.'

'Well, maybe it is,' he says. 'Or it will be, in time.'

I can't believe that things will ever be normal again.

'Michael seems to have no issues with it, with any of it. It's like he was almost expecting it.'

'Perhaps he was,' says Simeon gently. 'I mean, if he's known for all this time that your mum wasn't actually dead, then I suppose he might have been waiting for her to show up. And it makes sense that she's appeared now. If you were her, wouldn't you wait until your father died before risking an appearance?'

I hadn't thought of it like that but I guess he's right. Michael would never have gone searching for her because that might have hurt me, but he must have known from the moment I found the postcards that I'd get to the truth by myself. He's had the last few months to prepare himself for what I have had to deal with in a couple of hours.

I can't process any of it. I have no idea what to think, how I feel. It won't come into focus in my head. All that feels important is this moment, being here on the moor, hearing the birds sing, feeling the breeze on my face.

Simeon squeezes my hand in his. It feels like it belongs there.

'Do you think you can forgive her?' he asks. 'Not today, or even for a while, but eventually?'

Can I? I think of the sadness in her dark eyes as she told us her story, of Michael's tears at the Tate, of Ursula's graphic descriptions of their torrid home life. They have all held their pain deep in their hearts while I have blissfully sailed through my life without even an inkling of what they have each gone through for me. But a childhood without a mother; a lifetime of lies. That's going to take more to get over than I have to give right now.

We have reached the swastika stone, a Bronze Age rock carving on a flat outcrop of millstone grit. I lean on the iron railings that now surround the ancient site and stare down at the stone, tracing its shape with my eyes.

'Did you know that the swastika was a symbol of good luck before the Fascists got hold of it?' Simeon says.

The regular curves and cups of the carving, barely visible now after millennia of rain and wind beating down on them, are so beautiful that it seems impossible to connect them with the horrors of the twentieth century.

'Maybe this is an auspicious day for you too, Cara. The start of something good?'

His question hangs in the air between us. I squeeze his hand now. I think he might be right.

We stand in silence and look out over the valley, where the town nestles safely in the hills beyond. A small patch of the dark cloud lightens, like a scoop of vanilla ice cream on a slate. Then, just for a moment, the sun breaks through and sends a single shaft of pale light down to bathe the lucky field below in long-sought-after sunshine.

EPILOGUE

I sold the house. Not straightaway. They say you shouldn't make any decisions too close to a bereavement, don't they, so I hung fire for a while; but the impracticalities of living alone in a big place over three floors soon started to add up, especially with no Mrs P to keep on top of things for me. So I stuck it on the market and it was snapped up within weeks. The estate agent's details called it the 'perfect family home', which made me raise an eyebrow.

I never did go through the stuff in the attic either. I think at one stage I really intended to but, in the end, it just didn't feel relevant somehow. Dad's amazing labelling meant that I could stick the whole lot on eBay without ever opening a box. If its contents weren't clear from the label it went to the tip. I wondered once or twice about the little blue angel but if she was ever up there then she's gone with the rest of the stuff.

Annie (I can't seem to get the hang of calling her 'Mum', like Michael does) was at the house quite a lot after the funeral. It was like she didn't know what to do, how to behave with me; and if I'm honest, I didn't exactly make things easy for her. Beth offered to come round the first few times so that I wasn't on my own with her, to save us getting caught in those awkward silences that a lifetime of thinking that someone is dead can produce.

Anyway, we skirted round each other for a while, Annie and I, and then we settled into an uneasy equilibrium, which seems to work as long as neither of us refers to anything that might send us tripping down memory lane. We don't argue; I'm being terribly grown-up about the whole thing. Raking over each other's past doesn't take us any further. It's easier just to leave well alone. I find that I don't need to know what she was doing for all those years without me. So we stick to the present and the future and that seems to work just fine.

She went to see Ursula and met Skyler so we can talk about them and swap stories about our times in San Francisco. Ursula sent me an email filling me in on the visit. Her style is slightly chattier these days, though not much. She said that Skyler was delighted to meet her Aunt Annie. I got the impression that Ursula was less enamoured but that didn't surprise me, given everything. They are both planning a trip over here to see me and to meet Michael and his lot, which I'm really looking forward to. I want to show Ursula my dresses. I think she will understand that part of me better than anyone.

Not long after Annie arrived back in our lives, a flat came up for sale in an apartment block near Michael's place and she moved there. He's never said so, but I assume Michael bought it for her. Maybe he used his share of the old house; I didn't ask. It seems to be working beautifully for them all. Annie enjoys babysitting, I gather, and I can go and see her any time, if I want.

The front door bangs shut and Simeon calls out.

'It's only me. How's my princess?'

He appears at the door with his arms full of stuff.

'They only had these. I wondered if they might be a bit small but then I decided that too small was better than too big. Did I choose right? I can go back if you think the others would be better. And this kind of fell into my basket.'

He winks at me. There are dark shadows around his eyes that weren't there before but he never stops smiling. He holds up a tiny pink dress on a tiny white hanger. It's all frill and froufrou and totally impractical but it's very sweet.

'She's far too little for dresses,' I say. 'By the time I've wrestled her into it, it'll be time for bed.'

He screws his nose up.

'I know but I just couldn't resist. Please indulge me.'

He comes and sits down on the sofa next to us. Lily, momentarily distracted, stops sucking and looks up briefly but then she's back on task. Simeon takes her tiny foot in his hand and strokes the back of her heel.

'The nappies will be fine,' I say. 'And I'm sure we'll go somewhere where she can wear the dress.'

He grins. He's going to be a great dad. I can tell already.

'Anyone in need of tea?' Mrs P shouts through from the kitchen. I call her Angie to her face now but in my heart she'll always be Mrs P. 'It's thirsty work, feeding babies,' she adds, and she's right.

Simeon kisses me on the top of my head and then goes off to help her with the drinks, kicking the packet of nappies along the floor as he goes.

Lily must have had her fill because she pulls her mouth away from me and I wince. For a moment, she looks up at me with her deep-blue eyes and then she's asleep, a tiny smile that looks like contentment but is probably wind on her rosebud lips.

'Don't you worry,' I whisper into her dark curls as I hold her tiny body close to mine. 'Mummy's here.'

ACKNOWLEDGMENTS

As a mother of four children, I have to admit to having occasionally contemplated running away – and it was wondering what might make a mother leave her children that was the spark for this book. Since that initial idea struck me, the story has undergone a number of transformations and I would like to thank authors Patricia Duncker and Jenny Parrott for their valuable help with my plotting. Thanks must also go to editors Roisin Heycock, Celine Kelly and Victoria Pepe, together with my team at Lake Union for all their support and guidance in this adventure.

Closer to home, I would like to thank my writing buddies Carole Richardson and Lee Knight for their constant encouragement and the Wobble Wonk Group for keeping me smiling.

Finally, thanks must go to my family: to my parents for always believing in me, even when I didn't; to my children for learning when to leave my study door closed; but mostly to John for supporting me tirelessly as I typed and enthused and wept and shouted my way to this point. I could never have done it without you.

BOOK CLUB QUESTIONS

Do you think Michael was right to keep secrets from Cara?

In what circumstances would a mother leave her children behind?

Were you surprised by Cara's response to her mother when she finally meets her?

Ursula and Annie both respond differently to their father's bullying. Which approach is more successful?

Cara struggles to remember the past. Do you think she would have been more open to her mother's return if she could remember more of life before her mother left?

To what extent is Mrs P a substitute mother? Do you think Cara sees her as such?

Malcolm, Joe and Greg are all controlling men. Pam, Annie and Beth all respond differently. To what extent do you think a man's ability to control a woman is governed by her response to him?

ABOUT THE AUTHOR

Imogen Clark lives in Yorkshire, England, with her husband and children. Her first burning ambition was to be a solicitor and so she read law at Manchester University and then worked for many years at a commercial law firm. After leaving her legal career behind to care for her children, Imogen turned to her second love – books. She returned to university, studying part-time while the children were at school, and was awarded a BA in English literature with First Class Honours. Imogen loves sunshine and travel and longs to live by the sea someday.